Duets

Two brand-new stories in every volume...twice a month!

Duets Vol. #99

Veteran Harlequin author Pamela Browning makes her Duets debut this month with a delightful, splashy Double Duets volume. Sisters Karma and Azure O'Connor undergo their share of woe with men in this pair of fun, quirky stories set in trendy South Beach, Miami. Enjoy *Life Is a Beach* and *A Real-Thing Fling!*

Duets Vol. #100

Duets is having a celebration this month! This smile-inducing series, featuring gifted writers and stories, is one hundred volumes old. Look for two terrific tales by fan favorites Jennifer Drew and Holly Jacobs. *You'll Be Mine in 99* and *The 100-Year Itch* are both set in the crazy small town of Hiho, Ohio, where anything can— and will!—happen when people fall in love. Happy reading!

Be sure to pick up both Duets volumes today!

Life Is a Beach

"I'll challenge you to a game of Scrabble," Slade ventured.

Karma nodded and they settled down on the couch with the board between them. The room was illuminated only by the dim wavering light from the hurricane lamp nearby. Outside the wind rattled away and the ocean waves repeatedly battered the pilings beneath them. Every so often, the house would draw itself up, suck in its breath and give a shudder.

Karma tried to ignore the hunky cowboy opposite her and studied the letters in her rack before slapping down the word *east*. Slade promptly added the letters *B* and *R*, making it *breast*.

She raised her eyebrows.

"It's a word, right? It's legal." His expression was one of pure amusement.

Karma added an *O* and one *S*, then a second *S*, making *toss*. *Ah-ha*, she thought, *he's beat*.

Slade reached over and, using an *S*, a *K*, followed by an *I*, he answered her with *kiss*.

"Which," he said softly, with the sexy look that she was coming to know so well, "wouldn't be a bad idea."

For more, turn to page 9

A Real-Thing Fling

"Azure," Lee began, thinking the pretense had gone too far.

How could she ever trust him again if he didn't come clean about who he really was? He swore he'd never lose this woman—this smart, sexy, though a little wonky, lady.

Azure turned on a radio in one corner of the large, mostly empty retail space. "But I want to help. I want to do *something*," she said over the loud, lively music. Then she bent and dipped her brush in the paint, and applied it to the wall with a professionalism that put Lee's meager effort to shame.

He liked it that Azure had a generous side, but when he glanced at his watch he realized the painters—the real ones—would be returning in a mater of minutes. There was only one thing he could do, he figured, and that was to paint as fast as possible, the sooner to get them out of there and not have his secret identity discovered.

Plus, there was the way she was wearing those coveralls, and how they curved around Azure's delectable derriere that made working beside her a pleasure.

Or correction: make that behind her.

For more, turn to page 197

HARLEQUIN DUETS

ISBN 0-373-44165-7

Copyright in the collection:
Copyright © 2003 by Harlequin Books S.A.

The publisher acknowledges the copyright holder
of the individual works as follows:

LIFE IS A BEACH
Copyright © 2003 by Pamela Browning

A REAL-THING FLING
Copyright © 2003 by Pamela Browning

This edition published by arrangement with Harlequin Books S.A.

® and TM are trademarks of the publisher. Trademarks indicated with ® are registered in the United States Patent and Trademark Office, the Canadian Trade Marks Office and in other countries.

Visit us at www.eHarlequin.com

Printed in U.S.A.

Pamela Browning

Life Is a Beach

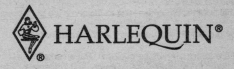

HARLEQUIN®

TORONTO • NEW YORK • LONDON
AMSTERDAM • PARIS • SYDNEY • HAMBURG
STOCKHOLM • ATHENS • TOKYO • MILAN • MADRID
PRAGUE • WARSAW • BUDAPEST • AUCKLAND

Dear Reader,

There *I* was on a flight to Miami reading the airline in-flight magazine. There *she* was, a professional matchmaker, smiling up from the page in all her glossy perfection. Cool job, I thought.

I recalled an elderly friend telling me how her happy marriage had been arranged by a yenta, the yiddish term for the neighborhood busybody who excelled at finding marriage partners. The phrase Rent-a-Yenta sprang into my mind, and thus the Rent-a-Yenta dating service was born.

As you read the stories of Karma and Azure O'Connor, the heroines in my Double Duets volume, I hope you'll agree with me that even if true love comes along only once in a blue moon, it's always worth the wait!

Best wishes and happy reading,

Pamela Browning

Books by Pamela Browning

HARLEQUIN AMERICAN ROMANCE
786—RSVP...BABY
818—THAT'S OUR BABY
854—BABY CHRISTMAS
874—COWBOY WITH A SECRET
907—PREGNANT AND INCOGNITO

Don't miss any of our special offers. Write to us at the following address for information on our newest releases.

Harlequin Reader Service
U.S.: 3010 Walden Ave., P.O. Box 1325, Buffalo, NY 14269
Canadian: P.O. Box 609, Fort Erie, Ont. L2A 5X3

For Judith Arnold,
who knows from bubbeleh and blintzes,
and for the guy who walks like John Wayne.

1

SLADE BRADDOCK WAS JUST a big old lonesome cowboy, and he was bound and determined not to be that way for much longer.

Big? Well, that was one thing he couldn't change, he reckoned. He was six foot three, so tall that he kept bumping into things in his cousin Mack's houseboat, where he had squatter's rights for as long as it took to find himself a wife.

Old? He was thirty-five, which was part of the problem. All the young women in Okeechobee City, Florida, were married. The older ones tended to mother him. So even though in some circles cowboys were said to be babe magnets, Slade had not found this to be true. He had heeded his cousin Mack's suggestion to seek out a Miami Beach dating service.

Lonesome? The dating service should take care of that.

Slade sauntered across *Toy Boat*'s salon, which was a high-class word, he figured, for a living room. He twirled his Stetson off the wall sconce where he'd tossed it after getting royally drunk with a couple of rowdies from South Beach last night, and he stopped for a moment to squint critically into the floor-to-ceiling wall mirror.

Yeah, he looked all right. He wasn't suave. He wasn't dapper. He was a little worn and tattered around the edges. But he'd do. The woman he was looking for wouldn't mind that a scar bisected his left eyelid, and she'd let him love her the way a woman was meant to be loved. He wanted a shy, sweet, old-fashioned girl to take back to Okeechobee City with him, to help him run the ranch. A small woman who would make him feel manly. And he'd find one before he left Miami Beach. He was determined.

He was so determined, in fact, that as he was striding purposefully toward the deck, he forgot about the low door-way and whacked his head.

A COWBOY DRESSED OUT in full regalia was not exactly what anyone expected to see ambling down a street in Miami's trendy South Beach on an ordinary morning.

But that was exactly what Karma O'Connor saw. This guy looked as if he'd galloped in fresh off the range after herding a bunch of cattle or chasing rustlers or something.

"Your aunt Sophie, she wanted you to inherit the business," said Uncle Nate as he admired the new brass plate beside the door.

Rent-a-Yenta, it said. Karma O'Connor, Matchmaker.

Very reluctantly, Karma peeled her eyes away from the cowboy and bent down to bestow a quick kiss on the little man's cheek.

"Thank you, Uncle Nate," she said warmly. "You could have closed up Aunt Sophie's office. You two could have let me go on being unemployed instead of scooping me up practically out of a welfare line and—"

"Never," said her great-uncle. "A girl like you should have a chance. Sophie thought about leaving the business to your cousin Paulette, but, well, she respected you, a single girl trying to make it on her own."

"Paulette is single. She's trying to make it on her own, too."

"Ah, Paulette. She's a go-getter, that one."

Privately Karma thought that her cousin Paulette was an overbearing little snip. She adopted an expression of mock dismay. "Hey, Uncle Nate—you're hurting my feelings. Aren't I a go-getter, too?"

He blinked up at her, a wizened little gnome with eyes that crinkled charmingly around the edges. ''You are, *bubbeleh,* you are. Sophie said you reminded her of herself when she was young,'' and with that pronouncement, he launched into an emotional reminiscence about his late wife, who had died six months before.

Karma listened, and she agreed with Nate that her greataunt had been a kind, charming, and, in fact, brilliant woman. While Nate rattled on as was his wont, she distracted herself from his monologue by searching for the cowboy's Stetson above the sleek blond heads of a bunch of roller-skating beach bunnies.

The hat was there, all right. It shaded the cowboy's face so that she gleaned only a quick impression of craggy cheekbones, a strong straight blade of a nose, and a tan that put those beach bunnies to shame. Wide shoulders, too. And, farther down, slim hips slung with a pair of well-worn jeans. Almost as if he knew she was watching him, the cowboy headed in her direction.

''How cool is *he?*'' she murmured to herself in awe.

''It's hot today like always in Miami,'' Nate said as he eased himself down on the bench beside the door to the corridor that led to her office.

Karma kept forgetting that she had to speak loudly so that her uncle could hear. He wore a hearing aid but often forgot to turn it on.

''No, I wasn't talking about the weather. I was admiring that cowboy heading our way.''

Nate scoffed at this. ''You should be thinking about business, not some *meshugeneh* cowboy. Like I told you before, Sophie managed to make fifty good matches a year and you haven't made any yet.''

''I wish I could have trained with her for a while,'' Karma said wistfully. Unfortunately Aunt Sophie had been too sick during her final illness to work, and the business had gone downhill fast.

"An apprenticeship with my Sophie might have helped. Then again, maybe not. No offense, Karma dear, but a two-time college graduate like you doesn't necessarily know the human factor."

"My degrees *are* in psychology," Karma reminded him gently as the cowboy continued toward them.

"Psychology, shmycology. You got to know people. Not that you don't," he added hastily. "Sophie thought you had potential. 'That girl has real potential,' she'd always say after we saw you at one of those family dinners at your parents' house."

This was nice to hear, but Karma couldn't remember a single one of those dinners in which she'd been able to get a word in edgewise, what with all the big talkers in the family. She'd always been the quiet one, the too-tall sister who passed the hors d'oeuvres while her three siblings noisily showed off their piano-playing and dancing talents.

And since when had any of her relatives thought she was anything but a loser compared to her talented and brilliant sisters, not to mention that colossal suck-up, Paulette? "I hope I can live up to your expectations," Karma murmured.

Truth to tell, her full attention was drawn to the cowboy. In a tropical climate where people customarily wore sandals or even went barefoot, this man was clomping along Ocean Drive in cowboy boots. A couple of children hung back on their mothers' hands and stared.

"Come along, Chuckie," urged one of the mothers, tugging.

"Aw, Mom, I want to see the cowboy."

So did Karma. She wanted to see him up close. And it looked, at this very moment, as if she might have that opportunity.

His boots were finely tooled leather, elaborated worked. She'd heard you could tell a lot about a cowboy by his boots. These were clearly expensive, maybe even hand-made, and definitely too dusty. The boots didn't jingle, however. This cowboy wasn't wearing spurs. Which she supposed made sense, since she didn't see a horse around anywhere.

"I guess I better stop talking about Sophie, I'm getting hoarse."

"Horse?" Karma said, caught off guard.

"Yeah, my throat itches. Sit down for a minute, Karma, while I catch my breath."

Karma felt her own breath grow shallow as the cowboy's gaze fell upon her. Up it went, then down. Never mind that this took a few embarrassing seconds because of her height. Was she blushing? No, she wasn't that susceptible to nuanced glances. She was twenty-seven years old and the veteran of more than one ill-fated heavy relationship. She was dedicated to carving a career for herself out of the matchmaking business. So why did this man make her heart beat like—well, like thundering cattle hooves?

Because he was possibly the handsomest man she had ever seen. Because his cowboy boots had stopped right in front of the bench. Right in front of her.

The cowboy stuck a hand in one of his back jeans pockets and rummaged around. *Going to roll a cigarette,* Karma thought. That's what cowboys always did in the movies, and the movies were the only place she'd ever seen a cowboy. She watched spellbound, expecting him to extract a fistful of rolling papers and some tobacco. Instead he pulled out a red bikini bra. A very ample red bikini bra.

He stared at it and then, with a puzzled and pained look, he crumpled it up and stuffed it back in his pocket.

As Karma watched, her mind was racing faster than a spooked mustang. She wasn't exactly thinking about this cowboy. What she was thinking was that things never came easily to her. Not graduating from college nor getting a master's degree, and certainly not holding a job. People always thought that if you were a natural blonde, you were home free in life. Well, nothing was free, and at the moment, Karma didn't have a real home. What she did have was a couple of possibly useless degrees in psychology, a generous great-uncle and a third or fourth chance to make something of herself.

She jumped up from her seat, feeling absurdly like a jack-in-the-box. She said to the cowboy, "Sir, I don't suppose you could use the services of a matchmaker, could you?"

He looked her over. It was impossible to tell what he was thinking. "That's exactly what I need," he said.

"You've come to the right place," Karma said, praising whatever gods were in charge of lucky coincidences.

The cowboy angled his head toward the shiny new sign on the building behind them. "That your place?"

"Yes. As of two months ago." She held her breath, half expecting him to walk away.

"The thing is, you'll have to tell me something. Just what exactly is a yenta?"

Nate stood up. "It's a Yiddish word. In Jewish communities, where marriages used to be arranged, you would go to a yenta that you trusted to find the right person for you. It's a family tradition, like with my Sophie. She was a good businesswoman, Sophie was. Knew how to change with the times."

"So Rent-a-Yenta is a dating service?" the cowboy asked politely. His voice was deep and rich, slightly raspy. It reminded Karma of Clint Eastwood's but with considerably more expression.

Nate's head bobbed up and down. "Yes, you might as well think of a yenta as someone who matches people up with their significance."

The cowboy looked slightly confused.

Karma found her tongue. "He means their significant others," she injected hastily.

"Hmm," said the cowboy. He appeared to be thinking this over.

Two things occurred to Karma in the next stretch of thirty seconds or so. One was that she wanted to make a success of this matchmaking business that had so providentially and unexpectedly landed in her lap. The other was that this was a client—a real walking, talking, live client.

"Won't you come into my office?" she asked, smooth as silk. Despite the bra in his pocket, this man needed her services. He'd said so.

"Sure," said the cowboy. He had a way of smiling that lifted one corner of his mouth and cocked the opposite eyebrow, and the effect was intriguing.

"I'll just amble along," said Nate. "Leave you to business." Karma knew he was running late for his daily game of pinochle at the café down the street.

"If I'm interrupting," said the cowboy.

"No, no, you two go right ahead," said Nate. He patted Karma's arm. "See you tomorrow, *bubbeleh.*"

"Well," Karma said as she watched Nate disappear in the throng of people on the sidewalk. She spared a look at the cowboy. He looked more resigned than eager, which was typical of the clients that she'd dealt with so far. She supposed that resignation was the last step before jaded. She hated jaded. It was so hard to win those folks over.

She aimed her brightest smile up at him. Up at him was a miracle, since she was almost six feet tall herself. Ever since puberty, her smiles had been mostly aimed downward. "Follow me," she said.

Karma had been told that she had nice hips. This was a good thing, considering that the cowboy's eyes never left them as they walked up the flight of stairs to the tiny cubicle that was Rent-a-Yenta. She'd rather have him staring at her hips, or, more accurately, her derriere, than, say, her feet, which were overly large. Or her mouth, ditto. Or her breasts, which weren't. That bikini bra in his pocket had looked like about a 38DD.

She dug the office key out of her purse and promptly dropped it.

The cowboy immediately bent down and picked it up. He didn't immediately straighten, however. That took a while. His eyes moved up, up, studying her ankles, her calves, and what he could see of her thighs, which was probably too much considering the fact that her skirt was very short. She had a hard time finding clothes that were long enough.

"Thanks," she said dryly as he handed her the key. At the moment that their hands touched, their eyes locked. His were the bluest eyes she'd ever seen. They were brilliant, sparkling like sunlight on the sea, heating up like a blue flame. They took her breath away.

She made herself shove the key in the lock, but the door opened before she turned the key. She'd better get that lock fixed one of these days, but it was low on her list of priorities since there wasn't much worth stealing in the office at present.

The cowboy was right behind her. She followed his gaze as he took in the half-painted lime-green wall, the plastic bead curtain that screened off the supply closet, the TV alcove for viewing client videos. She supposed the decor was startling, but this was her style. After downsizing the office into a mere one and a half rooms due to lack of funds, she'd painted over plain vanilla walls, banished Aunt Sophie's heavy mahogany desk, thrown out the dusty chintz curtains at the windows so she could look out at the multicolored pastel facade of the Blue Moon Apartments across the street where she lived.

"You—um, well, you could sit down," she said.

He looked puzzled. Oops! She'd forgotten that she'd sent the couch and client chairs out for cleaning yesterday. The only places to sit were on a couple of floor cushions that she'd brought over from her apartment and her desk chair.

Omigosh, she thought, *if I sit in the chair he'll be able to look right up my skirt.*

"There, ma'am?" the cowboy asked politely, staring down at the nearest floor cushion, the bright orange one.

"Why, yes," Karma said, acting as if nothing was amiss. "I'll take the pink one."

Looking disconcerted, the cowboy lowered himself to the indicated cushion. The position he took, knees upraised, back straight, strained the jeans tight against his thighs and calves. He didn't look at all comfortable. What he did look was sexy.

Karma's secondhand 1940s rattan desk was covered with an assortment of papers, old diet-drink cans, a dried-up paintbrush, and a dead hibiscus blossom awash in a jar lid half full of water. Karma yanked a form from a stack and, trying not to appear as ungainly as she felt, she also sat down on a cushion. Maybe she was crazy for going ahead with this. Maybe she should tell this man to come back tomorrow when the couch would be here and the chairs would have been delivered. But to dismiss him might mean losing him, and the business couldn't afford that. Clients had been very few and far between, and this might be her last chance to succeed. At anything.

"What do I have to do to sign up?" asked the cowboy.

Karma fumbled in her tote bag for a pen. "At Rent-a-Yenta we chronicle your personal information, collect a registration fee and then we videotape our clients. We'll study our database and pull up clients of the opposite sex that we think would be a good match for you." There was no "we"; there was only her. But she thought it sounded more impressive than admitting that she did everything herself.

"And I get to watch videotapes of the clients you pick?" He looked visibly cheered by the thought.

"Right. And they'll watch videotapes of you."

"Okay. That sounds like a good way to go about it."

"Oh, it is, I assure you."

After he wrote out the check, he folded his arms across his chest. A very broad chest. "Well, let's get started."

"Name?" she asked brightly.

"Slade," he said.

"Is that your first name or last?"

"Slade's my given name. Braddock's my last." His voice rumbled deep in his throat.

"Slade Braddock," she repeated, liking the sound of the name almost as much as the way he said it. She wrote his name down on the form.

"Age?"

"Thirty-awful."

She blinked. "Excuse me?"

"Thirty-awful. Too old for the young ones, too young for the older ones."

She tried not to smile. "Should be thirty-awesome, if you ask me," she retorted before she thought. She was always retorting before she thought, and before the words were out of her mouth, she wished she hadn't said that.

He grinned, expanded it to a smile, then let out a hearty guffaw. She tipped her head uncertainly.

"That's pretty good," he said. "Thirty-awesome. I'll remember that one."

She wanted to laugh, too, but this was a client. She cautioned herself to remain businesslike, but her next words sounded like a reproof. "Are you going to tell me your age, or should I leave this line blank?"

He sombered up then. "I'm thirty-five," he said. "Now I've told you my age, how about you telling me yours?"

"You're not supposed to ask a lady that," she said.

"But I just did."

Those eyes again, piercing right through her. They demanded an answer. "I'm twenty-seven," she said.

"A good age," he said thoughtfully.

She made herself look down at the form. "Address?"

"Sunchaser Marina. Route three, Okeechobee City."

"That's the whole address?"

"That's two addresses."

She forced herself to look at him. "Let's get this straight. What's your primary mailing address?"

"That would be the Okeechobee City one, ma'am. The marina one's sort of borrowed."

This, then, explained the cowboy outfit. Okeechobee City was cattle country, a small town on the shores of Lake Okeechobee some miles west of Palm Beach, that much she knew.

She wrote down both addresses. She knew the Sunchaser Marina well; she'd bicycled past it many times. It was home base for pleasure yachts, houseboats and assorted other watercraft, all of them expensive, none of them suited to a guy who dressed like he'd recently thundered on horseback right out of a John Wayne movie. Bermuda shorts in assorted pastel plaids and Gucci loafers with no socks were the preferred mode of dress at Sunchaser Marina.

Slade Braddock shifted on his cushion. She'd better rush this along or he might cut the interview short.

Karma fixed the cowboy with what she hoped was a serious and businesslike gaze. "And what brings you to Rent-a-Yenta?" she asked.

"I want to get married," he said doggedly. "I'm ready to find myself a bride."

Karma swallowed. She wasn't accustomed to clients who came right out and stated their purpose. Most of them weren't too sure what they'd be getting into when they signed with her, and they usually said something vague. "Introduce me to somebody nice to date," was the usual statement. Sometimes they added embellishments, such as "He has to have a platinum Visa card with his picture on it," or "I don't go out with anyone who doesn't know how to refold a map," but that was about as specific as they got. No one, in the months since she'd become a match-maker, had flat out said, "I want to get married."

Slade Braddock looked so earnest that Karma was sure he meant it.

"To what kind of woman?" she blurted.

"Oh, I've got a woman in mind. I can describe her if you like," he said as a dreamy expression filtered out the fire in those remarkable blue eyes.

This wasn't standard operating procedure, but Karma was fascinated by his honesty. Honesty was all too rare in this business, she'd learned. "Go ahead," she said, realizing that she was holding her breath. She let it out slowly, wondering if it was too much to hope that he'd describe a five-foot-eleven natural blonde with large feet, green eyes and breasts slightly on the small side.

"She'll have light hair. Yellow, like sunbeams. Kind of like yours, only straighter." He studied her. Appraised her. She didn't know exactly what that look meant, but she took it that he didn't exactly disapprove of what he saw. Until he went on talking, that is.

"She'll be tiny. A little bird of a woman. And her voice will be sweet. Maybe she'll like singing in the church choir."

Karma couldn't sing a note. And tiny she wasn't. As her hopes faded, she said stoically, "Go on."

"She'll be comfortable on the ranch, know how it works. Or be willing to learn. I don't expect her to rope and brand cattle, but she should understand that this is part of what I do. And she'll be crazy about me. From the very beginning if possible. I aim to have me a wife by this summer."

"What's happening this summer?"

He looked at her as if she was crazy for asking. "Why, our honeymoon. I've already signed us up for an Alaskan cruise."

"Oh." Karma was nonplussed.

He zeroed in on her astonishment. "What do you mean, 'oh'?" Is there something wrong with that?"

"Occasionally a wife likes to help choose the honeymoon spot," Karma said, holding back the sarcasm with great effort.

She judged from the perplexed expression in his eyes that this had never occurred to him.

"I figured that if the woman loves me, then anyplace is all right with her. For the honeymoon, I mean."

She took pity on him. "In some cases, that's true," she relented, and his smile warmed her heart.

Her heart had no place in this. She willed it to stop leaping around in her chest and pretended to make a notation on the form. But as she concentrated on her task, one side of her was having an argument with the other side. Sounding very much like her aunt Sophie, the yenta side counseled, "You've got yourself a client. You've got a paying customer on the hoof. Don't scare him away." The Karma side hissed, "Stupid! This is a really great guy. Why give him away to someone else? Why not keep him for yourself?"

A disturbing thought. She'd given up on men two or three relationships ago.

She cleared her throat. She cleared her mind. Or attempted to, anyway.

"Mr. Braddock. This is certainly enough information for me to match you up with some charming clients."

He beamed. "Now that's good news." He produced a money clip and peeled off several bills. "Here's the registration fee."

Karma's eyes bugged out at the wad of cool cash. Most people paid with a credit card. Most people didn't carry that much money around.

He put the money back in his pocket. "I can't tell you how downright scared I was coming in here today. I'd rather face a nest of full-grown rattlers than do this, I can tell you.''

She turned the full wattage of her best smile on him. ''Oh, everyone feels that way at first, I'm sure. The next step is, of course, our videotape session. Normally I'd be able to do that today, but my video camera is out for repairs. So I hope it will be convenient for you to come back tomorrow?'' She'd play soft sitar music on the boom box, wear something flowing. She'd make carob-and-pine-nut brownies and serve them with flair. She'd—but of course she wouldn't. She wasn't in the market for a guy, even one as appealing as this one.

Slade Braddock unfolded himself from the floor cushion, rising with spectacular grace. He looked down at her, a half smile playing across his well-sculpted lips.

''No problem, but why don't you stop by the marina this afternoon? There's a video camera on the houseboat. No point in wasting time. Got to get me a bride by June, you know?'' His smile so unnerved her that she levered herself upward, stumbling over the corner of the cushion and catching herself on the doorknob, barely averting an unladylike sprawl across her desk.

''You okay?'' he asked, frowning slightly.

''Y-yes. And where will I find you at the marina?''

''I'm staying on what they call Houseboat Row in a floating palace called *Toy Boat*. Silly name, isn't it?''

''Well,'' Karma said, unsure how to answer this. She didn't want to hurt his feelings. Guys sometimes got very attached to their boats.

''I didn't name it. That honor belongs to my second cousin's wife. Renee thought it was cute.'' He grinned, and Karma was totally charmed. Never mind that he had already told her the type of woman who appealed to him, and never mind that she wasn't it. All her misgivings about men evaporated in that moment.

''I'll be glad to stop by the marina,'' she said. ''Would

five o'clock suit you?'' She'd bring hors d'oeuvres, wear something revealing. She'd—yeah. She'd make a fool of herself. Again.

"Five o'clock. Right. Thanks, Ms.—O'Connor, is it?"

She scooped one of her cards out of the jumble on her desk. "Karma O'Connor. Like on the sign out front."

He looked at the card, looked at her. "Nice name, Karma. What does it mean?"

"Destiny," she said, staring him straight in the eye, and despite her reservations, in that moment she was certain that she had found hers.

AFTER SLADE HAD LEFT HER OFFICE, Karma immediately dashed across the street to the Blue Moon, where she rented a tiny three-room pad.

The Blue Moon was exactly the kind of place Karma would have chosen to live even if it hadn't been right across the street from Rent-a-Yenta. The building had seen its heyday in the late 1940s. It was painted pale pink, the doors and windows were outlined in aqua, and a lavender-blue stripe circled the top of the building. A blue bas-relief half moon hung over the door. Karma had heard the place variously described as "an iced pastry," and "a Wurlitzer jukebox done in pastels." After the heavy dark brick of her apartment block in Connecticut, she loved it.

Goldy, manager, desk clerk, custodian and security officer all rolled into one, sat inside the doorway behind a counter. She glanced up from her knitting with rapid-blinking brown eyes. Her short spiky hair gleamed in the sunlight from the nearby window; it was an energetic shade of copper this week. In the background a radio blared some sixties girl group singing, "Today I Met the Man I'm Going to Marry."

Was the song an omen? Maybe. Karma believed in omens.

"Hi, Goldy, anything new?"

"I read the tarot cards for you today. Something big's coming up. Something major." Her voice was tiny, like a little girl's.

"Like being able to pay my office rent?" Slade Braddock's registration fee made that a sure thing.

"Hmm. Could be bigger than that." Goldy set aside her knitting and adjusted the voluminous folds of one of the huge flower-print muumuus she liked to wear.

"Nothing's bigger than paying the rent."

"I thought since you gave up the five-room office suite, you'd be okay."

"Only if I bring in more business. Things fell apart fast when Aunt Sophie was sick. She may have left me her business, but I've got to revive it. After quitting a market research job, being laid off from *Psychtronics Magazine* and getting fired from The Bickerstiff Corporation, it's a welcome opportunity."

"Maybe you should have your chakras read, get some direction. I have time late this afternoon." Goldy's shtick was anything New Age, and she never let anyone forget it.

"Can't. I'm busy."

"Well, there you go. Business must be picking up," Goldy said with an air of idle speculation, which was how Karma knew that Goldy, from her vantage point by the window, had seen Slade Braddock.

"I have a new client," Karma said reluctantly.

"Is he anyone that Jennifer might be interested in?" Jennifer was Goldy's niece, and she'd signed up with Rent-a-Yenta the first week after Karma had taken over. Jennifer was hard to place because she had no real interests other than herself. Her favorite pastime seemed to be playing "Boxers or Briefs" while guy-watching with her best friend Mandi on Collins Avenue, and Karma privately thought that her brain was so empty that she ought to wear a Rooms for Rent sign on her forehead.

Karma managed a casual shrug. She couldn't see Slade Braddock with Jennifer. Or maybe she didn't want to.

"Well, how about Mandi?" Goldy asked.

Karma had experienced some success in placing Mandi, who also lived in this apartment house, but most guys backed off after they realized that artfully streaked hair, acrylic fingernails, and weekly massages did not come without a steep price.

"Could be," said Karma noncommittally. She turned to go.

"Oh, by the way, Geofredo's probably in your apartment right now. He's respraying the whole third floor."

Karma stopped and frowned. "I told you I didn't want that exterminator guy coming into my place. You know I don't believe in killing anything."

Goldy spared her a meaningful look. "You told me you had a family of roaches living under your refrigerator."

The roaches were palmetto bugs, enormous and all too prevalent in the state of Florida. These were big brown insects the size of hummingbirds, and they also flew. For palmetto bugs and spiders, which creeped her out bigtime, Karma was able to relax her standards slightly as long as she didn't have to do the killing.

Goldy said, "You tell Geofredo to check the supply room on your floor for spiders."

"Will do."

Karma started up the stairs to the third floor; there was no elevator in the building. She figured the stairs were good exercise, which she needed now that she was going to be sitting behind a desk every day. Not that she had done much sitting so far, since the chair was usually piled high with papers. Most of the hours she had put in at the Rent-a-Yenta office had been spent painting and cleaning, with an occasional client thrown in for good measure.

Speaking of clients, Goldy's niece Jennifer was skipping toward her down the stairs, probably on her way home from visiting Mandi. Jennifer's hair was long, straight, and bouncy. She wore a tight cutoff Planet Hollywood shirt with low-slung white capri pants that showed off her silver navel tassel.

"Hi, Karma," she said, stopping before they passed. "Hey, are those real?"

"Are what—?" Karma began before she realized that Jennifer was unabashedly staring at her breasts.

Karma shook her head as if to clear it. Was she supposed to answer such a question?

"I don't mean the boobs, silly. If they were fake, you'd have chosen bigger ones. No, I mean the nipples."

"What?" Back in Connecticut, where Karma came from, people didn't ask such personal questions.

"Oh, well, I guess they must be. Forget I asked—I was only wondering if your nipples were fake because I'm going to buy some if I can figure out where to get them, and I thought you could tell me."

"Sheesh, Jennifer, what are you talking about?" Karma had thought, erroneously it appeared, that she had outgrown being freaked by the wacko characters in Miami Beach.

Jennifer tossed her head so that her hair gave off the overpowering scent of mango-coconut shampoo. "Nipples, silly, you can buy fake ones to stick on. My own are kind of puny, and the idea of all these guys I'm going to meet through Rent-a-Yenta has been making me think. Do I want a steady boyfriend? Yes! Do I want to use every means at my disposal to attract one? Yes! Guys love huge nipples, Karma, believe me. It's a major drawing point. Point, that's funny!" She laughed uproariously.

Karma made herself keep a straight face. "I can't help you, sorry. But if I were you, I'd try that place advertised on the big billboard near the airport—The Booby Trap 'n Boutique." The billboard featured an overendowed winking woman wearing nothing but a large pink feather.

"Oooh! Good idea! Thanks, Karma." With that, Jennifer

resumed her skipping down the stairs, and Karma read-justed her blouse so that it didn't cling.

The exterminator, Geofredo, was backing into her apart-ment with his bug-spray equipment as she arrived. Karma considered if maybe this was the man she was going to marry, like in the song. She also considered readjusting her blouse so that it *did* cling, but she quickly gave up the idea until she knew more about him.

As he went around her apartment spraying and smiling shyly between squirts, Karma decided that if this guy had any intention of marrying her, he wasn't letting on.

He gave her one last bashful smile at the door. "*Hasta la vista?* Baby?" he said, looking more tentative than forceful.

"Don't forget about the spiders in the supply room," she said, doing a finger-play demo of the kindergarten song about the itsy-bitsy spider. "In el rooma de supply." This was the best shot she could give Spanish; she'd taken French in high school.

Geofredo shoved the bug bomb he was carrying into his pocket and grinned widely, exposing a row of teeth as white and as straight as a row of Chiclets. "Spi-der," he said, mimicking her actions. "*Araña.*" That's when Karma spot-ted the wedding ring on the third finger of his left hand and realized that he wasn't the man for her.

"*Hasta la vista* to you, too," she told him, and then she shut the door behind him fast.

Besides, she really dug cowboys. Or at least she had ever since she'd set eyes on Slade Braddock.

2

SLADE SETTLED BACK in a deck chair, popped the top off a Guinness, and resigned himself to listening to intermittent jabber and Cuban music wafting over from D Dock. He was trying his best to impersonate a yachtsman, but even after two days in residence on *Toy Boat,* he felt like an interloper. The habitues of the Sunchaser Marina were a tight-knit group. They didn't so much ignore him as act as if he didn't exist.

Well, his clothes might have had something to do with it, but whenever he shucked the jeans and boots for one of Mack's designer swimsuit outfits, he felt like a complete idiot. Silver reflecting sunglasses and a cabana shirt thrown open at the throat weren't his style.

Still, he might have gotten along with his companions better last night if he'd been dressed in Miami Beach mode. The two guys he'd met at the beach had taken one look at his boots and hat and mistaken him for a rube. They'd invited him along on a little bar-hopping jaunt, set him up with a sumptuous redhead at a party, and tried to steal his money in a back alley. Bad mistake. The guys were nursing aching heads today, no doubt, and not as a result of hangovers. As for the redhead, she'd split, yelling at the top of her lungs. Good riddance.

He was by nature soft-spoken and quiet, and he was well aware that it gave him an advantage to be seen as naive. He'd never thought it necessary to advertise the fact that he'd graduated from the University of Florida and been a star on the rodeo circuit for a couple of years afterward.

Slade Braddock had seen enough of the world to appreciate who he was and where he'd come from, which was why he knew he wanted to live in Okeechobee City for the rest of his life. Here in Miami Beach, he felt misplaced. Like a fish out of water, so to speak. He didn't belong here, he didn't really want to be here. He'd made progress today, though. He was on the way to finding himself a wife.

The marina was bustling with activity as boats came back from fishing trips, people returned to their houseboats from their day's activities, and fishermen weighed in their catch. The breeze felt good after this typically stifling September day; it wafted with it the scent of the ocean. Across Biscayne Bay, an orange sun cast the skyline of Miami into golden relief, and Slade was momentarily homesick. To his way of thinking, sunset in the Glades was a much more inspiring sight.

He allowed himself to daydream as he thought about the wife he had come here to find, heard her soft voice whispering in his ear. It would be good to have a wife at last, good to have a sweet little cutie to laugh with in bed at night, to cuddle happily for a few quiet moments in the morning before he rode out to check the fences and the herd.

He pictured the Diamond B Ranch in his mind—brilliant blue sky, acres and acres of green grass punctuated by palmetto hummocks, and in the distance, Everglades saw grass shimmering green and yellow in the bright sunshine. It was a special place, that ranch, carved out of the Glades by Slade's grandfather, built to its present greatness by his father, and he wanted a special woman to share it with him.

Slade spotted Karma O'Connor as she rounded the curve from the parking lot on her bike. Now speaking of women, there was an interesting one, he thought. But quirky. Karma didn't at all resemble the wife he intended to find—she was too tall by far, and not fragile. Definitely not fragile. The word he would choose to describe her would be robust. He did have to admit that her hair was much the same color as what he had in mind. It wasn't straight though, and he had a thing for fragile-looking women with long straight blond hair—Southern-belle type, if possible. On the other hand, on Karma that bouncy mop of curls looked good.

He stood up to get a better look at her, and to his surprise, she didn't stop pedaling when she reached the grassy strip dividing the parking lot from the dock, nor did she stop on the narrow band of asphalt that passed for a sidewalk. She rode her fool bike right onto C Dock.

He treated himself to another swig of beer as she bent her head down in determination and kept pedaling past the line-up of houseboats, a big Amazon of a woman. The boards of the dock creaked under her bike wheels. That fluttering purple thing she wore scared a lazy pelican off one of the weathered pilings, and the bike's back wheel clipped a bait box, but still she pedaled on.

Slade couldn't figure for the life of him what kind of garment Karma was wearing. You could see through part of it, but not any part that mattered—the sleeves and at least the bottom part of the legs were transparent like a nightie. He remembered her legs. He'd gotten a pretty good gander at them when she was walking up the stairs to her office this morning. And her hips, ditto. They'd looked like a couple of melons in a croker sack. Very firm melons.

Then: disaster. Slade saw what was going to happen before Karma did. An elderly guy named Phifer in C-22 was making repairs to his boat, puttering around on deck as he had all afternoon. Phifer must not have seen Karma because he tossed a line toward the dock. The line seemed to hover for a moment before it descended, a kind of slow motion free-fall, and as the rope looped toward her through the air, Slade yelled, ''Look out!''

Karma looked up. The trouble was that she looked up at

Slade all the way down in Slip 41, not at the line, which fell neatly over her foot, snagging both it and the bike pedal in a kind of a bungee hang-up. Karma went flying. So did the bike—both of them right into the drink with a huge splash.

Slade was up and off *Toy Boat* in a flash. But by the time he reached the space where Karma had gone in, all that was to be seen of either her or the bike was a circle of purple chiffon floating on the top of the water.

She surfaced right away, sputtering and flinging a tangle of hair out of her eyes.

"I'll throw you a life ring," Slade hollered, grabbing one from a hook on one of the pilings and tossing it at her.

She yelled back, "I can swim," but when the life ring landed beside her, she latched on to it anyway and began kicking in the direction of the dock. By this time, bystanders had gathered. "What happened?" asked the old guy who'd thrown the line.

"She was riding a bike. Lost control of it," Slade said, not wanting to get into a conversation with Phifer. At present he was much more interested in Karma, who was now treading water directly below him. "Swim over to the piling, I'll lean down and give you a hand up."

She looked wary. "I can't do that. I don't have on anything but my underwear. That's my sari," and she pointed at the purple chiffon, which was being borne away by the outgoing tide.

"What'd she say?" asked Phifer.

"I believe she said she's sorry," Slade told him.

"I should think she's sorry," huffed Phifer. "Riding a bike on the dock."

The other onlookers agreed with him, and one by one they wandered off to their barbecuing or their beer on ice or whatever it was that they'd planned to do. "Me, I've got fish to clean," Phifer said grumpily before slapping off down the dock in his worn old boat shoes.

No one else came over to see what was going on, which told Slade something about how these Miami Beach people lived. Sure, Miami Beach folks lived a laid-back lifestyle, but in his opinion, they should have more concern for their neighbors. In Okeechobee City, this situation would have drawn a bunch of spectators, all of whom would feel inclined to give advice and, probably, help. But then, Okeechobee City was a small town. Miami Beach was not.

He turned his attention back to the woman in the water. She was floating amid the flotsam, including but not restricted to a tangle of dirty fishing line, and assorted fish parts. "Um, ma'am?"

"Yes?"

"Did you really say that you don't have on anything but your underwear?" he asked.

"Do we have to keep talking about it?" she said.

He was sure that this was a rhetorical question, so he decided to change his tack. "You can't stay in there forever."

"Wait and see," Karma said, and he thought she looked kind of comical in her determination. The key parts of her anatomy that he could see under the surface of the water looked nicely shaped and tan. Why they were tan, he could only speculate. Maybe she did a lot of topless sunbathing, like some of the models he and his companions of the night before had seen on South Beach yesterday. He tried not to think about Karma with no top on, but the image stuck in his mind.

As if she could read his thoughts, Karma hugged the life ring to her chest, covering up what was interesting him. "I'll come out when it gets dark. I'll slink away into the night. Look, why don't you forget you ever met me? I'm sure you can find another matchmaker in this town."

Slade had no interest in shambling through the whole dating service sign-up process again. It was embarrassing enough to have to enlist help to find a wife in the first place.

Besides, at the moment he was fascinated by Karma O'Connor, though he couldn't quite figure out why. Mascara was running down her cheeks in rivulets, and she'd lost an earring. But with her hair plastered to her head like that so that he wasn't distracted by her wealth of curls, he could better assess her beauty. And Karma was beautiful. Her complexion was pink-and-white and flawlessly textured; her nose was aristocratically narrow. She also had very white and very straight teeth. As a connoisseur of horseflesh, he knew you could tell a lot about an animal by its teeth.

This, however, was a woman. A woman in distress. He said as comfortingly as he could, "Don't go anywhere. I'm going to get a robe and throw it down to you."

Karma opened her mouth, then shut it abruptly just prior to being sloshed by the backwash from the propeller of a passing outboard. Before she took it into her head to object, Slade took off at a trot back toward *Toy Boat,* passing Phifer on the way.

"Fool woman. Had no business riding a bike on the dock," grumbled Phifer, who by this time was tossing fish heads to a circling flock of gulls.

When Slade returned with one of Mack's monogrammed white terry cloth robes, Karma had moved to the piling and had commenced clinging to a metal ring affixed to the post.

Slade bundled the robe into a neat ball. "I'm going to throw this down, and you can put it on. Then you can come out of the water," Slade said.

Karma said something like "Hmmpf," and he tossed the robe down. He tactfully turned his back as she put it on, but he heard her splashing around and it seemed to take her an overly long time to get into the robe. "Everything all right?" he called over his shoulder.

"You must realize," she said, "that this thing has soaked up a ton of water. Yes, I've got my arms through the sleeves, if that's what you want to know, but I think it's going to pull me under. Like an anchor.''

Slade turned around. She was suitably swathed, but she was now riding slightly lower in the water and her expression was anything but pleasant.

He knelt down on the dock, held his hand out to her. She grabbed it.

He supposed that it was some peculiar flight of fancy that tied in with his earlier fantasy about finding the right woman for him, but all the same, he could have sworn that a bolt of electricity flashed through their connected hands. It was so strong that he almost let go.

But he didn't let go. He hung on for dear life even as he tried to sort this thing out. He concluded as he gave a mighty heave and yanked her up onto the dock that he had been mistaken. He couldn't possibly have felt anything. He was out of his mind for thinking so. He wasn't at all attracted to this woman. She wasn't his type.

And yet when she stood dripping in front of him, her eyes searching his face, he did feel something, an emotion that he finally identified as relief. No harm had come to her and he was glad. That was all.

''I guess I can say goodbye to that bike,'' Karma said ruefully.

''Well, maybe not. I'll see if the marina manager can do anything about it,'' he told her.

Karma shrugged, sending a veritable Niagara sluicing over his bare feet. ''Come on,'' he said, shaking his feet to rid them of water. ''I reckon we can find you something warm and dry to wear.''

She walked glumly and wetly beside him back to *Toy Boat.* ''I brought some things,'' she said. ''They're at the bottom of the bay along with my bike.''

He stepped down onto the boat first, handed her onto the deck. ''What things did you bring?''

"Crackers. Spicy tofu-cilantro garlic spread. Things like that."

Slade had never heard of spicy tofu-cilantro garlic spread, but it sounded downright unappetizing. He hadn't thought this was a social call. Wasn't it supposed to be business? To videotape him so she'd have something to show her female clients as a kind of sales pitch? He narrowed his eyes at her. She was now dripping all over the teak deck.

"Maybe you could, uh, wring yourself out," he ventured.

She eyed the yards and yards of wet white terry cloth doubtfully. She made as if to wring out one side of the robe, but he quickly directed her toward the side of the boat. "Over the side," he said helpfully. "If you don't mind. These teak decks take a heap of maintenance, according to Mack."

"Who's Mack?"

"The cousin who belongs to this boat."

"And where is he?"

"I dunno. He made it rich selling off his share of the family land, used the money to buy this boat and a lot of other things. I expect he and Renee are flying around in his Lear jet."

"A Lear jet," Karma repeated.

"Yeah, well, Renee hates flying in it."

"That's why it's important to find the right wife," she said. "That's why you came to Rent-a-Yenta. So that you wouldn't find someone who isn't suited to you, that is." She reached up and fluffed her hair, which was already drying in the breeze off the bay.

Slade thought it was cute that even now, sodden and miserable and annoyed about losing her bike and the tofu whatever, this woman could still inject a plug for her business into the conversation.

"Let's go into the master stateroom. Mack's wife's

clothes are there. Maybe some will fit you." He realized when she shot him a skeptical look out from under her eyelashes that this might sound like a come-on. "You can go in there alone. I'll stay right here on deck like a gentleman."

She looked heartened by this statement. "No funny business?" she asked.

"No funny business. I'll even leave the boat, walk over to the marina office and see if I can rustle up the head honcho around here, ask him about your bike."

"That might be a good idea," she allowed, and so as she made her way through the salon, scattering a narrow path of water droplets on the woven-to-order rug, Slade went to find the marina manager, who might know what you had to do to salvage sunken bicycles.

Wow, KARMA THOUGHT AS HER eyes popped at the sumptuous master stateroom. Slade Braddock certainly wasn't slumming. The boat looked like a picture right out of an upscale travel magazine, the kind of publication she'd read maybe once in her whole life. There was teak everywhere, and cove lighting, and some kind of pale shimmery fabric draping the portholes. The bed was huge and covered with a subtly patterned spread. The bouquet on the built-in dresser was composed of fresh flowers and hothouse variety at that.

She walked across the cushy seafoam-green carpet to the closet and flung the door open. Inside was a whole wardrobe of clothes arrayed on matching padded hangers. She pulled out a dress and a pair of slacks; they looked as if they'd been made for a midget. Slade's cousin's wife was apparently a nutritionally challenged size two.

All right, so she couldn't wear these clothes. She threw open the next closet and found more promising duds; the trouble was, these were Slade's.

She yanked a worn denim shirt out of the few hanging

there and held it up for inspection. It was the typical Western-style shirt with two pockets in front and a yoke in back. It snapped instead of buttoned. The best part about it was that it would fit her.

Well, almost, anyway. After a longing look at the shower in the adjoining bathroom and mindful that Slade hadn't said she could make use of it, she shrugged out of the wet robe and into the denim shirt. It came down to the middle of her thighs.

A glance into the full length mirror on the inside of the closet door reassured her that the shirt covered all the important points. She bent over experimentally and realized that she'd have to find something to wear underneath it. She kept looking and settled on a pair of stretchy black exercise tights that tumbled off the closet shelf. They probably belonged to the petite Renee, but they stretched to cover Karma's long legs.

She decided that there was nothing to be done about shoes, since her own sandals were swimming with the fishes at the bottom of the bay and none of the ones here fit. But she *could* do something about her bedraggled hair, and that was to dry it with the use of a hair dryer that was conveniently mounted next to the sink in the bathroom, which she supposed, since it was on a boat, would properly be called the head.

The only head she was prepared to worry about at the moment was her own. She wore her hair shoulder length, and when wet it tended to frizz. The dryer had one speed— hot. That frizzed her hair even more, and when she was finished, she looked as if she'd just unplugged herself from an electrical socket.

Never mind, she told herself. You've already blown any chance you might have had with Slade Braddock. She cast one last resigned look into the mirror and went outside to wrap this up.

When she emerged from the salon onto the deck, Slade

looked up appreciatively from the magazine he was reading.

"This belongs to you," she said apologetically, lifting the edge of the shirt.

"I never filled that shirt out so well," he said.

"What did you find out about my bike?" She was worried now about how she would get home. She didn't have cab fare, and it was a long walk back to the Blue Moon.

"The manager's son is a certified scuba diver, and he'll go down to look for it tomorrow morning. No problem. You'll get it back. Come and sit down, you might as well relax. Care for a beer?"

"No, thanks. I want to videotape while we've still got good light."

"There's the camera. I set it up on the tripod."

The camera stood on one corner of the deck. Karma went over to inspect it, surreptitiously looking Slade Braddock over as she pretended to note all the buttons and knobs on the camera. He wore only jeans and a white T-shirt, and instead of the boots, he wore deck shoes.

Under that T-shirt, his chest muscles rippled as he stood up to stretch. He was tall, even without his boots. Taller than she was, which was really saying something.

"Need any help in figuring it out?"

"This is different from mine," she managed to say although her mouth had gone dry.

"I've used this camera a few times before, so let me show you how it works." He closed the gap between them in a few steps, a maneuver that somehow mysteriously caused her heart to speed up. This attraction to a client, she knew, was wildly inappropriate. She shouldn't be breathing hard and heavy merely because he was standing close to her. It was unprofessional, it was unlike her—and it was a great way to be feeling after a long time without a special man in her life.

"This is the way you adjust it," Slade said, stepping

behind the camera to demonstrate, "and this is the button you press to make it start."

While he was concentrating on the camera, her gaze lingered for a moment on the cleft in his chin, drifted slightly higher and came to rest on his lips. She did not want to concentrate on his lips. Or any of the rest of him. Which was why she didn't think she could go through with this.

"Do you still want to do this videotaping, or would you rather stop by my office and do it another time?" she said on a note of desperation. Using her work to advance her own personal agenda with this man had been a mistake. She needed to go home and calm herself with some deep breathing exercises, maybe on the beach so the salt air could become a type of inhalation therapy. She needed a soothing cup of herbal tea. Maybe she even needed to have her chakras read.

"The camera is ready to roll," Slade pointed out with a twinkle. "You gonna deprive me of my first, last and only chance to be a star of my own video?"

"Um…no." Because she didn't know what else to do, she edged around the back of the camera and fiddled with the lens.

"Hey, didn't I explain it right?" Slade asked. "I've already focused it on that chair over there. What do you say I sit down and we get on with it?"

She punched a button by mistake, and the camera made a frenzied whirring sound. "What's that?" she said in alarm.

"Easy there," Slade said. He slid around behind her. The heat of his body sizzled right through the denim shirt she wore.

"I—I—" she stammered, forgetting what she had been about to say.

"Let me check to make sure it's still in focus," he said, and he bent and fit his eye to the camera. Karma was treated to a view of how his hair curved along his nape.

"Now," Slade said as he straightened. "Wait till I'm seated, and then push the red button." His body brushed against hers as he edged past her and out of the tight corner. As he passed, she was assailed by pure, clean masculine odor. Not fragrance, as in aftershave or cologne, but a natural male scent of musk and a couple of other unidentifiables. This disconcerted her almost as much as his touch. She'd expected him to smell good. But not great.

He smiled in that engaging way of his, one eyebrow cocked, one corner of his mouth higher than the other. She had noticed his smile before; why did it seem so appealing now?

She made herself concentrate. Peer through the lens, focus, and next all she had to do was push the little red button. It was when she looked up that she realized with astonishment that Slade had gone all remote. His face was immobile, his eyes glazed over. He looked like a clone of Mount Rushmore.

It had happened before: Freeze-up. Some people might be affable and congenial as all get-out before you switched on the camera, but as soon as they realized they were being taped, they were afflicted with the inability to move their tongues and lips in any semblance of casual conversation. They became so self-conscious in front of that lens that nothing, but nothing, could make them snap out of it.

This was all she needed. At the moment she wanted to get this taping over with and scurry home to the Blue Moon, which seemed like a safe haven after this debacle.

"Slade," she said, because she'd learned in some psychology course eons ago that using a person's name gave you an edge, made him really pay attention to you, "we're just going to chat normally."

He nodded, but stiffly.

"So," she said as she pulled a chair over to one side of the deck out of camera range. "How about stating your full name first?" This was usually easy for clients who were wary of the camera. People always were able to say their own names with a minimum of stage fright.

"I thought we already did that." His tone was flat, his voice expressionless.

"Excuse me?"

"On the form you filled out today. I gave you my name."

"This is for the tape."

"Uh."

"So go ahead and tell me your name." She smiled her encouragement.

"My name's Slade Braddock. Do I need to spell it?"

This was proving to be even more difficult than she had anticipated. "No, that won't be necessary." She could edit out the comments that didn't need to stay in. She'd had to edit like crazy for Jennifer and Mandi, especially Jennifer, who had given a very realistic imitation of an orgasm on tape. Or maybe it wasn't an imitation—who knew?

"Now, Slade, we'd like to know what you do for a living."

He stared at her for a moment. Not that she minded. She liked it when he looked at her. But they weren't getting anywhere with this video.

"Slade?"

He licked his lips. "I guess you know I don't like this much."

"That's okay. Just answer the questions the best you can."

"You wanted to know what I do for a living?"

"Yes."

"I run a herd of cattle up Okeechobee way."

It was like pulling teeth to get the man to talk. If she hadn't known he was perfectly capable of conversation, she'd be willing to quit. Some part of her was exultant at this development, though. The worse he looked on the video, the less appealing he'd be to the likes of Jennifer and Mandi. Still, it was her duty as the matchmaker to display him at his best.

Maybe if he talked about his work in more detail, he'd forget his self-consciousness.

"And what kind of cattle are they?"

"Why, they're Braford cattle, most of 'em."

"I don't believe I've ever heard of that breed of cattle."

"That means they're part Brahma, part Hereford. Braford."

He'd warmed up a little, but not much. "And how big is the herd?"

"Oh, it's plenty big."

"Perhaps you could describe the ranch," Karma said encouragingly.

He smiled genuinely for the first time since the interview had started. "Well, there's a big old house. Not real old, mind you. My daddy built it in fifty-eight, so it's got what they call mod cons. It overlooks a pond where you can see ibises and great blue herons and sometimes a little 'gator that we call Abner. Cute little guy. 'Course, Abner could be a girl. Hard to tell. There's a barn beyond the live oak trees, and you can just barely see it through the Spanish moss. That's where the horses stay, and once we had some goats. They sure were fun to raise. And—"

He went on about the chickens that his mother had kept and how he liked to gun his pickup through the ditches, and all Karma could think of was that now that she'd gotten him started, he was going to be hard to shut up. His face was lit up, alive, and he was so sexy when he talked about something that was clearly near and dear to his heart. She couldn't imagine why this man hadn't been scooped up by some girl, someplace, some time ago.

"And I guess that's about all you'll be wanting to hear about the Diamond B Ranch." He looked slightly embarrassed.

"Our clients might like to know more about Okeechobee City," she prodded gently.

"Well, Florida is a major beef producer in this country. Lots of grass up Okeechobee way, and it grows lush and green all year 'round. Why, the western states have nothing on us, since we had our own range wars, rustling, and fence-cutting to worry about back in the late 1800s. Life on the north side of the lake has calmed down a tad now, but it's still cow country. And how do I fit in? Admirably. Right now, I'm just one lonesome cowboy lookin' for a wife," he said.

"Your hobbies? The things you like to do in your spare time?"

"I don't know if you want to hear about that." He gazed down at his feet.

"Of course we do. Our clients like to get an idea of what they might be talking about on a date if they choose to follow up on you."

"Oh, okay, then I might as well tell you. I like to watch birds. That's my hobby."

She wouldn't have been surprised if he'd said he liked to practice bull riding or steer roping or even sky diving, but bird watching? There was no way she would have guessed that this big rawboned cowboy was interested in birds, of all things. She had to admit that she was fascinated.

"I like to get up in the morning, walk out into the sunrise when it's just skimming a bit of gold light over the pond. That's when I see the best ones. I saw a rare roseate spoonbill a couple of weeks ago. They're about as fanciful as a bird gets. You ever seen a picture of one?"

Karma shook her head, entranced.

"They're bright pink in color, kind of like a flamingo. Prettiest thing you ever saw, but a roseate spoonbill has got a funny clown face. Almost makes you laugh when you see it."

"I see," said Karma. What she saw was a man who felt passionately about something that was important to him. If she had thought that Slade Braddock was shallow, and she conceded that maybe she had, she knew better now.

"But I'm sure you don't want to hear anything more about that," he said, lapsing into silence.

"Oh, no, I was interested. It's just that—that we don't like to let our videos get too long. A short interview usually lets our clients know enough to make a choice." She got up and stopped the camera, removing the cassette. "I'll take this back to the office and edit it. I should be able to offer this for my female clients to view next week."

"Next week! What do you mean, next week?"

"I have to process your application. I need to check out references, edit the videotape—"

"You need to find me a wife," he interrupted.

Her chin shot up. "That's exactly what I'm planning to do. And if you'll stop by the office tomorrow, I should have my psychological profile forms back from the printer. You'll need to fill one out."

"Psychological profile?"

"I'm a psychologist by training. The profile is something new that I've added to Rent-a-Yenta for the betterment of our services."

"All right, all right. I'll fill out the form. But what am I supposed to do between now and the time you set up my first date?"

Karma looked at him. She looked at the water and the sunset and the boats out on the bay. She looked back at Slade and said the first thing that popped into her head.

"You could have your chakras read," she said.

3

HIS SECOND CHAKRA was twisted. At least that's what Goldy told him.

"Excuse me?" Slade said, feeling foolish.

Goldy sniffed. "The second chakra is the center of sensation and feeling. It's blocked."

He didn't see how his second chakra could be blocked, since when he glanced over at Karma, who was fiddling with flowers in a vase on the file cabinet, he felt a definite sensation. He likened it to the way a bull must feel when he saw a cow after a long dry spell. Only cows didn't have calves like Karma's. Her legs were shapely and well-defined in those tights she had borrowed from Renee's closet.

He forced his attention back to Goldy, who had tilted her head and was toying with the strands of beads around her neck.

"And what do I do to unblock my, um, chakra?" he said distractedly.

"Embrace the flow," Goldy said.

"Embrace the flow," he repeated. Needing more guidance than he was getting from Goldy, Slade glanced at Karma, who nodded in agreement. Her hair rippled into motion, and he had the sudden inspiration that if he tried to run his fingers through it, she'd let him. Not here, of course. Not now. But sometime.

The phone rang and Goldy answered it. She became in-

volved in a conversation that looked as if it might be pro-
longed.

"Movement would help," Karma said to him as she
plucked dead leaves off the flowers in the vase. "To unblock your chakra, I mean."

"Movement? Like walking? Talking? Riding a horse?"

"No, nothing like that. The kind of movement that frees
up blocked emotions. You could join a yoga class."

Slade shook his head to clear it. This didn't eliminate his
growing attraction to Karma, however, and he had to remind himself sternly that she wasn't his type. This conversation was more than enough proof of that.

"What is yoga?" he asked. He had a vague idea that it
was something that Hollywood types did when they came
out of drug rehab.

"The word yoga means 'yoke,'" Karma said. "It's a
discipline that yokes the individual with the divine through
practice that joins our mundane and spiritual lives."

"Okay, so explain what a chakra is."

"Chakra means 'wheel' or 'disk.' A chakra is the sphere
of bioenergetic activity coming from major nerves in the
spinal column. You have seven chakras stacked in a column
of energy from the base of your spine to the top of your
head."

It was worse than he thought, this stuff, plus if there had
been chakras wrapped around his spine, he was sure they
would have been shaken off by all that rodeo riding he'd
done.

Karma kept talking, and she might as well have been
speaking a foreign language. "What goes on in the chakras
influences our minds and bodies. Maybe Goldy can explain
how your second chakra is blocked."

Goldy rolled her eyes at them and pointed at the phone
while mouthing the words, "New tenant." Slade ran an
impatient hand through his hair and wondered distractedly
if he could get a takeout somewhere around here for din-

ner—a nice quiet dinner during which he could enjoy his own company.

"We could go to the delicatessen on the corner. I could explain more about your second chakra," Karma said, looking him straight in the eye. This statement was a direct answer to his unasked question, and for a moment he thought she might be able to read his mind but immediately discarded the notion. He was letting all this New Age stuff get to him, which was ridiculous.

"You want to?" Karma gazed at him hopefully.

He hadn't a moment ago, but it struck him that her eyes had green depths that he hadn't noticed before, and her neck was extremely graceful, putting him in mind of a snowy egret's. Plus, all else aside, he was hungry.

"I sure do," he said, and he was rewarded by a mega-watt smile.

"I'll run upstairs and change clothes," she said.

"Is that necessary? You look fine."

"Well," Karma said, glancing down at what she wore, "these clothes aren't mine."

She had already gone upstairs and come back down earlier wearing a pair of sandals on her previously bare feet, whose toenails were lacquered sugar-pea green with silver sparkles. He had an idea that if Karma disappeared into the mysterious upper levels of the Blue Moon Apartments, he would have a long wait before she reappeared. She would want to wash her hair, dry it, and slather on makeup. She would agonize over whether to wear the red outfit or the hot-pink outfit and decide after half an hour to wear the blue-and-green print one instead. In the meantime he would have to be polite to Goldy, who sounded like Minnie Mouse on helium. And that was presuming that she got off the phone; if she didn't, he'd have to rock back on his heels and pretend to admire what appeared to be distressed panels of coat-hanger art on the wall.

"You're gorgeous just the way you are," he said, appropriating Karma's arm and propelling her toward the door. He even waved goodbye to Goldy in a way that he hoped inspired trust and confidence.

"Shall we take the car?" He'd left his Chevy Suburban at a parking meter.

"Oh, let's walk," Karma said, and he swung into step beside her.

He realized before they had taken five steps that people noticed Karma. Men stopped and did a double take after they'd passed; some of them gave her a quick once-over as soon as they saw her. It must be because she was so all-fired tall. She'd dominate any group; she'd stand out in a crowd. He walked taller himself because he was walking beside her, and before he knew it, he was taking pride in being with her. He didn't mind being envied by other men; in fact, he kind of liked it.

"You see, you have to release emotional energy to free the body from its grip," Karma said, marching along to the beat of a steel-drum band playing reggae on the street corner.

"I don't think my emotional energy needs to be released," he ventured.

"That's what people think. But we all have repressed emotions."

"Do you?"

"I'm not so different from everyone else," Karma said seriously, though this was a statement he could have refuted. There was no opportunity, though, because they had reached the delicatessen. He opened the door for her, and she sailed through, hair bouncing, breasts ditto. A guy on the way out gaped at her.

"Would you look at that," the guy said to his friend. "Would you look at her!"

This was a compliment, but Slade was sure that Karma hadn't heard it. Or if she had, she was playing it cool.

Once they were seated in the restaurant booth, Slade

studied the menu. He was in the mood for a big broiled steak, but there wasn't anything remotely resembling one on this menu. Instead there were things like a corned beef-with-chicken liver sandwich on pumpernickel, and cheese blintzes, and humongous desserts with names like Double Chocolate Disgrace. On the table were two bowls in a metal holder, one containing small whole pickled green tomatoes, the other containing sauerkraut.

The waiter returned, and Karma ordered a veggie-and-cream cheese sandwich.

"Are you ready to order, sir?" The waiter stood with his pencil poised.

"What do you recommend?" Slade said, throwing himself on the waiter's mercy.

"We just made a batch of fresh chopped chicken livers. The chicken liver sandwich is very good."

The idea of eating a whole sandwich made of chicken livers made Slade slightly sick to his stomach, so he glanced wildly at the menu and chose the first thing he saw, corned beef on rye.

When the waiter had left, Karma ladled sauerkraut into one of the small bowls stacked on the table. "Want some?" she asked.

Slade shook his head. "I never liked sauerkraut, and I can't imagine eating green tomatoes."

Karma pulled a face. "I can't imagine not eating them. I'm a vegetarian, so maybe that's why."

"You don't eat any meat?" He'd never known a vegetarian before; he'd always thought such a person must be slightly deranged. Not to scarf down a thick prime rib, drowned in natural gravy? Not to sink your teeth into a big juicy burger with all the trimmings? Never to know the joys of pork tenderloin cooked on a grill, or leg of lamb, or succulent spare ribs?

"Nope, no poultry, no mammals. I eat fish, though. I love fish."

Fish. He'd been known to eat catfish in the Glades, and he liked a tuna sandwich now and then, but he couldn't imagine fish as a steady diet.

"I've never eaten in this place," he said, looking around at the clientele, who ranged from jewel-encrusted elderly matrons with shellacked hair to sunburned tourists whose skin looked like raw hamburger.

"My uncle—you met him this morning—and my aunt used to like to bring me and my sisters here when we visited as children. I guess I came by my liking for Kosher food naturally, since my mother was Jewish."

He welcomed the chance to know more about Karma's personal life; he couldn't imagine what could produce a woman like this.

"With a surname like O'Connor, your father was Irish, right?"

"Mmm-hmm. He and my mother married in college. Both families predicted the marriage's immediate failure, but my parents had four daughters, including me, and lived happily for years. Until my mother took up cake decorating, that is, and they split up. She changed her name to Saguaro, like the cactus, and moved to Arizona."

"They divorced because she became a cake decorator?"

"Kind of." Karma seemed reluctant to elaborate.

"I've heard of many reasons to divorce, but that one takes the cake." He grinned at her, pleased with his play on words.

The corners of her mouth twitched as if she were suppressing a smile. "Dad didn't approve of Mom's new occupation. You see, she worked for a bakery that specialized in cakes that look like body parts." She looked embarrassed and seemed as if she expected him to be shocked, but he was still operating in the dark.

"You don't mean—"

"I do mean," she said. "The body parts weren't arms and legs, if you get my drift."

He did. He tried to picture in his mind a cake that looked like a pair of breasts or—well! He cleared his throat.

"So, uh, what does your father do?" he asked, sensing that they had reached a conversational cul-de-sac.

"My father found a new life after Mom left. He works on a cruise ship, plying wealthy widows with booze and blarney while pretending to enjoy teaching them the tango."

Slade chuckled. "We should all be so lucky."

Their food arrived, and they dug in. Once the corned beef sandwich had taken the edge off his hunger—and it was a delicious sandwich—Slade managed with some difficulty to overcome his aversion to the subject of his chakra.

"Suppose you tell me more about my second chakra. Like, where it is, for example."

"Your second chakra is located in your abdomen."

"Why would it have problems?"

Karma inhaled a deep breath, and looking as if she doubted the wisdom of explaining, she plunged ahead anyway. "Well, you know how these days we store information on disks—with computers, I mean? I told you that chakra means 'disk.' So it stores information, too. If a chakra is blocked, it needs reprogramming."

"Reprogramming," he repeated, thinking that this was worse than he thought.

"The issues of the second chakra are change, movement, pleasure, emotion. If the chakra is blocked, it can be difficult to form attachments, difficult to experience the right emotion. I can match you up with the perfect person," she said, "and if you can't change, or get no pleasure out of the relationship, or can't emote—"

"Emote?" Slade said, wary about this new direction she was taking. All he wanted was a wife. He didn't expect to have to change, and he wasn't sure where movement fit into this whole thing, and he wanted to feel pleasure, but wouldn't that come naturally when he found the right person?

"You want to run that by me again?" he said.

"Emotion is a building block," Karma explained before she took the last bite of her sandwich.

"I see," he said, turning this over in his mind.

"Are you sure you don't want one of these tomatoes?" Karma said, shoving the dish across the table at him.

"No, thanks. And just between you and me, I think this whole chakra stuff is a bunch of nonsense."

Karma stopped conveying a tomato from the dish to her plate and let it drop with a weary thump back into its dish. "Great," she said. "Fine. See if I try to help you any more."

"You're supposed to find me a wife," he said, losing patience.

Karma started to slide out of the booth. "Don't you think I know that? Don't you understand that this is what our conversation is all about? Don't you think the fact that you haven't managed to turn up a likely candidate so far might have something to do with some kind of—of mind block?"

"I don't see the connection," Slade said honestly and a little desperately as he slapped a large bill on the table and followed Karma as she charged out of the restaurant.

"You wouldn't, since your chakra has for all intents and purposes shut down," Karma said. Her long legs ate up the sidewalk as she barged her way through bunches of blondes and a gaggle of tourists all gawking and talking excitedly.

Slade caught up with her. "You told me that I'm supposed to express emotion. Wouldn't you say I'm expressing emotion by telling you how I feel about all this chakra-babble?"

She slanted a look toward him. "What do you think emotion is?" she shot back.

He had to think about this for a moment, but the answer

seemed clear enough. ''Well, I'd say that emotions are instinctual reactions,'' he said.

She seemed taken aback, surprised at his response. ''Okay. At least you know one when you see one,'' she conceded. ''That's a start. To take it a bit further, our feelings are our unconscious reaction to situations or events. We organize our feelings through emotion. We can choose the way we react to emotions, but the feelings themselves are quite separate.''

Karma had slowed her pace was now walking almost sedately at his side.

''My emotional response to all this is that you and me should go in one of these bars and discuss this over a drink or two.'' Karma looked at him with rank skepticism. ''So I can learn more about this,'' he amended.

Ahead of them, a group of people spilled out onto the sidewalk from a neon-lit doorway. ''How about here?'' he said.

He thought he might be becoming more sensitive to others' emotions when he recognized a whole raft of them flitting across Karma's mobile features. Confusion, distrust, sheer terror—not to mention a brief blip of yearning overlaid with what he thought might be desire. But desire for what? For a beer? For his company? For more, even, than that?

''We can stop for a drink,'' she said. ''I don't want to be out late, that's all.''

He took her elbow, and she tensed as if she might shake his hand loose although she did not. They made their way into the club, where hot salsa music accompanied scantily clad bodies gyrating on a minuscule dance floor. Karma slid into a booth, and he slid in beside her.

''How do you know so much about all this chakra stuff, anyway?'' he asked her after they'd ordered drinks.

She smiled at the waiter as he slid her glass of white wine toward her. ''I guess you could say I was born into the territory. My parents met on a commune in the late sixties. My sisters and I were raised on soybeans, sprouts, tofu and a lot of other things that you've probably never heard of. Chakras, yoga, the freedom to be you and me, and so on. Commune life ended when we all had to go to school and they moved us to Connecticut where my father got a job in an aircraft factory.''

"That sounds normal enough," he allowed.

"Oh, but there's more. Life in suburbia was modified by my parents' history. Jewish woman married to an Irish Catholic and spending their marriage's first years grubbing around in an organic garden equals not just your ordinary family.''

"Are your sisters like you? Do they have unusual names like yours?''

"My oldest sister is named Azure, the youngest one is Isis, and the middle one is Mary Beth.''

"Karma, Azure, Isis, and Mary Beth?" he said, smothering a chuckle at the incongruity of it.

Karma picked up on his amusement. "Go ahead. Laugh if you want to. We're used to it.''

"Where did the Mary Beth come from?''

"Mary Beth was named after the midwife who rode five miles on a snowmobile to deliver her. Consequently, Mary Beth has always considered herself lucky that she was born in the middle of the worst winter storm to hit upstate New York in twenty-three years.''

"Are their occupations as interesting as yours?''

"Isis is married to a dentist and they're raising his three sons by his first wife, all model students and soccer enthusiasts. Azure is a management consultant based in Boston. Mary Beth is a rabbi. I love to ride by her synagogue and see 'Mary Beth O'Connor, Assistant Rabbi' on the sign outside. I imagine that the unexpected juxtaposition of our Irish surname to the title of assistant rabbi merits a few second glances from passersby.'' Karma grinned.

Slade laughed. He couldn't help but be charmed by this woman with her tumultuous hair, offbeat personality, and unusual background. It occurred to him that he hadn't met an interesting woman in ages. Years. It was why he had come to Miami Beach. It was why he had signed up with a dating service.

"What about you?" she asked.

"I'd say we've pretty much covered that during the interview."

"Not about your childhood. Or your family," she pointed out.

Slade took a sip of his beer before answering. "Grew up in Okeechobee City, went to college, worked the rodeo circuit for a while and eventually came back to run the family ranch. My dad is ready to retire from ranching. He and Ma can't wait until I come home with my fiancée so they can do some traveling."

"This fiancée you hope to find," Karma said carefully. "Do your parents have right of refusal? I mean, what if they don't like her?"

"They'll like anybody who decides to put up with me. They're so eager for a daughter-in-law that they'd accept the bride of Frankenstein if she'd marry me."

"I hope I can do better for you than that," Karma said seriously.

He was about to say, I hope you can, too. However, he looked at Karma, really looked at her in that moment, and something in her expression made him bite back the words. He thought she looked regretful, even a trifle upset.

"Now about the way I move," he said after they had watched the dancers for several minutes. "Why don't you let me show you that I know how?"

She regarded him with a puzzled expression. "Excuse me?"

"Let's dance. In the interest of freeing up my chakra, of course."

"Don't make fun of it," Karma said sharply. "If you don't believe in the theory, fine. Lots of people do, that's all."

"I guess I need to know more about it before I make up my mind. But for now, what about dancing?"

Karma bit her lip. "Well," she said. "I was thinking it was time for me to go home."

"You won't turn into a pumpkin, Cinderella. Humor me."

"Any reason why I should? You're my client. I'm not supposed to—"

"But that's exactly the point. I *am* your client."

"I should be finding the perfect date for you. I shouldn't be out having a good time and forgetting that this is a business relationship." She seemed troubled.

"Are you having a good time, Karma?" he asked softly, letting the words sink in. Because I am, too. I'd have a better time if you'd dance with me."

After a moment's hesitation during which Karma seemed to weigh the pros and cons, the pros must have won out. She got up and Slade followed her onto the crowded dance floor. No sooner did they get there than the song that was playing stopped and segued into a smooth ballad.

He took her in his arms, liking the solid feel of her, liking the way she melted into him. She was lighter on her feet than he would have expected, and he led her to the center of the floor where lights from a revolving glass ball overhead played across her features.

"So, Karma, tell me—do I move all right?" he asked after they'd been at it for a few minutes. He was teasing her to see what she'd say.

He expected a saucy retort, maybe a challenge. But she surprised him. "Oh, yes," she murmured.

"So do you. But in case I don't express myself enough to bring my most repressed feelings out into the open, what should I do?"

"Our previous discussions make me suspect that this is an insincere question."

"Insincere is as insincere does," he said.

"Meaning what?"

"Meaning that I asked for advice, and if I take it, you'll know that I'm far more interested than I've let on."

"This is a verbal sparring contest."

He tightened his arm around her waist. "At the moment, it's more physical than verbal as far as I'm concerned."

"Yikes," was Karma's inelegant remark. "Double yikes."

"So?"

"Well, if you really want to do something about movement and gain a little inner peace as well, you could try yoga, like I mentioned before."

"And where would I learn this yoga?"

"We hold yoga classes on the roof at the Blue Moon on Tuesday nights. Eight o'clock sharp." She spoke with a breathy little hitch in her voice that he found unbelievably sexy.

He pulled her even closer, felt her breasts pushing against his chest. "And you will be there, I suppose."

"I suppose. I mean, definitely. Unless I have something else to do."

What would this woman do in her spare time? he wondered. Make tofu-cilantro goodies such as the ones she'd lost at the bottom of the bay along with her bicycle? Hang out with Goldy in the lobby of the Blue Moon? Go on a date?

It occurred to him that Karma O'Connor might have a boyfriend. Or worse. She might be engaged. If she ran a dating service, she could have her pick of clients.

"You're not taken or anything, are you?" he demanded out of the clear blue, surprising himself as well as her.

"Taken?" She moved away and blinked at him. He noticed that her eyelashes were curly and long.

"As in going steady. Or engaged. Or something," he said, stammering around and feeling stupid.

"No." She moved closer now, tightening her arm across his shoulders. This gave Slade an exultant feeling that he would have been hard put to describe. He knew she wasn't his type. But he also knew that he might have a chance to get lucky for tonight. Or maybe the next few nights, if he played this right.

Not that it was only sex he was interested in. He wanted to know what made Karma O'Connor tick. He wanted to know why she thought the way she did, why she danced with her eyes closed. He wanted to know why she was running a place called Rent-a-Yenta and what she'd done before that. He wanted to know—

"You could come tomorrow night."

He had to think for a few seconds to put this statement in its proper context. "To yoga class, you mean."

"Yes, it would be good for you."

"If I promise to be there, will you leave here with me now?" he said, sounding more urgent than he intended.

"And where would we go?" she asked. In another woman, this might have sounded coy, but he didn't think Karma was capable of coyness.

"Somewhere away from the music, the smoke and other people. A walk on the beach, maybe."

"You like walking on the beach?"

"I think so. I haven't had many chances to do it." Well, there was last night, but he'd rather forget that whole fiasco.

"It's another way to bring movement into your life. Okay, you're on."

They broke apart, and Slade felt a pang of regret for the fact that he no longer held Karma in his arms. Watching the way she moved as they traversed the area between the dance floor and the door was some compensation, however, and putting his arm around her once they were outside on the sidewalk was even more.

They had turned to walk down the street toward the beach when he caught a glimpse of red hair sprouting from a knot on top of a head. The woman under the hair was on her way into the club that they had recently left, and it wasn't just any woman. It was, he realized with a sinking heart, the woman he'd met last night, the one who had accompanied the men he was with into the alley as they tried to rob him. The woman whose bikini top had ended up in his pocket.

There are certain moments in life that you can see coming from a distance away, and when that happens, the best thing to do is avoid them at all costs. And he didn't want to meet up with this redhead, whose name, he recalled, was Brenda.

But it was too late. Brenda had already seen him. Not that he was all that inconspicuous, as tall as he was and with the flamboyant Karma O'Connor on his arm.

"You!" Brenda shouted. "Come back here!"

"Looks to me like we'd better get out of here," he muttered close to Karma's ear. Fortunately at that moment a bunch of men wearing red fezzes on their heads tumbled out of a charter bus between him and Brenda, who let out a squawk of outrage.

Karma craned her neck. He had no doubt that she could see over the heads of the men in the red hats.

"That woman," she said. "Is she trying to talk to you?"

Brenda hollered something, the words indistinct.

"I think so," Slade said. "We'd better run for it."

He hadn't anticipated the effect these words would have on Karma. Instead of agreeing with him, or better yet putting one foot in front of the other as fast as could be managed, she dug in her heels and said, "Why?"

"Because that woman and her companions tried to rob me last night. Because I decked the two guys, and she went off screaming down an alley."

Karma narrowed her eyes. "What preceded this? I mean, why would you—"

Yesterday replayed itself in Slade's memory. Plenty had happened, but there was no way he could explain it to Karma in the few moments remaining before Brenda clawed and climbed her way over the wedge of men who were still good-timing their way out of that bus.

"It was a matter of survival," he said. "Let's go!"

Karma was not to be hustled, however, and to his horror, he saw four of the men lifting Brenda up and passing her over their heads until she was gently set down on the other side of their still-moving line.

Brenda let out a little "Yow!" of triumph and bounced toward them. "Slade! Isn't that your name?" she said, sparing a quick assessment of Karma, who stood mutely at his side.

Slade tried to edge away, but Karma was firmly rooted in place. She was staring at Brenda's chest, which was a fine example of silicone art at its worst.

"You have my bikini top," Brenda said without further preamble. "I want it back."

"I don't—"

"You do! You grabbed it up off the floor when I was dancing! I saw you!"

"But—"

"Hef gave it to me as a token of his esteem when I was Playmate of the Month!" Brenda was getting decidedly red in the face, almost as red as Slade remembered the disputed bikini top to be.

"Slade, is any of this true?" said Karma through tight lips.

"Some of it," he admitted.

"Great. I've just signed up a pervert at Rent-a-Yenta," Karma muttered under her breath, but at least his admission did what he hadn't been able to do. It got Karma moving.

She set off down the sidewalk at a pace that could only be described as rapid.

Slade turned to face Brenda, thinking that he might be able to talk her into being reasonable. "Your swimsuit top is at the houseboat. Stop by tomorrow and I'll give it to you."

"No," said Brenda, stubbornness flaring in her eyes. "I want it now."

"Tomorrow. No problem," he said, backing away as placatingly as he could.

"Now! We're going there right away! If you think I'm going to let you keep any article of my clothing for any length of time, you're nuts. After what you did to my friends—"

"They deserved it," he told her. "They tried to take my wallet."

"I don't care," Brenda said, on the verge, he was sure, of another tirade or maybe hysterics from the look of her. But then fate intervened in the form of a very large woman walking a very large and very hairy dog, which began to sniff around Brenda's feet in the way that dogs checked out fireplugs.

Uh-oh, thought Slade as the dog lifted its leg and Brenda curdled the air around them with a high-pitched scream. The dog panicked at the sound of Brenda's ungodly shriek, and it began to run around in circles. The woman yanked on the leash and yelled, "Heel! Heel!" Brenda kept on screaming. And he, Slade, made tracks.

Fortunately there were a lot of strollers out indulging in South Beach ambiance and the brine-scented night air, and fortunately, he spotted Karma's head about a block away. By the time he'd caught up with her, she had exceeded loping speed and was jogging along quite efficiently.

"Karma," he said, grabbing her arm. "I can explain."

"No explanation necessary. I saw you pull that red bra

from your pocket this morning when you stopped to inquire about Rent-a-Yenta.''

"It's not a bra. It's a bikini top."

"It serves the same function. Don't worry, I'll refund your registration fee."

"I don't want a refund," he said, glancing over his shoulder as Brenda's screams abruptly stopped. "I want a wife."

"Fat chance," Karma said.

He saw that red topknot flopping its way toward them. "I don't want to talk to this woman. I can explain. Where can we hide?"

"Like they say, you can run but you can't hide," Karma said grimly.

"It was all a fluke. I grabbed her bikini top off the floor when she threw it off while she was dancing on the hood of a cut-down '57 Chevy that was used as a couch in an apartment with some strange people I didn't know. It's true, I swear it."

Karma stopped dead in her tracks in front of a yellow-stuccoed apartment house and stared at him. "That story sounds absolutely too bizarre to be made up," she said.

"I didn't make it up. I have no interest in Brenda. Isn't there somewhere we can go?"

Karma's eyes moved sideways and took in their pursuer, who was now only half a block away. They were standing in the slim shadow of a palm tree, so there was a chance that Brenda hadn't actually seen them yet.

"In here," said Karma, yanking him into the lobby of the yellow-stuccoed place. Slade had the impression of dusty potted ficus trees and tables piled high with dog-eared magazines. A bunch of elderly men sat around tables playing dominoes.

"Hello, Karma dear," one of them said, his words punctuated by the sound of dominoes slapping on wood. "Your uncle Nate is out."

"I think he went somewhere with Mrs. Rothstein. He borrowed my Old Spice," said another. The rest of the men barely looked up.

"I'll just drop by his apartment," Karma said, edging toward the elevator and pulling Slade along with her. The men, focused on their game, barely paid attention.

Slade darted an anxious look at the front door. No sign of Brenda, or had she already passed by?

The elevator door opened, and Karma tugged Slade into it. "It's okay. We can cut through my uncle's apartment to the fire escape. From there we can—"

"I appreciate this," Slade said. "You don't know how much."

Karma stared straight ahead. "Don't try to weasel your way back into my good graces," she said. "I can't place any weirdos with my female clients."

He looked over at Karma, a slight smile playing across his lips. "I am entirely normal," he said. "In every way." Her mouth was unusually full, and her cheeks were flushed. Without knowing why, he bent his head, hesitated and kissed her full on the lips.

He thought she might have gasped beneath his mouth, but he was so intent on lengthening and deepening the kiss that he wasn't sure. What he was sure about was that her lips were softly pliant, her mouth was warm and willing, and she was one sensuous woman.

The elevator bumped to a stop, and he released her. Without saying a word, she walked out. He followed her, his mouth tingling, his ears ringing. And all from just one kiss.

Looking rattled, Karma led him into her uncle's apartment and raised a window before turning to face him. "You shouldn't have done that," she said.

"It was good for me. Wasn't it good for you?" He affected an air of studied innocence.

"It was unnecessary and uncalled for. And—"

"—and very nice," he murmured, gazing deep into her eyes, which dazzled him with their complexity of feeling.

She bit her lip and appeared to collect herself. "Let's go," she said, and she stepped out onto the metal fire-escape stairs.

"Now what?"

"We go that way," she said, pointing toward the next roof.

It was easy, clambering across the roof, and the next one, and the next. Throughout their curious journey, with the city of Miami Beach spread out before them, with the scent of the sea in his nostrils, all he could think was that he wanted to kiss Karma again. And soon.

"This is the Blue Moon," she said when they had reached a roof where lawn chairs were set along the edge of the building facing the ocean. The chairs on the sun deck were occupied by couples doing—well, who knew what? Slade had an idea, but he doubted the advisability of asking Karma if she would like to indulge. He was pretty sure she'd say no.

Karma marched across the roof and opened a door leading to a narrow hallway inside. "I suppose you want to be invited into my apartment for a drink or something," she said, squarely facing him under the glare of an unshaded bulb dangling from the ceiling.

"Yes," he said because he had never wanted anything so much in his life. "Yes, I reckon I would like that just fine."

Karma sighed and massaged the back of her neck. "I'll have to think this over," she said. "I don't know."

"I'll call you tomorrow," he said.

"You might want to come in to the office and look at some of my female clients' videos," she said.

"I thought you fired me," he said. "As a client, I mean."

"I did. But now I think you're okay."

"Because I kissed you?" he said, opting for the bold approach.

"No, because I believe that you didn't have any psycho reasons for having that bra—"

"Swimsuit top."

"—swimsuit top in your pocket. I saw your expression when you pulled it out this morning. You looked surprised. That's enough for me."

At the moment, screening videos of her other Rent-a-Yenta clients didn't appeal to him at all. "How about lunch tomorrow? Or dinner?"

"Or yoga? Remember, I said we'd have a class here tomorrow night."

She must be testing him. He didn't want to go to a yoga class. He hated anything New Age. But he did want to see Karma again, and desperately.

"I'll be there," he said.

She favored him with a decisive nod. "Good. Now I'd better walk you out of the building. Goldy doesn't take kindly to unescorted men rambling around in here."

They walked down four flights of stairs and found Goldy in the lobby, sitting behind her desk watching TV.

She looked up briefly, showing absolutely no surprise that the two of them had descended from on high rather than walking in the front door.

"Your aunt Sophie is here," she said.

Karma's eyebrows flew up. "My aunt Sophie is dead."

"Well, she's here anyway." Goldy gestured in the direction of a cardboard bucket of the same ilk as the ones that fast-food fried chicken came in.

"What in the world are you talking about, Goldy?"

"Your aunt Sophie. They delivered her ashes. That's them right there."

4

THE NEXT DAY WHEN KARMA met her uncle Nate at the neighborhood ice-cream parlor, she informed him about the fried chicken barrel now reposing on top of her refrigerator.

"Okay," he said, "so I should have ordered an urn. But what difference does it make? Sophie wanted her ashes scattered in the ocean. She loved the ocean."

Karma took time out from licking her raspberry frozen yogurt on a stick. "And you're going to scatter them, right?"

Nate looked uncomfortable. "No, not me. You, Karma."

Karma stopped stock-still in the middle of Ocean Boulevard. "Why me?"

"I pretend like she's buried. I go to the cemetery every day to see her grave, God rest her." He pulled her out of the path of a speeding dune buggy. "You should watch where you're going, Karma. I don't want to be going to any more funerals for a while."

They resumed their stroll. "With me out of the way, you could give Rent-a-Yenta to Paulette," Karma said while thinking that scattering Aunt Sophie's ashes was something Nate should do.

"I don't want you out of the way, Karma. Your cousin Paulette was second choice. Anyway, she already has a job counting money for a big Wall Street firm."

Lucky Paulette, Karma thought glumly. She probably had a boyfriend, too. But not someone as handsome and charming as Slade Braddock, she'd wager. Not that Slade was her boyfriend, but he *had* kissed her. He was a good kisser, too.

"Anyway, Karma, I like to go to the cemetery and look at Sophie's grave. I sit there for a while and I talk to her."

"Aunt Sophie doesn't have a grave. She's in that fried chicken barrel."

"Barrel? Don't call it a barrel. It's a fried chicken *bucket*. Sophie wouldn't need a barrel. She was as slim on the day she died as she was on the day I married her. And anyway, I picked out a grave that looks like it *could* be Sophie's. Sometimes I drive Mrs. Rothstein to the cemetery, too, so she can visit her husband's grave nearby. There's a pretty bottle-brush tree, and we like to sit under it on a nice wrought-iron bench. Let me have my fantasy that Sophie is there, *bubbeleh*. Don't spoil it for me."

"But Uncle Nate—"

"Your aunt Sophie was my life. I miss her." Nate wiped a tear from his eye.

Karma slid an arm around his shoulders. "She'd want you to make a new life, Uncle Nate."

He sighed. "I know, I know. That's true." He cheered up slightly. "So when can you scatter the ashes?"

Karma finished the rest of her frozen yogurt and tossed the stick in a trash can painted with a purple palm tree. "I don't know. I'll have to figure out a way. I think I'll need a boat, since you can't really toss ashes from shore without the prevailing winds throwing them back at you."

"You let me know what you're going to do."

"I will, Uncle Nate. Thanks for the frozen yogurt." She bent and kissed him on his wrinkled cheek.

"You've got your yogurt class tonight, don't you?"

"Yoga. I *practice* yoga. I *eat* yogurt." Her uncle had never been able to tell the difference between yoga and yogurt, which had been endearing at first, but now it was beginning to wear on her.

"Okay, yoga. Didn't I hear that the big cowboy was coming to class?"

"Where did you hear that?" Karma uttered in surprise.

"Goldy mentioned it. Is it true?"

"I invited him. Not sure if he'll be there tonight," she hedged.

Nate's eyes twinkled. "He will be. I saw the way he looked at you the other morning."

"From your mouth to God's ears," Karma said, but Nate only laughed.

"That's my line," he said, and it was true. Her uncle was always saying that.

After she and Nate parted company at the corner, Karma walked slowly back to her office, wondering where would be the best place to hire a boat. She was still mulling this over as she climbed the stairs. The door swung open before she inserted her key.

"Hi, Karma." Jennifer, the same Jennifer who was eager to find a date who was husband material, had parked her sexy self in front of the TV in the alcove where clients were welcome to browse through videos of possible matches. "Aunt Goldy sent me over to take delivery of the couch and chairs for you, and I figured it's a chance to check out new prospects. I've just met one, in fact."

"Oh?"

"He said his name was Slade Braddock. He was looking for a psychological profile form and took one off your desk. I hope that's okay."

Karma's spirits fell. She wished she hadn't missed him. "I guess it's all right. Um, Jennifer, why aren't you at work?"

"I switched to the night shift."

"They have night shifts for ear piercers?"

"Uh-huh. That's when all the teenagers come in, and we're having a special—two for the price of one."

"Two ears? You charge per ear?"

Jennifer rolled her eyes. "No, silly. Two people for the price of one. You should come get your ears pierced while the sale's on. Your belly button too. I'm not supposed to do belly buttons, but I'd make an exception for you."

Ouch! But, "I'll think about it," Karma said. To her dismay, the very video cassette that Jennifer now cradled in her eager little hands was labeled Slade Braddock, Client 1811.

"This guy was *soooo* cool. I think I'll pop this cassette in the VCR and see what he has to say."

"I haven't edited it yet."

"I don't care. Want to watch it with me?"

Karma shook her head. "I've got things to do," she said.

Jennifer leaned forward, her breasts surging out of her vee neckline. They were conical in shape and tanned all over, at least from what Karma could see, which was considerable. Furthermore, it looked as if Jennifer had succeeded in her quest for artificial nipples. They were standing up straight and proud. Did guys really like that look? It seemed that as a matchmaker she ought to know such things.

Jennifer noticed her scrutiny. "Yes, Karma, I did get them. Do you want to know where? I could—"

"No, thanks," Karma said hastily.

Jennifer treated her to a knowing smile. "They'd help you in the guy department, believe me. By the way, I took a message for you." She bounced over to the desk and ripped a pink message sheet off a pad. "The caller said she was your cousin Paulette. She said she was recently fired from her job in New York and wants you to call her back."

"Paulette? Call her back?" Despite Karma's immediate sympathy for anyone who'd lost a job, this wasn't anything she wanted to do. Paulette had been the butt of jokes from Karma and her sisters during their childhood. Karma knew she had never been completely forgiven for dipping the sleeping Paulette's hand in a pail of warm water on the first night of sleep-away camp when they were both eight; Paulette had wet her bed, which was what Karma had been assured would happen. After that, Paulette's nickname around camp had been P. P., which ostensibly stood for her initials, since her full name was Paulette Parham. But all the campers had known what the nickname really stood for, and the counselors probably did, too.

"Come on, Karma, sit down and watch with me." Jennifer tugged Karma into the alcove and pushed on her shoulders until she sat on the chair.

"Roll tape," Jennifer sang out as she pushed the play button, and Slade's face popped up on the screen. A good-humored face, an animated face—until Karma asked him the first question and he froze up.

As Slade hemmed and hawed his way down into the conversational skids, Karma slid a glance in Jennifer's direction to gauge her reaction. "Not much of a talker," was all she said.

"Mmm," Karma said noncommittally.

"Still," Jennifer mused as Slade started running on about birds, "he's a hottie. I can't see what's the big whoop about roseate spoonbills and great blue herons, they sound boring to me, but I think I'll give Mr. Slade Braddock a whirl."

Karma's heart sank.

Jennifer switched off the tape. "Set it up for Friday night, won't you, Karma?"

"Well, I—"

"I mean, why not?" Jennifer skewered her with a look.

"I'll have to check to see if he's busy," Karma hedged, getting up and shuffling through a pile of papers on her desk.

"Aunt Goldy says she's met him. She says he's nice. What do you think? Are we well suited, he and I?"

"Why don't I study your personality profiles in relation

to each other and get back to you on that? Of course, I won't see his until he brings it back.''

Jennifer shrugged, which went a long way to show off her breast assets. ''Oh, don't bother with that psychology stuff. I want to go out with him. Friday night is good because my mother is trying to set me up with her best friend's son, Sheldon. If I already have a date, Mom won't insist.'' She flipped her hair back off her shoulders, and Karma was nearly blinded by the shimmer of it in the slant of sunshine coming in the window. Slade, she thought sourly, would go crazy at the sight of Jennifer.

''So do you promise to set it up?''

''All right,'' Karma said reluctantly. ''I'll do it.''

''Tell Slade to pick me up at seven,'' Jennifer said airily on her way out the door.

When she had gone, Karma collapsed onto her desk chair and pillowed her head on her arms in dismay at the thought of setting Slade up with Jennifer.

''Well, he may be a client, but Jennifer won't like him,'' counseled the Aunt Sophie side of her. In fact, the voice in her head sounded so much like her aunt's that Karma's head jerked up in surprise.

Whereupon the Karma side of her cautioned, ''Why wouldn't Slade like Jennifer? She's blond, sexy and eager.''

Unfortunately it was the Karma side of her that made the most sense.

Still and all, Friday was still four days away. Karma could only hope that Jennifer, who could usually be counted on to show her fickle side, would decide before then that Slade wasn't a real possibility.

SLADE BRADDOCK SHOWED UP at the rooftop sundeck yoga class right on time that night. He strode in wearing those cowboy boots, jeans and a white T-shirt that made his tan look darker than ever. He nodded to Karma, balancing his hands on his hips and looking the group over.

"Who is that?" Mandi asked as she unfurled her purple yoga mat.

"Oh, just someone I invited to join us," Karma answered.

"Mmm-*mmm*. I sure would like to hear him say, 'You know you want it, baby. You know you do.'" Mandi lowered her voice in imitation of a male consumed by lust, which might have been funny if Karma were in the mood for it.

"Don't they all say that to you?" Karma asked innocently. Mandi let out a sort of halfhearted giggle as Karma unfolded herself from her mat, where she had been sitting in Half-Lotus position. She strolled over to where Slade stood.

He grinned at her, the light in his eyes rivaling the moonlight spilling down from a clear night sky, his grin revealing teeth that gleamed whiter than the promise of any toothpaste commercial on TV. "Didn't think I'd show up, did you?" he asked.

What to reply? She had and she hadn't, both at the same time. One thing for sure, she had developed a dry mouth from merely being in his line of sight, and at that moment, she wasn't sure she'd be able to open it to speak.

"Uh, glad to see you," she managed to say after what seemed like a couple of eons. Slade looked out of place, she thought, in those jeans. "Be better if you'd worn fewer clothes," she said, not realizing until the words were out of her mouth how they sounded.

His delighted laughter boomed out over the assembled regulars, most of whom were gawking at him with their jaws hanging down to their knees. Which was not an approved yoga pose as far as Karma knew.

"Most things," Slade said wickedly but in such a low tone that the others couldn't hear, "are better without so many clothes. You mind telling me which items you'd like me to discard first?''

She blushed. She couldn't help it. ''Your boots for a start,'' she said crisply.

The instructor, a powerful bare-chested yogi from The Om Place whose previous address was listed as an ashram in India, sauntered over. ''A new student?'' he asked in precise tones as he inspected Slade from head to toe.

''Prashant, this is Slade. Slade, Prashant.'' Karma made her introductions as quickly as she could and scurried back to her mat.

''How do you happen to know that big hunky guy?'' Mandi wanted to know. Her favorable assessment of Slade and his muscles and his tan and his white, white teeth was undisguised and avid.

''Oh,'' Karma said with a vague wave of her hand, ''we met on the street.''

Jennifer arrived, running late as usual. She stopped to talk to Karma. ''Isn't that Slade Braddock talking with Prashant?'' she asked, aiming a come-hither look and up-standing nipples in his direction.

''Yes,'' muttered Karma. ''I'm afraid so.''

''Should I introduce myself? Or do you want to do it?''

''After class,'' Karma told her.

''Mmm,'' said Jennifer, her gaze still on Slade. ''Boxers for sure.''

''Briefs,'' Mandi corrected. ''He's a briefs kind of guy.'' Having made that pronouncement, Mandi leaped up, her melon-sized breasts jostling each other for room under her Om Is Where The Heart Is T-shirt. She undulated over to the corner where Slade was approaching the stack of spare mats.

''Need some help?'' Mandi asked.

Karma wondered, *Help? Help with what?* Deciding whether he wanted a blue mat or a purple one? Putting one foot in front of the other until he reached the rest of the group? Oh, pu-leeze!

Karma shut her ears to the byplay between Slade and Mandi and forced herself to breathe deeply, trying to find her center. The trouble was that by the time Slade, looking like every dream man in every one of her fantasies since she was twelve years old, began to spread his mat out beside hers, her center seemed to have moved downward considerably to that warm place between her—

"Karma," Slade whispered under his breath while fielding admiring glances from virtually every woman present without so much as acting as if he noticed. "Karma, what am I supposed to do?"

She opened her eyes. "What Prashant says."

"Oh," Slade said in a puzzled tone. He glanced from her to Prashant. "He likes you, I think."

"Prashant? That's doubtful."

"He certainly came running when he saw us talking. Defending his territory, maybe?"

The observation was too ridiculous to be worthy of reply, and Karma was saved by Prashant's settling down on his own mat at the front of the group and welcoming them all to the lesson.

Prashant began the class by chanting an Om. "Allow yourself to go with the flow, and then you will find what you've been looking for," he said afterward with reverence.

"I'll be damned if I think that's going to get me a wife, which is what I'm looking for lately," Slade muttered under his breath. Karma threw him a reproachful look.

"Well, don't I have you to find me what I'm looking for?" he whispered.

"Go with the flow anyway," she whispered back.

Prashant coached them through a few simple warm-ups. With Slade beside her, Karma, for the first time ever in yoga class, found it difficult to concentrate. As they progressed through various poses, he doffed his shirt, revealing a torso that was leaner, harder, and more muscular than she could have imagined. And she had been imagining it plenty, starting from the first moment she saw him.

It was an intense class, and the members of the group, most of whom were intermediate students, flowed from pose to pose with little recovery time in between. Sun Salutation, Warrior, Downward-Facing Dog…and Slade, who seemed to be struggling valiantly to keep up, looked slightly more musclebound with each pose. Musclebound was not good with yoga. Flexible was good. Agile was good. Slade seemed to be neither.

"Are you doing all right back there, Slade?" Prashant asked once, and Slade replied with what looked like a grin superimposed on a grimace. "Fine," he gritted through clenched teeth, but the next pose, a backbend, drew an incredulous intake of breath from him as he lay on his back and attempted to lift himself up.

"Karma, you are the best at backbends. Will you please demonstrate?" suggested Prashant.

"Well, I—" she began, but Mandi said, "Yes, Karma, do!" and was rapidly echoed by Jennifer.

All eyes were upon Karma, but the only ones that mattered in that moment were Slade's. He lay on his mat looking up at her with a challenging grin, and all she could think at the moment is that if they were in bed, this is what he would look like—well-muscled and fit, his grin fading into passion as he reached for her and pulled her down across his body, the better to kiss you, my dear.

"Backbends are important," intoned Prashant, breaking into her reverie. "They help our bodies release emotion in a positive way."

"Wouldn't backbends be good for me?" Slade urged. "Since my chakra is blocked, I mean?"

He might have something there, but the thing that finally decided Karma was that if she were in a backbend pose, she wouldn't have to look down at him and thus wouldn't be tempted to reach over and unbutton his jeans, a behavior that surely would be frowned upon.

Karma forced herself to lie down on her mat; she closed her eyes and inhaled a deep breath, then exhaled as she firmly planted her hands behind her ears and her feet flat on the floor. While inhaling the next breath, she hoisted herself up into a backbend, keeping her eyes closed and wishing she'd never invited Slade to class. Slowly she walked her feet in a bit closer and arched her back even more, thrusting her breasts up. She knew that the quickly inhaled breath next to her came from Slade, and too late she realized that she was exhibiting more of the very thing that he probably wanted to see if Jennifer were correct in her thinking. Karma was wearing a thin exercise bra along with tight shiny leggings. Neither did anything to disguise her womanly attributes. This could be good. This could be bad. But all she could think about at the moment was that she wanted to get out of this pose.

As she began lowering herself to her mat, she was horrified to hear the separation of stitches somewhere along her front. Then she felt a quick rush of air in a private place and realized with horror that her leggings had split somewhere south of her belly button.

Thump! She hit the floor abruptly and sat up, yanking her mat up to cover herself.

"Excellent," Prashant was saying. "Only next time do not come down so quickly. You could get dizzy that way."

"Oooh, Karma, did you rip your new leggings?" Mandi said in a loud voice.

"Oooh, Karma, that's too bad," echoed Jennifer.

"I—I think I'd better go change clothes," Karma said, running the words all together and hoping she wasn't wearing the panties with the lace panel in front. They would reveal too, too much.

She scrambled to her feet, clutching her mat in front of her as she sidled sideways toward the door. Slade was staring at her, his eyes wide, a devilish grin on his face. Without a single word to him, she turned and darted inside the building.

"Unfortunate," she heard Prashant murmuring. "Shall we try the backbend one more time and then rest for a few moments in Child's Pose before our final relaxation?"

Karma slammed the door behind her and looked down. Sure enough, more of her was exposed than Slade Braddock needed to see. She owned one pair of lace panties, only one pair, and guess what?

She was wearing them tonight.

Unexpectedly she burst into tears. Prashant was right—backbends promoted the release of emotion. Too bad that in her case, backbends made her blubber.

SLADE DRAGGED HIS ACHING carcass along to the Blue Moon's lobby after the class. He was still reeling from his meeting with someone who had claimed that she was his Friday night date, a woman who had introduced herself as Jennifer Something and looked so artificial that she terrified him. He couldn't believe that Karma would set him up with someone completely wrong for him, someone that he would never in a million years take home to introduce to his parents. He'd fled as fast as it was possible to flee without being downright rude.

Goldy hunched in her chair behind the desk, knitting. She blinked at him over the top of her half-glasses when he entered the lobby.

"How was the yoga class?" she asked brightly.

"I think," he said slowly, "that I'm feeling freer all the time." This was not necessarily untrue, though what he was feeling freer about was pursuing Karma. She might not be the sort of woman he had hoped to find in Miami Beach, but she had certain—attributes, all of which had been more in evidence tonight than at any previous time.

"I received a lot of energy in the class," he offered

helpfully. *And a novel view of Karma,* he thought to himself.

"That's good," Goldy said, and she beamed.

"There are a few things I'd like to discuss about it. About the expression of this energy, I mean. But Karma won't answer my knock."

"Maybe she's not in her apartment."

"She left class early. Did you see her go out?"

"No, I didn't see Karma leave. Not that I would, necessarily. Not if she went out the back. She often slips out that way to walk on the beach, especially when she's feeling all mellow from yoga class. The door's down that hall." Goldy inclined her head toward her left.

"Thanks, Goldy," Slade said. He grinned at her, and she grinned back.

"You know, Slade, I seem to recall that you live on a boat."

"At the moment, that's so," he said.

"Karma has need of a boat. She wants to scatter her aunt Sophie's ashes at sea."

Goldy's intent was not lost on Slade. She was giving him another boost, a clue as to what he could do to capture Karma's attention, possibly even her undying gratitude.

"Like I said, Goldy, thanks. I owe you."

"Remember, you can't escape your Karma." She winked.

He winked back before loping off down the hall.

The door at the Blue Moon led to a narrow alleyway that culminated at a boardwalk leading down to the sand. The beach at this hour was deserted except for a lone figure walking along the high tide line about a hundred yards south. Karma.

He jogged to catch up with her. As he approached, she wheeled around, startled. Her eyes were wide, her lips parted. Her hair stood out around her face and seemed to snap and crackle with energy. He thought he had never seen anyone more beautiful in his life.

The breakers were rolling in at a fast pace, giving rhythm to the night. This part of Miami Beach seemed far away from the hoopla of South Beach night life.

"What are you doing here?" she demanded, stopping dead in her tracks.

He thought he saw the tracks of tears dried on her face, but perhaps he was mistaken. "I came to offer my services," he said.

Karma started to shake her head, but on the off chance that she wouldn't object, he captured her face between his hands. "Or rather," he added, captivated by the confusion this brought to her eyes, "the services of my boat."

"I don't need—" but she stopped talking in midsentence, all the better for him to explain.

"So you can scatter your aunt Sophie's ashes," he said gently, moving his head closer and tilting it into kissing position.

"How did you know about that?" she breathed, and her breath was sweet and soft upon his lips. Her eyes were deep and unfathomable, and she didn't pull away.

"When a person opens himself up and begins to receive energy, all sorts of things happen," he murmured, and then he kissed her.

As soon as his mouth touched hers, he wanted her. He wanted her with all the passion and depth of a man in full pursuit even though he warned himself again that she wasn't his type. Yet the image of her nipples straining against the fabric of that brief top she'd worn to yoga class was burned into the part of his brain that governed reason and good sense; he wanted her. Perhaps this lustful feeling was the ultimate expression of the energy he was experiencing?

Slowly his lips explored hers, and before he knew it his tongue was seeking new territory and his hands were tangled in her hair. She was a full participant, her tongue meeting his, her teeth nibbling at his lower lip, her hands pressing against his back to draw him closer.

When she pushed him away it was with less conviction than he had expected.

"You're a client," she said, the words approximating a gasp of passion. "I shouldn't be doing this."

"If you'd like, I'll resign as a client," he said. "I could be just plain Slade Braddock, man on the loose."

She braced her hands against his chest and shoved, forcing him to take a step backward.

"More like Slade Braddock, man on the *make,*" she said.

"Anything wrong with that?" he asked amiably.

"You're supposed to go out with Jennifer on Friday night."

"She told me. What if I don't want to go?"

"That will get me in trouble with Jennifer, not to mention Goldy, who is her aunt. Don't do that to me, Slade."

"Goldy is the one who told me you might be on the beach."

"She may not know that Jennifer has dibs on you."

"I have free will. I can see—or not see—any woman I please. So do you want to go out in the boat with me or not?"

"A houseboat isn't something you'd take out to sea," she said, casting a look in his direction. He didn't know the meaning of that look, but it was definitely not one that said *go away,* so he kept walking along beside her.

"*Toy Boat* has a dinghy," he told her.

"So you're planning on rowing out to sea? That's not advisable, you know. The waves can get pretty big offshore."

"Maybe it isn't called a dinghy. I don't know because I'm not that experienced a boater. It has a motor."

"And what strings are attached to this offer?"

"Absolutely none. Maybe while we're in the boat we could talk about freeing me up. Maybe we could talk about freeing *you* up."

He saw her rolling her eyes. "I'm as free as I want to be," she said. She swiped at her nose with a tissue that he hadn't realized she carried in her hand, increasing his suspicion that she'd been crying.

"Maybe that's the problem. You need to feel attached to someone," he said hopefully. She could be lonely, he supposed. She could be shedding a few tears because she had no one to walk with on the beach on a beautiful and romantic night such as this one, which could play into his purpose really well.

"I don't think I want to be attached in the way you're thinking about."

"Perhaps you need to free up your chakras, all seven of them. Have you ever thought about giving yourself permission to feel, Karma?"

She shot him a skeptical glance.

Realizing that this line of discussion wasn't going any further, he changed the subject. "How far do we walk? When do we turn around and go back?"

She seemed on the verge of smiling when she looked up at him. "Why? Too much exercise for you, cowboy?"

"Not at all," he said firmly, wishing suddenly that she could observe when he and Lightning, his prize quarter horse, were cutting cattle. She'd see that he was a superior athlete, an experienced horseman. He was out of his element in sea-sand-sky territory, that's for sure.

"I usually stroll to the next lifeguard station, then head back. You're welcome to go back now, if you like. These walks of mine are usually solitary."

"Too bad," Slade said.

"Not really. Solitude is good sometimes."

"Karma, when a woman looks like you, acts like you and kisses like you, there's no reason to be alone."

She emitted an exasperated sigh. "Maybe I want to be alone. Maybe I like it that way."

"And maybe I'm the king of Siam, but I don't think so."

"I don't think there is a king of Siam anymore. For that matter, there's not a Siam anymore. It's called Thailand these days."

"You get my point," he said.

They had almost reached the lifeguard station, and Karma slowed down. She drew a deep breath before speaking. "I know what you were looking at in yoga class tonight when I was doing that backbend, and I might as well tell you that unless you concentrate on being centered, you're not doing your blocked chakra any good."

He turned back toward the Blue Moon when she did and wondered what she would do if he kissed her again. He decided not to chance it. "I believe I feel my chakra becoming unblocked," he said, not believing that he was actually speaking these words that flowed so easily from his lips. "I feel a certain—a certain—" He struggled to think of something that would convince her that he was making progress.

"A certain letting go?" Karma supplied.

He grinned and punched a fist into his opposite hand. "That's it! A 'letting go'!"

"Maybe it *is* working. Maybe you are getting better. Backbends are good for releasing emotion."

She walked on, a frown marring her features. "You'll have to keep doing yoga. It will help you dramatically."

Maybe his muscles would stop screaming out in agony by next Tuesday night, maybe he'd be able to twist himself into a damned backbend—a real one this time, not a weak imitation.

"I should practice," he said. "Other than backbends, I'm not sure what poses would be best, though, so perhaps you could help me."

"No funny business if I do," she said firmly.

"What do you mean, funny business?" he replied, all innocence.

"Kissing me," she said. "Becoming unduly familiar."

"Now wait a minute. I don't want to make promises I can't keep."

"If I'm going to find you the wife you want, you can't sully the process," Karma said in a reasoning tone.

He didn't know what to say to that. The kind of wife he wanted had slipped his mind. The sweet, delicate little Southern-belle type didn't seem so desirable anymore. He knew he should ask when he could view some videos of female Rent-a-Yenta clients. He knew he should be more eager to make contact with other women. He ought to be encouraged by the thought of having a date with Jennifer. And yet when he stole a glance over at Karma walking along beside him, when he took in that curly blond mass of hair and those breasts straining against the cotton of her blouse, when he thought about what had been revealed through those lace panties when her leggings split—well, *she* was the one he wanted to know more about. *She* was the one for him.

At least for the short term.

When they reached the boardwalk, he stopped to pull on his boots. As if against her better judgment, she waited for him.

"How about if I pick you up Thursday afternoon at three to scatter your aunt's ashes?" he asked, taking the bold approach.

She looked down at her bare feet. "I don't know if I can be ready by three. I have work to do in the office."

"Three-thirty, then."

"Well, only if you learn how to motor that boat."

"I'll learn." Slade finished pulling on the boots and stood up. At the moment that he was ready to slide his arms around her, she stepped up on the boardwalk. It was an evasion, but he wasn't going to let her get away with it.

"Not so fast," he said, the words coming out more gruffly than he had intended. He grabbed her wrist, the handiest thing to grab, and twisted her around. His heart was thumping against his ribs as he pulled her close. He'd bet his last dollar that her heart was hammering, too.

"Slade," she said, the word more of an assent than a denial. And then he kissed her thoroughly, liking the way her head was on a parallel with his because of the increased height standing on the boardwalk gave her. If she were tiny, like the woman he'd come here to find, kissing her wouldn't be nearly as satisfying. As it was, when he opened his eyes they were gazing directly into hers. He liked what he saw there because it wasn't anger or defiance or anything but a kind of hushed acceptance of what was and maybe could be.

He released her reluctantly and dug a paper out of his back pocket. "I brought you my psychological profile," he said. "It, um, may give you clues to my emotional identity." He wasn't sure what an emotional identity was, exactly, but it was the kind of term Karma would use.

She merely stared at him, then took the sheet of paper from his hand. It quivered a bit, and not entirely from the ocean breeze.

"See you tomorrow," he said, and then she was off, scampering up the boardwalk like a runaway heifer.

All in all, he thought jubilantly as he headed for the parking lot, the evening had gone tolerably well. Except for yoga class, and even that had had its redeeming features.

Like lace panties that left little to the imagination.

HE KNOCKED ON KARMA'S DOOR at three-thirty on Thursday afternoon. She opened it, clutching a flyswatter in one hand.

"I'm chasing a palmetto bug," she said, leaving the door

open and taking off into the tiny kitchen, which he could see courtesy of a pass-through to the living room.

He closed the door. "I learned how to run the boat," he called after her. His words were followed by a loud *Splat!*

"Good," she said distractedly. "Damn! I missed it."

"Didn't I hear something about an exterminator service around here?"

"Yes, which is personified by a guy named Geofredo. He's tried his best, and now the exterminating is up to me. The thing about palmetto bugs is that you can't treat them nicely. One becomes two, which become four, and pretty soon you've got a bunch. It used to be against my core beliefs to kill anything, but I've had a change of heart." She flicked the flyswatter back and forth.

"Why?"

"Because this particular roach and his kinfolk were waving their feelers at Aunt Sophie's bucket," Karma said, angling her head toward it. The bucket sat on top of the refrigerator amid a tangle of dish towels, a blender base, a potato ricer and a tape deck.

"Fear not. Bwana will hunt down palmetto bug. Bwana will kill."

Karma shook her head. "Thanks, but this is my fight. If he'd only show his face, I'd nail him."

"I think I see him poking out from under the baseboard." The palmetto bug—an enormous one—scurried across the kitchen floor, straight toward Karma.

"Eek!" she squealed, backing fast and furiously until the back of her knees hit the couch. She rallied, feinted, and swung the flyswatter down hard.

"Dead," she pronounced solemnly. She scooted the carcass out the sliding glass door with one foot. "How about some lunch?"

He rocked back on his heels. "It's not the most appetizing idea at the moment. Anyway, it's a little late for lunch."

"Call it an early supper if you like. I haven't eaten because I've been busy trying to balance my checkbook all day.'' She went into the kitchen and began shoving pots around on the stove. "I've made linguine," she called over her shoulder. "With shrimp sauce."

He noticed with bemusement that she had set the table with turquoise-blue place mats and yellow plastic plates. There were napkin rings that looked like carved fish painted red and pink, and she'd stuck a branch laden with white oleander blooms into an old wine jug. The effect was, well, interesting.

He sat down at the table, and she bore a huge platter of pasta into the little dining area. While he was waiting for her to pour iced tea, he had a chance to look around the apartment. Furniture consisted of what appeared to be flea-market finds, but it was a creative mix. An old couch had a fringed silk shawl thrown artistically across the back, and a shelf on one wall held bottles and jars in jeweled colors, which were lit from within by tiny Christmas tree lights. A coir rug was underfoot, and his sharp eyes didn't miss the fact that the binding was ripped in the corner behind the rocking chair that almost, but not quite, hid the imperfection from view.

"Nice place," Slade said. He meant it. It looked comfortable and reflected Karma's personality.

"Thanks. I hit a dozen yard and garage sales when I arrived here. I didn't move much down from Connecticut with me since I wasn't sure I'd stay."

"Why not?"

She shrugged and sat down across from him. "I didn't know if I could make a go of the business. I still don't. There's so much to do that I hardly have time for anything but work."

She passed him the linguine, and he helped himself. "As busy as you are, you wouldn't have had to provide food," he said.

"It's the least I can do when you're going to so much trouble for me."

As she tucked into the food, he studied her. She was wearing a knit short-sleeved polo shirt, yellow, and navy-blue shorts, and her hair was pulled into a ponytail. She looked wholesome, like a camp counselor, but her expression was decidedly businesslike. Taking his cue from her, he concentrated on eating and making small talk, which turned out to be enjoyable enough. He told her that her bike had been retrieved from the bottom of the bay, and she seemed relieved. She was even grateful when he told her that he'd asked the marina manager's son to make sure it was rideable and to fix it if it was not. They talked about her uncle, who seemed special to her. It occurred to him as he helped her clear the table that he was really enjoying her company.

By the time Karma climbed into the Suburban beside him clutching the bucket of her aunt's ashes firmly between her breasts, Slade had already planned what they would do when they returned from their task. They'd have a late dinner on the houseboat, then a walk in the moonlight alongside the bay and perhaps a nightcap before he took her home. And maybe, if he got megalucky, he wouldn't have to take her home. There was plenty of room in the master stateroom's bed for two people.

The runabout, fourteen feet long, was painted in the houseboat's colors and had been given the cutesy name of *Toy Boat's Toy,* which was no doubt the idea of Mack's wife Renee. Karma smiled when she saw the name lettered on the stern, though, and then she spotted her bike, which he had propped against one of the pilings near the houseboat's mooring.

"The bike looks fine," she said, giving it a quick once-over before climbing down the ladder to the runabout. "Maybe I'll ride it home."

Maybe not, Slade thought involuntarily as he steadied the

runabout. After the romantic evening he'd planned, she might want to rethink things.

Phifer had shown him how to start a cold outboard, for which Slade was grateful since his knowledge of boats was sadly limited. Phifer had also loaned him charts and had given him instructions about where to go. As Slade, feeling optimistic about the afternoon and evening to follow, aimed the runabout's bow toward Key Biscayne, Karma settled herself and her aunt's ashes in the middle of the boat facing him.

There were a number of boats on the bay, as usual. Karma angled her head so that the sun's rays fell more evenly on her features, and Slade made himself concentrate on working the throttle as they chugged past Key Biscayne and out into open water.

Once there, Karma shaded her eyes with her hand to squint into the distance as he consulted the marine chart in his lap. "How far do you think we need to go?" she asked.

"Phifer told me to watch for a certain buoy, and when we get past it, that would be a good place for the ceremony."

Karma seemed disconcerted. "I didn't think of having a ceremony. I don't know what to say. Let me give it some thought, okay?"

They rode in silence; how long they went without speaking, Slade lost track. "There's the buoy," he said after a time, pointing ahead and levering back on the throttle. Beyond the buoy lay deep channels, marked by their indigo color.

Karma stared at the cardboard bucket at her feet as he jockeyed around the buoy and cut the throttle. The boat drifted on gentle swells in the sudden silence. Slade waited to see how she would handle this.

"Aunt Sophie wasn't at all religious, but I wouldn't feel right if I didn't say something—well, ceremonial—about her," Karma said.

"I think you should."

She seemed to be thinking. Finally she clasped her hands in her lap and said, "I want to talk about Aunt Sophie's life."

"Fine with me." Slade was captivated by the animation of her expressions, the slight crinkling of her forehead. The way she tucked the tip of her tongue between her lips before she spoke. The tilt of her head as she waited for his replies. He was enchanted by Karma, everything about her, all of her.

"Well," Karma said finally. "My aunt Sophie was born in Brooklyn, and she thought she'd grow up to work in a sweatshop like her own mother. But when the neighborhood yenta was arranging the marriage of her eldest brother, Sophie became fascinated by what the matchmaker did, by the magic she wrought in people's lives. Sophie tagged along after the woman, annoying her at first, then making herself useful, and finally absorbing every facet of the business. And when the old yenta died, it was Sophie who took over. She was too young, people said. She needed seasoning before she could be entrusted with such serious business.

"'Ha!' Sophie told them. 'It's not the years that make a good yenta! It's what's in the heart.' So she proceeded to make some very fine matches for the people in the neighborhood, and soon the talk died down. But she herself didn't marry.

"'What kind of yenta are you?' people used to ask. 'If you were a good one, you'd find your own self a husband.' Aunt Sophie said, 'Ha! When a good husband comes along, I will marry him.' She didn't meet my uncle Nate until she was thirty-four, which was old in those days to marry. He was a button salesman, and he had never been married, either. It was an extremely happy union for both of them, though they always wished they'd had children.

"Aunt Sophie took an interest in her clients, always telling them that they were like her children. 'But you don't know what it is to have children,' people said. 'Ha!' Aunt Sophie told them, 'it's what's in the heart that ties you to children, and these clients of mine are in my heart.'

"Then, when she knew she was dying, she told Uncle Nate that she wanted to give me Rent-a-Yenta. 'Karma is in my heart,' she told him, and later she told me that too. Giving me Rent-a-Yenta was a loving act, the nicest thing anyone ever did for me. I will never forget it, and I will never, ever forget her. And sometimes I feel that she's right beside me, guiding me as I try to make Rent-a-Yenta my own."

Karma paused, biting her lip.

"That's beautiful, Karma." Slade was touched by Karma's simple but eloquent words.

Karma released a sigh. "Now I should scatter the ashes, I think." She picked up the container and hesitated. "Like I said, my aunt wasn't religious. But I don't feel right about not saying anything about God. She did believe in God."

Slade cleared his throat. "All I can offer is to repeat the Twenty-Third Psalm. I had to learn it in Sunday school when I was a kid."

Her smile was grateful. "That would be perfect, Slade."

He recited the psalm, stumbling a couple of times but getting most of it right. When he had finished, Karma removed the lid and held the container up over her head. When she lofted the ashes into the wind, they rose and glimmered briefly, then caught the golden rays of the sinking sun before swirling away on the breeze.

"Goodbye, Aunt Sophie," Karma murmured. "I love you." In her eyes, tears shimmered unshed, and she fumbled in her pocket and said, "I didn't bring a tissue. That was dumb, wasn't it?"

It was as he handed Karma his handkerchief that Slade first noticed the rolling black clouds churning toward them from the west. "Whoa," he said. "What's that about?"

"It's that I really loved my aunt Sophie," Karma said before blowing her nose.

"No, I mean those clouds," he said, jerking a thumb westward.

Karma stuffed the handkerchief in her pocket. "Yikes," she said, looking alarmed. "Looks like a major storm."

Slade squinted toward the setting sun, almost obscured now by the encroaching storm. "Phifer didn't warn me about storms. He told me about the channels and how to start the motor and about staying out of the path of big boats, but he didn't say a word about storms."

"More fool Phifer," Karma muttered under her breath. She shoved the tissue into her pocket, keeping her eyes on the changing panorama to the west.

Slade shot her a skeptical look. "Look, if you think you can get us out of here better than I can, feel free," he said.

She backed off at that, sinking further down onto her seat. "Nope, I know little about boats. All I can say is that we'd better make a run for it."

Without saying another word, Slade hauled anchor and started the boat's motor. It sprang to life, and he turned the bow back toward land, keeping a sharp eye on the clouds, which were trailing gray curtains of rain over the surface of the sea. He was aware that no other boats were in sight and that they were alone—completely and utterly alone and at the mercy of the elements.

"Slade," Karma called to him over the noise of the motor and the keening of the rising wind, "do you think we'll make it before the storm hits?"

He tried to sound reassuring, though he was feeling anything but optimistic as the blue of the sky above was obscured by scudding clouds. "I hope so," he said.

As he spoke, a wave splashed over the side of the boat. The seas had risen alarmingly, and the wind had begun to blow in strong gusts.

Karma wrapped her arms around her against the sudden

chill in the air. It looked to her as if Slade were having trouble keeping the runabout on course. She regarded the advancing rain with trepidation. It had not escaped her that the runabout was equipped with two life vests, and she reached under the seat to drag them out.

"Good idea," Slade told her.

It was a struggle to get into the life vest with the boat rising and falling on choppy waves, but she managed, and when she again looked at Slade, he was wearing his. As a gust of wind swerved the boat around sideways, Karma gripped the gunwales and held on tight. Rain began to pelt down out of the sky in rapid, stinging drops.

"What's that?" Slade called, waving his arm toward her left.

She let go of the gunwale for a moment to wipe the rain out of her eyes. "I think that's Stiltsville," she said, raising her voice to be heard over the wind.

"I give up—what's Stiltsville?"

"A bunch of old houses on pilings. They're built in the shoals, abandoned now."

The boat was being hammered by repeated gusts, some of them so strong that the bow bucked up and down like an unruly horse, slapping back down again with enough power to toss them from the boat. "We'd better head for the houses. They're shelter," he shouted over the keening of the wind.

Rain had soaked Karma's hair, and she huddled in the bottom of the boat, hanging on as best she could. Slade did his best to turn the runabout toward the houses in the shallows. There looked to be seven of them, though the rain was pouring down from the sky in such heavy sheets that visibility was severely limited. A huge wave lurched over the side of the boat, and all he could do was hold on.

"You okay?" he shouted.

Karma nodded, but he saw that she was scared. She began to bail with the bucket that had held her aunt's ashes.

Spunky woman, he thought, and then he turned his full attention to getting them to one of the houses that had appeared so providentially out in the middle of the bay.

Rain stung his eyes, water swirled around his feet in the bottom of the boat, and a wind gust whipped them around counterclockwise. So much water spilled into the boat that he almost couldn't maintain his grip on the throttle, and as he dashed the water from his eyes, he realized that the anchor line was washing overboard. He made a last-minute grab for it and missed.

Karma shouted—he couldn't hear what she said—but the next thing he knew, the motor choked and died, which was when he realized that the anchor line had become fouled in the propeller.

He was no sailor—that was obvious by now to both of them. If anything the storm was growing stronger, the seas higher now, their little boat pitching and yawing frantically as it tossed upon the swells.

With a sickening feeling in the pit of his stomach, Slade realized that they were in an extremely precarious situation. The clouds overhead were thickening and seemed more sinister; the water was as black as night.

For the first time he wondered if they would make it to safety.

5

THEY WERE AT THE MERCY of the sea, and he hunkered down in the bottom of the boat, moving closer to Karma so he could protect her.

"...jump? We could swim to the houses," she shouted directly into his ear, but in Slade's judgment, they were less than a hundred yards away from the nearest house and it would be foolhardy to leave the boat when they were so close.

He wrapped his arms around her, holding her tight, becoming aware of her warmth. She had given up bailing, and she clung to him, too.

Lightning rent the air above them, which was frightening but illuminated Stiltsville so that he could see that they were closer than he'd thought.

"Give me the oar!" he shouted to Karma, and she pushed it toward him.

He paddled as best he could, but it was the waves that provided the most momentum. In a matter of minutes, they had banged up against one of the pilings attached to an abandoned house.

Despite gulping more seawater than he'd thought he could hold, he managed to help Karma crawl toward the stern of the boat and the piling, which was studded with boards that made a kind of ladder.

"You go up first," he gasped, and she climbed ahead of him while he prayed that she would not slip on the wet wood.

When he saw that she was safely clinging to the platform surrounding the house, he secured the runabout as best he could with what was left of the anchor rope and made his way upward.

Karma pulled him up the last two rungs. "The house is locked," she shouted, bracing herself against the railing as a particularly hard gust rocked her sideways. "I already tried the door."

For an answer, he removed one of his soggy boots and dealt the window in the door a heavy blow with the heel. Then, cushioning his hand and wrist with his sock, he reached inside and unlocked the door.

They blew in on a gust that he would have bet was gale strength, and it slammed the door behind them.

"Here," Karma said, yanking a blanket off a couch right inside the door. "Stuff this in where the glass is broken."

While he tended to the window, Karma caught her breath and assessed their quarters. It was a small cottage, equipped with basic furnishings—long wood table for dining, small cubbyhole of a kitchen, and through a door, a bedroom.

"This place will do," she said. "If it survived Hurricane Andrew some years back, it'll make it through this storm." She pulled off the life vest and tossed it beside the door.

Slade did the same. He also yanked off his other boot and sock. "Damn right it will, but the last thing I expected was to find a fully equipped house out here in the middle of Biscayne Bay." He was dripping on the floor, but that was a minor problem. They were lucky that they weren't lying at the bottom of the ocean, or at least the part of it that they hadn't swallowed while trying to survive the storm.

"Uncle Nate told me about these places," Karma said. "They were built in the 1930s, starting with a bait and sandwich shop that catered to fishermen. My uncle knows a guy who worked here." She slid the band from her hair and tried to fluff it without much success.

"All these houses to serve fishermen? No way."

Karma went and peeked into the bedroom. The furnishings consisted of a double bed, its spread old and rumpled, and a scarred wooden trunk in a corner. She turned back around. "Later more houses were built, and one of the charms of the place was that it was out of the reach of law enforcement so that people could gamble. Families kept vacation homes here in the fifties and sixties, but Hurricane Andrew leveled all but seven of them."

He looked past her into the bedroom, wheels beginning to turn in his mind when he saw the bed. He didn't have any trouble picturing the two of them in it.

Karma stood at the window gazing out at the roiling sea, now mostly blotted out by the rain. He walked up behind her, which seemed to make her so uncomfortable that she slipped out of the space where she stood and sort of hopped sideways. Graceful it wasn't, but it was amusing.

He'd noticed that she was shivering, and he cleared his throat. "I think we should scout around for dry clothes, and I'll check to see if there's food and candles or hurricane lamps. We may have to stay here for a while until the storm lets up."

She looked concerned, but Slade felt exactly the opposite. To be shipwrecked with Karma somewhere where she couldn't run away—or hop out of reach—was his idea of really good luck.

"SO DO YOU WANT CORNED BEEF hash or corned beef hash? There's only one can of food in the pantry," Karma called to Slade from the kitchen. She'd found a tank top—too small—in the trunk in the bedroom, and she wore it with a pair of shorts—too big. Still, she was dry, and that increased her comfort level considerably.

"Fortunately I like canned hash."

She shrugged. "I won't eat it, so it's all yours."

"Oops, I forgot you're a vegetarian. But you'll have to

eat something," Slade called from the bedroom. He emerged wearing nothing but a pair of shorts—too small. The sight of his bare chest, braided with muscle and deeply tanned, flooded Karma with the kind of heat that had nothing to do with the temperature of the room. She wheeled around and concentrated on opening the can with the primitive can opener. That way she didn't have to look at him looking at her, which was what he was doing. And her tank top didn't cover much.

Slade began to rifle through the kitchen cabinets. "Don't know who owns this place, but I'll leave them a check to cover the food and damage. Say, here's a rice cake. You can have it," he said. He tossed it on the table, where it landed next to the hurricane lamp he'd lit earlier.

The rice cake didn't sound appetizing, but she supposed beggars couldn't be choosers, as Aunt Sophie would have said. She busied herself freeing a saucepan from the tangle of pots underneath the counter while Slade prowled around the cabin, whistling tunelessly between his teeth. On further thought, it wasn't so tuneless. The song he was whistling was an old one and had lyrics along the lines of, "Oooh baby, you're so sexy." If he was trying to send a message to her, it was getting through loud and clear.

She slammed the cover on the hash.

"Here, I'll take over," he said, moving closer.

She sat down at the table and unpeeled the rice cake, keeping her arms up to cover her breasts. This would hide the fact that her nipples were puckering beneath the thin fabric.

"You don't want any of the hash?"

She took a bite of the rice cake, but it was so dry that she almost spit it out. "No, thanks. I wish we could go fishing." She eyed a fishing pole that was propped in a corner.

Slade gave the hash a stir. "We're not going to do any fishing with this storm going on. But, my friend, when you come to Okeechobee, I'll take you to a great catfish restaurant."

"I never said I would go to Okeechobee," she told him.

"I never invited you, but I'm inviting you now."

She made herself eat the rest of the rice cake. Would he still want her to come once he'd gone out on a date with Jennifer? She studied his back in the flickering lamplight.

"Will you go to Okeechobee with me?"

"I don't know yet. I'm mostly concerned with getting out of here. It doesn't look as if we're going to be rescued any time soon."

"This may be a big storm front. There won't be any recreational or Coast Guard boats coming along until it's over, I reckon. We may be stuck here until morning."

Her watch had stopped over an hour ago. "What time is it?"

"Almost eight o'clock."

When the hash was hot, he brought the pot to the table and spooned half if it onto his plate.

"The rest of this is yours if you want it." He held the pan out toward her so that she got a hearty whiff.

"I told you, I won't eat it." It smelled wonderful, though, and the rice cake sat in her stomach like lead.

He sat down across from her, straddling the bench. "Suit yourself."

The food on Slade's plate steamed invitingly, and she found herself staring at it.

Slade grinned. "Your hunger is showing," he said.

"I was thinking that I could pick out the pieces of potato and eat them," she said grudgingly.

"Go with it." He went to the stove, scraped the rest of the hash onto a plate for her, and handed it over.

She separated some of the potato from the meat. Her stomach rumbled, and she nibbled at a potato chunk. "It tastes pretty good," she told him when she noticed how intently he was watching her.

"Well, sure. Why don't you try a taste of the meat?"

"Oh, I don't know," but her mouth was watering and

she couldn't help wondering what canned corned beef would taste like.

"You want it. You know you do," he teased.

Wasn't this what Mandi had said she wanted to hear him say? What guys usually said to Mandi? Mandi hadn't, Karma was sure, wanted Slade to utter that particular phrase in the context of food, but she certainly would have been impressed that Karma had heard him say it. This made her smile. "Stop being funny. I can't think, I'm so hungry."

Slade became more serious. "You'd better eat whatever you can. If we have to push off in our own boat, you may need all the strength you can muster."

"The anchor line is caught in the prop. I doubt that the boat will take us anywhere."

"One word, Karma. Oars. As in row, row, row your boat."

She groaned. "I'm hoping for a luxury rescue by a sleek cabin cruiser on a fishing trip."

"Don't depend on it."

Seeing how serious he was and realizing that he was right, she took a small bite of the hash, meat included. It tasted heavenly and was all crispy on the bottom where Slade had browned it.

She saw that he was waiting expectantly for her reaction, and she didn't disappoint him.

"I think it's the best thing I ever ate," she said fervently, forking in another mouthful. So much for principles. So much for sticking to them.

Slade laughed uproariously. "That's very funny. Canned corned beef hash wouldn't be on anyone's list of favorite meals."

"That depends on how hungry they are."

"Don't scarf it all down at once," he teased. "Make it last. You never know when you'll get a chance to eat meat again."

She entered into the spirit of fun. "I'll savor every bite.

And I'll make them real small bites so that there will be more of them.''

Once her plate was empty, Karma wished she hadn't eaten so fast because it suddenly occurred to her that after they ate, there wasn't much to do.

She got up and rinsed off her plate. Slade did, too. She was certain from the way he studied the curve of her backside in those ridiculously baggy shorts that he had something in mind for a pastime and that she'd better find something to do—fast.

She dried her hands on a dishtowel and went to the bookshelf that divided the kitchen from the living area. She knelt on the floor to browse through the pile of games on the bottom shelf.

Slade went to look out the window at the thrashing sea. "I think our boat's still there," he reported.

"That's good news. I guess." She couldn't feel too hopeful about their prospects of leaving anytime soon.

He came to stand beside her. "Any interesting games?"

"A game of Candyland much the worse for wear, a box of dominoes with only six dominoes in it. Oh, and Scrabble."

"I'll challenge you to a game of Scrabble. Loser has to sweep the floor."

She thought about it. "That's fair," she agreed finally.

They settled down on the couch with the Scrabble board between them, illuminated only by the dim wavering light from the hurricane lamp nearby. Outside, the wind rattled the windows. Waves repeatedly battered the pilings beneath them, and every once in a while, the house would draw itself up, suck in its breath, and give a little shudder.

Karma ignored the weather as much as she could and studied the letters in her rack before slapping down the word EAST. Slade promptly added the letters B and R to the beginning of it, making it BREAST.

She raised her eyebrows.

"It's a word, right? It's legal, right?" His expression was one of mild amusement.

"Uh-huh," she had to admit, and she added an E and an A downward from the T to make the word TEA.

"Oh, this one's easy," Slade told her. He added a T to the end of T to make the word TEAT, looking up at her afterward with an air of studied innocence.

"Slade," she said, suspecting that it wasn't by accident that his two words so far had sexual connotations.

"I know what you're going to say, but keep in mind that I'm a cattleman and that cows have udders."

This was too much, and she wasn't about to let him get away with it. "I'm pretty sure that the Diamond B has beef cattle, not dairy cattle. Your experience with udders is probably nonexistent."

"Udderly true," he said with a straight face. "And besides, it's your moo-ve."

It was all she could do not to throw a couch pillow at him. Instead she slapped down an O, an S, and another S next to the last T in TEAT, creating the word TOSS, which was what she would do at this point to get rid of him if she could.

He got it. She thought he might comment, but he didn't. Instead he made good use of the last S and arranged a K, and I, and another S above it, making the word KISS.

"Which," he said softly and with the enterprising look that she was coming to know so well, "wouldn't be a bad idea."

Ignoring the tingle that rose from somewhere she'd rather not think about at the moment, Karma made a show of arranging her letters on her rack. "You agreed to no funny business," she reminded him.

"That was when all we were talking about was taking your aunt's ashes out to sea. That was before getting caught in the storm and washing up in this extremely cozy little place far away from the rest of the world. It was before survival became an issue.''

''It's not an issue. We're going to be fine.'' The word thrummed in her ears like a heartbeat—*fine, fine, fine.* But were they? Was she?

''Of course we are. But in the meantime—''

Without hesitating, Karma plunked down a T and an O and a P after the second S in KISS. This created the word STOP. ''Which means the game is over,'' she said, springing up and dumping the board and its contents into its box.

But it wasn't, and she knew it.

''Does this mean that you sweep? Or do I?''

''I'll do it.'' Karma went to the closet and hauled out a broom, which she proceeded to wield with great efficiency. Slade forced himself to remain silent as he sorted out the board, racks and letter tiles.

When he straightened from putting the Scrabble game back on its shelf, Karma was spreading a large beach towel on the floor.

''What's that for?'' he asked.

''I could use some calm and lucidity,'' she said. She sat down on the towel and crossed her legs in a position that he recognized as the Half-Lotus, eyes closed, hands placed palms up on her knees.

''Guess I'll try some of that too,'' he said. He went in the bedroom, found a towel in the old trunk, and spread it out near hers. ''There's nothing,'' he said, ''that I need so much as some freeing up.''

She opened one eye. ''It seems to me,'' she said, ''that you're getting much too freed up as it is.''

''I don't understand why, if I'm good enough for those clients of yours, I'm not good enough for you.''

She opened the other eye. ''I didn't say you're not good enough for me. I want to protect our matchmaker-client relationship, that's all.''

Slade settled himself on the towel. ''What if I told you that's not important anymore?''

The light from the lamp flickered across her face, gilding it with light. ''We have a contract. I'm supposed to find you a wife.''

''What if I told you—''

''Please, Slade. Don't tell me anything. I'm not in the mood to hear it.''

''Even if I said you have some of the prettiest hair I've ever seen? If I told you that your figure really turns me on?'' From this angle, the shorts gave him a view up the inside of her thigh. He tried not to look, but he was, after all, a normal guy. She wasn't wearing panties; apparently she hadn't found any dry ones in the trunk.

Karma seemed to be ignoring what he'd said. He knew she'd heard him, however. How could she not? They were only three feet apart. He could have reached over with his hand and flicked a bit of lint off her tank top. He wondered if he dared to hope she'd do another backbend today.

Reluctant to push her too far, he tried to concentrate on his own Half-Lotus position. That only brought to mind his extreme discomfort—his hips ached and his knees hurt, for starters, and on top of that, the foot that was angled across his thigh had gone to sleep. At the point when he was ready to shout for mercy, Karma rose fluidly to her feet.

''Now what?''

''Now a few Sunrise Salutations. You can follow along with me if you like,'' she said. She lifted her arms up high so that her nipples stood out against the jersey, and then she bent backward as Slade contended with another stiffness, this one in a place that could cause serious embarrassment for him if she noticed.

While he struggled to subdue his errant anatomy, Karma bent and planted her hands on the floor on either side of her feet (which meant that he had a great view up the back of her shorts), shot one foot and then the other out behind her (so that her breasts hung downward, looking lush and full), and then gracefully angled up, chest out, buttocks down (so that he could imagine other uses for this particular position).

"Remember? We did this in class."

"Uh—yeah. Sort of." In class he hadn't been able to observe Karma this closely as she went through the motions of the Sunrise Salutation, and now, watching her buttocks rise high in the air as she assumed the position called Downward-Facing Dog, he swallowed hard. With Karma's derriere propped so enticingly in the air in front of him, he could think of a lot of things he'd rather be doing right now than yoga.

"And that's all there is to it," she said when she had finished. "Now you try it."

His desire for her had settled into an ache in his belly, difficult to ignore with her standing so close and looking so fetching. He could see, however, that she wouldn't take no for an answer.

He positioned himself with his hands pressed together in front of his chest in the Prayer Position, feeling stupider by the second. No self-respecting cowboy would be doing something called the Sunrise Salutation. No rancher had any business doing yoga. He wasn't comfortable with New Age stuff, and he opened his mouth to tell her so.

Then he realized that she was prepared to do this right alongside him, and for the life of him, he couldn't summon the wish to make her stop. He wanted to see her go through the whole thing from Prayer Position to Downward-Facing Dog to the conclusion of the exercises, to watch every sensual move as her body so effortlessly flowed from pose to pose. To imagine how her body would move against him if they were—

"Ready?"

He nodded and thought how good they would be together. How utterly and completely in tune they would be physically. He knew she was keeping the skill level moderate for him as they progressed through the yoga sequence, that she deliberately held herself back to accommodate his slower pace. Which is what he would do if they were in bed together. He would take his time, savoring it, letting her learn about him as he learned about her, and he would make sure she found her pleasure before he took his.

"No, no, no," she said, scrambling up when they were side by side in Plank Position, bodies perpendicular to the floor, feet supported on toes, arms straight down, hands with fingertips spread on the wooden floor. "You're sagging in the middle."

She bent and reached under his torso to tap him on the belly. "This is supposed to lift up, and it's right above your second chakra. You won't be getting the full benefits of the pose if you don't do it right."

The touch of her hand was what did him in. He felt so attuned to her, so ready to emote, that to his horror his stomach sagged, his toes curled, and his elbows relaxed. He felt as if he were watching from a long way away as his hands slipped, flew out from under him, and he fell.

Down he went, taking her with him, landing on top of her with a gentle *"Umph!"*

Well, not on top of her, exactly. On top of her arm. He turned his head so that he could look full into her face. She made no attempt to move, only stared deep into his eyes. She looked startled. Bewildered. And, to his amazement, overcome with—lust?

While he was registering the heretofore unlikely possibility that Karma might actually be as hot for him as he was for her, he also dealt with the fact that the fall had knocked nearly all the air out of him. He gulped a couple of gasping breaths to refill his lungs.

"Are you—are you okay?" he stammered when he could finally speak.

"I don't know," Karma replied softly. "I seem to have

found new benefits to that pose.'' She had made no attempt to reclaim her arm, no move to put distance between the two of them.

''You—have?''

Solemnly she nodded. He didn't want to move himself off her arm. He liked it where it was. But he rolled over on his side, never taking his eyes from her face.

''Karma,'' was all he could say, the only word in his vocabulary, the only thought in his mind. ''Karma.'' He reached out and brushed his fingertips along the curve of her cheek.

He saw her swallow. She was so close that he could see that the tips of her eyelashes were golden, so close that he could smell the scent of her sea-washed hair.

''We shouldn't—'' she began, but he didn't want to hear it. And so he did the only thing he could do to stop her. He lowered his mouth over hers and gathered her into his arms.

His skin warmed to hers, his arms molded her to his body, and he was gratified by her quick intake of breath and the tremor that followed it. *Right, this is right,* he thought to himself, glorying in all the long length of her as he guided her hips closer to his. The texture of her mouth was soft and smooth, her lips full and silky against his. Outside a roll of thunder shook the little stilt house on its pilings, but it was a mere echo of the thunder pounding in his own blood.

''You can tell me to stop,'' he said roughly, ''if you want to.''

''This isn't—one of—the standard yoga postures,'' she said between nibbles on his lower lip. Her voice was low and laced with the slightest hint of huskiness.

''Thank goodness for that,'' he said, because now all he felt was pleasure from his head to his toes.

He was surprised to feel her lips curving beneath his,

and then she laughed. He had never heard a more welcome sound.

He laughed, too, from pure enjoyment, and as he moved to hold her even closer, she said, "Maybe we'll invent some new postures, what do you think?"

"I think," he said unevenly, "that sounds like a real good idea."

6

NEW POSES ELUDED HIM, however, as his fingertips feathered up her back to tangle in her hair and his mouth sought out all the places he had dreamed of kissing since the moment he realized that he was attracted to her. Her nape, her earlobe, the hollow of her throat, the other earlobe—warm and salty to the taste, all of them.

Karma was definitely the more experimental one. She was as curious about his body as he was about hers, and she was definitely not the type who laid back and let the man do all the work. She kissed his eyebrows, his nose, ran her hands along the muscles in his back and tunneled her fingers through the hair on his chest. She bit his neck and laughed when he was startled.

"Let's call that position Bug Looking For Bites," she said as she rolled over on her back and pulled him on top of her.

"Only if we call this one Dog Lying On Treats," he told her, and was pleased when she laughed.

"Once you get started, are you always this eager?" he asked playfully, staring down at her.

Her eyes became serious, her expression somber. "No," she said. "No, Slade, I'm not."

He would have liked an explanation, but he didn't want to talk. Instead he crushed his mouth down upon hers, their lips fusing until he felt her tongue unfurling against his. He didn't know when he had ever known a woman to take the lead as Karma did. Somewhere in the back of his mind, he filed away the thought that this wasn't merely biology—

two people mating. It was chemistry—two people so attuned to each other that their mating promised complete gratification. That wasn't something he had expected. But it was something that he wanted. Oh, yes, he wanted this to be more, to be everything, to be all.

He wanted this to be love.

But how could he think about that now? With Karma touching him, teasing him, smiling at him in that tremulous way? Shaken by the depth of his feeling for her, he bent and kissed her nipple, which was pebble-hard beneath the thin jersey of the top she wore. If she had objected, he would have stopped, but instead she guided his mouth to her other breast, raking her fingers through his hair and making a sound deep in her throat that let him know that he was doing this right.

He slid his hand up under the jersey and trailed his fingertips along the bottom curve of her breast. Her eyes opened wide, and he said, "Do you like this?"

"How could I not?" was her reply. His eyes never leaving hers, he pushed the fabric up and out of the way so that both breasts were exposed to view. They were pale in the dim light, the nipples long and rosy.

He jolted back to reality. "I don't have any protection. I didn't expect this."

"It's okay. I won't get pregnant. I take birth control pills. Not because I need them for—well, you know. I haven't had a boyfriend in a long time. I kept taking them for my complexion."

"I'm glad you did," he said. He reached for her again.

"Wait," she said, and he moved to one side, propping himself on his elbow as he watched her slide the shirt over her head in one lithe movement and toss it to one side.

He reached out to cup one breast in his hand, his thumb rolling upward to tease the nipple. "You have," he said unsteadily, "the most beautiful breasts I have ever seen."

"Doubtful," she said, looking down at herself, and at

the expression on her face, all he could do was pull her into his arms.

"I'm being honest. I wouldn't tell you that if it weren't true."

"They're too small," she murmured as he took one nipple into his mouth and explored it with his tongue and teeth. She closed her eyes and braced her hands against her shoulders.

"Not too small," he said. "And the perfect shape. Let's stop talking and enjoy. And lean forward."

She did, and he filled his hand with one breast while kissing the other, pulling her over him. It seemed that his senses were full of her—touching, tasting, smelling, seeing—and he was glad that she wasn't that tiny delicate woman he had come to Miami Beach to find. No, he liked Karma, and he liked her the way she was—a woman he could sink into, a woman who could match him length to length, a woman like no other he had ever known.

A woman with a desire as strong as his if her present occupation was anything to judge by, because she was pulling the waistband of his shorts down.

"Boxers," she said.

He thought he hadn't heard her correctly. "What?"

"You wear boxers, not briefs. White silk. And the pattern's kind of cute."

His lips twitched. "That's our black Diamond B Ranch brand. My father once ordered several dozen pairs of boxer shorts with our brand and handed them out to every guy who works at the ranch."

She smiled. "You've got to be kidding."

"Nope. You'd have to know my father. He has a sense of humor. But I admit that I like silk underwear."

"It's very sexy," she said.

"I'll pass that information along to our ranch hands," he said with a grin.

Speaking of hands, he wanted Karma's to be caressing something more relevant than the silk of his boxers. He slid quickly out of them, shoving them aside as her hands closed around him. Her fingers were cool against his heat, calm against his urgency.

"We could move into the bedroom," she suggested, her words all breathy and rushed.

No, they couldn't. Not with her hands working their magic on him, not with her body so eager to be explored. Even one minute apart from her, even one second, would be too long. For an answer, he tugged a pillow off the couch and positioned it under her head. "Later," he said.

"Well, then," she said, and before he knew it, she had slid out of her own shorts. He couldn't speak, he was so moved by her beauty. Her skin was creamy and white where her bikini had protected it from the sun. The small trim triangle of hair at the apex of her thighs was pale and soft, and when he was touching her there, he felt her frisson of anticipation, her eagerness that he would bet was every bit as strong as his.

"I would never have guessed that you were a highly sexed woman," he said. "I wouldn't have known from the way you acted."

"Maybe that's why I acted that way," she said softly. "Maybe I knew that there would be no turning back."

"That's not an excuse I've ever heard before," he said, kissing her between her breasts and moving lower.

"It's not an excuse. It's true," she said as his hands moved to the cleft between her legs and parted them.

And then he didn't talk for a long time. A long, long time, during which he learned about every part of her body and she learned about every part of his. But even learning, even finally knowing, wasn't enough. He wanted to touch her in every conceivable way, to drive her to heights that she had never before imagined and that he hadn't imagined either. He only knew that there were things about this woman that he needed to know in this lifetime, and the sudden thought occurred to him that even a lifetime might not be long enough.

Before he had time to settle that thought into a part of his mind where he could revisit it at leisure, Karma sat and urged him up with her. Her arms folded around him, pulling him closer, and he couldn't believe it when she murmured with the utmost good humor and a twinkle in her eyes, "Now, cowboy, you're going to teach me how to ride." And then she slid over him, bearing down all warm and wet and ready, laughing gently when all he could do was gasp and circle his arms around her hips.

Ride him she did, flowing into the act so naturally that it seemed as if they had been indulging in this sweet pastime forever. He drew her into a kiss of passion, tongues tangling in haste, their worlds merging with exquisite delight. He lost himself in her—no, not in her, but in the newness of being truly one with another human being, with Karma.

Her fingernails bit savagely into his back, urging him on, and when her breath quickened, when she arched her back and cried out his name, he drove himself into her with a fury unmatched by the storm raging outside. She surrendered to him with a recklessness that was matched only by his own, and he couldn't draw enough air into his lungs, his blood screamed in his veins, his heat threatened to ignite them both. He rose up and bore her to the floor, never letting her go, and as he pinned her beneath him, her cry of release set him free and allowed him to plunge into her with a fierceness that brought on his own climax only seconds after hers.

He collapsed on her, his whole weight, wanting their bodies to fuse, wanting to be part of her for more than this one night. He felt her trembling beneath him, and he whispered in her ear, "Karma?"

"Oh," was all she said, and then again, "oh."

He lifted himself up so that he could see her face. Her eyes were closed, her lips slightly parted.

"Is that all you can say?" he asked tenderly.

She swallowed and repressed a smile. "It's better than, 'Oh, no!'"

"What? Are you having regrets already?" His mock seriousness didn't produce the reaction he'd hoped for. She frowned.

"You're a client. You're supposed to go out with another client on Friday night. I have really screwed up, Slade." She pushed him off and rolled away.

"I wouldn't say you've screwed *up*, exactly, but—"

"You don't understand. You couldn't possibly," she said, pulling on her shirt and then her shorts. He was stunned that there were tears shining on her eyelashes.

"I'm willing to try," he said in total bewilderment. He reached for her, wanting nothing so much as to kiss those tears away and to enfold her in his arms.

"Oh, Slade," she said, breaking into sobs. "This is my one chance to succeed. Rent-a-Yenta fell into my lap, a gift from my generous Aunt Sophie and Uncle Nate. I didn't have a—a job, and I—I needed one, and so I came to Miami Beach to be a matchmaker. And—and I'm failing at that, too!"

She grabbed her clothes before jumping up and running into the bedroom, slamming the door behind her.

Slade pushed himself to a sitting position and raked a trembling hand through his hair. He had just participated in the most memorable lovemaking session in his life with the most sexual and exciting woman he had ever met, and she was pushing him away. He didn't know what to think.

Oh, yes, he did! Gritting his teeth in determination, he yanked on his shorts and strode into the bedroom.

Slade burst through the door to find Karma sprawled across the bed, her clothes obviously pulled on haphazardly. She had lit a candle and set it on the table beside the bed, and he saw that her face was puffy, her eyes swollen. It was clear that even though some women might be attractive when they cried, Karma was not one of them. This endeared her to him somehow. Who would want a woman who was perfect in every way? It would take too much energy to try to measure up to her.

"Karma?"

"Don't talk to me right now, Slade."

It took all his restraint not to drag her off that bed and pull her into his arms. Instead he sat on the bed beside her and brushed the damp hair back from her hot face. "Do you wish we hadn't made love?" he asked gently.

She eased over on her back. Her blotchy face was beautiful to him, and her eyes, though exceedingly red of rim, spoke volumes. "If that had been making love, I wouldn't mind so much."

"It felt like it to me," he said.

She stared. "It did?"

He nodded. "I'm thirty-five years old, and I haven't exactly been celibate. But Karma, I'm telling the truth when I say that it's never been like that for me. Never. I care about you."

She swallowed and tentatively touched his arm. "I'm scared, that's all."

"Scared of me?"

"No. Scared of what this means. I've wanted to make a success of this business, and I can't do that if I'm going to rip off my best clients for myself."

This disconcerted him. "How many clients have you slept with?" He realized after he said it that this was none of his business.

She sat up. "None, except you. And I don't intend to do it again. Oh, Slade, I'm not clear about exactly what's going on here."

He leaned closer and took her hand. "Neither of us knows what has begun, but why don't we find out?" He drew a deep breath. "Come home to Okeechobee City with me, Karma. Meet my parents. See my ranch."

She closed her eyes for a long moment, then opened them. "You're inviting me to meet your parents? Isn't that a bit hasty?"

He regarded her seriously, his eyes searching her face. "I don't think so."

"Well, I can't go."

"Why not?"

"I have a business to run."

"We could go this weekend. Surely you don't keep office hours on the weekend."

"You have a date with Jennifer tomorrow night. She wants you to pick her up at seven o'clock." He was learning to recognize the stubborn set of her chin.

"I don't want to go out with Jennifer. I want to be with you."

"I promised her! You have to go!"

"No, I don't. I didn't promise anything. Karma—"

He stopped talking when she buried her face in her hands. When she lifted it again, she was steely-eyed.

"Obviously you don't understand how important the business is to me. If you don't go out with Jennifer, she'll pass the word around that Rent-a-Yenta doesn't follow through on its promises. Who would come to a dating agency that lets its clients down? What kind of memorial would that be to my aunt Sophie?"

"I hadn't thought of it that way," he allowed.

"Now that I've pointed out the problems, you'll take Jennifer out. Won't you?"

He shook his head. "You're invited to Okeechobee over the weekend, like I said."

She clenched her teeth. "I haven't said I'd go."

"That makes two of us. I'm not going out with Jennifer and you're not going to Okeechobee. But you and I are going to make love again. For sure." He stood up and turned his back on her, striding into the kitchen to check a leak in the roof, going to the door to make sure the blanket that they'd stuffed in the hole where they'd broken the glass was still keeping most of the water out. But his mind wasn't really on those chores. He was thinking about how he could get Karma to Okeechobee.

After a while, she came to the door of the bedroom, an afghan wrapped around her shoulders. "Slade?"

"Yes?" He fixed her with a no-nonsense gaze like he did with one of the horses when it got out of line.

"Maybe we could compromise."

"What do you suggest?"

She walked over to where he stood and placed herself directly in front of him. "You go out with Jennifer tomorrow night, and I leave with you for Okeechobee City on Saturday morning."

He stared at her. "You know, you really drive a tough bargain."

"It's a fair one, I think."

He sighed. The thought of squiring Jennifer around Miami Beach was unappealing, but perhaps she'd agree to go home early. And as a result, he'd get Karma where he wanted her—on his turf back home where she could see what he was really all about.

"All right," he said unenthusiastically. "I'll go out with Jennifer. Not because I want to, you understand."

"I understand," she said heavily.

He afforded her a curt nod and watched as she walked back into the bedroom. He should have felt as if he'd won something, but he couldn't when he felt as if he'd had to pay too high a price.

KARMA MADE HERSELF as comfortable as she could on one side of the double bed. She'd cocooned herself in the afghan because the spread and the sheets on the bed smelled musty and felt damp. She wished that they would be rescued soon. She wished the storm hadn't forced them to take shelter in Stiltsville.

She wished she hadn't made love with Slade Braddock.

No, that wasn't true. What she really wished was that she hadn't fallen *in* love with Slade Braddock, and that was a different thing altogether.

They were a mismatch, that's for sure. He was a cowboy,

and she was a city girl at heart. He liked small women, and she wasn't. He wanted a wife, and she wasn't a candidate. Their lifestyles were so different, and how would they ever reconcile those differences? Why, he ate meat. He raised beef and sold it, for Pete's sake! He was a nice guy, and he was sexy—but it didn't take a couple of degrees in psychology to know that he wasn't for her.

Feeling depressed about the whole thing, she rolled over on her other side and pillowed her head on her hands. She must have dozed because the next thing she knew, Slade was sitting on the bed beside her and offering her a cup of hot tea.

"I thought you might be cold," he said.

This thoughtfulness so endeared him to her that she could only stare.

"Are you all right?" he asked, his forehead pleating into a frown.

She pushed herself to a sitting position and accepted the cup from him. The tea tasted good, warmed her from the inside out.

"Mind if I stay here?" he asked.

She gestured toward the pillow on the unoccupied side of the bed. "Feel free," she said.

He plumped the pillow a few times and lay down beside her.

"What time is it?" she asked.

"After midnight."

She sighed. "A long time until morning."

"The storm seems to be on the wane."

"Any signs of boats out there?"

"No."

"We might as well get a good night's sleep."

"Right."

"You can stay here if you like."

"I was planning to." He turned toward her. "I'm glad you're going to Okeechobee with me. My folks will think you're wonderful."

"I'm not so sure."

"Once I find me a wife, they're going to retire to a little house in town, enjoy life."

Karma pictured a gray-haired couple, the man with a paunch, the woman's hair pulled into a bun. With her unconventional background, Karma would have little in common with such people. What would they talk about? What could *they* like about *her?*

"I'm not the kind of wife they'd want for you."

"You don't know that." He seemed pretty sure of himself.

"Anyway, maybe you'll like Jennifer better. Maybe you'll invite *her* to go to Okeechobee."

"Not a chance," was his flat reply. "Jennifer wouldn't know the front end of a horse from the rear, and she probably doesn't have any interest in birds."

Karma greeted this statement with silence, but Slade seemed oblivious to her withdrawal, talking enthusiastically about Abner the alligator and his horse, Lightning, and something about barrels that Karma became too sleepy to follow.

She fell asleep with her head pillowed on Slade's broad shoulder, thinking that she had been a fool to agree to go to Okeechobee with him but oddly excited about the prospect anyway.

MORNING. SOMEONE SNORING softly beside her.

Snoring? Karma sat upright and edged away from the man who slept on the other half of the bed. His hair was rumpled, and his mouth hung slightly open. Dark stubble covered his cheeks and chin, but even so, Karma still thought he was the handsomest man she'd ever seen in her life.

It was Friday morning. He was supposed to take Jennifer out tonight.

Putting the thought out of her mind, she slid out from under the afghan and padded lightly to the window. Dawn was tunneling experimental fingers of light through a heavy fog. At least it wasn't storming anymore.

"Karma?"

She turned to find that Slade had sat up and was stretching. "How does it look out there?"

"Like we're inside a wad of cotton."

He got up and joined her. "Well," he said philosophically, "once the fog burns off, we'll start seeing some boats. Rescue can't be far away."

This statement was punctuated by the growl of Karma's stomach. She blushed, embarrassed. "We don't have any food," she said glumly.

"Maybe there's another rice cake somewhere. I'll look."

While Slade methodically went through the kitchen cabinets, Karma picked up the towels off the floor where they had made love last night. This morning she could hardly avoid the fact that she had acted reckless and wanton. What if she had made a fool of herself? It would have been far better, she thought with crystal clear hindsight, to let him lead the way.

"No more rice cakes, but I found a package of peanuts." He poured half of them into his hand and handed the rest to her.

She sat in a chair and huddled down into the afghan. She began to eat the peanuts.

"Karma," Slade said, watching her as he spoke. "I really like you. A lot."

Fortunately her mouth was full, and she didn't have to speak. She didn't know what she would have said.

"I want you to know that I'm glad we ended up in Stiltsville. I'm glad we made love last night. I'm glad—"

She never learned what else Slade Braddock might be glad about because they heard an approaching boat motor outside. They exchanged a startled look and ran to the nearest window, where a boat was closing in through the remaining shreds of fog.

In a matter of seconds, they had thrown open the door

and were outside on the deck shouting and waving their arms at a Coast Guard cutter like two people in the latter stages of dementia. Someone on the boat hallooed back, and in a few minutes, a couple of Coast Guardsmen were climbing the makeshift ladder.

"Looks like we've been rescued," Karma said brightly, mostly because Slade was looking sad.

He pinned her with a meaningful and way-too-serious look. "I meant what I said in there. I'm glad this happened."

Her heart took a little leap and started to beat faster. The truth was that she was glad, too. But she wouldn't tell Slade. At least not yet.

THE COAST GUARD CUTTER delivered them to the Sunchaser Marina with *Toy Boat's Toy* in tow, a phrase that Karma tried to say really fast, which made Slade look more cheerful though he couldn't say it any better than she could.

Phifer came running over as soon as he saw them disembarking from the Coast Guard boat, and he and Slade got into a lively discussion about the weather.

"I've got to take Karma home," Slade told Phifer, but by that time, Karma was checking her bicycle tires to see if they had enough air.

"I don't want a ride home," Karma said, straightening and taking hold of the handlebars.

"Don't be silly. Of course I'm giving you a ride."

But Karma adamantly refused. "I need some space," she said. "I need some time."

"You've got until tomorrow morning when we go to the ranch."

She groaned. "Don't remind me." Now that they were away from Stiltsville, going to the ranch loomed as a major ordeal.

"You'll love the Glades, you'll see."

Karma drew a deep breath. "Don't forget to pick Jennifer up at seven tonight."

"The only reason I'm going is that I promised. After what happened between you and me at the stilt house—"

"Nothing happened, Slade."

He rolled his eyes. "Yeah, and I was there when it didn't."

"Goodbye, Slade." She started walking her bike up the dock, but she knew that he watched her as she passed the marina office. She heard Phifer say grudgingly, "At least she's walking her bike this time, not riding it. It's against the rules to ride a bike on the dock you know. Against the rules." She couldn't hear Slade's reply.

As Karma cycled back to the Blue Moon, she mulled over the past twenty-four hours. She felt terrible that she had made love with a client; she felt happy that it had been Slade. She felt sad that she had been given the task to scatter Aunt Sophie's ashes; she felt happy that Slade had been with her. She felt sad that—

Well, she didn't feel as sad about any of it as she should. She mostly felt happy that she and Slade had been together for such a long time.

"I don't want to fall in love with him," she said out loud, so caught up in her own thoughts that she didn't realize that a stoop-shouldered little old lady on a bus bench heard her.

"Well, you don't have to fall in love with anyone if you don't want to," the little old lady hollered after her, and all the rest of the way to the Blue Moon, Karma made sure that she didn't voice any of her thoughts out loud. But she wasn't sure she'd had any choice in falling in love with Slade Braddock. It had just happened, and now she had to figure out what to do about it.

"I guess you and Slade had a good time last night," Goldy ventured when Karma walked into the lobby pushing her bike. Karma could tell that it wasn't lost on Goldy that her hair had dried stiff from the salt water and that her clothes were still damp, but she kept walking and wheeled the bike into the storage room where she kept it.

"Jennifer says she has a date with him tonight," Goldy called after her, clearly fishing for information.

At that, Karma slammed the closet door and backtracked to Goldy's counter. "That's true."

"Jennifer won't like to know that you're dating Slade Braddock."

"We're not dating," Karma said, immediately on the defensive.

"That's not what my tarot says. Either you're dating now or you will be soon," Goldy said with satisfaction, waving a careless hand over the cards spread on her desk.

"Listen, Goldy." Karma made invisible circles on the counter top with an index finger.

"Yes?"

"I'd appreciate it if you wouldn't mention that prediction to Jennifer."

"I wasn't going to. He doesn't look like her type." Goldy resumed laying out tarot cards, and Karma started up the stairs.

At the second floor landing there was a clatter from above, and Jennifer and Mandi hove into view. Jennifer was wearing a magenta-sequined bandeau and matching mini-skirt with an orange denim jeans jacket thrown over her shoulders. Mandi was resplendent in a lizard-print Lycra sheath worn with crystal-beaded platform shoes and was chatting on her cell phone as she descended the stairs.

"Oh, hi, Karma," Jennifer said. Mandi gave her a half-hearted wave.

"Hello," Karma replied, not feeling positive about this encounter. She needed a shampoo and a shower, and, under Mandi and Jennifer's scrutiny, she felt like she'd recently been keel-hauled and looked it.

"Did you tell Slade about our date? He hasn't called me." Jennifer smiled, and her prominent bicuspids, though perfectly capped, gave her a slightly predatory look.

"He will," Karma said wearily. "I promise."

"I'm going to suggest going to hear Shemp," Jennifer

said, naming the new band playing at the nightclub down the street.

Karma didn't want to know where Slade and Jennifer were going on their date. "That's nice. Now if you'll excuse me—" She tried to brush past this Dim Duo, but they didn't move aside.

Mandi clicked off her phone. It was scary to watch up close as a thought sprang into her mind. "Jen and I are going shopping. You really should come with us, Karma. Looks like you could use some new clothes." Mandi popped a green Tic-Tac into her mouth and rolled it around on her tongue, which also became green. In a weird way, it complemented her Lizard Lady outfit.

"Some other time," Karma said. She pushed past them, and as she started up the next flight of stairs, she heard Mandi say, "Sounds like Karma woke up on the wrong side of an empty bed this morning," and Jennifer tittered.

If they only knew, Karma thought, her cheeks pinkening as the two of them continued on to the lobby.

At her apartment, she showered and, inspired by the clothes Jennifer and Mandi had been wearing, changed into shocking pink slacks and a navy-blue bustier with a sheer white blouse worn over it for effect.

"You look nice," Goldy observed when Karma tried to sneak past her on her way out to tell Nate that she'd completed her mission of scattering Aunt Sophie's ashes. "I don't think you should dress so—um, *colorfully*—when you meet Slade's parents, though."

Karma skidded to a stop. "How did you know?"

"Know what?"

"That I'm going to meet his parents."

Goldy held up her tarot deck. "These told me."

"Well, don't let them tell anyone else," Karma said.

"I wouldn't, Karma, you know that. When you meet his parents, why don't you wear your pretty linen sundress? I've only seen you wear it once."

"You don't think my vintage sixties caftans are appropriate? You wear them."

"*I'm* not going to meet a man's parents. The linen dress is safe, Karma. That's all I'm saying."

"Thanks, Goldy. I'll think about it." Karma breezed out the door before Goldy could impart any more helpful advice.

She walked briskly to Nate's hotel, where his buddies in the lobby told her that he and Mrs. Rothstein had gone to the cemetery. She left a note for him and hurried back to the Rent-a-Yenta office, where she supposed it was time to write checks on her meager bank account, a chore she always dreaded because the available funds never seemed to stretch far enough to cover the expenses.

She ran up the stairs and pulled out her key. But she didn't need to use it because the door was already open.

I really must get that lock fixed, she told herself, and then she stopped cold in the doorway, staring in disbelief.

The slim, small-boned woman with the sleek auburn hair who was sitting at Karma's desk with her back to the door swiveled around and grinned up at her.

"Hello, Karma! Long time no see," chirped her cousin Paulette.

7

PAULETTE HAD IMPROVED considerably since their child-hood days back in the old neighborhood. She had stopped biting her fingernails. She had straightened her hair. With her Blahnik shoes and short tight skirt, she could have been an advertisement for the TV show, *Sex and the City*. And she was in need at the moment, which was why Karma felt true sympathy for her.

"I got fired because the boss's wife was jealous," Pau-lette said philosophically over lox and bagels at the deli. "Not that I was anyone to be jealous of, mind you. But then my boyfriend broke up with me because I couldn't pay my share of the rent, so I not only lost him but the roof over my head. I've been through my share of misery, and when I told Uncle Nate that I wanted to drive down to Miami Beach—"

"Uncle Nate knew you were coming? He didn't mention it."

"I phoned to tell you, Karma, but you never called back."

Guiltily Karma recalled Paulette's phone message. "I *am* glad to see you, Paulette. Come on, I'll show you my place." She slid out of the booth.

Paulette looked pathetically eager. "I'd like that," she said, and on the way back to the Blue Moon, she tripped eagerly along in Karma's wake like a puppy.

"With all the pink and aqua and blue paint everywhere, I feel like I'm visiting Barbie's Dream House," Paulette exclaimed when she saw the Blue Moon, which Karma felt was stretching its allure considerably.

As Karma ushered her into her little apartment on the third floor, Paulette oohed and aahed over the minuscule view of the ocean. She loved Karma's shower curtain, which was fashioned from Indian print fabric bought at a yard sale. She exclaimed enthusiastically over the three-paneled shoji screen that Karma had set up to divide the dining area from the living room, and she especially liked the lace curtain that Karma had draped over it for softness.

"Karma," Paulette said in a pleading tone, "would you mind if I stayed with you? Uncle Nate has a guest room, but I'd rather be here. He's sweet, don't get me wrong, but you and I have a lot more in common."

Karma dumped a package of soy nuts into a dish and tried to think of a reason why Paulette was not welcome. She could think of none that would hold water. "Okay," she said, then wondered how long it would take her to regret it.

As it turned out, Paulette had left her yellow VW bug in the Blue Moon's parking lot and her duffel downstairs behind Goldy's desk, and before Karma could change her mind, Paulette had shlepped her duffel into the living room, where she swore she didn't mind sleeping on the pull-out couch.

Karma, though busy with Paulette, had thought that maybe Slade would call that afternoon. He was supposed to go out with Jennifer that night. But he didn't call, and she grew more jittery as afternoon segued into late afternoon and late afternoon shifted into dusk and dusk became darkness.

"Let's go out and you can show me South Beach," Paulette said eagerly after dinner. "It looks like a fun place."

Karma finished drying the few dishes they'd used and started putting them in the cabinet. "Oh, I'm not in the mood for a big night out,'' she said, the fear that they would run into Slade and Jennifer heavy on her mind.

"Come on, Karma, I've heard so much about South Beach,'' Paulette wheedled, pulling the pout that Karma used to hate so much.

Karma kept her tone brisk. "You can go if you like. I'll phone a couple of my friends, see if they'd like some company.'' She knew that Mandi was probably free tonight, since Jennifer was out with Slade.

Even thinking about Slade and Jennifer together made Karma feel miserable, and to know that she herself had set it up made her feel slightly sick to her stomach. Right now Slade and Jennifer were probably dancing cheek to cheek to a wonderful band, and Jennifer was rubbing her artificial nipples against Slade's shirtfront, and Slade was wondering, *what the hell—?* Later, they might kiss, their tongues getting tied up in the traffic of it. The thought of Slade's tongue tangling with anyone else's made her drop a plate, which broke into little bits that scattered across the tiny kitchen's floor. She knelt to pick them up.

"Karma?'' said Paulette, coming to the door of the kitchen. "You look so pale.''

"I—I—'' but at that moment, a mental image of Slade wrapping his arms around Jennifer burst across her mind, and all she could think of was that she had made a terrible, stupid mistake. She had thrown the two of them together, and if Slade fell in love with Jennifer, it would serve her, Karma, right. He wouldn't know those were artificial nipples. He wouldn't know if Jennifer was good in bed or not. So why wouldn't he want to find out? Why wouldn't he go as far as Jennifer would let him, which was probably about as far as you *could* go?

At the thought of Slade's making love to anyone else, especially Jennifer, Karma suddenly burst into sobs and groped her way onto the kitchen stool, the seat of which happened to be covered with dishtowels and scraps of old aluminum foil that she'd been planning to put away as soon as she found a place for them. It wasn't so comfortable, but maybe she wasn't supposed to be comfortable. Maybe she was supposed to suffer for not being more encouraging to Slade.

Paulette, whom she'd almost forgotten about in her teary-eyed travail, was kneeling beside her and peering up into her face. "Karma? What's wrong? Karma, I've never seen you like this."

Karma yanked one of the dish towels out from under her and blotted her eyes. "Paulette," she said, never dreaming that she was going to say it until the words were out of her mouth, "I—I think I'm in l-love."

"I *hate* it when that happens," said Paulette, her eyes wide. "Want to tell me about it?"

Karma gulped. "I have no business being in love with this man. We're so different, and I have to make a go of Rent-a-Yenta, and—and—" She began to sob again, undone by the sheer impossibility of the situation.

"Come into the living room and spill the details," urged Paulette, and Karma could almost believe that her cousin was the one with the degrees in psychology, so empathetic and helpful was she. And so Karma told Paulette about Slade and how she had met him and how they had gone out in *Toy Boat's Toy* and been stranded in the storm. She told about the stilt house and the game of sexual Scrabble, which made Paulette howl with laughter. And she even told Paulette how they had made love and how special it had been for her and for him.

This interested Paulette more than Karma had anticipated, but then, women talked about these things. It was just that Karma had lacked a man to talk about for a really long time.

"Why was it so special with Slade?" Paulette wanted to know.

"Well, you know."

"No, I don't, actually."

Karma twisted the damp dishtowel in her lap. "He, um, knew all the right buttons to push, so to speak."

Paulette's eyes widened. "You mean—?"

"Yes. The very spot. The Gosh-he-found-it spot. The Goody-he-knows-what-to-do-with-it spot. *You* know."

"Golly gee. I think I do."

They looked at each other and laughed.

"He sounds marvelous," Paulette said when they had both calmed down. "So what's the problem?"

"I told you—we're too different for this to work out."

"He's looking for a wife. Why *can't* it be you?"

"Maybe he thinks so, but I don't. And get this, Paulette, he invited me to his ranch. To meet his parents."

"You're going, of course."

"I have to," Karma said. "I had to promise I'd go before he'd agree to a date with Jennifer. And now they're living it *up* together somewhere on South Beach, which I suppose is better than *living* together, but who knows what could happen?"

Paulette managed to look very wise. "If he's been chasing after you as diligently as you say, I doubt that he's enjoying his date with this Jennifer."

Karma sniffed disconsolately. "She looks exactly like the ideal woman he described to me. Besides, she has artificial nipples."

Paulette was mystified by this statement until Karma haltingly explained the conversation wherein Karma had told Jennifer where to shop for such embellishments, and then Paulette started to whoop with laughter again.

"It's not funny," Karma said, beginning to feel huffy.

Paulette managed to contain her mirth. "Of course not. But listen, Karma, I'll take care of Rent-a-Yenta while you're at the ranch with Slade. I'll finish painting that wall, the one that's half lime-green, and I'll see if I can straighten out the checking account for you. And if Jennifer comes around, I'll find her a date with someone, anyone, to get her off the scent of Slade Braddock. How does that sound?''

"It sounds like a godsend," Karma said, beginning to feel more hopeful.

"I'll neaten up this apartment too, and get a lot of your stuff put away. It'll be fun. I need something to do to keep busy, and I'm a good organizer, you'll see. Now how about if you show me where to find the sheets for this bed? We could both use a good night's sleep, I think.''

Karma and Paulette made up the couch bed, and then Karma headed for the bedroom. Before she went to brush her teeth, she paused in the doorway and turned toward Paulette, who was propped up against the back of the couch reading the *Wall Street Journal*. Her heart softened toward her cousin. She and Paulette weren't the first women in the world to bond over guy troubles, but it was a pleasant surprise that the two of them had reached a point in their lives where they could actually be girlfriends.

"Paulette," she said slowly, "I really appreciate your help. You're a lot different than you were when we were kids, and you're being a good friend to me.''

Paulette lowered the newspaper. "I know," she said with an arch little smile.

Well, people might change for the better, Karma thought wryly, but if they were smug to begin with, they were likely to remain smug later.

Whatever, she was glad that Paulette had turned up. She'd meant what she'd said—that Paulette was being a good friend. And it was wonderful to have a girlfriend in her camp right now.

THE NEXT DAY, SLADE ARRIVED to pick her up for the visit to the ranch. Paulette walked them to the lobby, and while Slade and Paulette were chatting, Goldy beckoned to Karma. "Here," she said, lowering her voice to a conspiratorial tone as she pressed a small brown package into Karma's hand. "Inside are four crystals. Put one in each corner of your bedroom at Slade's house, and they will increase the good vibes."

"No," Karma hissed. "His parents are bound to be very conservative. What if they found out? They'd think I'm nutsoid."

Goldy took the crystals back. "Suit yourself. The sundress looks lovely, by the way." She winked at Karma as she waved them off.

Karma wasn't so sure, but at least the dress showed off her suntan, and she had to admit that it was an appropriate choice for meeting Slade's parents.

Because of the usual Miami Beach traffic, it took them a while to get across the causeway to the mainland. After they passed the upscale buildings and lush foliage along the bayside drive, Miami showed its grimy backside in a blur of glaring strip malls and fast-food places, making it a relief to emerge on the west side of the city where traffic thinned out. Slade headed the Suburban northwest on a route that pierced straight through the Everglades toward Lake Okeechobee.

The Saturday afternoon sun glinted on the shallow water flowing between the spears of sawgrass in the canals on either side of the road. Overhead the sky was a soaring blue dome, and Karma, fresh from declaring her love for Slade to Paulette, tried to relax as she rode along beside him.

It wasn't easy to remain calm. She felt self-conscious; she felt in awe of this man. His hands gripping the steering wheel were strong and sinewy, and his jaw looked rock-solid.

"Relax," he said, reaching over and clasping her hand in his. She knew that he must have sensed that she was nervous, and her palm immediately began to perspire. Should she pull her hand away? If she did, would he read

that as rejection? Or should she let their joined palms grow
sticky in the spirit of togetherness? Maybe she could
squeeze his hand and then pull hers away, pretending that
she needed to brush her hair back from her face. But that
wouldn't fool him—she had another hand that would work
for that.

He solved the problem by dropping her hand and giving
it a little pat. What did *that* mean? She felt like an awkward
teenager out on her first date with the captain of the football
team.

"Tell me what Paulette offered to do again?"

"She said she'd balance the Rent-a-Yenta books, rear-
range the client videos in alphabetical order, and that she'd
play pinochle with Uncle Nate. She also cleaned my toaster
oven this morning."

"Well, hey, she sounds okay to me. Why don't you get
along with her?"

Karma shrugged, feeling guilty. "When my sisters and
I were kids, Paulette was always so prissy and perfect. She
tattled about everything we did, and we made her the butt
of our jokes. But now..." Her sentence tapered off as she
recalled Paulette's eagerness to help.

"Now you feel sorry for her, right?"

Karma nodded. "I've been fired before. It's not fun."

"Did she say how long she's staying?"

"No, but Paulette's parents aren't prepared for her to
move home to Connecticut. Which Paulette doesn't want
to do anyway." But Paulette had not yet met a palmetto
bug, so she was still enthralled with Florida. So far, anyway. And she had urged Karma to stay in Okeechobee as
long as she liked.

"Don't worry," Paulette had said over toast and juice
that morning. "Maybe I'll even figure out a way to make
Rent-a-Yenta more profitable. I didn't get a degree in business for nothing."

"You're a real peach, Paulette," Karma told her.

"I know," Paulette had replied, but Karma was getting used to that.

Slade cleared his throat. "I guess you're wondering about my date with Jennifer," he said.

It took Karma only a New York nanosecond to decide that noncommittal was the key here. "Mmm," she said, though she hoped he wouldn't tell her more than she wanted to know. It wouldn't do for her to burst into tears the way she had done last night with Paulette.

"First of all," Slade said slowly, "she isn't my type."

"You said you wanted someone petite and blond."

"Never mind what I said. And she took me to this place with a band called Shrimp—"

"—Shemp," Karma corrected him. "It's called Shemp."

"Right. Anyway, she wore a dress that looked as if it was made for a six-year-old, judging from how short it was, and too much jewelry. And no underwear."

"*Eeek!* How did you find that out?" She was almost morbidly curious, considering the fake nipples.

Slade cut a look sideways at her. "I didn't find out the way you're thinking I did. She kept falling out of the top of the dress, that's how. I have no knowledge of whether she was wearing panties, but I suspect not."

"I think," Karma said faintly, "I'd rather not hear any more." It wasn't ethical or prudent to talk about one client with another. But if Jennifer kept falling out of her dress, and if she had been wearing artificial nipples, wouldn't Slade have seen them? And if so, would he remark about them, or would he spare her the anguish of hearing that particular detail?

"Jennifer is so far from what I'm looking for that she might as well be from outer space. In fact, we'd be better off if that's where women like her lived. They could mate with aliens, who might be more to their taste than ordinary guys like me."

Slade was far from ordinary, but Karma liked hearing this part. Still, she kept her mouth clamped tightly shut until Slade suggested hitting a Burger King drive-through for lunch, and he almost convinced her to order a Whopper.

Karma had never in her life eaten a Whopper, and when she saw the mouthwatering picture of it on the order board, she almost caved. She made herself ask for a salad and a large order of fries instead, but the scent of onion and pickle and catsup and most of all, meat, stayed with her. Ever since scarfing down that corned beef hash at the stilt house, Karma hadn't been able to shake her craving.

Slade was in a hurry to get to the ranch, so they ate on the way. Karma found it interesting that as they drew closer to Okeechobee City, the serene Everglades scenery, complete with expanses of saw grass and cypress tree hammocks rising out of the saw grass like a mirage, changed to fenced green pastures.

"This is all Braddock land," Slade said expansively as he waved an arm out the open window of the Suburban. "As far as you can see."

Karma smoothed her skirt nervously, wondering what Slade's parents would think of her. Before she'd left her apartment, she had vetoed her chartreuse feather earrings as too outrageous, and she had removed her green nail polish. The sundress was a relatively innocuous teal-blue; it wasn't low-cut enough to show off anything much.

"Here we are," Slade said. She inched forward on her seat as Slade slowed the vehicle and turned down a blindingly white shell-rock road. The sign spanning it said Diamond B Ranch.

"I can't wait for Ma and Pop to meet you," Slade told her, and Karma wondered what he'd told his parents. By this time, she could hardly wait to meet the elderly couple who had sent their son off with their blessings to find a wife in Miami Beach.

The Suburban followed the drive as it curved around

palmetto trees and pines, thickets and a pond. Once their passage startled a covey of quail, which scattered into the brush. Another time they skirted a pasture where curious cattle hung their heads over the fence and watched until they were out of sight.

Soon the ranch house loomed up behind a copse of scrub oaks festooned with long beards of Spanish moss, and Slade drove over a cattle guard with a startling *thump-bump!* "Keeps the cattle from straying into the yard and eating Ma's prize double hibiscus," he said in answer to Karma's questioning look.

When he stopped in front of the house, Karma was in awe. It was a big two-story building constructed of old brick. Four sturdy columns reaching to the height of the second story's roof fronted the porch, and on the porch sat an assortment of rocking chairs, their cushions covered in a bright flowery print. The effect was charming.

As Karma climbed down from the front seat of the Suburban, she heard a motorcycle approaching hell-bent-for-leather down the driveway. It raced around the oaks, flew over the cattle guard, and screeched to a stop inches from Karma's feet.

The petite rider unstraddled the seat and yanked off the helmet to reveal a short cap of wispy platinum-blond hair. She unbuttoned the top buttons of her black leather vest to reveal ample cleavage and a tattoo of a fawn's head, all the while treating Karma to a brilliant smile.

"Whee, doggie!" she whooped, slapping Karma on the back so that Karma had to grasp the open door of the Suburban to keep from sprawling headlong in the dirt. "It looks like Slade has finally found him a bride."

Slade strode around the car and threw out his arms. "Hi, Ma," he said.

8

So much for the gray-haired traditional mother that Karma had been expecting. She learned in short order that Bambi Braddock was a former exotic dancer with a Ph.D. and a liking for Jack Daniel's. She had married Slade's father, Norton, after he wandered into a conference room in Las Vegas where she was presenting a paper on neutron something-or-other, and he had fallen madly in love and married her that very weekend in a little chapel down the road. They were still crazy about each other, to hear Bambi tell it.

"Oh, he's my man, no doubt about it, and always will be. He rides a Hog, too," Bambi had explained as the three of them became acquainted over drinks. Sure enough, before long Slade's father roared up on his own Harley-Davidson. He was as tall as Slade, suntanned and fit, with piercing blue eyes and a silver stud earring in one ear. He strode into the living room, greeted Karma, and poured his own Scotch, all the while expressing his enthusiasm for Karma, for Slade, for marriage, and for the prices he'd get for his cattle at market.

Karma, still in shock at her inaccurate assumptions about Slade's parents, sipped a demure lemonade containing a sprig of mint while wondering why Slade had never mentioned that his parents were as unconventional as hers, albeit in a different way. Why, she could have worn her earrings with the feathers on them; she could have shown up in a G-string for all these people would have cared.

After drinks, Bambi showed Karma to her room before she went to supervise the cook, who was preparing dinner. "You go ahead and make yourself comfortable," Slade's mother told her. "Kick back and relax some. After all, this will soon be your home."

"Oh, but—"

Bambi hugged her, and her eyes sparkled. "I'm so glad Slade has finally found the perfect person for him. We can talk about the wedding later."

"I don't—"

"Not now, dear. Josefina will call you when dinner's ready." And with that, Bambi was gone, trailing the scent of what smelled a lot like Chanel No. 5, an oddly traditional choice for such a free spirit.

Karma liked Bambi. She liked Norton. But they'd have to understand that she was only visiting and was not Slade's intended bride.

Karma's room had its own bath with a whirlpool tub and overlooked the pond behind the house. Accommodations at the Braddocks' house were sumptuous and charming, she thought as she sat down at the vanity and bundled her hair into a scrunchy. Her conservative sundress made her snicker. So much for hoping to impress Slade's elderly parents. Boy, had she got that wrong.

"Karma?" It was Slade knocking on her door.

She went to the door and flung it open. "Why didn't you tell me?" she demanded as he leaned against the door frame, his arms crossed and regarding her with a mild grin. "Parents who ride motorcycles. A mother with a tattoo. You let me think they were ordinary folks."

He looked disconcerted. "Aren't they?"

She let out an exasperated sigh. "No, they're not. They're a little on the wild side."

He guffawed at this. "Can't wait to tell Ma what you think of her," he said.

"Don't you dare! I like her. But, Slade, your parents seem to think that we're engaged."

He eased into the room and quirked his eyebrows. "I'll explain to them later that we're only having sex. If that would make you happy, that is."

Karma reminded herself that this was serious business. "I know you're joking. I know you wouldn't do that. And besides, we only had sex once."

He came over and slid an arm around her shoulders. "Couldn't you refer to it as 'making love?' Also, I intend to address the lack-of-frequency problem ASAP."

"I wouldn't feel right about making love, as you so quaintly choose to call it, in your parents' house."

He became suddenly serious. "It *was* making love. For me, Karma, it was a beautiful experience. I'd hoped it was for you, too."

"Oh, Slade, things are happening so fast. Yes, it was wonderful. It was magic, it was firecrackers on the Fourth of July, it was all the things a woman dreams about. But I haven't known you long. I've been caught up in the excitement of it from the very first moment I set eyes on you, and I'll admit that it's a heady experience, but—" She let the words dangle, not knowing how to finish and afraid that she had said too much.

Slade smoothed a loose tendril of hair back behind her ear. "I don't want you to be uncomfortable around me, Karma. Ever."

She drew a deep breath, let it out. She felt suddenly shy, didn't know where to look. She wasn't ready for a heavy discussion about her emotions; she wasn't prepared to hear about his and thought maybe she should be. "Well," she said shakily, attempting a smile. "Now what?"

His expression was tender, and understanding glimmered in the depths of his eyes. He adopted a light tone. "As it happens, I told Josefina to hold dinner. Want to walk over to the barn and meet Lightning?"

Karma grasped at this idea, a lifeline. "Your horse? Sure."

Taking her hand in his, he led her down a flight of service stairs and out through the laundry room into the steamy outside air. A mockingbird flitted up out of a palmetto tree, and on the pond, a flock of white ducks paddled lazily. They walked around a large screen pool enclosure where the pool, bordered by colorful patterned tile, shimmered in the sun. The barn was almost hidden behind a grove of pine trees and, once they left the pool enclosure, was reached by a pathway paved with mellow old brick.

"I didn't know you lived on such a grand scale," Karma said as she walked alongside Slade taking things in. The house seemed enormous after her small apartment, and from here, she could see the two wings that were hidden from the front. "You never mentioned that you had servants."

"There's only Josefina, though she hauls in squadrons of nieces and nephews when it's time to clean house."

"Like spring cleaning? Do people still do that?" she asked.

Slade laughed. "Don't you?"

"Cleaning house isn't high on my list of priorities."

"Maybe that's why you're so interesting, Karma. You don't get bogged down in details."

Karma followed him down the central passageway through the barn to a stall in the rear as her eyes adjusted to the dim light. As they approached, the horse's head nosed over the top of the half-door. "Lightning, this is Karma," Slade said as she reached up a tentative hand to stroke the horse's neck.

The horse was coal-black with a distinctive zigzag patch of white down the center of his face. He whinnied and pawed at the straw on the floor. "See?" said Slade, looking pleased. "He likes you."

"I don't know much about horses," Karma said doubtfully, though horses didn't look nearly as big to her as they had when she was a child.

"You've never ridden?"

"We had horses on the commune when I was a kid. I remember that I liked riding them until one scraped me off under a low tree limb. That was the end of my horseback-riding days."

"You'll ride Millie, who wouldn't hurt a fly. Come over and meet her."

Millie was a docile mare who hung her head over the door of her stall with interest when they walked up. "She'll take to you even more if you give her this," Slade said. From his pocket he produced a carrot.

Karma held the carrot flat on the palm of her hand until Millie's lips and teeth ever so gently removed it.

"She looks so appreciative," Karma said. "As if she didn't expect someone to come along and give her something special."

"It's easy to tell what horses are thinking. Unlike most people. Except for you, of course."

Karma ignored this pronouncement and scratched Millie behind her ears, then took her time walking slowly down the row of stalls, inspecting the horses within. When she reached the door to the outside, she noticed dark thunderclouds rolling in from the west.

Slade saw her watching them and started toward her. "I forgot to tell you. Here in the Glades we have a shower almost every afternoon."

"At least we're not out in a boat," she said as raindrops began to patter down into the dust outside, leaving little pockmarks.

"Yes. We're in a nice comfortable barn." He moved closer, so close that she could feel the heat from his body.

"So you claim to know what horses are thinking?" she asked. He was making her nervous, standing only a few inches away.

"Oh, most of the time."

"And how did you arrive at this ability?"

"I've always had it. If you ask me, horses are so much easier to understand than women."

"Except for me, right?"

"Right. I can pretty much figure you out." She didn't doubt that he thought he was speaking the truth, but the statement smacked of arrogance and seemed to require a challenge.

"Even though I'm not a lot like you? Even though I'm a vegetarian and don't ride and have never set eyes upon the Everglades before today?"

To her dismay, the last couple of words caught in her throat as Slade moved closer and planted one hand on the wall on either side of her, effectively caging her there. Outside, the rain began to pour down in sheets, steam swirling up from the warm ground.

"I like to think I know you," he said evenly. "Some people you feel as if you've known forever."

"It could be karma," she breathed. "Destiny."

"Oh, it's Karma, all right. You."

"What makes you think that I'm your type, anyway? I'm certainly not what you ordered." She wished he'd move his hands; she wished his eyes wouldn't burn into her like that. This certainly wasn't the way to slow things down.

"Karma, I think you're my type because I can't be around you without wanting to kiss you and hold you. And you can't tell me that you don't recognize the chemistry, otherwise you wouldn't have such a hard time breathing when I'm around."

He was much too perceptive. She struggled to think of something, anything, to say. Over in one of the stalls, a horse bumped against the wooden wall. Outside something cried, "Help! Help!"

Startled, Karma asked, "What was that?"

"Oh, just one of the peacocks. That's their cry. They're taking cover because of the rain."

"You have peacocks? You never mentioned peacocks."

"I have the hots for you, Karma O'Connor, and I don't believe I've mentioned that either."

The way Slade was looking at her made her feel as if she were melting. It was only the heat, the steamy heat, she told herself, but it felt as if the air was on fire between them. Worse yet, her neck itched. She tried to move within the confines of his arms, but he refused to budge. A horsefly buzzed around her head, but neither of them brushed it away. It flew out into the rain, leaving them behind in the somnolent barn where the only sound now was their breathing. In her own ears, she heard the primitive pounding of her blood. It was almost enough to blot out everything else, but she forced herself to ignore it.

Slade's head dipped lower, and his lips parted. She knew how he kissed now, slow and sexy and as if he couldn't get enough. Hungrily. Demandingly, sometimes.

"You're going to kiss me, aren't you? Well, go ahead. Get it over with. And then we can go into the house and eat dinner. And I can try to act as if nothing happened out here at all."

He chuckled under his breath. "You want me to kiss you?"

"Yes." The word was a whisper. Her neck still itched. Her heart was pounding. It occurred to her that what she felt was more like an allergic reaction than a sexual attraction. All that was missing was a sneeze, and she could manufacture one of those easily enough if she inhaled deeply enough of the dust in the air. Straw dust, it was. Stable dust. She drew in a breath, sucking it deeply into her lungs. The dust-heavy air tickled her nostrils, but she didn't sneeze. She closed her eyes, feeling heavy and slow. If she'd had to run, she wouldn't have been able to. The torpor that had settled down upon her licked at her resolve with an edgy excitement, a flutter of desire.

"Open your eyes, Karma." His command came as a surprise, but she obeyed it. Slade's face was so close that she could have reached out and flicked his lips with the tip of her tongue. A crazy notion, one that she should ignore. But the funny thing was, she found herself doing it. Without thinking about it, without even knowing why she did it, she slid her tongue out of her mouth and touched it daintily to his lower lip.

"Oh, Karma," he said, and while she was still regretting this ridiculous thing she had just done, wishing she could scratch her neck, wishing she didn't always ruin everything by doing something stupid, he folded her into his arms.

He was undone by her, by her simple sensuality. Through the familiar scents of stable, of horses, of hay and feed and saddle leather, of rain and green growing things, Slade could only smell the fresh sweet scent of Karma, and it was the scent of a woman who was ripe and ready for love. The quiet involuntary moan in the back of her throat let him know that she liked this, that she wanted it. He had known that, of course. He really did believe he knew what she was thinking. Right now, for instance, she was wishing he'd nuzzle her neck, and so he did. He let his lips roam upward to the curve of her jaw, to her lips.

She didn't realize that she was kissing him back until her arms went around him, urging him closer. He smelled of soap, and sunshine, and of his own undefinable scent—something woodsy, leathery and a little bit dangerous. His hands came up and slid the straps of her sundress of her shoulders. The fabric fell away, and then his palms were reverently cupped around her breasts, lifting their weight, his thumbs caressing her nipples.

Her pulse beat in her ears, and it said, "Yes, yes, yes," all the while her common sense was telling her no. She wavered, knowing that this was not the proper time or place for making love, except that at the moment any time or place seemed right.

Slade dipped his head to kiss one breast, then the other. "Karma," he said. "Oh, Karma." His breath seared her nipples, made them hard. She went giddy with the sheer voluptuousness of her body, with the knowledge that he could have her here and now, right up against the wall. If she'd let him. If she said yes.

She clutched at her dress, pulled it up.

"Slade, we should go back in. The rain's letting up."

He brushed her hands aside so that the fabric fell down again. "Not yet."

She swallowed and made herself think. It wasn't easy, not with his hands working sweet magic upon her body, his words wrapping themselves around her mind and tangling with her resolve. "I told you how I feel about making love in your parents' house, and I won't go sneaking around."

"What if I told you that they wouldn't mind?"

"I *would* mind."

"Do you mind this? And this?" He nipped at one nipple, tweaked the other.

"No," she said, making it a moan deep in her throat. Her hair fell out of the scrunchie and lay hot against her neck.

He chuckled. "That was the kind of 'no' that I can live with," he said. He straightened, and to his surprise, she said meekly, "Could you—could you kiss my neck again, please?" A watery sun peeked out from behind the clouds; the rain had stopped, and the only sound was the dripping of water from the roof.

"Your neck?"

"It—it itches," she said, and at that he laughed out loud. He lifted her hair and buried his face in her neck, playfully rubbed his late-day beard growth against the tender, soft skin from her temple to her jaw, nibbled lightly and felt her answering pulse beating against his lips.

His impulse was to sweep her into his arms and carry her into an empty stall, making a saddle blanket their bed. But, "That's quite enough, thank you," she said into his hair.

He couldn't help laughing as he held her away from him, willing his body to subside. She jerked the shoulder straps of her dress up and smoothed the wrinkles out of the bodice.

"Anything else you want? Anything else you need?" He knew what he needed, knew that she could supply it as no one else could.

"A kiss before dinner," she said with a certain primness that only made him wild for her.

"Just one?" He liked teasing her, liked the consternation that always flitted across her features during the split second during which she tried to figure out if he was serious or not.

"Maybe two."

"And after dinner? My parents go to bed really early."

"We'll see," she said, lifting her lips to his.

He grasped one of her hands and moved it lower until her fingers touched the hardness beneath his jeans. "I want more than a kiss," he said, his voice gone rough and husky. She didn't pull her hand away, and he felt himself throbbing against her palm. She felt it, too. There was no way she could not.

"Oh," she said as if surprised. "Oh." But she didn't remove her hand.

He kissed her then as she had asked him to do, a warm, deep, velvety kiss, a kiss that made him dizzy, made the world disappear, made him weak in the knees and overwhelmed by desire for her body, all of it.

But it was more than a kiss. It was a promise of things to come.

And he felt that promise in her kiss, too.

"SO," SAID NORTON AT DINNER as he passed the hearts-of-palm salad. "I hear you're going riding tomorrow."

It was a scene of normality that surpassed surreal in the aftermath of what had happened earlier in the barn. Karma, still off balance, had no idea how Norton knew about their plans. "Well," she said, buying time as she dished salad into the bowl beside her plate, "I haven't ridden a horse since I was a kid."

"She's going to ride Millie," Slade said.

"Are you sure you don't want to ride my Harley? Take a tour around the ranch that way?"

"Ma, it scares the wildlife."

"Yes, well, a horse moves too damned slow," said Norton. "By the way, Karma, I'm not sure Slade told you that when you two are married, we're going on a two-month motorcycle tour of the eastern United States."

"But—" Karma began, mentally telegraphing a harried call for help to Slade.

Bambi held out a plate loaded with short ribs. "I know you two probably want a simple wedding, since Slade has never been fond of ceremony. The thing is, we want you to take that Alaska cruise, and then we're off on our own adventure. Ribs, dear?"

"I don't think so," Karma said faintly, though they smelled wonderful. The ribs were glazed with teriyaki sauce, and it was all she could do not to salivate all over the plate.

"Roast beef, then," said Norton, hefting a huge platter toward her.

Slade continued forking beef into his mouth as if there was no tomorrow, but he looked interested in Karma's crisis of conscience. It was clear, however, that he wasn't going to explain that she was a vegetarian or help her to remain one.

"I think I'll pass," Karma said faintly.

"Well, of course there's the chicken, but I must say it's a travesty to eat chicken on a beef ranch."

"You could try it," Slade suggested under the guise of being helpful, but she sensed that he wanted to laugh at her dilemma.

Karma considered her predicament. Why hadn't Slade told his parents that she was a vegetarian? She shot him a helpless glance, which went unheeded as he helped himself to a huge helping of mashed potatoes, and then she reached for the chicken.

"Josefina fries it in peanut oil. It's better than any fried chicken I ever ate," Norton said, smiling approvingly as she selected a leg and a wing. "Taste it. Tell me what you think."

She lifted the chicken leg to her lips, studying the crust, trying to seem nonchalant. She regarded it for a moment, then sank her teeth in. The crust crumbled delectably onto her tongue, setting off little bursts of flavor. Her taste buds awakened to a new treat. She didn't have to think about it to make her teeth slide the tender meat from the bone, gently and then not so gently. She thought that never in her life had she tasted anything so good.

"Well?" demanded Norton. "Is it as good as I said it was?"

Karma could hardly speak for chewing and swallowing. "Oh, yes," she breathed before taking another bite. The chicken seemed imbued with a hundred flavors she had never tasted before. It slid into her stomach, which sang songs of praise to the cook. Her brain segued into a hosanna of joy. Her mouth couldn't seem to stop biting off more tender flaky chunks of chicken, her teeth couldn't seem to stop chewing, her throat couldn't stop swallowing. Before she knew it, she had devoured the meat off not only the drumstick but a wing and a thigh, and she had started in on a breast.

Josefina, a slim, wiry Hispanic woman with eyes that sparkled when she talked, stuck her head out of the kitchen. "My chicken is good, no? I use secret spices, better than the Colonel's. I will bring more." She disappeared into the kitchen again before Karma could say that she'd had enough.

Not that she had. Not that she wanted to eat anything else—nothing else tasted anywhere near as good as that fried chicken; not the potatoes mashed with cream, butter, and green onion tops fresh from Josefina's garden, not the salad, not the fresh beans prepared with almonds or the fluffy yeast rolls.

Throughout this orgy of eating, Karma distractedly fielded interested questions from Bambi and Norton. "You have a business, don't you? I assume it's the kind of operation that you can pick up and bring with you to Okeechobee City," said Norton.

"Oh, don't bother her with details like that," scoffed Bambi. "I'm sure she has that all planned out, don't you, Karma?"

Karma's mouth was full, so she didn't answer.

Norton grinned at her. "Of course, you may want to take up gardening. All these plants around the house take a heap of care, don't they, Bambi?"

If they only knew that the only thing Karma had ever been able to grow with any success was mold in her refrigerator, they'd give up on the idea of Karma's becoming a gardener. She was prepared to make a statement to that effect, but, amazingly, Bambi went on to the next topic, which was the planned motorcycle tour.

Slade made a face at her when both of his parents weren't looking, and she knew she would get no help from his quarter. But apparently, as long as she continued to feed her face and Bambi and Norton could keep up an intermittent but ongoing discussion about their planned tour, extensive conversation was neither needed nor expected.

When Karma could absolutely eat no more, Bambi leaped up from the table and began to clear it. Karma started to help, but Josefina appeared as if by magic and shooed her away.

"Josefina rules," Norton said to her in an aside. "She must like you. She's eager for Slade to marry, you know. Says she wants some children around here. That's okay with you, isn't it?"

Karma's mouth dropped open, and Bambi, who was passing by en route to the kitchen, patted her on the shoulder. "Don't let him rush you. It's up to you and Slade to decide when you're ready for kids."

"You'd better tell them we're not engaged," she hissed at Slade, darting a furtive glance toward the kitchen door when the others had disappeared behind it.

"You tell them."

"I—"

Bambi and Norton returned to the dining room, the kitchen door swinging behind them. "Now you two will want to be alone, so Norton and I are going to do our own thing for a while," Bambi said.

Norton slid an arm around his wife's waist. "We've told Josefina to go home to her family, and we're going to clean up."

"Oh, let me help," Karma said, thinking that if she could be alone with them, she could explain.

"Absolutely not," said Norton, looking stern. His face softened. "Plus Bambi and I like doing things together, don't we, babe?"

"Karma and I will sit around the pool, maybe have an after-dinner drink," Slade interjected smoothly.

"Fine idea," said Norton approvingly.

"You'll find your clothes unpacked when you go back to your room, Karma, and if there's anything you need, please ask," Bambi told her.

"Th-thanks," Karma stammered. There didn't seem to

be any way to talk to these nice people. They kept talking *at* her, not *with* her. It was frustrating.

As his parents again retreated into the kitchen, Slade went to the bar between the dining and living rooms and swung the upper cabinet doors open. "What would you like to drink, Karma?"

"Nothing," Karma said, feeling agitated and manipulated and annoyed.

"How about kahlua? It's Ma's favorite."

"Fine." She went to the window and stared out at the night.

Slade handed her a small glass and took her hand. He carried a snifter of brandy.

"Come with me," he said.

The air was warm and heavy with humidity outside the air-conditioned confines of the house, and it smelled of water and green things growing. The pool was dark in the moonlight, its outline shadowed and still.

Slade pulled two lounge chairs close together near the pool house, a small structure that housed an apartment for guests as well as bathrooms and changing rooms for swimmers.

Karma took a sip of kahlua. "Slade, I don't know how to react when your parents say things like 'It's up to you to decide when you want kids.'" Her imitation of Bambi was so accurate that Slade chuckled as he pulled her down onto the lounge next to his.

"You reacted perfectly. Josefina makes great fried chicken, doesn't she?"

"Yes, but stop changing the subject. We were talking about kids."

He cocked an eyebrow. "Oh, I'm in favor of them. I'd like to see a couple of munchkins running around here. How many boys and how many girls do you reckon you want?"

He was exasperating, but it was hard to muster enough

anger to tell him off. Out around the pond, bullfrogs were cranking up a chorus, making it hard to think.

While she was framing a tart retort, he picked up her left hand and studied the fingers one by one. He paused at the ring finger, circling it loosely with two of his. "I don't care how many boys and how many girls," he went on. "I'd like to wait at least a year before the first one, though. So that you and I can get to know each other."

She felt her breathing stop. So far, there had been a lot of teasing but nothing concrete. Was this a marriage proposal? It wasn't as if she'd had a lot of experience in fielding such offers.

He appropriated her glass and set it beside the snifter on the table. Then he turned toward her on the lounge, making it squeak loudly. "Come over here," he said.

"Bambi and Norton..." she said, glancing toward the wing of the house where she believed their bedroom to be.

"...fall asleep as soon as they hit the mattress," he said, finishing her sentence. The windows in that wing were dark, the draperies pulled shut. His hand reached over and cupped her chin.

"I'm absolutely crazy about you," he said. "Not only do I think of you every waking moment, but you're the one I've been looking for all my life."

"It's not me," she said. "It was never me. Someone blond and tiny and with a good singing voice, that's what you specified on your registration form."

"You *are* blond," he pointed out. "But I've never heard you sing."

"You don't want to. I sound like those bullfrogs out there in the pond."

"I'm not much of a singer, either. No big deal. By the way, I thought we'd head out early tomorrow morning so I can show you some of my special places around the ranch. But for now, can't we stop talking?" He feathered a line of kisses down her cheek, inhaled a deep breath. "You smell so good, Karma. Your skin is so soft."

"Oh, Slade," she said, giving up on trying to converse, giving in to the warm slow heat rising from deep in her belly. It was so easy to surrender to the sensations that she was learning to enjoy so much, to let her mind go numb and her will go weak under the onslaught of his kisses. Helplessly, longingly, she opened her mouth to his, trembling with excitement as his hand slid up from her waist to contain her breast. This was slow, too, as if they had all the time in the world.

Outside, the night beat around them, the fecund scent of saw grass and mud and cypress stirring something primeval in her breast, the chir of crickets and tree frogs and other denizens of the swamp echoing her own heartbeat. They might have been miles from civilization, from people. Her heart seemed to swell with the pleasure of wanting and with the sweet urgency of need.

When he reangled his body, she moved fluidly to meet him, her arms circling his neck, surrendering as he pressed her backward onto the lounge. She had tried to be sensible, and she had told herself that he wasn't for her—but none of it had worked. Had she been too deep in denial to realize how incendiary their relationship could be if they both went with the flow? If they threw away all their preconceptions and took each other for who they were and what they were, good sense be damned?

She heard the peacocks, sounding as if they were far away. "Help, help!" they cried, and she thought it was too late now. She was beyond help, was set on this course that she had chosen, and she was glad.

Slade slid her sundress strap off her shoulder and kissed the place where it had been. Then he was peeling the dress away, murmuring in the hollow of her throat, and she was helping him remove his clothes too. It was cool in the pool house, and dark, and she felt hidden away from everyone in the shadows, even from the moon and the starry sky above. Only the two of them, only their breathing, only the two of them exploring each other with a kind of edgy excitement.

He toyed with her nipple, angled his bare leg between hers. Somehow all that remained between them was a thin bit of fabric. Slade's hand rested there, waiting, she knew, for her assent. Not that she wanted to speak. She was too caught up in sensation, in the drive to feel him, all of him.

She slid her hand over his and guided it inside her panties to the part of her that ached to receive him. The silky wetness there made him inhale sharply as she arched under his touch, and she drew him into a deep kiss as she lifted her hips so that he could strip away the last barrier.

His lips were moist against her neck, hot as they traced the hollow between her breasts, his beard rough against skin that was excruciatingly sensitive. Suddenly frantic with desire, she reached for him, but he said huskily, "No. Let me. I want you, Karma, all of you," and he pressed her back onto the cushion as his mouth moved lower, dropping a kiss on her navel, brushing the soft hair between her legs, parting her thighs before moving higher. She gasped as his tongue traced her softness, as his lips found her most sensitive spot.

Never had she been loved like this, never. The joy of it overwhelmed her, brought tears to her eyes, made her wonder if she had ever known what lovemaking was all about. Lost in sensation, in bliss, the world around her seemed to implode upon itself, drawing her into it, a place with no end and no beginning, just Slade's mouth seeking her center as she rocked against him, his name on her lips. And then, when she thought the sensation could not become more intense, she felt a groundswell of heat surging from deep inside, or did that heat originate with Slade, his mouth, his lips, or—oh, could this be real? Could it be honest and true and right? She opened her eyes to the starry sky whirl-

ing above, and the starlight and moonlight swirled and converged with the heat to spin her away on a tide of pleasure
unlike any she had ever known. Amazed that this feeling
could have existed somewhere in the world without her
ever knowing about it, she was filled with a delirious sense
of wonder.

When she thought it couldn't get any better, Slade feathered kisses across her belly, leaving a damp trail across her
breast, and tenderly smoothed her hair back from her face.
She began to spiral back into reality, but before she could
speak, he pinned her arms above her head and drove into
her with one long stroke, suddenly plunging hard and fast,
slick and hot. His ragged breath was warm in her ear, and
she found the rhythm and worked it with him. She wrapped
her legs around his hips, holding him tight, their breath
mingling as their bodies glistened slick with sweat. Now
he gave her no quarter, demanding as well as taking, and
she met him thrust for thrust.

She didn't think she was capable of another climax, not
now, but to her amazement, she felt herself losing control,
felt her muscles clamping around him, wanting him so deep
within her that it hurt. The pounding of their bodies became
her heartbeat, and soon there was nothing but that beat, or
maybe it was his heart that she heard, or were their hearts
beating in synchrony, the two of them one? His mouth
crushed hers, and she felt him let go, felt him soar along
with her to the heights, to the place where two hearts and
minds and bodies truly became one.

One. Not two. One.

Their climaxes came within moments of each other. She
convulsed as his seed pulsed into her, and then, with a
hoarse cry, he collapsed onto her, spent.

He clutched her tightly to him, seemingly loath to let her
go. It was delicious, this feeling of having her fill, of peace
and optimism and another emotion that startled and surprised her.

"Dearest," he said unevenly as she paused in her reflection to wonder at this new pleasure, and before she could decide what her feelings were telling her, his face was above her, his kisses on her lips, and she was clinging to him as if she would never let him go.

Their hearts subsided together, but he held her fast. She was glad for that. She could not imagine being parted from him ever again.

"Marry me, Karma," he said unsteadily. "Say you will."

How could she deny him anything now? How could she think this thing through, figure out what it meant, decide?

His eyes were fierce in the darkness. "Say you'll be my wife," he said, his voice urgent in her ear.

"Say you'll be his wife," said another voice, which sounded remarkably like her aunt Sophie's and seemed to originate inside her head.

And so help her, Karma said, "Yes."

9

AT KARMA'S INSISTENCE, they slept apart that night, but Slade greeted her exuberantly in the kitchen the next morning, stealing a kiss in the pantry when no one was looking.

"My dearest love, at least you've made me an honest man." His eyes were bright.

She twisted away. "What are you talking about?" But she wanted to kiss him again, and soon.

"You're now my fiancée," he murmured before slipping away to carry a tray into the dining room for Josefina.

"Sure you won't tour the ranch on our motorcycles instead?" Norton boomed out during breakfast, which was a spread of eggs and sausage and pancakes and bacon unequaled in Karma's experience.

Karma finished chewing her sixth link sausage and swallowed. "Maybe after I get the hang of riding a horse, I'll take on a Hog," she said, and everyone laughed.

After breakfast, Slade saddled Millie as well as Lightning, and he took Karma on an unforgettable tour of the Diamond B Ranch. They saw the cattle chutes and the barrels where Bambi practiced racing for amateur rodeos. They saw the pastures and the tractors and the equipment shed. They looked unsuccessfully for Abner the alligator in the pond, disturbed a couple of playful otters, watered their horses from drainage ditches and counted head of cattle.

Once they stopped at the edge of a palmetto thicket for a breather. "You don't mind that I raise beef cattle?" Slade asked, eyeing her keenly.

"Mind?"

"It's what I do, Karma. I raise beef for people to eat. The cattle go to market and come out as food. As a vegetarian, I figured you might have moral objections to this business."

"I don't think I'm a vegetarian anymore," Karma said, thinking of Josefina's chicken and the sausage she had eaten for breakfast.

"You're not giving in because you feel pressured?"

"Slade, my parents were the ones who taught me not to eat meat. I didn't know that it was so good. Now that I do, I'll set my own standards. Okay?"

"Okay." He smiled at her.

"It's a big job, taking care of this ranch," Slade said later as they rode the fence line of the largest pasture.

"And as your wife, what would my job be?"

"To supervise Josefina, who doesn't need much direction. To be my helpmate, my friend. And to do whatever it is that makes you happy."

At the moment, it seemed as if loving Slade would be enough to keep her happy as long as she lived. But niggling at the back of her mind was the notion that she had to have her own life. And how could she transplant a Miami Beach dating service to this little town in the Everglades? It was something to consider, the difficulty involved. But in her happiness, she pushed it to the back of her mind.

That night they went out, the two of them, to a catfish restaurant on the edge of the lake, a wide expanse of silvery water stretching clear to the horizon. The next morning they got up before dawn and pushed off into the slough in Slade's dugout to observe birds. With the binoculars glued to her eyeballs, Karma learned the difference between a heron and an ibis; she watched a hawk swoop down upon his prey on a lonely hammock covered with scrub pine and edged with cypress. Later they returned to that hammock and made love lazily in a shady fern-filled glen with palmetto fronds rustling overhead in the cool, water-scented breeze.

Another day, when Slade and his father had business in town, she watched Bambi practice barrel racing on the course behind the barn. The next afternoon, Slade took her to a rodeo in Indiantown, and they cheered as Slade's mother won the event. Toward the end of the week, Karma visited a sugar mill on the other side of the lake where the land was checkered with sugar cane fields and where she met some of Slade's friends, who owned the operation. She attended a church circle meeting with Bambi and to her surprise, she relished the experience almost as much as she liked the people. Karma even offered to teach the members of the group a few yoga poses when they expressed interest.

Slade was in his element in his home town. He had been a standout in Miami Beach, but here he was in charge of a large cattle operation, commanding and well-respected. Karma, seeing him in this new way, felt only joy that he had chosen her to share his life.

And so one day slid into another. Karma kept in close touch with Paulette by phone, relaxing over Paulette's handling of Rent-a-Yenta when she realized that her cousin was not only capable but as smart as a whip and not afraid to show it. They talked at least once a day and sometimes more.

"It sounds like you love it at the ranch," Paulette said one day during a lull in the conversation.

"Oh, I do," Karma said. "I have to admit that I'm enchanted by everything I see and everyone I've met."

"Are there lots of cowboys galloping around? A corral? Desperadoes to be headed off at the pass?" Paulette seemed to have the idea that Okeechobee City was similar to a TV rerun of the *Bonanza* show.

"There are ranch hands who do all the hardest work. There's more than one corral and not a desperado in sight, unless you could count Josefina, who is an angel. Why,

Paulette, with Josefina's cleaning squad arriving at convenient intervals, I'll never have to chase another dust bunny as long as I live!''

''As if you ever did,'' said Paulette, but she spoke fondly and indulgently. ''So what do you and Slade do all day?''

''We go bird-watching, or I ride out with him to the pastures, or we go somewhere special, like the rodeo. Oh, and Josefina taught me to make Slade's favorite casserole yesterday. I've eaten beef bourguignon and developed a taste for calves' liver simmered in wine. I'm going to learn how to run the barrels with Bambi, and—''

''Karma, slow down. Isn't the pace a little too frantic? Don't you think you might be trying too hard to fit in?''

Paulette, Karma was learning, could home in relentlessly on the key point of a conversation. ''Oh, I don't know. I admit I feel a little overwhelmed by the suddenness of getting engaged, but Slade is being so helpful. He suggested moving the honeymoon cruise up a few months so we can be married sooner, which made me stop and think for a minute, but I told him it would be okay. At least, I think it will be okay.'' She'd been telling herself over and over that things were fine, that Slade was a good man, and that she truly loved him. So if he wanted to marry her sooner rather than later, how could there be anything wrong with that?

''Karma, I detect some doubt. Are you *sure* everything is all right?''

Karma peeked around the corner of the kitchen to see if Josefina was working there, and when she saw her putting the finishing touches on a pie crust, she quietly let herself out the front door and sat on one of the porch rockers, lowering her tone. ''I think so, Paulette. I *think* so.''

Paulette's reply was sharp and to the point. ''What do you mean, you think so? Are things okay or not?''

Karma sighed, watching a kingfisher as it lit on a utility pole near the barn. A week ago, she hadn't even known there was such a bird. She had come a long way in a short time, that was for sure.

"All it is, Paulette, is that I find it hard to accept my good fortune in finding a wonderful guy. I've been single for so long, and now I'm going to be married, and I worry about Rent-a-Yenta and what will become of it, and I worry about getting to know the names of all the ranch hands, and I wonder if Josefina is going to want to help me as much as she helps Bambi, and—oh, Paulette, please tell me I'm out of line here."

"Gosh, Karma, you're not. These are normal apprehensions when you're changing your whole life around to be married to a guy you've only known for a couple of weeks."

"Maybe that's it," Karma said, feeling guilty for not putting a more positive spin on her situation.

"Have you talked to Slade about all this?"

"No, of course not. The honeymoon's supposed to be in June. This is October. He thinks a December wedding would be perfect because all his relatives will be in town for Christmas. We can get married in his church, he says."

"Well, what's wrong with that?"

"I never wanted to be married in a church. If I were going to be married in a house of worship, it should be my sister's synagogue. Besides, I've always wanted an outdoor wedding, but now it makes more sense to do what Slade says, I guess. Except if the wedding is in December, it will be too cold to go to Alaska on the honeymoon cruise like he planned. We'll go to the Caribbean instead. I was kind of getting into the idea of Alaska myself."

Paulette let out a sigh of exasperation. "It's *your* wedding and *your* honeymoon. You should have some input."

"I don't want to spoil Slade's enthusiasm. He's so excited about getting married. You wouldn't believe how much he talks about it, how often he tells me he loves me." She saw Slade's Suburban bumping down the driveway toward the barn, and she stood up, wanting to wind this conversation up before he arrived.

"That's all well and good, my dear cousin, but why don't you talk things over with him before things are set in stone? Slade is a reasonable man, and if he loves you, he'll understand and make allowances."

"Do you think he'll go for a longer engagement? So I can get used to the idea of getting married? So we can plan a wedding that we're both happy about?"

"Karma, if he loves you he will."

"He loves me. I know he does. I'd better run, Paulette. He's coming in from the feed store, and I'd rather he didn't know we've talked about this yet."

"Any time you want to hash it over, give me a ring."

"Right. And thanks. You're a good counselor."

"I know."

Karma smiled to herself before running down the steps and over to the barn to greet Slade. It didn't occur to her until she was halfway there that Paulette hadn't mentioned Uncle Nate, and she made a mental note to ask how he was getting along next time they talked.

THE CONVERSATION SHE intended to have with Slade weighed heavily on Karma's mind, but because ranch life was busy and their days full, it was a couple of days before she was able to broach the subject of her misgivings.

They had just made love, long and languorously, beneath a spreading scrub oak tree not far from a creek in an isolated section of the ranch. Slade was lying with his head in her lap, and she was leaning back against the tree trunk, half drunk with love and happiness.

They watched a great blue heron take flight on the opposite shore of the creek. "I never knew two people could be so happy," Slade said, taking her hand in his. "You *are* happy, aren't you, Karma?"

She stroked his hair and waited a moment before speaking. "Yes, Slade, I am," she said softly. "But I do think I could be happier."

She felt him tense, and he sat up. "What do you mean?" He stared at her across the space between them, his skin dappled by the sunlight streaming through the branches overhead.

"I've been wanting to talk with you, Slade. This is all so wonderful, and I am thrilled to be engaged. I want you to know that. But I think I need more time before we get married."

"More time? Why?" A frown marred his features, and Karma's heart lurched in dismay. She hadn't expected him to look so upset.

"I have an idea about Rent-a-Yenta, about how I can stay active in the business after I move to the ranch. It will take time to implement the new plan." He looked doubtful, but she plunged ahead. "And—and I had my heart set on a honeymoon in Alaska, not the Caribbean."

Slade ran a hand through his hair. "Well, Karma, I reckon we can still go to Alaska. The honeymoon doesn't have to follow the wedding. It can be a few months later."

"Six months is how much later it would be if we get married in December. Slade, I don't think I can be ready to get married in only two months."

He seemed taken aback. "Why? What's the problem? You buy a white dress, you line up Paulette to be your bridesmaid—"

"I have three sisters. I always planned for Isis to be my only attendant, like I was in her wedding last year. And during the Hanukkah and Christmas holidays, I doubt that anyone in my family will be able to travel to Florida. Azure lives in Boston, Isis is in California and will be entertaining her husband's family, Mary Beth is always busy with something at the temple, and as for my father, who knows where he'll be? Probably on a ship somewhere, and Mom needs more than two months' notice if she's going to be at our wedding.''

Slade swallowed and seemed to think this over. ''I thought you wanted to be married soon, like I do.''

She rested a placating hand on his shoulder. ''A long engagement would help me make the transition from thinking like a single person to thinking like one half of a married couple.''

He attempted a laugh. ''I'm already thinking like half of a married couple.''

''It's different for you, Slade. You expected to find a wife. I'd given up on relationships long before I met you. I'm crazy about your parents, I look forward to my life with you on the ranch, but I have important things to do before I take the big step of getting married.'' Her eyes pleaded for understanding.

''Karma, I thought you'd made the final commitment when you said yes to my marriage proposal.'' He had retreated into stoniness, and she tried again to explain.

''I did make that commitment. When I said yes, I didn't know you meant you wanted to be married so soon, that's all.''

He stood up and walked over to the edge of the creek, his agitation evident in every step. She stood too, following after him, planting one foot in front of the other in grim determination.

''It doesn't sound to me as if you feel the same way about me as I do about you,'' he said under his breath when she was standing beside him.

''I love you. You should know that by now.''

''Should I? When you're backing off like this?''

Karma fought the tears that stung the back of her eyelids. This was going wrong, all wrong. ''I'm not backing off. All I'm saying is that I'm not comfortable with this whirlwind of a courtship.''

''I'm not comfortable with a woman who doubts her love

for me. Oh, God, Karma, don't turn on the tears. I can't stand it.''

She couldn't help her quick retort. "So I should hide my emotions because it makes you uncomfortable? I expected honesty in this relationship, Slade.''

He threw his arms out in a gesture of helplessness, but what she really wanted was for him to wrap those arms around her. He made no move to do so. Instead he blew out a breath, ruffling the hair that fell so endearingly over his forehead. "All right, Karma. Give me honesty.''

"Maybe—maybe we need to spend some time apart. Maybe going at it hot and heavy has obscured our true relationship.'' The words popped out before she had a chance to think them over, which she knew was one of her failings—but he *had* demanded honesty.

"Karma, I—''

"I think I should go back to Miami Beach for a while. That will give both of us time to think things over.''

"There's nothing for me to think over. I'm totally in love with you, Karma, and I want us to be married as soon as possible.'' He took her shoulders in his hands and gazed deep into her eyes. Then he kissed her, and her arms went around him to hold him close. She must be crazy to suggest being apart, she thought. She must be out of her mind.

He released her. "I'll drive you back to Miami Beach tomorrow, and you can take as long as you like to figure things out. If you still want a long engagement, we can discuss it later.''

"Later?'' The word came out in a squeak.

"Not too much later, I hope.'' He said this with a wry grin, then became more serious. "I'll be here waiting for you when you're ready to come back.''

This hadn't gone at all the way Karma had planned. She had expected a careful, measured response to her voiced apprehensions. She had expected thoughtfulness and understanding. But now she realized with some bewilderment that she had wounded Slade's pride and that by giving her an easy out, he thought he was accommodating to her needs.

She considered trying one more time to explain how she felt, but she sensed that Slade wasn't ready to hear it. So she only turned back toward the Suburban, blinking so that her tears would not fall.

Slade walked slightly behind her, and she didn't dare turn around to look at him. She didn't think she could bear his crushed expression, the anguish in his eyes.

She sat stiffly beside Slade on the ride back to the house, not talking and staring resolutely out the window on her side of the car. When he pulled up in front of the house, she climbed down and hurried inside. She didn't speak. She couldn't. She had the feeling that she had ruined everything by speaking her mind.

She had hoped to reach her room without having to talk to anyone, but as she crossed the hallway to the stairs, Josefina ran out of the kitchen clutching the phone in her hand. "A call for you, Karma," she said.

Since they talked often, Karma wasn't surprised to hear her cousin's voice. At first she intended to tell Paulette that she'd call her back later, but she was arrested by Paulette's distraught tone.

"Karma, oh, you have to come home. It's Uncle Nate— he's had a heart attack!"

It was late that night before she and Slade arrived in Miami Beach after a tense ride in from the Glades. At the hospital, Karma was allowed to see her uncle right away, and the first thing she did was to send Paulette home for a good night's sleep. Paulette had been with Nate since he'd checked in, and she looked exhausted. Then Karma, after Slade left for the houseboat, sat holding Nate's hand until morning.

Her uncle was hooked up to tubes and bags and bottles,

and his face looked pale and wan under his suntan. But when he woke up, he had enough energy to greet her the same way he always did.

"Vus machts du, bubbeleh?"

"How are *you* doing, Uncle Nate?" she said, enunciating loudly into his hearing aid.

"Getting better," he said, and the attending physician told Karma when he made his regular rounds that morning that he expected Uncle Nate to make a full recovery.

She called Slade to report the good news, and he sounded as glad as she felt.

"And how about you? How are you holding up?"

"Fine," Karma said, though she wasn't so sure. She missed Slade terribly.

"If you need me, call me," he said firmly.

"I thought you were going back to the ranch."

"Not now. Not with Nate so sick."

She knew he wasn't staying in Miami Beach for her uncle's sake but for hers, but she still had a bleak feeling when she thought of the rift between them. But there was no time to dwell on what had gone wrong even though she was awash in regrets that she hadn't planned her approach more carefully.

By the third day, Nate's friends were allowed to visit, and Mrs. Rothstein was the first to show up. Paulette happened to be in the room when the woman arrived surrounded by a cloud of Shalimar cologne, and with a meaningful glance, she pulled Karma out into the hall.

"I think we'd better give Uncle Nate and Mrs. Rothstein some privacy," Paulette said in an undertone. "Under the circumstances."

Karma, who always took the all-night shift, napping in a recliner while her uncle slept, was feeling as wrung out as an old dishrag, and she didn't understand. "Circumstances?" she repeated. "What circumstances?"

Paulette moved closer and dropped her voice to a whisper. "When Uncle Nate had the heart attack, he was in Mrs. Rothstein's bed!"

"You don't mean it," Karma said in astonishment.

Paulette grinned. "Yes. And it was Mrs. Rothstein who called the medics and made sure he got to the hospital."

"I knew he was seeing her," Karma said slowly. "But I didn't know he was—"

"Shh," said Paulette, putting on a smile. "Here she comes."

As Karma drove Paulette's car back to the Blue Moon, she kept having to wipe a grin off her face, and she was thinking, *Why, Uncle Nate, you old rake!*

Karma usually slept all day and then went back to relieve Paulette around dinner time. When she woke up late that afternoon, she noticed the answering machine's light blinking and found a message from Slade.

"Call me," he said. "I miss you."

When she called, Slade answered right away. After inquiring about Nate's progress, he asked how she was.

"I'm tired. Too little sleep and too much stress."

"Poor darling. This has been hard on you."

"And on Paulette."

"If you feel that you can take a night off, I'd like to take you to dinner," Slade said.

She longed to see him. She really did. But she couldn't leave Uncle Nate. "I can't just yet. I wouldn't feel right about it."

He was quiet for a moment. "Your uncle needs you. I know that."

Not as much as he needs Mrs. Rothstein, evidently, she thought, but she wouldn't feel comfortable telling Slade about that.

"You don't mind if I call you every day, do you?" Slade asked.

"No, of course not. I like it."

"Have you had time to think about—well, what you wanted to think about?"

"I still want a longer engagement."

"I think we can work this out," he said. "But not if we never see each other."

Karma bit her lip, knowing that he was right. "When Uncle Nate gets out of the hospital, we'll talk. In the meantime, I meant it when I said you might want to go back to the ranch."

"I'm not leaving, Karma. I love you and I miss you and I'm not going to let you get away." She was glad to hear a note of humor in his voice, and she smiled into the phone.

"As if I want to," she said warmly.

"I'll hold that thought, dearest," he replied.

Mrs. Rothstein was at the hospital when Karma arrived that evening, and Uncle Nate was sitting up and laughing.

"My, you look so much better," Karma told him.

He grinned happily. "From your mouth to God's ears."

"Have you been out of bed this morning?"

"Twice, dear. Leah helped me. It's easy when she's around—she tickles my funnybone."

Mrs. Rothstein said, "I'd like to tickle a little more than that, Nate," which made Nate laugh raucously and caused Karma to flush with embarrassment.

"Are you sure you're supposed to be laughing so hard?" Karma asked him. "Won't you dislodge a tube or something?"

"No, I'm getting along much better, and they let me eat some of Lee-Lee's chicken soup. That's the best medicine so far."

"I've got even better medicine for you when you're well enough," Mrs. Rothstein said encouragingly, and there was no mistaking what she meant.

Fortunately, at that moment Paulette stepped back into the room. "I'm leaving, Karma. Oh, hello, Mrs. Rothstein. It's good to see you."

"And you." Mrs. Rothstein nodded cordially, and Karma had to admit that the woman was attractive. She would have been beautiful no matter what her age, which was upwards of seventy, though you wouldn't know it from her figure, which was svelte, or her skin, which was tan, or her face, which was tucked and nipped in all the right places.

Karma followed Paulette into the hall. "If you could, Paulette, would you mind returning the Rent-a-Yenta phone calls that the answering machine has picked up? I didn't have time before I left."

"Sure. Oh, and by the way, I have a message from Goldy. She wants to know if you want her to read your tarot. I think she's gotten wind of a rift between you and Slade."

"How would she find that out? Did you tell her?"

"No, of course not. She must have read it in the cards."

"The cards should have told her that it's not a rift, exactly, it's only a time out that hasn't turned out to be what I thought it would be. Slade refuses to go back to the ranch. And with Uncle Nate so sick—" She lifted her shoulders and let them fall.

Paulette grinned. "So maybe you'd better have your tarot read after all, Karma. It wouldn't hurt."

"Tell Goldy to read the cards for our esteemed uncle instead. I'll take a chance on being able to sort things out with Slade after Uncle Nate goes home. And that won't be a moment too soon for Lee-Lee in there."

Paulette burst out laughing. "Aren't they great together?"

"Absolutely, only why does she only show up when I'm here? Why aren't you treated to the sights and sounds of two septuagenarians in love?"

"Mrs. Rothstein can only be here at night. During the day she runs a food bank." Paulette shrugged. "You're just lucky, I guess. See you, Karma.'' With a wave of her hand, Paulette was off and running.

Karma had already resigned herself to an evening with her uncle and Mrs. Rothstein. She had to admit that their banter was cute, even clever, but as she listened, Karma felt like odd man out. She realized that she could have probably ducked out for a couple of hours every night, but she knew that Aunt Sophie, if she were alive, would have been there around the clock looking after Nate. As grateful as she was for what her aunt had done for her, Karma could do no less.

But one thing that Aunt Sophie wouldn't have had to put up with was the cooing of the two lovebirds, who even now were stealing kisses every time Karma turned her head.

Karma managed to turn her head as often as possible in an attempt to be helpful, but she had an idea that it was going to be a very long night.

''DON'T WORRY ABOUT A THING, dear,'' Mrs. Rothstein said briskly a few days later as Karma settled Nate on the couch in front of the TV in his apartment. ''I've found someone to take my place at the food bank, and I'm happy to look after him. I think I'll make my blintzes for lunch, Nate, what do you think?''

Uncle Nate, his eyes dancing, reached over and took her hand. ''Anything you want, Lee-Lee. Only you'd better use low-fat sour cream. Doctor's orders.''

''You see, Karma? Your uncle's going to be fine, just fine.''

Karma wasn't worried about leaving her uncle in Mrs. Rothstein's capable hands, which were all too eager, she thought, to find their way back to parts of Uncle Nate's anatomy that Karma didn't want to think about. After slightly more than a week in the hospital, Nate was eager for his life to get back to normal. Karma could only hope that normal wouldn't kill him next time.

"So are you and that cowboy of yours going to see each other tonight?" her uncle asked.

"Mmm, I don't know," she hedged, although she planned to call him later to tell him that Nate had gone home.

"Slade told me on the phone when you were at the ranch that he was going to buy you a big diamond as soon as you two came back to Miami Beach."

"I think the diamond ring might be slightly premature," Karma said. She hadn't mentioned the current state of affairs to her uncle, knowing that it would only worry him.

"Premature?" scoffed Nate. "You're engaged to be married! Get a big diamond, Karma. You deserve it, and your cowboy wants to buy it for you. He told me at least two carats."

She decided to go along goodhumoredly with this line of discussion. "Two carats? What would I do with a two-carat diamond, Uncle Nate?"

"Wear it as a proud symbol of the man's love for you, *bubbeleh*." He laughed, sounding exactly like his old self.

She bent and kissed his forehead. "Dear Uncle Nate, what would I do without you?" she said fondly.

He grinned. "Fortunately, Karma, you do not have to find that out yet."

Mrs. Rothstein walked her to the door. "Now I mean it, Karma. Don't worry. And come for dinner this weekend, why don't you? Bring Slade."

"I'll let you know. Thanks for letting me use your car, Uncle Nate."

"No problem. I'm not going anywhere for a while."

"Goodbye, Mrs. Rothstein."

"Leah. That's what you should call me, dear." She hugged Karma in farewell.

At least Mrs. Rothstein hadn't insisted on being called Lee-Lee, Karma thought with amusement.

She drove Nate's car back to the Blue Moon, where she parked it under a poinciana tree beside Paulette's little Volkswagen bug.

"Hi, Karma," said Goldy as she walked through the lobby. "How's Nate?"

Karma stopped to chat for a moment. "Uncle Nate is doing well," she told Goldy.

"Paulette told me you wanted me to read the tarot for him," Goldy said with a hint of archness in her expression.

"And what did the cards predict?"

Goldy set aside her knitting and leaned closer, lowering her voice. "Let me put it this way, Karma. Nate won't need to sign on with Rent-a-Yenta to find the perfect mate."

"You don't mean—you aren't saying—?"

"Yes. Mrs. Rothstein. They're going to tie the knot, wait and see."

Somehow Karma wasn't surprised, but she was delighted. "That's wonderful, Goldy."

"I think so too. Your uncle is a fine man, and he doesn't have to be lonely anymore."

"I know, and I'm happy for him. By the way, have you seen Paulette today?"

"She went over to the Rent-a-Yenta office earlier. She said she'd be back soon."

"Oh, okay. See you later, Goldy." Karma ran up the stairs, light on her feet. She thought maybe she'd fix lunch for Paulette, who had been working hard at Rent-a-Yenta without asking for so much as a paycheck. Business was picking up. Paulette, amazingly, had signed up twelve new clients while Karma was at the ranch, which was more than Karma had signed up in two months.

On her own floor, she burst through the door from the stairwell into the hall and almost mowed Jennifer down.

"Karma! I was looking for you. I put a certificate for a

free ear piercing under your door. The special will be over soon, and since it's two for the price of one, I thought you and Paulette could come together.''

''I'll ask Paulette,'' Karma said, taking in Jennifer's Outrageous Outfit Of The Day, which consisted of a scarlet exercise bra, much too tight, and silk boxer shorts, white with a black design that consisted of—of the Diamond B Ranch brand?

What?

No. It wasn't possible.

Karma squinted at the shorts, hoping that her eyesight was failing. But there was nothing wrong with her vision. The design on those shorts was unmistakably a diamond shape enclosing a letter B, the Diamond B Ranch brand. She had seen those boxers before. On Slade Braddock.

Karma went numb even as she spoke. ''Um, Jennifer,'' she said.

Jennifer, snapping her fingers in time to the rhythm of her chewing gum, tried to brush past, but Karma adroitly blocked her way.

''I really have to go, Karma, I'm running late for the Dolphins' cheerleader tryout practice. I'm trying out, did I tell you? Wow!'' She bounced and executed a dance step in her pristine white sneakers.

''Before you go, would you mind telling me where you got those shorts? Those very *distinctive* shorts?'' Karma was hoping that Jennifer would tell her that she had bought them at a Salvation Army store, though she was sure that was the last place Jennifer would shop. She was hoping that Jennifer would say that the shorts were a factory outlet store bargain, though she didn't know of any that sold silk underwear imprinted with the Diamond B brand.

Jennifer reached down and fingered the fabric. ''These? They're Slade's. See you, Karma.'' She pushed past Karma and through the door to the stairwell, letting it slam behind her. The sound reverberated through the long hallway like a shot.

Which Karma felt as though it penetrated her heart.

Karma couldn't think. She couldn't feel. She couldn't do anything but let herself into her apartment and stand staring woodenly at the tiny wedge of seascape on the other side of the sliding glass door. The ocean seemed flat and one-dimensional, and the apartment where she usually felt so comfortable was oppressive. Jennifer and Slade, she thought, her mind refusing to move past their names. Jennifer and Slade. She didn't want to believe it. But she had to believe it, considering the proof.

After a minute or two, she walked over and slid the door open, hoping that the fresh sea breeze would revive her, would make her be able to think and feel again.

But it didn't.

She moved to the balcony railing and stared down at the cars in the parking lot. During her long nights at the hospital, she had often imagined Slade driving into that parking lot. In her mind's eye, he would climb out of the Suburban looking tan and fit and cowboyish, wearing his boots and faded jeans and a big smile, and she would welcome him with open arms. She would tell him that she regretted hurting his feelings by asking for time apart and that she really wanted a June wedding, and he would tell her that she was absolutely right and that he'd been out of line to expect her to be married in a church in Okeechobee City in December. And then, arms around each other, they would phone Isis and ask her to be Karma's attendant, and they would inform Bambi and Norton that the wedding would be on the beach near the Blue Moon, and Slade would call the travel agency and put her name on the ticket for the honeymoon cruise to Alaska.

And all the while she, Karma, had been longing to see Slade, to reconcile with him, Jennifer had been wearing his silk Diamond B Ranch boxer shorts.

Life wasn't fair. Not that this was news. If life were fair, Karma would have been born that sexy little ectomorph that Slade had been seeking in the beginning, and maybe then he wouldn't have committed the act that resulted in Jennifer's wearing his boxer shorts.

There was no doubt in Karma's mind that Slade had slept with Jennifer, none whatever. Well, what could she expect, now that his second chakra was unblocked, thanks to her? She didn't think that he had had sex with Jennifer the night of their one and only date, which she herself had arranged. She didn't think he was capable of sleeping with Jennifer and then taking her, Karma, home to meet his parents and making love to her. No, it had probably on one of those long balmy nights when Karma was keeping her vigil at the hospital with Nate. Slade would have had plenty of opportunity, and he had been lonely, and Jennifer was all too available.

But that didn't give Slade the right to sleep with her. Not when he was supposed to be engaged to Karma, when he was telling her that he loved her and he missed her. They'd never agreed that they weren't going to get married. They hadn't agreed on when and where, that's all.

Anger began to percolate behind Karma's eyelids, a slow-burning, white-hot variety of anger such as she had never known before. Whenever it had happened, whatever had happened, Slade Braddock was the lowest of the low, the rattiest of rats, the king of the cockroaches. Worst of all, she loved him.

She whirled as she heard a key turn in the lock and Paulette breezed in carrying a stack of file folders.

"Hi, Karma. I brought some work back here, I thought I could sit out on the balcony in the sun while I—Karma? Is anything wrong?" Her cousin stopped and set the folders down on the wicker trunk that served as a coffee table.

Karma looked at her bleakly. "You won't believe it," she said.

''It's not you and Slade, is it?''

''Yes,'' Karma whispered, willing herself not to fall apart.

''Oh, Karma, I'm sorry,'' Paulette said, looking stunned. Karma bit her lip. ''He—he slept with Jennifer.''

''With Jennifer? Oh, you must be mistaken.''

Feeling as if someone else were telling the story, Karma related how she had seen Jennifer wearing Slade's boxer shorts and how Jennifer had blithely admitted that Slade had given them to her.

''That's incontrovertible evidence, I'd say.'' Still numb, still operating on autopilot, Karma walked past Paulette into the apartment.

''What are you going to do?'' Paulette's expression was somber.

''I'm not going to call him, if that's what you're asking.''

Paulette slid an arm around her waist. ''I don't blame you. Come sit down, Karma. I don't suppose you have any cookie dough, do you? I like to pig out on cookie dough when something is getting me down. It's my ultimate comfort food.''

''No cookie dough, I'm afraid.''

''Too bad. I'll make you a cup of herbal tea.'' She searched through the cabinets. ''Do you want chamomile or sarsaparilla?''

''I don't care,'' Karma said distractedly, wrapping her arms around herself and feeling awful. She made herself drink the tea that Paulette brought her, knowing in her heart that it didn't matter how much you loved a man if he couldn't be faithful, if he lied, if he exploited. Because when all was said and done, if he didn't love you back, you were setting yourself up for a life of heartbreak and misery. Uncle Nate had said of Aunt Sophie, ''She was my life.'' And unless and until Karma found a man who could make her, Karma, his life, she wouldn't marry him. But oh, it was so hard to come to grips with the fact that it was over with Slade, really over. Despite their recent difficulties, it seemed strange to think of her life going on without him.

It was an hour or more before she hauled herself up from the couch and told Paulette, "I'm going to lie down for a while, and then you and I are going out, Paulette."

"We are?"

"Yes. We're going to celebrate being ourselves. We're going to rejoice in being single. And we're going to work out a plan that keeps you here in Miami Beach to help me with Rent-a-Yenta."

"Oh, Karma, I would love that!"

"Me, too. And if Slade calls, tell him I'm sleeping, tell him I'm busy, tell him anything you want. I don't want to know about it. I don't want to even hear his name."

"But Karma, don't you and Slade need closure?"

Karma groaned. "Let me be the psychologist around here, okay?"

Karma retreated into the bedroom and shut the door. She told herself that she hated Slade Braddock. She told herself that she'd been fine before she met him and she'd be fine again. She told herself that she was lucky to have found out what a jerk he was before she married him and moved to the ranch and began to share his life, a life that was now lost to her forever. At the thought of the marriage that was not to be, the tears rushed in like a torrent, and it was a long time before she could stop sobbing.

When she did, she told herself that if she never saw Slade Braddock again, that would be too soon.

SLADE HUNG UP THE PHONE after calling Karma's apartment and talking with Paulette, wondering why he felt so uneasy. Yes, Nate had gone home from the hospital earlier, but Karma was taking a nap and couldn't talk to him, Paulette had said.

"I'll call her later. Maybe she'd like to go out," he told

her, and Paulette had responded much too quickly, "Oh, I doubt it, Slade."

Something in Paulette's voice had given him pause. She had sounded prickly, annoyed, and the slightest bit disgusted.

And it seemed odd to him that Karma hadn't called him herself to tell him that she was free tonight. On the other hand, Karma was worn out from taking care of her uncle, and she could be expected to need some extra rest.

Well, no matter what Paulette said, he would call Karma later, and even if she were resting and he didn't talk with her, he'd try to get an idea from Paulette what was going on.

He heard a step on the deck of *Toy Boat* and went to the door of the salon. It was Phifer, grinning ear to ear.

"Hey, Slade, want to go out tonight and let me buy you a couple of drinks? I caught a sailfish today, my first. It's an occasion, man. Let's do it!"

"Sure," Slade said, feeling lackluster in spite of Phifer's enthusiasm.

"I'll come by later. See you then." Phifer left, looking jaunty.

Slade wish he felt more upbeat, more enthusiastic about the evening ahead. Maybe he'd feel better after a shower and shave.

He headed for the master stateroom, unable to shake the feeling that something was seriously wrong.

10

___

KARMA AND PAULETTE TREATED themselves to dinner at Fontaine's, the best restaurant in town, famed for its snow crab. It was also known for its Fountain of the Dancing Waters where multiple lighted water jets rose and fell to beautiful music every half hour. Fontaine's was where Karma would have asked Slade to take her if they had gone out on this night, and she was determined that dressing up in her blue sari with the gold edging and going there with Paulette would banish thoughts of him from her mind.

Not that it worked, however. She thought of Slade—and of his betrayal—every minute.

That didn't stop her from outlining her plans for Rent-a-Yenta to Paulette, a plan that had begun to seem like a possibility back at the ranch and took shape on those long nights at the hospital with her uncle. And, with Paulette in need of a job, she kept thinking that Aunt Sophie would have approved. It also seemed to her that her aunt would have approved even more if marriage to Slade were still in the works, but even so, Karma's idea had merit for both Karma and Paulette.

"If you could handle the business side of Rent-a-Yenta," Karma told Paulette, "I could handle the rest of it. You know, the psychological profiling. The contacts with people who have expressed an interest."

"That would work," Paulette said excitedly. "Why, it's perfect. You're good at the psychological side of things, and I've enjoyed every minute of looking after the accounts and organizing the office.''

"Together, we can bring in more business. Rent-a-Yenta will be a going concern again.''

"I want to put all the accounts on computer. You can enhance the psychological profiling.'' Paulette looked as if she could hardly contain her glee.

"It's a deal then?''

"A deal.''

"To Rent-a-Yenta,'' Karma said, raising her glass of wine, and they drank a toast to their joint venture.

Feeling reckless, Karma ordered steak, which made Paulette regard her with doubt. "Are you sure you want to order meat in a restaurant known for its snow crab?'' she asked skeptically.

"Sure,'' Karma said, beckoning to the waiter so she could order another glass of wine. "I like meat. I didn't know it before, that's all.''

"Until you went with Slade to the ranch?''

"I don't want to think about him. Or the ranch. Or Bambi and Norton or the Alaska cruise.'' She drained her glass.

Paulette leaned across the table. "Karma, should you be drinking so much?''

"Why not?'' Karma retorted. "Please don't go judgmental on me, Paulette. We're celebrating.'' This didn't feel much like a celebration, though the wine was helping. She wanted to forget about Slade and Jennifer for a while, and if a heavy dose of merlot could accomplish that, more power to the grape. She lifted the new glass of wine to her lips.

"I don't know, Karma. I realize you're upset, but I'm not sure it's wise to make yourself sick over Slade Braddock.''

Paulette could be irritating at times, and her present diatribe made Karma want to grind her teeth in order to drown out her voice.

"I'm not making myself sick." She stood up. "Be back in a minute." The Fountain of the Dancing Waters outside the window with all its tinkling and trickling made her want to go the ladies' room.

She headed for the back of the restaurant, realizing that she was going to have to walk through the bar to get where she was going. She felt big and bulky in her trailing sari, but at the same time she felt as if she were shrinking away inside, recoiling from the pain she felt over Slade's deceit.

In the rest room, she stared at herself in the mirror. She looked slightly wild-eyed, so no wonder Paulette kept carping about the wine. Well, too bad. It wouldn't hurt to drown her sorrows this one time.

On the way back to the table as she was negotiating the twists and turns through the cluster of tables in the bar, she saw Mandi waving at her across the room. Mandi detached herself from a group that was watching some sporting event on TV and headed toward her.

"Karma! Want to watch the golf match with us?" Mandi wore high-heeled gold boots and a tiger-print bodysuit. Her sparkly eye shadow appeared to have been layered on with a trowel.

Karma's knees were feeling slightly wobbly, and she managed only a brittle smile. "Who's us?" she said, expecting that Jennifer would be part of the group.

"Oh, me and some friends."

"Paulette and I are having dinner. And I'm not eager to see Jennifer right now."

"Jennifer? I didn't say Jennifer was here."

"The two of you are usually together."

"That was before Jennifer found a guy. She's out with him tonight."

My guy, Karma thought to herself. "Yes, well, they can wear their matching underwear all around South Beach.

They'll look so cute together in their black-and-white diamond-print boxer shorts.''

"Black and diamond—?'' Mandi seemed mystified, but Karma wasn't up to any more discussion. She wheeled and started to walk toward the dining room, her path slightly wavery. Behind her Mandi bleated something about Jennifer and how she was in love with this way hunky guy and how her mother was so pleased and—well, the bleating stopped when Karma reached the dining room where a group of waiters gathered around one of the tables to sing "Happy Birthday," blocking Mandi's entry.

Karma sat down at the table and drew a deep breath. "What do you say we chugalug a whole bottle of that wine?" she said to Paulette.

SLADE ORDERED BOURBON and water from the bartender at Fontaine's and thought briefly about moving closer to the television set in one corner before discarding the idea as too much trouble. He wished he'd stayed home. This glitzy watering hole felt all wrong, out of character, out of sync.

He stood up, thinking that it was time to call Karma at home. He'd tried earlier, but no one had answered, not even the answering machine. As he headed away from the bar, someone called his name.

"Mandi," he said as she worked her way through the crowd toward him.

"Hi, Slade," she said with more than her usual share of perkiness. "You're here looking for Karma, right? Well, I just spoke to her. She's in the dining room."

In the dining room? Here? Karma was supposed to be napping. Slade tried to hide his surprise.

"She seems a little strange, Slade."

He eyed Mandi in her tiger-print bodysuit, gold boots and thick eyeliner. Mandi thought Karma was strange?

He stuck his thumbs through his belt loops. "You want to elaborate on that?"

Mandi shrugged. "Saying crazy things. Acting like she's snarfing magic mushrooms or something. Like, I told her Jennifer was out with her boyfriend, and she said something about they'd look cute in their matching black-and-white diamond-print boxer shorts." Mandi fluttered her hand and rolled her eyes. "Weird."

"She talked about matching diamond-print boxer shorts?"

"Yeah, go figure that one out."

Diamond-print boxer shorts. Jennifer. Matching.

It dawned on him then, a flash of horrified realization. "Whoa," he said unsteadily.

"Whoa?"

He slugged back his drink. "Excuse me, Mandi, I'm out of here." Mandi shrugged and began to make her way back to the group.

Phifer was holding fort at a table surrounded by guys. "Phifer, look, I've got business to tend to. You can get back to the marina on your own, right?"

Considering that he had interrupted Phifer's fish story, the man was amazingly goodnatured. "Sure, Slade, is anything wrong?"

"Only everything," Slade said through gritted teeth, and he stalked out of the bar.

SLADE SPOTTED KARMA SITTING at the table with Paulette. She looked beautiful, her hair caught up in a jeweled clip, her eyes bright. In that moment, he realized how much he loved her and how all her unusual attributes made her so special. He had been a goner from the word go, captivated by her charm, her style, and her easygoing personality.

As he approached the table, she lifted her eyes to his face. But her immediate scowl signaled that she wasn't happy to see him—far from it.

"You!" she exclaimed, throwing her napkin on the floor and leaping to her feet.

Well, scratch her easygoing personality. But she was majestic in her anger.

"Yup, it's me," he said mildly. "Would you mind explaining why Paulette told me you were napping?" Paulette sat quietly, looking stricken, her gaze bouncing back and forth between the two of them.

"Sure," Karma said, and he realized as she slurred the word that she must be slightly tipsy. "As soon as you explain why you slept with Jennifer."

It seemed in that moment as if a hush fell over the room and as if every pair of eyes was focused on him.

"Karma, I didn't." He kept his voice level, his gaze straightforward. He touched her arm, but she shook his hand away and began to stride toward the entrance.

"Wait! I can explain!"

She only tossed a scalding look over her shoulder and kept walking past a group waiting for tables at the entrance. Outside, the quiescent Fountain of the Dancing Waters lay in front of them. Its shallow pool, the size of a basketball court, glimmered aquamarine in the lights from overhead.

"Karma," he said, his way blocked by a group wearing name tags.

"I have to get the car," she said tightly. She clutched a ring of keys in her hand.

Several people were making their way toward a tour bus to their right, and a limousine glided to a stop in front of him. Behind it, another car blocked the exit.

"Karma, I didn't sleep with Jennifer," he said, getting desperate.

"He didn't sleep with Jennifer, he said," a blue-haired dowager declared loudly to her companion. "Imagine that!"

Karma, meanwhile, was threading her way through the vehicles. "Go away, Slade. I can't handle this right now." Her gait was none too steady.

She reached the rim of the fountain and paused, seemingly unsure what to do next.

Slade wished for a lasso so he could rope her and reel her in. Lacking that, he wrenched open the limousine door. The driver let out a strangulated yelp, and the couple in the back seat shrank back into the luxurious upholstery as he scrambled over their feet.

"Excuse me," he said politely, taking care not to slam the door on anyone as he exited on the other side.

By this time, Karma had climbed up onto the fountain rim, which was about two feet high. It looked to Slade as though she were planning on walking along the rim to the parking lot, since the traffic in the driveway was so congested.

She spotted him as soon as he emerged from the limo. "I told you to go away," she said.

"I won't. I can't. I love you, Karma. I didn't sleep with Jennifer, you have to believe me."

Karma, balancing carefully, began to mince along the fountain rim. She held her long skirt up with one hand. He jumped up onto the rim so he could talk to her without shouting, and at the precise moment when he could have reached out and touched her, the car keys she had been holding sailed into the pool. He saw them glittering on the bottom, too far away to fish out.

"I dropped my keys," she said unnecessarily.

"I'll get them. And then we need to talk." He sat down on the rim and pulled his boots off. Then he swiveled around and jumped into the knee-deep water. The people watching, and there were many by this time, let out a collective gasp.

He bent over to retrieve the keys and was stunned by a jet of water squirting into his face. The jetting water was accompanied by a clash of cymbals, and he realized that the Fountain of Dancing Waters had begun to dance. Sure enough, the bright overhead lights dimmed and softer lights in red and blue and green and a whole host of colors in between winked on below the water's surface.

He started to reach for the keys again, but he couldn't see them below the frothing water. Karma, who had been watching silently, had clasped her hands in front of her chest, and her mouth had assumed the shape of the letter O. He saw Paulette and Mandi running, and they stopped in astonishment when they spotted him in the pool and Karma balanced so precariously on its rim, the colors of the lights flashing rainbowlike across her face.

"Karma!" yelled Paulette so that Karma jerked her head around to look, losing her balance in the process. In slow motion, she toppled and fell, her gown spreading out around her like wings, her hair loosening from its clip.

As other jets began to dance and sway all around, as the music rose into succeeding crescendos, Karma landed in Slade's arms with a gentle *"Oof!"* Not one to overlook random blessings, he clasped her to his heart.

The song blaring from the surrounding speakers was something he didn't recognize, but it seemed to require a lot of splashing, spurting water.

"I told you to go away," Karma said thickly.

He held her fast. His hair and face were wet. He didn't care. "Never, my darling. I can explain everything."

"She was wearing your Diamond B Ranch shorts. Your silk underwear."

Out of the corners of his eyes, Slade saw Paulette and Mandi leaning over the edge of the pool. "Jennifer didn't sleep with Slade. She's in love with Sheldon!" Mandi hollered.

Karma turned her head toward Mandi. Water dripped off the end of her nose. Her dress was soaked. He thought she looked wonderful.

"What?" Karma said.

Mandi leaned farther over the rim, and Slade hoped she

wouldn't fall in, too. He didn't know how many wet females he could handle.

"Sheldon! The guy her mother set her up with! And I can explain the underwear!"

"She can explain the underwear!" Paulette echoed. "You'd better listen to this, Karma."

"You'd better," Slade said, deciding that this might turn out all right after all.

They waited for another burst of music to play itself out, and Slade had to pull Karma back behind the bank of water jets that were currently pluming and spuming. The jets were between them and Mandi, and they made it harder to hear her.

"Karma, haven't you ever been on a scavenger hunt?" Mandi called.

"Sure, Scavenger hunts. You're at a party and you get a list, and the first one who returns to the party with all the items on the list wins."

"Well, Sheldon took Jennifer to a party, and their list included an item of underwear from the last person you dated. In Jennifer's case, that was Slade. So naturally she had to go to his houseboat and get a pair of underwear."

Karma glanced up at Slade. "Is this true?" she asked. Her mascara was running. He reached up and wiped a dribble of it away.

"I gave her the boxers. Jennifer said she'd bring them back, but I told her to keep them, I had lots more."

"Jennifer and Sheldon have been together every single night," Mandi said.

"Oh," Karma whispered, looking stricken.

Slade pulled her closer. "I don't want anyone but you for as long as I live, Karma, and as long as I love. Though I have to tell you that I get tired of rescuing you from watery places." He kissed the tip of her nose. "You're my destiny, Karma. You're my life." With those words, it was as if she melted, all resistance draining out of her.

She blinked at him. "I am?" Karma couldn't believe her ears. Those were the words she had wanted to hear from him, needed to hear. They were the words that Uncle Nate had said about Aunt Sophie.

"You are. And I've been thinking it over. We can get married whenever you like, go wherever you want on our honeymoon cruise."

She buried her face in his soggy shirtfront. "I'm so sorry I hurt your feelings about that," she said. "I never meant to." The pool was a cauldron of bubbles swirling around their knees.

"I was entirely too quick to make a big deal out of it. I should have listened. I should have been more sympathetic. I hated every minute of being apart. Karma, will you come back to the houseboat with me tonight?" He smoothed her hair tenderly back from her face.

She hiccuped. "I don't have any dry clothes there."

"That's the idea, my darling. You won't need to wear anything at all for what I have in mind."

She looked up at him, her cowboy, the man of her dreams. "I like the way you think, cowboy. And I love you, Slade, with all my heart."

The music drew to a close with a final crash of cymbals, and he swooped Karma up into his arms. He stood there in the sudden silence, letting her drip. In the group of onlookers, someone began to clap, and soon all of them were.

With one last effervescent flourish, the dancing waters became calm—as tranquil as Karma's mind, as peaceful as her heart now that she had found the love of her life.

Slade gazed down at Karma, his heart overflowing with emotion. "I don't know what the name of that tune is, my darling, but I think from now on, it's our song."

A FEW HOURS LATER, THEY LAY in bed on *Toy Boat,* the reflection of moonlit water shimmering across the ceiling.

"Slade," Karma murmured sleepily. "When did you know?"

"Know what?"

"That I was the one." She snuggled closer, curving comfortably against his side.

"When I got a look at those lace panties you wore to yoga class."

"No, be serious!" She smiled into the moonlight.

"It might have been when you rode your bike off my dock. How could I not love somebody who loses her dress before our first date even begins?"

"It wasn't a date. It wasn't a dress for that matter, it was a sari, like what I wore tonight."

"I like those. They peel off so easily, especially when wet."

"I'm not going to get a serious answer out of you, am I, Slade?"

"Only one. And it's that I agree to being married on the beach, since that's what you want. As long as I don't have to rescue you from drowning again, I mean."

"Oh, wonderful." She kissed his neck, and he curved his hand around her breast.

"Ready to go again?"

"No," she said. "Not until we sleep for a while."

"There are much nicer things to do," he said, gathering her into his arms.

Later, when they were about to drowse off, Karma said, "You know when I knew you were the one?"

"Mumphf," he said, almost asleep.

"It was when I saw you striding down the street wearing cowboy clothes—hat, boots, and everything. And then—"

"Karma, go to sleep. We have to call the travel agent early in the morning and put your name on the cruise ticket."

"You did say that you wanted someone who was crazy about you from the very beginning. And I was."

He kissed her cheek. "Remind me to call the ranch in the morning. I want to make sure we can use that extra room in the pool house for your office."

"Paulette and I will set things up so that I only have to come to Miami Beach every few weeks. I can handle my half of Rent-a-Yenta by phone and e-mail and computer."

"Good, because I'll miss you so much when you're gone."

Karma slid her hand into his. "You know, Slade, I think this is the best match I ever made as a matchmaker."

"It's the *only* match you ever made."

"That's what I mean."

"Good night, dearest." He pulled her closer so that they spooned together, her back to his front.

"And to think that I found a guy without springing for artificial nipples," murmured Karma.

Slade stirred, his breath fluttering warm against her neck. "What did you say?"

"Nothing important. Good night."

It was the strangest thing, but as Karma drifted into sleep, she saw Aunt Sophie floating between the ceiling and the porthole beside the bed.

"Ha!" Sophie said, which was how Karma knew that it was really her aunt. "This may be the best match *you* ever made, but it was the hardest match *I* ever made. You kept screwing things up."

"He was a client. I needed clients. I didn't think it was right to want him for myself."

"How do you think I got your Uncle Nate?"

"You mean—?"

"I was supposed to find him a wife. I found him one, all right—me. And by the way, Leah Rothstein is perfect for him."

"From your mouth to God's ears," Karma said.

"I'll make sure of that. In the meantime, Karma, take good care of your cowboy."

"Everything worked out okay in the end," Karma murmured, her eyelids growing heavier.

"That's right, *bubbeleh*," and Aunt Sophie smiled benignly and blew her a kiss before disappearing into a beam of moonlight.

Karma Melisande O'Connor
and
Slade Norton Braddock
joyfully request your presence
at the celebration of
their marriage vows
June 14, 2003
on the beach at the
Blue Moon Apartments
Miami Beach, Florida
Come barefoot!

Get FREE BOOKS and a FREE GIFT when you play the...

LAS VEGAS
GAME

Just scratch off the gold box with a coin. Then check below to see the gifts you get!

YES! I have scratched off the gold Box. Please send me my **2 FREE BOOKS** and **gift for which I qualify**. I understand that I am under no obligation to purchase any books as explained on the back of this card.

311 HDL DUYR   111 HDL DUY7

FIRST NAME	LAST NAME

ADDRESS

APT.#	CITY

STATE/PROV.   ZIP/POSTAL CODE

(H-D-05/03)

7	7	7	Worth TWO FREE BOOKS plus a BONUS Mystery Gift!
🍒	🍒	🍒	Worth TWO FREE BOOKS!
🔔	🔔	♣	TRY AGAIN!

Offer limited to one per household and not valid to current Harlequin Duets™ subscribers. All orders subject to approval.

Pamela Browning

A Real-Thing Fling

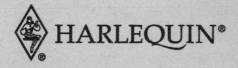

HARLEQUIN®

TORONTO • NEW YORK • LONDON
AMSTERDAM • PARIS • SYDNEY • HAMBURG
STOCKHOLM • ATHENS • TOKYO • MILAN • MADRID
PRAGUE • WARSAW • BUDAPEST • AUCKLAND

This book is dedicated to my fellow Frog Princesses
from Palm Beach High School—Lynne, Sheila,
Carole, Bette Anne and Charlene. Even though I
missed our Frog Festival reunion this year because
I was working on this book, I was there in spirit!
(Ribbit!)

1

Memo to Self: Get this wedding over with and fly home to Boston before freakin' family drives me out of my skull. Mom wailing that the wedding should not be held on beach. Dad full of himself; merry Irishman kind of thing. My sister Isis couldn't find her luggage or youngest stepson for a while (what's new?). Sister Karma also seems to have lost something—her mind. What else could explain marrying cowboy and moving to isolated ranch on edge of Everglades? Other sister, Mary Beth, spending the year in Israel, so not here. Something to do with her rabbinical duties. Lucky Mary Beth....

AZURE O'CONNOR TUCKED her PalmPilot into her purse and tried not to look jaded as the saffron-robed officiant who was uniting Karma and her beloved Slade in marriage began to ramble on about the glories of love. There was, Azure firmly believed, no such thing as love.

There was infatuation. There was lust. There was—

There was her uncle Nate, seventy-five years old or more, gazing soulfully into the eyes of the former Leah Rothstein, a woman of indeterminate age and with more than a passing acquaintance with cosmetic surgery. They had eloped a couple of months ago after his full recovery from a heart attack and were said to be blissfully happy.

Azure turned her head away, unwilling to witness any more bliss than necessary on this occasion.

"...and you may kiss the bride." The man in the saffron robe stepped back and beamed at the bride and groom.

Barefoot, flowers entwined in her bouncy curls, Karma turned to Slade, her eyes glowing, and Slade gathered her into his arms. Tenderly, joyfully, happily, they kissed. Tentatively at first, then with gusto.

Azure felt herself sinking deeper and deeper into the sand of Miami Beach on her stiletto heels. She had not taken off her shoes like most of the other guests. She agreed with her outspoken mother—a beach wedding wasn't the way to go. It involved smelly seaweed heaped everywhere, and curious uninvited gawkers, and it offended her sense of order with the chairs for guests scattered here and there, a flute player on one side, a lute player on the other, and bell ringers back on the promenade where you couldn't even see them. Plus a wind had sprung up and was teasing her hair out of its carefully twisted chignon to blow unwelcome tendrils across her cheeks. And dammit, there must be sand in her eyes. That's all it could be, right? She was not crying over this stupid wedding. She was *not*.

Azure blinked. To her horror, a tear rolled slowly down her cheek. Hoping that no one noticed this chink in her armor, she swiped at the tear angrily and repeated her mantra: *There is no such thing as love, there is no such thing as love, there is no such thing....*

When her vision cleared, she noticed a guy standing amid the knot of wedding guests on the other side of the makeshift aisle, which was marked by a row of conch shells. He was staring at her intently, a bemused expression on his face.

It was a familiar stare, that one. It held all the hope and

promise of a man's interest when he first sensed a possibility of—what? Getting laid, most likely. And she was definitely not a candidate.

Now the happy couple, arm in arm, faced their guests in front of an ocean turned the color of amethysts in the waning afternoon light. On cue, someone released a flock of birds—doves? sea gulls?—from a wicker basket, and they swirled toward the sunset, their wings afire with iridescent pink light. Karma kissed her new husband on the cheek, and he wrapped her in his arms and kissed her, too.

Azure closed her eyes against the sight of their happiness. *There's no such thing as love, there's—*

Her cousin Paulette stirred beside her. "That's so romantic, isn't it, Azure? I mean, I've never seen Karma look so great. She even looks smaller, don't you think?"

Leave it to Paulette to deliver a backhanded compliment! Anyway, Karma wasn't big. She was tall. And beautiful, especially to Slade, which was kind of touching when you thought about it.

Trying *not* to think about it, Azure turned to follow the other wedding guests down the aisle in the bridal couple's wake. The aforenoticed man, who was a tall, sandy-haired specimen with shoulders out to here, edged those shoulders toward her. He had, Azure noticed unwillingly, an appealingly crooked grin, which was exactly what you'd expect from a Lust Puppy like him.

Adroitly maneuvering so that Paulette's body was between them, Azure flicked a speck of sand off her tailored charcoal-gray gabardine suit, which now was beginning to seem like a questionable choice for this freewheeling wedding. The doves savoring their freedom overhead must have thought so, too, because one of them dropped a little wedding present—splat!—right onto her left lapel, where it sat quivering.

Great, thought Azure. *Karma gets married, and I get pooped on.*

Well, it could have easily been her getting married this month, if her fiancé, Charming Paco, had not absconded with a pair of boobs that just so happened to be attached to one of Azure's best friends. She supposed that it was better to know that Charming Paco was unfaithful now rather than waiting until after the wedding. At least that's what she'd been desperately reassuring herself for the past six months. But after a lifetime of kissing frogs in hopes that one of them would turn into a prince, she had been majorly disillusioned over the Paco defection.

Lust Puppy was so tall that he could see her over the heads of the other guests between them. He was still trying to catch her eye, she would swear to it.

Relentlessly broadcasting the message that she wasn't interested in what he had to offer, Azure pressed on through the crush of wedding guests heading toward the reception at the Blue Moon Apartments a half a block or so away.

She planned to spend as little time as possible making nice with family and friends. She could hardly wait to repair to Paulette's tiny apartment, also at the Blue Moon, and sleep off the jet lag she had accumulated on last week's trip back from London.

WOULDN'T YOU KNOW THAT KARMA would choose sitar music for her reception? You couldn't dance to it, at least not in the conventional way. You couldn't sing along with it. Maybe sitar music was an agreeable complement to making love, but that was a moot point as far as Azure was concerned. Making love was not on her agenda for the foreseeable future. Charming Paco had soured her on men, maybe for the rest of her life.

The Blue Moon was an art deco monstrosity built in the 1940s, and its roof garden was decorated for the occasion with potted palms and, as things progressed, equally potted people. Under the winking stars of a darkening twilit sky, Azure had dutifully kissed Karma on the cheek in a sisterly manner and shaken her new brother-in-law's hand formally in a subdued but friendly way. She had edged away from the conversation in which her mother was explaining to a fascinated and wide-eyed Goldy, the desk clerk/mother hen at the Blue Moon, that her occupation was creating cakes modeled after parts of the human anatomy. She'd murmured something polite to her father's latest conquest, a moneyed widow whom he'd met while he was teaching ballroom dancing on a Caribbean cruise ship. She'd listened to her grandmother's lengthy account of her latest visit to her chiropractor. Then she'd checked her cell phone in case there were any messages, conscientiously entered Karma and Slade's new address in her PalmPilot before she forgot, and unsuccessfully tried to remove the bird poop from her lapel with seltzer.

"Azure, Mom wants to see you," said a voice behind her, and Azure pivoted to face her sister Isis, who as Karma's lone attendant was wearing an outfit that seemed to be made of opaque blue cobwebs cunningly draped to cover the essentials. Close behind Isis was an elderly friend of their grandmother, who appeared to be in distress. It didn't take Azure long to find out why.

"I seem to have broken the buckle on my shoe. Barefoot is okay for you young people, but for me? No way," said Mrs. Hockleburg, wrinkling her forehead and knitting her brow.

Azure felt sorry for the woman, who had driven Grandma Rose all the way from Connecticut for the wedding. "Would you like me to take a look at it?" she asked politely.

Isis, looking happy to be off the hook, said, "I'll go find Mom," before rushing off.

Mrs. Hockleburg slowly eased her considerable bulk onto a chair. Azure sat down beside her as the woman slipped off the shoe. It took only a few seconds of studying the buckle to find out what was wrong. "It's okay. Look, the prong has slipped sideways. All I need to do is move it over, see?"

As Azure handed the shoe back to Mrs. Hockleburg, she saw the tall man who had been staring at her at the wedding regarding her with interest. Not wanting to encourage him, she focused her attention on helping Mrs. Hockleburg with her shoe and was therefore trapped when her mother pounced.

"Now, Azure, I hate it that our planes leave so early in the morning! I thought maybe we could get together for brunch, but all of us—Isis and the kids and her husband and me—have to be at the airport so long before boarding! Security, you know. Promise you'll drop by Sedona to see me next time you fly to Flagstaff."

"I promise, Mom. It won't be for a few months, though." Her mother, who had changed her name from Lois to Saguaro, like the cactus, after her divorce from Azure's father, patted her on the arm. "Whenever, whatever. And when you come, I'll make your favorite bulgur-and-goat-cheese casserole."

Azure didn't have the heart to tell her mother that bulgur and goat cheese had never been her favorite casserole. And, like her three sisters, she wasn't a vegetarian anymore, which her mother also didn't know.

"I'm going to bug out of this reception, Mom. I'll call you at your hotel before you leave in the morning, okay?"

"Okay, sweetie." Her mom hugged her before descending on Mrs. Hockleburg.

Azure moved restlessly toward the door and away from a barechested waiter who was bearing down on her with some kind of macrobiotic hors d'oeuvre. She stopped once to comfort a stray moppet who was crying because she had dropped her cracker on the floor. Azure plucked a cracker off the waiter's tray for the kid and packed her over to her parents, whose attention had been temporarily diverted from their offspring by Eamon O'Connor's demonstration of a ballroom dance step with his merry widow friend. The sitar player had stopped momentarily and was watching with the others, though his expression was more disapproving than not.

When the dance demo was over, Azure hugged her father, said goodbye to the widow, and refused her father's request that she accompany them to Key West for a few days. "You'd like the Keys," Dad said, but Azure doubted it.

Sleep beckoned, and pleasantly after this rooftop reception, which, though the view of the ocean and Miami Beach was stunning, had turned into a real ordeal. Sleep, however, wasn't the only thing beckoning. So was Paulette, who was wearing one of her most aggressive smiles as she accosted Azure slightly short of the escape route. That smile put Azure in mind of a set of shark's teeth she had once seen at the Smithsonian in Washington, D.C.

"Azure, darling," Paulette caroled, reminding her how much she hated her own name. And since when had Paulette ever called her darling, jealous as she was of Azure and her sisters, who had taken perverse pleasure in making Paulette's life a living hell back in their old Connecticut neighborhood? It had been easy to drive Paulette up the wall in those days, unfettered as the four O'Connor sisters had been after their parents, reformed hippies, had summarily snatched them from their early life on the commune and set them down in suburbia.

"Azure, darling," Paulette repeated as if for effect. "Azure, this is my client Mr.—" Paulette began, which was when Azure realized that it was Lust Puppy, the same sandy-haired fellow who had stared at her on the beach.

"Lee," the man interjected smoothly, his twinkling gaze resting on Azure's mouth before moving to her throat and even lower. Azure had the sudden and irrelevant notion that he was picturing her in a teddy or even less. Which was ridiculous because she didn't even own a teddy and furthermore never intended to.

She forced a grin and shuffled off to the right like a veteran vaudeville player. "Got to go grab some sleep! Jet-lagged from trip! Nice to meet you! 'Bye!" was what she blurted; at least that's what she thought she said. A path appeared through the crowd, a miraculous welcome path to the door, and she fled. At that moment, another miracle: An instant wall of people rose up between her and Paulette and Mr. Lee, and Azure made it through the door to the inside hall without being stopped.

She executed a quick beeline down the stairs to Paulette's apartment, where, as her cousin's house guest, she occupied the fold-out couch. She soon fell asleep to the sound of chatter and laughter from the party overhead. She couldn't hear the sitar music, but maybe that was just as well.

Memo to Self on morning after wedding: I'm never getting married. Major inconvenience for everyone else in family. Hate Miami Beach. Hot and humid and buggy. Can't wait to get back to Boston traffic jams where I can get high on fossil fuel fumes on way to office and work out at gym on way home. Hitting gym as soon as I arrive at airport. Didn't work out while in London and can feel abs flapping against ribs. Also, butt jiggles. Horrified to feel it yesterday when walking back to Blue Moon from wedding.

AZURE STUCK HER PALMPILOT back under her pillow and stretched in an attempt to wake herself all the way up. Paulette was making way too much noise in the kitchen, slamming doors, crumpling paper, running the disposal.

"Azure?" Her cousin came to the kitchen door, a pink sleep mask pushed up over her hair, which was colored Outrageous Raspberry to coordinate with her dress for yesterday's wedding. "I'm so glad you're an early riser. I knew we'd get along great."

Azure wasn't so sure, and she would have liked to point out to Paulette that she wouldn't have been an early riser if Paulette hadn't been making enough noise to wake a zombie.

"I've made coffee," Paulette said. "Come and have a cup. And then if you'd like, you can take my car and drive to Haulover Beach. It won't be as crowded as the beach here, and I won't need the car today anyway since I'm going to be going over the Rent-a-Yenta books."

Translation: Paulette wanted her out of the apartment. Getting out on her own sounded like a great idea, though.

"Mmm, okay, I'd like that," Azure said, going into the

kitchen and helping herself from the Mr. Coffee. Out of politeness she added, ''Why don't you go with me?''

Paulette waved her hand around, indicating too much to do. ''Busy,'' she said. ''Want me to fix you a scrambled egg or something?''

''Not necessary,'' Azure said after she gulped her usual breakfast of two stress vitamins.

Paulette downed the last dregs from her cup and wandered off in the direction of the crowded bedroom where she'd wedged a desk into a corner for working at home. ''Car keys on the table beside the door. The beach is south on—what's the name of that road? Hmm, I don't recall. Just follow the signs to Haulover Beach. You'll find it.''

Azure needed no more urging. After a quick goodbye phone call to her mother and her sister during which Isis's terminally cute youngest stepson recited a long and boring poem that he had written about a sand crab encounter on the beach, Azure folded up the couch bed and dug her swimsuit out of her suitcase. In less than half an hour, she was speeding south in Paulette's yellow Volkswagen bug, which was no more her style than, say, sitar music.

Boy, she reflected on the way, would she be glad to leave this place tomorrow and get back to Boston and her tidy little apartment, her conservative gray Camry sedan, and all her classical CDs. Plus, no one called her Azure there. They called her A.J., a truncated version of her given name, which, due to the folly of her parents, was Azure Jonquille. She'd been rebelling against it—and them—most of her life.

At Haulover Beach she jockeyed the bug into a slot in the parking lot, followed the tunnel under the road, and emerged into sunlight. The sight of the glassy ocean, the scent of brine wafting on the breeze, the wheeling of gulls overhead, were all so exhilarating that she didn't mind the trudge down the beach to a deserted area where she could bask in peace. She staked her claim on a few square feet of sand, slathered on a handful of suntan lotion, plopped down on her stomach, and pulled the baseball hat loaned to her by Paulette over her face, after which she promptly fell into a doze.

Azure was awakened by the laughter of people who were involved in setting up a volleyball net. She didn't look. She didn't have to. She already knew that they were placing the net much too close, and if she ignored them, maybe they'd move it. But they didn't. They went on talking and laughing, and when they started to play a game, the sand began to fly and she knew she'd have to vacate.

She eased over onto her back and pushed her hat back from her face. Aghast at what she saw, she blinked, sure that her eyes weren't focusing correctly. The volleyball game was proceeding full speed ahead, but every participant, male and female, was completely nude. Embarrassingly nude. Upsettingly and floppingly and wigglingly nude, and she wanted out of there.

That Paulette! Azure never should have trusted her. Not only was her cousin annoying in the extreme, but she clearly had an ax to grind, maybe because she resented all those jokes the O'Connors had played on her when they were kids. All the same, Azure would give Paulette a piece of her mind. She would—

Her attention was drawn to a handsome male specimen who was now sauntering out of the ocean. Openmouthed, she couldn't help but admire his physique, his deeply bronzed skin, his muscular structure. While she gawked, he stopped beside her blanket, showering droplets of water on her skin that, just from looking at him, had reached sizzling temperature. "C'mon," he said easily. "They need a couple more players."

Oh, no! She knew this guy. She hadn't recognized him at first because—well, the obvious answer was that he was stark naked. But his hair was slicked back and darker from swimming, and here on the beach he seemed even taller than he had yesterday. Also, she couldn't help but notice a sexy gap between his top two front teeth, and that those teeth were the whitest of whites. This was the guy who had kept trying to fix an eye-lock on her at the wedding, the guy Paulette had introduced her to in the moments before she fled the reception. Lust Puppy.

Speechless though she was, Azure knew she couldn't go on sitting with her eyes on a level with—well! From somewhere in the back of her mind emerged the thought that she did crave symmetry in all things in her life, and she did have to say this for the guy—he was symmetrical, all right. Two eyes, gray with silvery sparkles, already noted yesterday. Two ears, nicely formed, ditto. One thing she definitely had not had access to before was the tattoo slightly south of his navel. It looked like—it definitely was—a frog.

Warning herself not to get any further interested in this Mr. Lee's anatomy, she scrambled to her feet. He seemed to interpret this as assent to his suggestion and immediately grabbed her hand, propelling her toward the game.

"But I—I—" She objected to his appropriating her without her permission, though even as she offered it, she knew her objection was not as strenuous as it probably should have been.

"Watch out!" someone shouted. The volleyball was flying through the air with a pretty good chance of bonking her on the head, so thinking concussion, Azure warded it off in self-defense. It was what anyone would have done under the circumstances, but people clapped and cheered as if she'd joined the game.

Approval didn't seem so bad after the last couple of days spent fielding her family's tart questions about her love life, her work life, and her lack of hobbies—none of which she had answered to their satisfaction. But still. These people weren't wearing clothes!

"Don't you want to relax a bit more?" The guy who got her into this was staring down at her from his six-foot-plus height, laugh lines crinkling around those remarkable eyes that were both humorous and wry.

Translation: He thought she should shed her swimsuit, a staid and respectable flowery-print job. As if she would! Her mushy abs and jiggly butt were uppermost in her mind.

"Actually I've got to go," she blurted, marching with determination back toward her blanket where she gathered up her things, telling herself she'd better keep an eye on this man yet not look at him.

"Go where?" he asked, planting himself and his froggy tattoo and all his other considerable attributes directly in front of her.

"Um—" she started to say, thinking fast. She had the absurd idea that he didn't have to worry about jiggling, but when he shifted his weight from one foot to the other, she discerned that she'd been wrong about that. She felt a blush beginning below her jawline and moving upward.

"We could meet for a drink later," he suggested, layering on the charm, which was a mistake. She distrusted charm after her experience with the faithless Paco.

She drew herself up to her full five-foot-seven height. "I don't think so, Mr. Lee."

"Lee's my first name, not my last," he said, his words

interrupted by a beach-grooming machine that made a lot of noise and flung sand in their faces. It was a perfect opportunity to flee, which she did, noting too late the sign that she hadn't spotted as she arrived: Warning! Nude Sunbathing Ahead.

There are all kinds of fruitcakes around here, she thought to herself as she jammed the baseball cap on her head and charged toward the parking lot. Oh, she'd known from the beginning that there'd be a whole slew of oddballs at Karma's wedding. Thus this Lee character. Thus her present annoyance. Thus her murderous thoughts aimed directly at Paulette.

In fact, Azure was spitting fire by the time she cornered Paulette back at the apartment. Paulette, however, had a phone wedged against her shoulder and waved Azure away as she continued the conversation with an unknown client.

"She has one of those diseases that makes all her hair fall out. Her brother's a tattoo artist and he's tattooed all these little black scrolls all over her head." A pause while Paulette rolled her eyes. "No, it doesn't look like barbed wire. Scrolls, I said, and she's very attractive." Another pause. "Sure, Client Number 1799 loves to pull weeds. I'm sure she'll be happy to help you in your garden. I'll give you her phone number," and Paulette reeled it off, finally hanging up. "Whew," she said, heading toward the bathroom. "What some people will endure to get spousally enhanced."

Azure followed hard on her heels. "How could you send me to a nude beach?" she sputtered. "People playing volleyball with no clothes on, and—"

Paulette picked up a bottle of Evian water and began spraying it on her face. "It was a nude beach?"

"Oh, it was nude, all right. Nude boobs. Nude stomachs. Nude—"

Paulette stopped spraying and frowned. "Stop, I get the picture. Hmm, did you meet anyone?"

"Only that Lee fellow, and I wasn't too thrilled to see him there, particularly since he was stark naked. And speaking of tattoos, he had one. Right below his navel."

"I see. Or rather, I didn't see, which is probably all to the good. So how should I know that was a nude beach? I've never had time to go there myself." Paulette was maddeningly nonchalant. She set the Evian bottle down among the jumble of cosmetics on the vanity and, looking completely self-absorbed, pulled a few pixielike tendrils of hair to the front of her ears.

Slightly mollified, Azure sank down on a chair outside the bathroom door. "You didn't send me there to get back at me? For all the things my sisters and I used to do to you as kids?"

Paulette eyed her warily. "No, that's not why I sent you there. Anyway, I thought we'd forgotten about all that," she said pointedly.

"Well," Azure began, not sure what she was going to say.

"I hope you're not seriously thinking of telling me to put my tongue on the metal flagpole again when the temperature is only a few degrees above zero. If you are, look outside. It doesn't get down to zero here in South Florida. For which I thank my lucky stars." Paulette sauntered to her desk and began ticking numbers off on a notepad, clearly finished with the subject.

"Um, your tongue on the flagpole—did it hurt much?" Azure had always wanted to know, and truth be told, she had always felt some regret for that caper, which had earned her and her sisters a major restriction for a month when they were kids.

Paulette glanced up at her from beneath raised brows. "Hell, yes, it hurt, but not until I tried to pull it *off* the flagpole and left a significant amount of skin behind. Afterward I thought I shouldn't have been so dumb." Paulette was smiling, sort of.

"I'm sorry, Paulette. For that and the other things." Like the catfood sandwich they'd traded to her for lunch. And the time before their school's fall placement tests when they'd told the naive Paulette that smoking a cigarette would make her smarter, and Paulette had been caught puffing away in the basement by her horrified parents. Paulette hadn't ratted on them, though. She'd taken the punishment, which as Azure recalled involved raking leaves for days and days, maybe even weeks.

"Well, all is forgiven," Paulette said. "I might as well confess, though, that I've run a dating match on you. I'd like to set up a date for you with a certain client. Client Number 1851, to be exact."

Azure stood up. "No dates, Paulette. Charming Paco saw to it that I won't want to kiss any more frogs for a long time. Anyway, I'm leaving tomorrow."

"Oh, not so fast." Paulette scrabbled among the papers on her desk and produced a phone message. "This is from someone named Harry. He wants you to call him right away."

"Harry Wixler is my boss," Azure said, wondering why he would be calling her here. Then she recalled that she'd switched off her cell phone at the beach so she wouldn't be disturbed. Her time away from Wixler Consultants was supposed to be vacation time.

"Harry said he wants you to stay in Miami Beach for a

while. I'll be away at a seminar on small business practices in Orlando for most of this week, but you're welcome to keep bunking here if you like.''

Azure didn't like, but she thought she'd better find out what was going on, so she retreated to a lounge chair on the balcony and dialed Harry's office number on her phone. Out on the small triangle of rippling blue ocean that she could see from where she sat, she watched a large freighter ply its way north, trailing a creamy white wake. A scattering of pleasure boats caught her eye closer in, and she had the reluctant thought that there could be worse places to linger on the orders of her boss.

''Got a little problem, A.J.,'' Harry Wixler told her when he answered. ''A prospective client is vacationing in Miami Beach on his yacht, and I want you to wait there until he calls. He requires major sucking up to if we're to acquire his account.''

Azure rolled her eyes. ''I hate sucking up.''

''The man needs a business plan, and you're the one to do it.''

''What kind of business plan?''

''He sold his dotcom company for millions before dotcoms went bust, he's weary of traveling around on his yacht, and he's eager to begin a new venture, franchising his new idea. It's called Grassy Creek. He didn't tell me everything, but it's something to do with grass. In fact—''

''Grass? What kind of grass?'' she asked sharply.

''Not that kind,'' Harry said with a deep chuckle. ''You young whippersnappers always jump to conclusions.''

''I am not,'' Azure said tartly, ''a young whippersnapper. I am a thirty-year-old woman—''

''That's young. When you're my age, anyway. And you're one of the best consultants on board, especially with franchise start-ups. This client plans to franchise a bunch of health food stores specializing in wheat grass, if you can believe it. I've given him your phone number, so stay put until he calls. And rent yourself a set of wheels so you can pick him up and take him to dinner. Got that?''

''Got it,'' Azure said wearily.

''Good. Report back to me after you talk with him.''

''Hey, Harry,'' Azure said before he could get away. ''What's this guy's name?''

''Santori,'' Harry said. ''Goodbye, A.J. Don't get sunburned.''

''Wait a minute, Harry! Are you talking about Leonardo Santori?'' She'd read plenty about the man, who when still a college student had established an online mail-order music company and sold it for gazillions a few years ago.

''Right. He's the Dot.Musix fellow, a real brainy guy and a hell of an entrepreneur. He's kind of reclusive, always stayed out of the public eye. I don't need to tell you that it would mean a healthier bottom line for our struggling company if we snagged his business.''

''Why don't I call him?''

''Like I said, he's a very private person. He lives on a yacht, it would be best if he could talk to you at his convenience, not yours, and you're not to bother him.'' With that, Harry was gone.

At least Harry wanted her to rent a car. That would give her the freedom to get around on her own without having to depend on Paulette.

Who was at this moment standing at the sliding glass door and more or less smirking at her over a glass of papaya juice. ''*Now* will you go out on a date with my client?''

''Your client, Harry's client, the world's exploding with

clients,'' Azure muttered, getting up and leaning over the balcony railing. A huge bougainvillea vine trailed up a wall trellis, its branches overhanging the balcony, and Azure brushed them aside for a better view.

''I only tried to match you up with him because you seemed kind of down this morning.''

''I was nowhere nearly as depressed as I am at this very moment,'' Azure said darkly. She heaved a sigh. ''I'd better call and reserve a rental car. Phone book?''

''On the kitchen counter.''

Paulette trailed her into the kitchen and noisily scavenged in the freezer for more ice while Azure made arrangements for a car to be delivered to her at the Blue Moon.

''Problems, problems,'' Azure said after she hung up. ''The rental car company can't deliver the car until tomorrow afternoon, and who knows when I'll hear from the mysterious Mr. Santori? What am I going to do here for the next few days? The rest of the family left early this morning, I don't know anyone except you and Uncle Nate, who keeps wanting me to join in a pinochle game with him and his cronies, and—''

''You can help me at Rent-a-Yenta,'' Paulette said hopefully. ''I'll be leaving late tomorrow for the seminar I told you about, and I'm incredibly overworked because I'm signing up clients right and left.''

''So set one of them up with this guy you keep pushing at me.''

''I might have to. If *you're* not interested, there's always Mandi.'' Mandi lived upstairs, and Azure had met her before the wedding. Mandi had been wearing a black halter top with a short white see-through skirt, showing off her new diamond nose stud to anyone who would pay attention.

"Better Mandi Eye Candy than me."

"Like I said, I need help in the office. I'm way behind because of Karma's wedding."

"No way," said Azure. But then she thought of Paulette standing forlornly with her tongue frozen to that metal flagpole all those years ago while she and Karma, Isis and Mary Beth laughed their heads off. Guilt was a great motivator.

"On second thought," Azure said unwillingly, "maybe I could do some filing for you in the morning."

On third thought, she wished she hadn't offered. But Paulette did look pleased, you had to say that for her. And what could it hurt?

2

LEE SANTORI POISED ON THE bow of his 141-foot yacht, *Samoa*, soaking up the early-morning sunshine. The temperature at seven in the morning was a simmering 82 degrees, typical for summer in South Florida. Across the bay rose the city of Miami, its glass towers golden with the reflection of the rising sun. Behind him was Fisher Island, home base for many wealthy people, including more than a handful of bona fide celebrities. Beyond that lay the wide Atlantic Ocean, which Lee had crossed on the *Samoa* only two weeks ago on his way back to the U.S. from Portugal, where he had spent the winter.

He was glad to be back on this side of the Atlantic where he could elude the woman who had followed him around Europe uninvited, turning up everywhere he did for months. She had claimed to be a princess in exile, victim of some Balkan upheaval or other, though Lee had doubted the truth of the story. Anyway, he was free of her now, and all he could think about was the woman who had captured his interest at the wedding. Azure, her name was. Azure: the shade of the bay at sunset, the brilliance of the sky at noon, the color of his favorite crayon when he was a kid.

Lee breathed deeply before plunging from the yacht in a swift dive that took him beneath the cool sparkling waters of Biscayne Bay, and as he surfaced he felt encompassed in a bubble of blue, azure blue. Which only reminded him

A Real-Thing Fling

again that things had gone wrong, terribly wrong, between him and the one woman in the world who interested him at the moment.

The mellow muted sound of the ship's bell rang out over the water as he surfaced.

"Breakfast," Fleck called from above, where he was hanging over the railing and watching.

Lee swam with sure, powerful strokes to the yacht's swim platform and hoisted himself up the ladder. He still couldn't believe his good fortune at owning a yacht like this one, nor could he feel completely comfortable with the life of leisure he led after selling his company. Well, he was going to take care of that. He had plans, big ones. Not as big as his plans had been for Dot.Musix, but big nonetheless.

His friend Slade's childhood buddy Fleck, built as squat as a fireplug, grinned at him from under his mop of unkempt hair, frizzy and bleached almost white from the sun. "It looks like shrimp and cheese grits and scrambled eggs again for breakfast, pal."

Lee shook the water from his hair. It sprayed across the highly polished teak deck in a shimmer of fine droplets. He dried himself off with the towel handed to him by a silent steward. "I've ordered shrimp and grits to be served every morning, Fleck, as long as you're in residence."

"You know how to treat a guest, that's for sure." Fleck slapped him on the back as they made their way to a round breakfast table set up in the open air near the stern railing. The table was covered with a pristine white cloth, set with china embossed with the name of the yacht, and embellished by a colorful bird-of-paradise centerpiece, one of a series of fresh flower arrangements ferried out to their anchorage every morning by a local florist engaged for that purpose. Beside Lee's plate was propped yet another letter from his father, and he avoided looking at it. He hadn't spoken to his father for some time, nor did he intend to.

He turned his attention back to Fleck. "I was thinking," Lee said slowly, "that you might want to come on board permanently."

"As part of your security detail?"

"No, I've got the guys who man the boat for that if I need them, and I'm traveling incognito here in Miami. I want you to become my point man for my new venture."

Fleck appeared startled. "Yeah? You mean this new health food chain you told me about?"

"That's what I mean, all right." Lee drained his glass of fresh-squeezed orange juice and dug into the scrambled eggs, which were invariably cooked exactly the way he liked them—soft, but not runny.

"Hey, dude, what makes you want to take a chance on a reprobate surfer like me?"

"My old roommate Slade Braddock, for one thing. He assures me that you're through goofing off. He also told me what a fantastic job you did managing that resort over on the west coast until it went bankrupt."

Fleck's face clouded for a moment. "I got unsettled by that whole sad situation, and after the place went belly-up, I thought to myself, 'Hey, why not take up surfing again like when I was a kid?' That's why I set out to hang ten at every worthwhile beach in the world, and I made it to almost all of them before the accident."

Slade had told Lee all about Fleck's motorcycle accident, which had laid the guy up for a month and consumed most of his savings. Fleck's present poverty was why Lee had offered the hospitality of the *Samoa* for as long as Fleck needed it so that he could attend Slade's wedding. They'd gotten to know each other, he and Fleck, and Lee was impressed by Fleck's insight and by his down-to-earth business sense, which the veneer of his casual lifestyle and careless speech did not entirely hide.

"Are you ready to settle down?" Lee asked bluntly.

"Yep, I sure am."

"I'm planning to open my first Grassy Creek outlet right here in Miami. I want you to be in on this from the get-go, Fleck."

Fleck looked surprised. "Kewl," he said. "You got all your ducks in a row yet?"

"I'm staying on in Miami Beach so I can meet with an executive of a seed company, who will be flying in from South America for a business presentation on Wednesday. I've also rented a storefront in a strip mall on the west side of Miami, and the workmen are remodeling to my specs. Maybe we could go take a look one of these days."

"Any time, good buddy. And you are a good buddy. I mean it."

It always embarrassed Lee to be thanked effusively, and he wasn't about to give Fleck that opportunity. "Think nothing of it," he said, pushing his chair back.

"You going somewhere?"

"I've got to go onshore and check on the construction crew, but first I want to talk to Paulette from Rent-a-Yenta. She messed me up big time with Azure O'Connor."

"Azure O'Connor? Karma's uptight sister?"

"Maybe she's not so uptight. The last place I saw her was at a nude beach."

Fleck appeared nonplussed. "You don't say! And were there noteworthy girl parts under that business suit she wore to her sister's wedding?"

"I wasn't in a position to know."

"Uh, what position were you in, exactly, Lee?" Fleck asked with a sly grin.

"Let's just say that I didn't uncover any new territory, and this Paulette person has pretty much ensured that I probably won't ever get the chance. Azure thinks I'm below the level of pond scum at the moment."

"Care to spill the story?"

"I signed up with Paulette's dating service, Rent-a-Yenta, on Slade's advice. Ever since I sold my business, I've got women chasing me all over the globe. When women smell money, their whole manner changes. It's awful."

Fleck guffawed. "Too-oo bad! I wish I had your problem. Anyway, how did you manage to sign up with Rent-a-Yenta without giving yourself away as a billionaire?"

"I did what I do when I want to preserve my privacy. I used the name Lee Sanders."

"Kewl." Fleck seemed impressed, though there was nothing to be impressed about. Using an alias wasn't fun, but it was a necessity, especially since he'd rather be anonymous than have his movements curtailed by a security detail.

Lee got serious, and fast. "Trouble is, Fleck, I don't meet many women that I have something in common with, and trying to get them to be honest about who they are and what they're about is impossible. I'm thirty-seven years old. I'm ready to settle down. A dating service? Well, why not?"

Fleck shrugged. "Makes sense, I guess."

"So I spotted Paulette Parham at the wedding sitting next to this ice-maiden type who was punching entries into her PalmPilot right up to the minute Slade and Karma started to repeat their vows. I'm thinking, 'You're one coldhearted lady if you can't take a few minutes to appreciate the wedding thing.' And then she puts the PalmPilot away, and the bride and groom are saying 'I do' back and forth, and I'm watching this cool customer standing all stony-faced and aloof when suddenly I see a tear—one tear—trickle down her cheek. I thought, 'The ice maiden melteth.'''

"Yeah? So?" Fleck helped himself to a fresh-baked croissant.

"So there's a real human being under that gray suit. And she noticed me watching her. She looked straight at me, and I could have sworn that something clicked between us in that brief moment." He didn't know how to describe the compassion he'd felt for her, the sense of a tragedy in her life. Nor did he think he wanted to explain the deep-down urge he felt to comfort and nurture her. He was sure Fleck wouldn't understand.

As if to underscore that point, Fleck said briskly, "Well, cut to how you happened to be at the nude beach with her."

Lee forced the vision of Azure's tearstained face to the nether regions of his consciousness. "I asked Paulette about her, and it turns out they're cousins. Azure is Karma O'Connor's sister. Paulette tried to get a conversation going between us at the wedding reception, but Azure left in a hurry. After that, I asked Paulette to set up a date between us for the next day, and she suggested that if I went to Haulover Beach, I might run into Azure in the morning—that is, if she could convince Azure to go. I went for it."

"Hmm, I would, too."

Lee decided not to explain his feelings of anticipation as he drove to the beach, or the vision he held in his mind of Azure's heart-shaped face, her voluptuous figure. "I thought Azure was into nudity when I got there and saw signs posted that warned of nudity past a certain point on the beach. It was early in the morning, not too many people around, so I went for a long swim in the ocean thinking it over.''

"What was to think about?" Fleck said with an expression of incredulity.

"Whether I wanted to stick around. And whether she'd take her clothes off.''

"And she didn't?" Fleck appeared to be hanging on every word.

"Nope. I tried to get her involved in a volleyball game, but that only made her angry.''

"So she left?"

"Ran up the beach lickety-split. Don't ask me why, but she's all I can think about.'' He could have added that he'd noticed her looking after a crying child at the reception and taking the time to repair the shoe of an elderly lady. She might be standoffish where he was concerned, but he had seen evidence of a good heart, and this, in a world where selfishness often seemed to be the rule, appealed to him as much as her spectacular beauty.

Fleck appeared to be mulling over what he had said. "Seems to me that if I were you, I'd avail myself of the awesome chicks who hang around the marina waiting for a glimpse of you, not chase after someone who wouldn't give me the time of day.''

"It's precisely because she doesn't want me that I want her. I enjoy the chase, Fleck, and I get high on the challenge. If Azure would let her hair loose from that tight knot she wears, and if she'd wear something more suited to the climate, she'd be a knockout, a real babe.''

"Sheesh," Fleck said, shaking his head as he scooped up a forkful of food. "You sound like a man who knows what he wants.''

Lee pushed his chair away from the table. "At the moment, unfortunately, I'm a man who can't have it. Sure you don't want to change your mind and go ashore?"

"Thanks, but I'm going to have some more of these shrimp and grits. They don't make 'em any better than this."

As if by magic, a waiter appeared out of nowhere and began to spoon more of the delicacy onto Fleck's plate. Lee, after draining the last of his orange juice, grabbed the letter from his father and headed below decks to his stateroom where he surprised Miguel, one of the newly hired stewards, delivering a bag of laundry. Lee relieved Miguel of the laundry and went inside his stateroom, where he tossed his father's letter on a pile of similarly unopened ones and chucked the laundry bag on the bed. It wasn't until after Lee showered that he discovered that the laundry bag was full of Fleck's clothes, not his, and that his own dresser drawers were empty of tropical-weight garments.

He donned a sleeveless blue, softly faded tank top and shorts from the pile of clean laundry in the bag, smiling at the way he looked in the cabin's full-length mirror. Well, the Miami Beach lifestyle was famously casual, and this outfit would keep him cool.

Or "kewl," as Fleck would say.

THE *SAMOA*'S LAUNCH DELIVERED Lee to the marina where, wearing mirrored sunglasses and a nondescript canvas hat pulled down low over his face, he slunk past the waiting groupies while they all sidled up to Mario, his handsome first mate, who was sworn to secrecy and adept at diversionary tactics. It was around ten o'clock in the morning when Lee bounded up the steps to the Rent-a-Yenta office two at a time.

The door hung open, and he intended to barge in and demand an explanation from Paulette for the beach debacle. Then he realized with a start that the woman who was sitting in the alcove on the far side of the room was not Paulette Parham. It was Azure, and his video, the one that was supposed to introduce him to other clients of the dating service, was playing on the television set.

He strolled through the open door. "Ahem," he said and was rewarded when Azure's head turned abruptly. He leaned casually against the wall, stuffing his hands down in the pockets of Fleck's rumpled Hawaiian shorts.

"You!" she said, leaping up from the chair.

Judging from the go-eat-worms look she gave him, she was singularly unimpressed. Well, Fleck's clothes weren't much in the way of sartorial splendor, he thought wryly, and the old running shoes he wore had holes in the toes.

"I thought you were going to say that you didn't recognize me with my clothes on," he quipped, deciding that humor was the way to save face in this situation.

"No smart remarks, please. I recognize you, that's for sure. What are you doing here?"

"I'm a Rent-a-Yenta client. Enjoying my video?"

Her chin shot up. "I'm only interested in the lead-in information, and not because of any personal interest. I'm helping Paulette with some filing." Two spots of color had appeared on her cheekbones, or was that sunburn?

"Oh? And you decided to file my video in the VCR, right? With the button in the on position?"

She punched the button to turn off the machine, which spat out the video cassette. The cassette got tossed unceremoniously onto Paulette's desk, and Azure pointedly moved to a table in the middle of the floor and began collating papers that were stacked on it in little piles, balancing on high heels that showed off the slim curves of her ankles.

"Do you have real business here, or are you only being annoying?" she asked, looking flustered. Today her hair was arranged in a neat French braid, and she wore a dark skirt and a crisply starched white long-sleeved blouse— hardly the attire for a South Florida morning in June.

"I stopped by to see Paulette." He slowly eased himself off the wall and moved closer.

"Paulette has gone down to the corner deli to buy bagels."

"Wonderful. You wouldn't happen to know if she's getting poppyseed? They're my favorite."

Paulette breezed into the office, did a double-take when she saw Lee, and slowly set a white paper bag down on the table.

"As it happens, I didn't buy poppyseed. I bought sundried tomato and pumpernickel, plus two kinds of cream cheese. You're welcome to join us for bagels and coffee, Lee. I've invited Uncle Nate, too."

Azure cocked her head to one side. "Wait a minute, Paulette, I'm trying to get rid of this guy."

"Why not sit down and enjoy a cup of coffee and a bagel with him?"

"I've suddenly remembered that I have sightseeing to do," Azure said. She grabbed her handbag off a chair. "Give my love to Uncle Nate. Catch you later, Paulette."

Before Lee could react, Azure had all but run out of the office and was clattering down the stairs in those ridiculously high heels.

"Uh-oh," said Paulette. "Looks like she's not interested in being a match for you. On the other hand, I have a client who lives in my building. Mandi is her name. I bet she'd jump at the chance.''

"I met her at the wedding. Sorry, but she isn't my type.''

"You think Azure is your type? Well, unless you're into workaholics with no sense of humor and little idea of how to have a good time, I'm afraid you're wrong.''

"We'll see about that,'' Lee said, and then he was off at a fast lope.

He'd find Azure, wherever she'd gone. He'd always enjoyed a challenge, and Azure O'Connor certainly was one.

AZURE, WISHING BELATEDLY that she'd brought clothes more suited to the tropics, limped in her painfully tight high heels along a row of shops on Lincoln Mall. Jewelry shops, shoe stores, dress boutiques—all offering expensive wares in the most outlandishly bright colors. She could afford to buy those things, but the practical side of her balked at buying stuff that she'd never wear again.

The weather was hot, even for June, and beads of perspiration formed on her forehead. The stifling, humid air seemed to congeal in her unsuitable clothes, making them so soggy that they clung to her skin. Seeking relief, she ducked under a store awning and yanked an envelope out of her purse, then stood fanning herself with it as she scoped out a skimpy yellow crochet bikini on a mannequin in the shop window. She would wear something like that if she lost a few pounds, but she'd nix the yellow snakeskin boots shown with it, ditto the feather boa.

"That suit would look great on you,'' said a familiar voice, and she whirled to see Lee standing with his hands casually balanced on the waistband of his shorts. He was smiling in a way that was beginning to be all too familiar.

"Why do you keep turning up wherever I go?''

"I'd like to get to know you better." His eyes were sparkling with flashes of silver, and they were frankly admiring.

His admiration unnerved her. She swung around and out into the stream of pedestrian traffic on the sidewalk. "There's no point in furthering our acquaintance."

He followed her and, to her chagrin, kept talking. "Why not? We might be meant for each other."

Damn these shoes, anyway. They hobbled her so that she couldn't walk fast enough to leave him behind. "I'm not in the market for a relationship. I'm going home to Boston in a few days."

"So? What could be wrong with exploring Miami Beach with me for a while?"

She gave him a quick once-over. "Don't be funny."

"I'm serious. Believe me, I'm more serious than I've been in my whole life." He seemed sincere, that was the odd thing about this exchange. But it might be wise to let him know that he was distinctly not her type. Cruel? Maybe. But in the long run, the kindest way to handle bozos like this one was to be honest.

She drew a deep, steadying breath, noting, before she gave him a piece of her mind, that there was a firm set to his jaw. It bespoke determination, but she plunged ahead anyway. "I don't hang out with beach bums."

"Beach—?" He looked taken aback, then reached up and ruefully felt the stubble on his jaw. "Usually I shave. This morning, I was in a hurry."

She felt a prickle of self-doubt. The man had charm, but maybe that was the problem. After Paco, she distrusted personable men who thought they had the world by the tail, a description that fit Lust Puppy to a tee.

"Well, while you're hurrying, hurry in another direction.

Preferably away from me.'' She kept walking, expecting to see, out of the corners of her eyes, a crestfallen look. But instead, he seemed to be holding back laughter. This confused her, but then, none of this was going by the book.

"I don't have to hurry," Lee said. "We beach bums more or less take it easy." He'd never been mistaken for a beach bum before, and this put a new spin on things. Since he didn't want Azure to know his true identity, her mistake could work in his favor, for a while anyway. Later, after she had a chance to get to know him, he'd tell her the truth.

Azure's cell phone began to ring, and she dug it out of the depths of her purse. "Yes? This is she. Yes, you're supposed to deliver the car today. To the Blue Moon Apartments. Right."

She listened for a moment before clicking the phone off. "That's all I need," she said, tossing her head so that a few tendrils of pale hair, fine as spun glass, worked their way loose at the nape of her neck. "The rental company is short on personnel today and can't deliver the car."

"Are you sure there's one available?" he asked. He had the sudden urge to brush aside those downy hairs and kiss the skin beneath to find out if she tasted as delectable as she looked.

She started to walk again, but there was less swing to her step than earlier. "Oh, they've got a car, they just can't deliver it, and their office is way over on the mainland. I'd better flag down a cab." She saw one across the street and began to make tracks toward it, nearly getting run down by a bus in the process. Before she could reach it, the cab sprinted away in a cloud of exhaust fumes.

"Maybe I'll try some other rental car phone numbers," she muttered, stopping near a bench shaded by a potted palm. There was an unoccupied phone kiosk there, and she hefted the phone book up and began to thumb through the yellow pages.

Lee looked up the street in hopes of spotting another cab. Nothing. He looked down the street. Still nothing. If he offered to drive Azure to the rental car place he might blow his cover; he had rented a new Mercedes 450 for transportation while he was here in Miami Beach, and beach bums didn't drive luxury cars. Beach bums drove decrepit old convertibles. Beach bums drove...

...a car like Fleck's. A rag-top Mustang, candy-apple red and sporting a few dings and a missing bumper.

Lee cleared his throat. "I can drive you to the mainland to pick up your car. No problem."

Azure looked up from the phone book, a skeptical look on her face. "You can?"

"It so happens that I have business in Miami later. You're welcome to ride along." More than welcome, he added to himself as he studied the fetching curve of her cheek, the sensuous droop of her lower lip as she considered his offer.

"You're sure you don't mind?"

"No, of course not."

"Well—" She dropped the phone book back into its slot. "I have no choice. I need to be ready to meet a client."

"I'll go get my car and stop by the Blue Moon to pick you up."

Azure heaved a sigh and pushed the wisps on her neck back into place. In that moment, Lee would have liked nothing so much as watching that glorious hair tumble free from its pins or whatever she used to fasten it.

"Well, it's kind of you, and it would simplify things."

Would it ever, Lee thought. "Like I said, no problem."

She afforded him a curt nod. "All right. Can you stop by for me in an hour?"

"Sure."

"Fine. I'll see you then." She shoved her cell phone down into her purse and took off toward the Blue Moon while Lee started back toward the marina where the *Samoa*'s launch was waiting.

He grinned to himself as he thought about the fun he was going to have.

THE BLUE MOON APARTMENTS were located smack dab in the middle of South Beach, Miami Beach's much-touted art deco district. Azure couldn't figure out for the life of her how anyone could have thought it a good idea to construct such a building and then paint it pink, aqua, and lavender. A blue bas-relief half-moon hung over the door. Azure had, so far, wisely managed to keep her mouth shut about the place's overall garishness.

Goldy, general factotum at the Blue Moon, was hunched behind her desk studying tea leaves in a cup when Azure walked into the lobby.

"The tea leaves say I'm going to travel over water," Goldy said, adjusting the folds of her voluminous flower-print caftan. "They tell me I'm going to attend some sort of ceremonial occasion."

"You just did," Azure reminded her. "You went to Karma's wedding."

"This upcoming ceremonial event is something different. It doesn't have the same vibes. I wonder if it has anything to do with the spaceship."

Azure, confounded by this statement, stopped in her tracks. "What spaceship?"

"Well, I don't know *what* spaceship. Some guy on a

radio talk show said that an alien spaceship could come right here to Miami Beach, and there are followers of some Elvis-worshiping religion who plan to meet it when it arrives. A few of them stopped by the other day and wanted to know if I had rooms to rent for the occasion.''

Azure had grown friendly with Goldy in the few days that she had been staying with Paulette. It was hard not to like Goldy, though she had her oddball moments.

In order to call a halt to this line of conversation, Azure adopted her most businesslike attitude. ''Goldy, I'm expecting my ride to the rental car place to arrive shortly. Will you call me when he gets here?''

''Oh, sure.'' Goldy peered down at the tea leaves again. ''The man—the one who's going to pick you up?—lives on water. This whole reading has a lot to do with water.''

Azure laughed. ''Water is right. The guy's a beach bum. But he has a car, and I need a ride.''

''A beach bum? That would mean surfing?''

''Something like that.''

Goldy's eyes grew round behind her glasses. ''Maybe he's like the guys on *Baywatch*. You know, on television. Old reruns, of course.''

''Chances are he's not as hunky. Anyway, didn't you meet somebody named Lee at the wedding?''

Goldy pursed her lips and thought for a moment. ''I don't remember him.'' At that point, the phone rang, and Goldy answered it.

Azure, feeling fortunate not to participate in any further discussion that touched on Elvis worshipers or spaceships, hurried upstairs to Paulette's apartment. She took a quick shower, her second of the day. After she had dried off, she dug through her suitcase searching for clothes that would be more comfortable in this climate than the ones she'd been wearing. She came up with a navy-and-white blouse and a pair of navy slacks, part wool, that she'd worn in London. They'd be too warm to wear here.

In desperation, she flipped through the hangers in Paulette's closet, looking for something cool to borrow. Paulette had a lot of snazzy outfits, but they were all too short except for a pair of white pedal pushers that hit Azure a little high on the knee. No matter, they and the navy-and-white blouse would have to do. Fortunately she and Paulette wore the same shoe size, and she slipped her feet into a pair of sandals that wouldn't hurt her poor pinched toes.

Maybe, she thought unhappily as she stared at her reflection in the mirror, she should have gone on a shopping spree after all.

FLECK'S TRUSTY MUSTANG had its shortcomings. Like the ripped seat cover that leaked stuffing. Like the door handle on the passenger side that kept coming off. Like a missing bumper.

But that was all fine with Lee, and Fleck was delighted to let him use it.

"You mean we're trading cars? You drive the Mustang and I drive the Mercedes?"

"We're trading identities, buddy," Lee told him as he studied himself critically in the mirror in his mahogany-paneled stateroom. "As of this moment, I'm the beach bum and you're the owner of this yacht."

Fleck howled with glee. "For how long?"

"Until I say so. Unless you object, that is."

"Hell, no! I'm Fleck Johnson, impersonating a billionaire and waiting for women to swarm over the sides of the *Samoa* and have their way with me."

"It's not all it's cracked up to be."

"You get your ya-yas your way, I'll get mine my way." He paused and gave Lee a critical once-over. "Hey, if you want to be a bum, you've got to wear your hair differently. Except for the clothes, you look like you walked right out of an exclusive tennis club."

Lee's brown hair had been whipped blond by wind and sunshine on the long days he'd spent on the deck of the *Samoa*, but he knew the style wasn't quite right for the role he intended to play. He gave it an experimental flick with a comb. "You mean it should look like this?"

"Naw. Do you mind?" Fleck stood ready to wreak havoc on Lee's hairstyle.

Lee shook his head.

"Do it this way," Fleck said, churning his fingers around Lee's scalp so that the strands separated and stood on end. "And like this."

"Sheesh," Lee said. "I look—"

"Like a surfer guy. Chicks love the look."

"If that's so, why haven't you been the one they're swarming over the side of the boat to see?"

Fleck adopted an offended air. "We're talking about a different kind of woman, dude. The kind of women, see, who gravitate toward beach bums are kind of loose and free, and I do mean free. They aren't looking for a guy to support them. They're laid-back, like me."

"And the women who want guys like me are after my money, which is what I'd already figured out."

Fleck leaned back against the dresser, crossing his arms over his chest. "You're going to let Azure think you're poor?"

"Why not? It's a way to find out if she really likes me for myself."

Fleck cocked a skeptical brow. "From what you've said, she doesn't like you at all."

"You're right. Which means that I've got my work cut out for me." He gave his tank top a tug and stood back to admire the effect. His pectorals bulged under the jersey, thanks to regular workouts in the *Samoa*'s gym and vigorous massages from the live-aboard masseuse. His chest hair didn't look half light enough for a guy who was supposed to be surfing in the sun most of the time, but maybe Azure wouldn't notice.

He slipped his Rolex off his wrist. "Here," he said. "I can't wear this."

Fleck forked over his own ancient Timex. "You might have to gas up my car," he said in a cautionary tone. "I haven't checked lately."

"Will do. And take it easy on the women, Fleck."

Fleck laughed. "From what you say, I'd better hope the women take it easy on *me*."

Lee scooped up the car keys from the dresser. As he headed for the launch, Fleck was still chuckling.

3

To: A.OConnor@wixler.org
From: D.Colangelo@wixler.org
Subject: paco and tiffany

hi, a.j., we miss you at the office. guess what—i spotted charming paco alone and looking down in the dumps in the coffee shop today. i decided i was still speaking to him after all and asked him where tiffany was. he said he didn't know. you don't suppose she's gone somewhere and had a breast reduction, do you? you know she always talked about it. it would serve c.p. right, wouldn't it luv,
dor

Reply to: D.Colangelo@wixler.org
From: A.Oconnor@wixler.org
Subject: Re: paco and itffany
Dorrie:

I am as tired of thinking about Tiffany's breasts as I am of kissing frogs and hoping they will turn into princes! I never want to hear about her breasts again! And yes, it would serve Paco right if Tiff came back from wherever as a 30AA instead of her normal 40DD. But miracles like that don't happen in real life.

Speaking of real life, I'm stuck here in M.B. until my client calls, and I haven't heard Word One from him yet. More later.
A.J.

AZURE, EAGER TO CONCLUDE the whole car rental chore, waited impatiently by the curb outside the Blue Moon and tried to ignore the man with a slick black pompadour who was parading a chicken on a leash down the sidewalk. The chicken was being trailed by two teenagers, who were jokingly threatening to kidnap it for voodoo purposes. At least Azure *thought* they were joking, but then again, maybe not. According to Goldy, all kinds of weird things went on in South Florida, with santería, a specialized type of voodoo originating with the large Cuban population, being only one of them.

As she was contemplating calling the SPCA or whoever was in charge of the well-being of animals, Goldy came lumbering out of the Blue Moon, and as she did, a bright red convertible with its top down roared around the corner and screeched to a stop in front of them.

Lee jumped over the door on the driver's side. "At your service, ma'am. Beach taxi service. Our motto: We go where you go."

"Um, Goldy, this is Lee. Lee, Goldy."

Goldy batted thin eyelashes. "Nice to meet you. Hmm, I don't get the feeling that you're one of those Elvis worshipers. You live in a big place on the water, don't you?"

"How do you know where I live?"

She smiled mysteriously. "It was in the tea leaves. Nice to meet you, Lee, but I'd better get back to my desk. Stop by to see me sometime and I'll read the tarot cards for you. It could be most enlightening." With a little backhanded flutter of her plump fingers, she hurried back inside, her caftan flapping in the breeze.

Lee stared after her. "What was that all about?"

How to explain Goldy? Azure didn't have a clue. "She's

into New Age,'' she said, less than eager to expand.

"What in the world is an Elvis worshiper?"

Azure sighed. "Evidently there's a local cult, and that's all I know about it. Shall we go? I don't want to lose the reservation on the rental car by not showing up on time."

Lee courteously opened the car door, and she slid in. As he continued around to the driver's side, Azure knew she had no business looking down on the only mode of transportation that had presented itself, but it was plain to see that the vehicle was falling apart. The paint was peeling, revealing that in a previous incarnation the car had been green. Various parts were missing, and from the sound of it, the muffler needed to be replaced. If there was a muffler, that is.

When Lee climbed in beside her, he immediately threw the car into reverse, which was apparently not the way he wanted to go because he then slammed on the brakes hard enough to make her sunglasses fall into her lap.

"Sorry," he said as she jammed the glasses back onto her face. "Stick shift. Sometimes it actually does stick."

"Right."

Without too much additional effort, Lee managed to insert the car into the stream of traffic. "So," he said, keeping his eyes on the road, "how long will you be in town?"

Not that this was any of his business, but he *was* going out of his way to do this favor for her.

"I'm not sure," she said.

"You said you have a client here," he prompted, turning and treating her to the megawattage of his super-white smile.

"That's right," she said, deciding to offer no more information. He was entirely too cocky, and he was entirely too good-looking. Plus he had a lot of charm, which set off a cacophony of alarms in her head. It would be better if the man were mud-fence ugly; at least then she wouldn't be thinking about the way his hands, strong and sinewy, gripped the steering wheel. Or about the muscles of his thigh tensing and letting go as he worked the accelerator and the clutch.

She forced herself to glance away, to gaze out the window at the sign heralding their approach to the causeway, at anything. She hadn't been so rattled about any man in a long time. Since before Paco, and even he had never had quite this unnerving effect on her. Right now all she could think about was that tattoo of a frog below Lee's navel.

"You—you could tell me what kind of work you do," she said in desperation, stumbling over the words at first and then letting them out all in a rush.

He blinked his gaze in her direction for a moment, then back to the traffic. "A little of this, a little of that," he said vaguely. "Whatever it takes." He figured it was what Fleck would have said. Until now, he hadn't considered that pretending to be someone else would tend to limit self-disclosure.

"Look," he said, gesturing toward the water as they approached the bridge across the water. "Parasailing."

This distracted her for a while as she watched someone riding the breezes on a brightly colored parasail, and they were halfway across the long causeway before she spoke.

"I really appreciate what you're doing for me," she said. "Really." In profile, her delicate bone structure was even more evident.

He cranked up his nerve and made a move. "Enough to see me again?"

She swiveled her head around and frowned. "Are you serious? I already told you that I'm not interested."

"Would you go for a simple flirtation?"

"There's no such thing. Flirtations tend to get complicated."

He shot her a sidelong glance. "They don't have to. You're visiting Miami Beach, I'm visiting, why don't we hang for a while? Go out for a few drinks, maybe a bite to eat, and then we both head back to our respective homes, richer for the experience." He hadn't known he could wax so eloquent about a few simple dates, and he thought he had outdone himself until she let out a sigh of exasperation.

"Lee, I don't want a boy toy for a night or two. And I thought you lived here."

He had to think fast. "I'm only in Miami Beach for a while, like you."

"How did you happen to come to the wedding? Do you know my sister?" When she pivoted to look at him, the wind from the open convertible caught her bangs and mussed them attractively.

He shook his head. "I'm a friend of Slade's."

This produced a flare of interest. "Oh? And how did you two meet? You don't seem much alike."

He had to make a split-second decision as to whether he wanted to use the Lee Santori connection or the Fleck connection. He finally decided on the Lee Santori one. "Slade and I were college roommates," he said. It was true. They'd met in their freshman year at Florida State.

"What did you do after college?" she asked. For a moment, he thought she was sincerely interested, but judging from the way she was inspecting her manicure, he could scratch that notion. Still, he had to admit that it was better to attempt a conversation than to sit in awkward silence. "I worked," he told her.

"Worked?"

"Corporately," he said in a tone that invited no further discussion.

"But hanging out at the beach is more fun? Especially the nude beach?" She slanted a questioning look at him out of the corners of her eyes.

"I don't—" he started to say, thinking better of it immediately.

She called him on it. "You expect me to believe that you don't go there regularly? That it was a fluke when you happened to stroll stark naked out of the Atlantic Ocean and invited me to join a volleyball game?"

"Haulover Beach is not my usual habitat," Lee said desperately, wondering why he was inexorably attracted to someone who didn't give a flying fig that he found her fascinating. It was time for a quick review of what appealed to him: Her eyes, so breathtakingly blue. Her carefully hidden vulnerability, which he liked to think most people never saw.

"If you don't walk around nude with some frequency, why on earth would you have a tattoo in a place that is normally hidden by your clothes?" she asked in what he pegged as a sudden and welcomely whimsical mood. It was a new side of her personality, and he had to hand it to her— it caught him by surprise.

He laughed. He couldn't help it. "My tattoo is not for the admiring glances of everybody," he said. "It's for the inspection of people who get to know me in a more intimate way."

"Meaning people you have sex with," Azure said in a

slightly world-weary tone which earned her a sharp look from Lee.

"It's a conversation piece," he said. "It distracts them."

"Do they need to be distracted? And from what?"

He hesitated, unsure if this line of conversation was something he wanted to continue, but in the end he reminded himself that this might be the only chance he would have to get to know Azure and for her to get to know him well enough to see him again. And there were so many things that he couldn't be honest about as long as he kept up the pretense of being a beach bum. When he *could* be honest, he *should*.

"Sometimes," he said carefully, "when two people decide to become intimate, it can be awkward. Daunting. If there's something silly and inconsequential to talk about while you're warming up—"

"Warming up?" Azure looked askance.

"Proceeding through the preliminaries," he amended. "If you can joke or make light of things, then it makes it easier."

She turned a wide-eyed gaze upon him. "Oh, how considerate. What a swell guy you are! I am sure that the women of your acquaintance must grovel in gratitude when the fact of your thoughtfulness in getting a tattoo gets through to them."

It took him a moment to realize that she was being facetious.

"Okay, okay. I was only telling you one of the reasons I got the tattoo. You want to know the other one?"

She shrugged. "Sure."

"I was shanghaied into it on a night when I was drunk out of my mind. Two buddies hauled me into a tattoo parlor and next thing I knew, I was walking out of there stone cold sober with a patch of skin that felt like it was on fire.''

"I can believe the part about being drunk. But did it really hurt?''

"It was awful. I'll never get another one.''

"Why a frog?''

He shrugged. "Why *not* a frog? It's not like I knew what I was doing.''

"I once thought about getting a tattoo,'' she said thoughtfully, surprising him completely.

"You? No way.''

"Yes, way. Fortunately, I didn't go through with it.''

"Why not?''

This caught her up short. She had no intention of confessing what a fool she had been over Paco, nor did she feel like telling anyone that his nagging her to get a tattoo to match his, which was on the high inside of his thigh, had resulted in her making an appointment that she didn't keep after she found Paco having wild crazy sex in her bathtub with Tiffany, one of her closest friends. The only good thing you could say about that episode is that it had been easy to wash away all evidence of their betrayal with a long-handled brush and a few squirts of bathroom cleaner. Even so, Azure had showered at the health club for two whole weeks before she felt like using her own tub again.

She cleared her throat. "Let's just say that I didn't get the tattoo because circumstances changed.''

Thinking about taking showers at the health club reminded Azure that she needed to find a place to work out. She'd already asked Paulette, who appeared to stay devastatingly slim by snacking on Snickers bars, but the question about where to find the nearest gym had drawn a blank.

"Jim?" Paulette had answered vaguely. "Is he one of my clients?"

Azure turned to Lee, who certainly looked fit with those biceps bulging and those pecs positively pulsing in rhythm to the music from the radio. Or was that only her imagination? Maybe so.

"I don't suppose you know a gym near the Blue Moon where they welcome guests," she ventured, making herself look elsewhere besides those pecs.

"I usually—" he began, catching himself before he mentioned the gym aboard the *Samoa.* "I've noticed one two blocks up from Ocean Boulevard on Marco Polo Street."

Azure fished her PalmPilot out of its special pocket in her purse and entered the information.

"Do you take that everywhere?" he asked.

"Of course. Also my cell phone."

"I noticed," he said dryly.

"You have a problem with that?"

He thought about when he had been building his business, when he couldn't afford to be out of touch for even five minutes a day, juggling more tasks than most people would have found humanly possible. "No," he said quietly. "I don't."

She pulled a scrap of paper out of her pocket. "I'd better check the directions to the rental car place."

"Let me see," he said. She handed the paper over, and he studied the map she'd drawn on it. He was fairly familiar with Miami geography because he'd traveled there frequently on business. "I can find it," he said.

"I hope I'm not taking you out of your way."

"Nope," he said. After he dropped Azure off to pick up the car, he planned to check on the progress of the contractor who was renovating the store in the strip mall where he was scheduled to open the first Grassy Creek outlet. The painters were supposed to be working this week.

"There!" she said. "I see a sign for the car rental company. See? The arrow to our right?"

Sure enough, there was a directional sign pointing down a short side road and a larger sign on top of the rental company's office. It hadn't taken as long as he'd thought it would to get there, and he wasn't any closer to seeing Azure again than he'd been before they started out.

He pulled into the parking lot in front of the car rental office. "How about dinner tonight?" he said, figuring he might as well shoot for the moon.

"I told you," she said, "I'm not interested."

"In anyone?" Maybe there was someone else.

"In you. You know the old saying, you have to kiss a lot of frogs before you find your prince? I'm sick and tired of kissing frogs." Too late, she realized what she had said; too late, she remembered the nature of Lee's tattoo.

There was a silence that lasted a jot too long, and then Lee began to laugh. "I wasn't asking you to kiss it," he said. "I wasn't even suggesting that you see each other again."

"That is *quite* enough," she said tightly. She got out and slammed the car door, which is when its inside handle fell off. "Azure, wait," Lee called after her rapidly retreating figure, but she ignored him and continued into the car company's office building.

Lee swore softly to himself at his inability to refrain from smart remarks and slid over to the passenger seat where he set about reaffixing the handle to the door, which would have been easier if he'd had a screwdriver. A check in the trunk for a nonexistent tool kit made him realize that he'd have to do the job without tools.

He concentrated on getting the handle back on, thinking that he'd have a chance to make amends with Azure when she came out of the building, but the next time he looked up, he spotted her driving out of the lot in a jazzy white convertible. He watched helplessly as the car tooled around the corner toward the interstate.

Barring unforeseen bad luck, he thought that Fleck's Mustang might be fast enough to catch her.

LEE WAS SPEEDING ALONG the expressway keeping a sharp eye out for Azure in her white convertible when he spotted a farm truck with its bed full of cucumbers up ahead as it swerved into the next lane. He slammed on his brakes and saw that the truck had been trying to avoid running over an armadillo that was taking its time meandering across the six-lane highway.

To Lee's horror, the truck began to fishtail back and forth across all three lanes going north, and cukes began to rain down in front of the car in the passing lane, which happened to be—a white convertible?

Lee slammed on his brakes at almost the exact moment that Azure did. He managed to control his vehicle, but hers skidded on a mess of cucumber pulp and traversed all three lanes before blowing a tire and slamming down the bank toward a drainage ditch.

Lee, unable to slow his car in time to pull over at the site, shot an incredulous and horrified look back over his shoulder. He couldn't tell if Azure was okay. All he saw before he turned the steering wheel sharply toward the exit lane was a corner of the white car, which appeared, from what he could tell, to have avoided sliding into the ditch.

He drove as fast as was prudent across the overpass at the end of the exit and back onto the highway, and even though he passed the place where Azure had gone off the road after only a minute or so, a guardrail in the median prevented him from crossing over. That meant that he had to go all the way to the *next* exit and double back to where Azure was now, thankfully, pacing in the weeds at the edge of the ditch and haranguing someone on her cell phone. Her hair had fallen mostly out of its plait, and the wind was whipping strands of it across her face. Her shirt had come untucked. But she seemed unharmed.

She clicked the phone off and whirled around when he drove up beside her, and he was pleased that she looked relieved to see him. He jumped out of the Mustang.

"Are you all right?" he asked immediately, striding through the dusty weeds and oozy bits of cucumber until he stopped in front of her.

"I—I'm a little shaken up, but otherwise I'm fine," she said, staring at him as if he were the Skunk Ape, a relative of Bigfoot who was reputed to hang out in the nearby Everglades.

"I saw you go off the road. I was afraid you'd ended up in there." He jerked his head sideways in the direction of the ditch.

Azure fought to control her trembling. "It's a wonder I didn't," she said. She'd had to struggle to retain control of the unfamiliar car, and her vision had been obscured on the highway by all the cucumbers falling off that truck, and when her tire had blown, it had been with a loud *bang!* that scared her half to death.

"We'd better try to get you out of here," Lee said, assessing the damage to the car. Except for the blown tire, it appeared to be all right.

"Keys?"

She handed them to him and, while she bound her hair

up into a ponytail, he used the remote opener to pop the trunk. When he pried open the compartment where the spare tire was supposed to be, it was empty.

Azure felt a rush of consternation when she realized that there was no spare. "Oh, great," she said. "And I just talked to the people at the car place. They can't bring me another car, they can only arrange for a tow truck." Not only that, but something floating in the canal looked a lot more like an alligator than a log, the surrounding saw grass seemed like an ideal habitat for water moccasins, and the cars whizzing past on the expressway were cutting too close for comfort.

"I'll take you back to the Blue Moon," Lee said soothingly. "As long as you don't mind going with me on my errand."

She didn't hesitate. She went over to the Mustang, opened the door, and climbed inside before she realized that she was sitting on the door handle.

She eased herself up and extracted it from underneath her, treating Lee to a suspicious look. "What this means is that I can get into your car, but I can't get out, right?"

"Right," Lee said, flashing her a lightning grin, and in that moment she decided that maybe this wasn't so bad. Sitting in her disabled rental car waiting for the car people to rescue her from an alligator that might amble out of the canal at any minute would have been much, much worse.

LEE DROVE THE MUSTANG OFF the busy, bright street into the parking lot of a low-hunkering strip mall anchored by a convenience store plastered with signs touting the Florida lottery.

"Are we going to buy lottery tickets or what?" Azure asked.

"Or what." He continued driving around to the back of the building.

"What's happening?"

"I need to see a guy," Lee said, but he saw right away that the painter's truck wasn't parked there, so maybe the crew had gone to lunch. It didn't really matter, since Lee could check on the crew's progress anyway. This prototype version of the first Grassy Creek store had been configured according to his specifications, and he didn't want to show the place to Fleck until all equipment was in place.

"This won't take long," he told Azure, who was looking curious. "You're welcome to come in if you like."

"I might as well. It's too hot to sit in the car," she said. He liked the way her ponytail accentuated her piquant features and bounced when she moved.

Lee had a key to the building, and he let them into the store, which was blessedly air-conditioned. The back part was neat, with paint cans and various equipment sitting around in boxes, but he wasn't pleased with the way the front part of the store looked. Scaffolding had been placed along one wall, and the painters had finished painting the top of the wall mauve but had not started on the bottom. Someone had evidently intended to paint the opposite wall, which was going to be in a darker green to fit in with the wheat grass theme, but whoever it was had opened the paint can and then gone off and left the brush sitting in the can.

Azure, hands on her hips, was looking around with a good deal of speculation. "This is where you work?"

"In a manner of speaking."

"And you only work when you feel like it?"

He kept forgetting his beach-bum fiction, which was getting to be a burden. "Yeah, I guess you could say that," he heard himself saying. He bent to remove the paintbrush from the can so he could close it up. The paint was already beginning to form a skin across the top, and there was no point in letting it go to waste. He might have plenty of money, but he hadn't accumulated it by being reckless with either dollars or resources.

She raised skeptical brows. ''You were supposed to report to work today, weren't you?'' she asked in a slightly accusing tone.

And he had thought she was beginning to lighten up. ''Not exactly,'' he said, hedging.

Her eyes gentled, her face lapsing into the softer expression he had noticed when she had helped the child and the elderly woman at the wedding. ''You took me to get the car instead of going to work, Lee. Right?''

''I wouldn't say that.'' He felt unsettled by her probing, and he wished she'd stop asking questions that he didn't want to answer.

''Well, then,'' she said, going over and perching on one of the steps of a nearby ladder. ''You go right ahead and start painting. I don't mind waiting.''

He felt his jaw slacken in surprise but made a quick recovery. ''I—''

''If the man you were supposed to talk with is your boss, and if you were going to tell him you weren't coming in today because of me, that makes me feel very guilty, Lee.'' She cocked her head to the side, and the movement made her even more appealing than she already was.

Lee looked down at the paintbrush in his hand and then he looked at the prepped wall. Judging from the time, which was a few minutes after noon, the painters might return in half an hour or so, which meant that the coast was clear for a while. He had enough time to figure his way out of this tangled web of deception that he'd been weaving—maybe.

He walked over to the nearest wall and slapped a green patch of paint on it. He liked the paint shade even better on the wall than in the can, he decided after he stepped back and looked at it.

"Shouldn't you put on coveralls or something? So paint won't get all over your clothes?"

Lee looked down and for some reason was surprised to see that he was wearing Fleck's clothes. He had an idea that Fleck wouldn't care if they were returned in less than pristine condition.

"I was only going to finish painting this one wall."

"Still. You don't want to ruin your clothes."

In order to keep up the charade, Lee went over to the corner and pulled on a pair of paint-spattered white coveralls from a pile that the painters had left.

"That's better," Azure said, and she smiled. She didn't look as prim when she smiled.

"Don't you want to walk down to the corner? Buy a magazine at the convenience store or something?" He thought she might be getting bored.

"I could get both of us something to drink. What would you like?"

"Whatever they've got." He pulled out his wallet, but she waved him away.

"I'll pay for it. Be back in a minute." She slid off the stool and headed out the front door.

He heaved a giant sigh after she was gone. Her absence gave him a chance to concentrate on what he hoped to accomplish with this new Grassy Creek venture.

Ever since he had first tasted wheat grass juice at a juice bar in Mexico, he had wanted to start his own franchise business. It wasn't that he believed all the claims about wheat grass juice—that it cured serious illnesses, that it helped acne, that it kept hair from graying. He didn't know if they were true or not.

It was more that he had discerned a market niche for small convenience-type stores where people could buy macrobiotic snacks-to-go. In the past year, he'd studied the market, he'd added eight other vegetable and fruit juice specialties and a bunch of easy-to-prepare snacks to his offerings, and he'd instituted a testing program in traditional health-food outlets.

Now he had arranged for the first store to open in a high-traffic-volume area of Miami, and if it was as much of a success as he expected it to be, he'd begin franchising, first in the U.S. and later, perhaps, worldwide. He'd know more about franchising once he heard from the consultant that Harry Wixler had recommended so highly.

He was taking stock of the placement of electrical outlets when Azure came back with two bottles of lemon iced tea.

She handed him one of the bottles. "I bought us each a lottery ticket. Pick one, you choose," she said, holding them out to him.

"How much were they?" He'd never bought a lottery ticket in his life.

"A dollar."

He pulled out his wallet again, but she waved him away. "I'm paying. I appreciate your rescuing me today."

"But—" He didn't feel right accepting a drink plus a lottery ticket.

"Here."

"I don't mind paying you."

"Don't be silly. Anyway, you might win."

She didn't seem as if she were going to back down, so

he decided that in the unlikely event that he did win, he'd give her all the money. He took one of the tickets, folded it, and tucked it carefully into his wallet.

She resumed her seat on the stool and watched while he twisted the cap off the iced tea.

"When is the lottery drawing?"

"On Saturday. Don't let me interfere with your work," she said. He shrugged and finished the iced tea. Then, because there didn't seem any way out of this for now, he started to paint again.

Azure watched him for a few minutes before speaking. "That looks like fun," she said.

"I wouldn't call it that," Lee replied. He wondered how he was going to get them out of here before the painters returned. Claim that he had a charley horse in his leg? Remember that he was supposed to be somewhere else? Neither of those seemed like viable options.

Azure hitched herself off the ladder. "I could help. I'm a good painter."

"Oh, I don't think—" he began, but before he could get the sentence out of his mouth, she had marched over to the corner and was donning a pair of coveralls.

"You don't think I'm a good painter? Think again. I painted houses during summer vacations when I was in college. I got paid by the job, not by the hour. I suppose you do, too? That's good, because I can help you get done sooner. Got a spare brush? Oh, I see one."

"Azure," he began, thinking he'd better set things straight because this pretense of his had gone too far.

She walked to a radio in the corner and switched it on. "I want to do *something*," she said over the music, which was loud and lively. Then she bent and dipped her brush in the paint, slapping it on the wall with a professionalism that put his meager effort to shame.

He liked it that Azure had a helpful side, but when he glanced at his watch, he realized that the painters—the real ones—would return in a matter of minutes if his calculations were correct. There was only one thing he could do, he figured, and that was to paint as fast as he could, the sooner to get them out of there.

Plus there was something about those coveralls and the way they curved around Azure's delectable derriere that made working beside her a pleasure.

Or correction: make that behind her.

4

YOU'VE GOT MAIL!
To: A_OConnor@wixler.org
From: D_Colangelo@wixler.org
Subject: tiffany

i've been trying to reach you on your cell but you don't answer. tiffany called me today and told me that she and paco are on the outs!!! :-) :-) :-)

so what are you up to? have you found any frogs to kiss? dorrie

---

"WHEN I WAS WORKING MY WAY through college," Azure said as she dipped the brush into the paint again, "I worked odd jobs. Painting, wallpapering, dog walking. Mowing lawns. House-sitting."

The music blaring from the radio seemed to have loosened them both up. "I've never sat on a house," Lee said conversationally. "Is it more comfortable than sitting on a handle from a car door?"

She caught the sly mote of humor in Lee's eyes. "Definitely, but let me tell you about baby-sitting. It's—"

"I've actually sat on a baby before. It was in a dark movie theater, and I was munching my popcorn as I moved down the row after the movie had started. I saw an empty seat, and I sat down. It wasn't until the mother yelped that

I realized that the seat wasn't really empty and that I was about to squash this kid in a baby carrier.'' He laughed. ''I thought the mother was going to kill me.''

Azure rolled her eyes. ''Did you do any harm to the kid?''

''No, the baby was sound asleep and the mother yelled before I sat. I felt so bad about the whole thing that I went and bought the mother and her other kid a couple of cartons of popcorn. The kid wanted to go home with me. He was so cute that I almost let him.''

''You like children?''

''Yeah, a lot. I noticed at the wedding how you took care of that little girl, by the way. I thought it was a nice thing to do.''

''She was crying,'' Azure said. ''Anyone would have helped.''

He wielded his brush vigorously, moving closer. ''No one took notice of her but you.''

''Someone would have seen to her eventually.''

''I thought she might be a member of your family.''

''No, there are no small girls in the family at present, only my sister Isis's young stepsons. You may have noticed them at the reception—they were the ones who were doing their best to take a dive off the roof. They're a handful. And then of course, my father had eyes only for his lady friend, who none of us had seen before, and my mother was holding forth telling about her job decorating cakes baked in the shape of sex organs, and—''

''Would you mind repeating that?'' Lee said, stopping work entirely and trying without success to wipe the incredulous expression off his face.

''I certainly would mind repeating that! I mean, wouldn't you? If she were your mother? It's bad enough that Mom changed her name and left my father for a new life in Sedona, Arizona.''

"Why'd she do that? If you don't mind my asking?"

She concentrated on her painting. "Why should I? Everyone in our family has been asking ever since it happened. She and Dad were active in the community—Mom chaired a community action committee, and Dad led a Boy Scout troop. All I can say is, I think Mom was bored. We kids had already flown the nest, so her leaving didn't inconvenience us, but my father was devastated."

"I can understand that," Lee said slowly.

"*Soooo*, Dad now teaches ballroom dancing on a cruise ship."

Lee appeared reflective as he climbed a ladder to cut the paint in at the ceiling. "Have you ever appreciated how interesting your family is?" he asked, looking down at her.

Azure began to lay off the last section of wall she'd finished. "Interesting? I've been fighting against their eccentricities all my life. Karma and her fruity-granola New Age lifestyle never made much sense to me, and Mary Beth, my sister who is the assistant rabbi, seems to think about nothing but religion. Isis is probably the most normal, but she lives way out in California, and when she was twenty-two, she married a man who already had a family, so none of us sees her much."

Lee thought about his own family and wished in that split second that it was more like hers. "You're lucky," he said with conviction. "You don't know how lucky, that's all."

"I'm lucky that none of them live in Boston near me," she retorted, laughing as she said it.

He concentrated on the delicate business of painting the top edge of the wall without getting paint on the ceiling.

"You and your sisters should be glad that your parents didn't try to force you all into a mold. They obviously didn't want you to be cookie-cutter images of each other. You were each allowed to develop in your own way, to be anything you wanted to be. That's a kind of gift, Azure."

She appeared thoughtful. "I suppose that's true, but I still remember that when I was a teenager, all I wanted to be was like everyone else. I didn't want to have a sister who in her spare time did nothing but study for her bat mitzvah, and I didn't want anyone to know that our family was vegetarian, which pretty much cut out having class-mates over for dinner. I certainly didn't want anyone to know that Karma kept a statue of Buddha in the room we shared and—horrors!—insisted on sleeping in the nude."

"Do you suppose she still does?" Lee asked with frank admiration.

"You'll have to ask Slade. Who knows?"

"It—um—isn't a family custom, I take it?"

"No!"

He climbed down from the ladder. "Just thought I'd ask."

"You're much too nosy."

"I'm interested in how other families work," he said. "Mine was nothing like yours."

"I would have thought," she said consideringly, "that they might be very much like mine."

Lee's father, a businessman with international interests, had valued a college education so highly that he hadn't spoken to his only son for a full two years after Lee quit college to start Dot.Musix. He'd felt abandoned by his dad at a time when, brimming over with excitement for his new venture, he could have used some family support. He didn't want to get into all that at present, so all he said was, "My father is a dictator. He doesn't care much for anyone who colors outside the lines.''

Azure caught a hint of something in his tone that made her look at him sharply. ''I'll venture a guess that you've colored outside the lines all your life,'' she said.

''You'd be right about that,'' he replied. ''I was a non-conformist from the word go.'' He could have added that he'd also captured first place in his school's science fair two years in a row and that he'd won awards for citizenship and lettered in swimming. Those were things that he seldom told anyone, and in this case, he didn't want to reveal too much.

Azure stopped to finish drinking the rest of the iced tea in the bottle, tossing it in a trash barrel when it was empty. ''I was supposed to be a nonconformist, considering that I had a pair of ex-hippies for parents, but I struggled to give the impression that I came from a quote-unquote normal family.''

He shot her a wry look. ''Well, if you ever want to start a support group for Adult Children of Dysfunctional Parents, give me a call.''

''I'm not so sure mine were dysfunctional. Peculiar is more like it, and I've been struggling to be different from them all my life.''

''And pretty successfully, too,'' Lee offered. ''You're so staid, so dignified.''

At the moment, with her hair pulled back into a ponytail, her feeling had become one of playfulness, and wearing sloppy painters' coveralls, Azure felt anything but dignified. She realized as soon as Lee spoke that she had actually been having fun as they performed this chore, and one part of her wanted him to know that. Another part of her wanted to hang on to her sedate image, but as she tapped the paint off the end of the brush into the paint can, the fun-loving part overwhelmed the dignified part and she felt a surge of an unfamiliar emotion that she identified as glee.

"I'll show you staid," she said as she straightened. "I'll show you dignified." And with that she reached out with her brush and very slowly and deliberately painted a green stripe right down Lee's back.

He froze in surprise, and for a moment she thought she had made him angry. But then he turned, and with the light of hilarity springing into his eyes, he dipped his paintbrush and, as slowly and deliberately as she had done, he painted a wide stripe down her front.

She took this in for a split second. Then, "Oooh," she said. "You don't look so good in green. I bet you'd look a whole lot better in mauve."

"Mauve?"

"Mauve," she said firmly. She walked to the other side of the room and pried the top off a can of mauve paint that had been opened and almost used up. A fresh paintbrush sat beside it, and she swirled the brush through the paint before setting off toward Lee at a dead run and slapping the paint across his chest. She couldn't help laughing at the stunned expression on his face as he looked down at the mauve paint, now dripping onto the floor.

"Oh, you think you're such a great painter, right? Here's great," and he ran his brush down one sleeve of her coveralls.

"Green is not my color," she said with mock hauteur. "I look a whole lot better in something brighter, cheerier."

"There's nothing brighter and cheerier than yellow," he said, reaching down and peering into a discarded can. "And there's just enough here to brighten you up quite a bit."

He swiped a bit of paint out of the bottom of the can and headed toward her.

Moving swiftly, he bent and wiped the paintbrush on her coveralls at knee level. While he was doing that, she took the opportunity to daub some mauve on the back of his neck.

He danced away to the beat of the music from the radio, putting his hand to the back of his neck and staring at it when it came away covered with paint. ''How dare you! When I couldn't defend myself!''

She couldn't help laughing at the way his eyes glittered with the light of revenge, and she ran around to the other side of the ladder. He followed, but she dodged him, keeping the ladder between them as a shield.

''I'll get you back,'' he warned. He looked around. ''There's a can of black paint over there. What do you say we open that one up?'' He was laughing as he said it, and she began to giggle.

''You look like a clown,'' she said.

''So do you. Or worse. Whose idea was this, anyway?''

Suddenly the music stopped. A voice boomed out from the doorway leading to the back room. ''That's what I would like to know,'' said the man who had entered and pulled the plug on the radio while they weren't looking. He was at least six foot two and had burly arms and a shaved head.

Azure dropped her brush with a clatter. Lee cleared his throat as he tried to figure out if he knew the guy. It wasn't Dave Edelson, the general contractor on the job, with whom he'd had dinner only a few nights ago. It wasn't the painting subcontractor, either, because he had met him once in Dave's office. Still, the man looked vaguely familiar.

''Who are you?'' he asked, stepping forward.

"I'm the one who should be asking questions. Who are *you* and what right do you have to be here?"

"He's only doing his job, and I'm helping," Azure said. She had a sudden horrified vision of being dragged down to the police station and having to call Harry Wixler to bail her out.

Lee shot her a look that she figured meant he wanted her to be quiet. She had no intention of doing so, but then Lee started to unzip his coveralls.

"You and I should step outside so I can explain," Lee said to the guy.

"You can explain right here," the man snarled. "You and your girlfriend with the green hair."

Azure felt her hair; sure enough, the back of her ponytail was damp, and her hand came away green.

By this time, Lee had divested himself of his coverall and was walking toward the bald man, looking conciliatory and putting on a friendly face. *Charm*, thought Azure. *He's got tons of it. Well, if his charm can get us out of this, who am I to criticize?*

"It's like this," Lee said, putting a hand on the man's shoulder and urging him toward the back door. The man didn't seem to like being urged anywhere, but Lee made himself look as nonthreatening as possible and continued to move the guy along.

Once they were outside, Lee breathed a sigh of relief and backed off. "I'm Lee Santori," he said. "I own this place."

"Yeah? And I'm president of the United States. Believe it?"

Lee suddenly recalled where he'd seen this man before, but he was interrupted before he could remind him.

The guy stuck his jaw out in an attitude of belligerence.

"Well, I don't believe you, either. What I've heard around town is that Lee Santori lives on a yacht out there in the bay. He doesn't run around in beat-up old cars," and here he jerked his head toward the Mustang, "or bring his girlfriend over here to vandalize the place for fun."

"I saw you in Dave Edelson's office last week," Lee said, dragging his wallet out and opening it to his driver's license. "That's me right there," he said, tapping the picture. "I *am* Lee Santori."

With distrust written all over his face, the guy peered closely at the picture, glancing dubiously up at Lee and back again. "That looks like you, all right." He narrowed his eyes suspiciously. "What's going on?"

Lee folded the wallet and stuffed it back in the pocket of his shorts. "A little fun and games," he said, winking at the guy. "This is how my girl gets her jollies. You know?"

This statement earned him a look of rank skepticism. "By painting each other?"

Lee shrugged, adopting a man-to-man stance. "Sure."

"You're really Lee Santori?"

"You saw the picture, man."

A long pause, and then the guy held out his hand. "I'm Jake Gruber. I work for Dave. I came to check on the painters because I thought they might be slacking off. Dave wants this job finished on time."

"I appreciate that," Lee said. He reached for his wallet again. "And I'd also appreciate it if you'd let us finish up here at our own speed and make sure the painters clean up any mess." He peeled a couple of hundred-dollar bills off the stack in his wallet and pressed them into Gruber's hand.

"Hey, that's not necessary," Gruber said, but he took the money anyway. Lee had noticed ever since he'd had money to spare that not many people turned it down when he tried to give it away.

"Now if you'll excuse us," Lee said, "we'll pick up where we left off."

"Kink-*y*," said Gruber with barely concealed admiration.

Lee gave him a cocky thumbs-up, and then he went back inside the building and locked the door behind him just to make sure that Gruber didn't decide to follow him for purposes of observation. That would prove, he thought, slightly more kinky than he had in mind.

As soon as Lee and their visitor stepped outside, Azure shrugged out of her coveralls and found a rest room opening off the back corner of the storeroom. It was equipped with a sink and a soap dispenser, so she began to scrub the latex-based paint off her hands and wrists. She was studying the end of her ponytail and contemplating various ways to remove the paint when Lee called from the other side of the door, "Azure?"

"In here," she said, swinging the door open. "So are we busted?"

He nodded ruefully. "We're through for the day, that's for sure."

"Are you in trouble?" Her eyes were wide and solemn, though she appeared slightly comical with splotches of mauve and yellow paint embellishing her forehead and chin.

"No, everything's fine. Is the paint coming off okay?"

She held up the end of her ponytail. "Look. What do you think?"

He smiled. "I think you look beautiful with green hair."

She stared at him and for a moment he thought she was

going to hit him with a sharp retort, but instead she grinned. "You have weird taste," she said.

"Want me to help?" he asked.

"Help? I was helping you, and look where that got us."

He edged around her to turn on the water at the sink. "Bend over. I'll get that paint out for you."

After a dubious look, she leaned over the sink. He punched the soap dispenser a few times, releasing the antiseptic scent of institutional handwashing into the small room, and she wrinkled her nose. "I hate that smell."

"They don't provide orange blossom-jojoba shampoo in places like this." He held the end of her ponytail under the stream of water, carefully working the soap through the ends. The paint began to dissolve and wash away.

"How's it doing?" Her voice echoed hollowly back from the sink bowl, but he was so captivated by the pale skin of her nape and the softness of her hair that he didn't answer. It would be so easy to slide the restraining rubber band off her hair and let it tumble around her shoulders, a sight that he had been imagining ever since he spotted her standing so cool and aloof at her sister's wedding.

"I said, how's it doing?"

"Almost all through," he said, trying not to reveal how mesmerized he was by the intimacy of this service he was performing.

"Can you hurry it up?"

He squeezed the water out of her hair and grabbed a paper towel, sliding it around her ponytail so there wouldn't be any drips. She straightened and blotted at her hair for a moment and said, "Now you."

There was the problem of that mauve spot on the back of his neck. They traded places so he could stand in front of the sink, and he bent and held his head under the faucet.

He closed his eyes and let the warm water sluice over his face; he felt a trickle of it running down his chest, but he forgot all about it when her felt her fingers massaging the back of his neck. They were gentle, and soft, and it wasn't much of a leap to imagine how they would feel if they were touching other and more sensitive parts of his anatomy. He pictured it in his mind, lying completely naked under a palm tree on a deserted beach, reaching for her, pressing her close as she caressed him and whispered sexy sweet nothings in his ear.

Which was filling with water as it sloshed off his neck. He adjusted the slant of his head, and Azure said much too brightly, "All finished!"

He brought his head up and she handed him a paper towel. "I know an easier way," he said, and he turned on the hot-air hand dryer and turned the nozzle so that it was aimed at his head. He still had to crouch for the air to hit his hair, though, but this position had its advantages because it put his eyes on the exact level of Azure's breasts. Considering that he'd had his fill in the last couple of weeks of admiring the silicone implants that bloomed all up and down Miami Beach, it was heartening to see a pair that looked utterly and entirely natural.

She seemed unaware of his admiration. In fact, she was leaning toward the mirror, scrubbing at a small spatter of yellow paint. He concentrated on fingercombing his hair into the proper disarray a la Fleck, and when he straightened, he didn't realize that she would be leaning in his direction in order to toss a damp paper towel into the trash bin. Their heads collided with a solid *thwack!*

Lee didn't exactly see stars. The images that obscured his vision were more like spiraling luminous jellybeans.

"Lee? Lee! I'm sorry! I didn't mean to do that!"

When his vision cleared, when the jellybeans dissolved into the ether, he was surprised to see two of Azure, which was something of a benefit as far as he was concerned. Double eyes, lovely. Double nose, delightful. Double little pointed chin and high cheekbones and pale hair, all gorgeous. Both of her were staring up at him in horror, and that gleam of caring or solicitousness or whatever it was that had so attracted him at the wedding had kindled in her eyes, doubly.

To steady himself, he had no choice but to grasp her shoulders and lean slightly forward as the two of her slowly converged into the usual one. It may have been his imagination, but Azure seemed to lean toward him, too. Or else he was unsteady on his feet, which could be the case. It had been a fairly powerful punch.

"Are you hurt?" he asked, his voice coming out in a husky whisper. He wouldn't doubt that the crack on the side of her head hurt as much as the one he'd taken on his jaw.

She rubbed the side of her head. "No, not much. I should have been more careful."

His hands slowly came up and cupped her face. Pain receded, desire rushed in. He was so close that he could kiss her without the slightest inconvenience. And she was staring up at him, lips moist and slightly parted. Her skin felt soft as rose petals beneath his hands, soft as—

"Don't you think we'd better leave? The painters will be back soon."

This brought him sharply back to his senses. He didn't want to have to explain again, this time to the subcontractor painting crew, why he and Azure were on the premises. And this wasn't the most romantic place in the world for their first kiss, which he would prefer to be a momentous occasion that rocked her to the depths of her soul, one that she would remember for all time.

He dropped his hands. "I'll go clean up some of the mess," he said.

She was still staring at him, her eyes unfathomable pools of light. "Good idea," she breathed, but he realized in that moment that she didn't think it was a good idea at all. He knew then that she would rather be kissed, and he felt a surge of triumph at having brought her to this point against all odds.

He backed away, came up against the closed door. "So I'll go and do it."

She drew a deep breath. "I—I'll dry my hair." She gestured toward the hand dryer. "Under there."

He afforded her a sharp nod and backed slowly out the door, letting it close softly behind him while her eyes were still captured by his. Moments later, he heard the rush of air from the dryer.

He hammered the lids back on paint cans, tossed the coveralls in the corner where they had found them, and when Azure came out of the rest room and said she was going to go sit in the car, he told her he'd be out in a minute.

But before he joined her, he couldn't resist picking up one of the paintbrushes and scrawling a large and jubilant "Yesss!" on the blank white wall.

AZURE DIDN'T KNOW WHY she was doing this. She didn't know why she was attracted to this guy. She didn't know why she was, at that very moment, walking beside him into a noisy barbecue restaurant on U.S. 1.

She did know why she was ordering the honey-roasted baby back ribs, however, and it was because the waitress recommended them. At least some sanity remained to her, she thought. At least she was still sensible enough to gather data, evaluate it, and make a reasonable decision. She hadn't totally succumbed to this guy's considerable allure.

He sipped a beer and smiled at her from across the table, which was a picnic table covered with brown butcher paper. Beer arrived in large pitchers, country music blared from a loudspeaker on the other side of the big room, and people tossed their chewed-up rib bones in large buckets on the floor. It wasn't the kind of place that she would normally frequent much less have a good time, but nothing about her life was normal lately. This episode with Lee only underscored that fact.

It was an episode that she didn't regret so far. In fact, she joined him in laughing about her consternation when Jake Gruber showed up and tried to throw them out.

"I couldn't believe we'd been caught," she said.

"Did you see the look on his face? He looked so angry I thought he might have swallowed his tongue."

"His face changed colors. It was mauve. And neither of us even painted him!"

Lee laughed, but he sobered quickly enough. "I had fun," he said quietly, his eyes seeking and holding hers.

"So did I," she said. "It was good to be someone I'm not, if only for a little while."

"I know what you mean," Lee said softly.

She wondered why she couldn't look away from him. It was as if he had some sort of magnet behind his eyeballs, a pull that was impossible to ignore. At the same time, she was fully aware of his nose, so fine and straight, of his eyebrows, so expressive, of his mouth, so full and so— kissable? Was she actually thinking about how it would feel to kiss him?

Shaken by the rush of yearning that inexplicably welled up from someplace deep inside, she forced herself to look away, to gaze out the window at the heavy traffic, at the cashier stationed next to the door, at the child who was standing on the picnic bench across the room and being urged by his father to sit down.

Fortunately, before she could explore her thoughts too deeply, the waitress bore two huge platters of ribs to their table, and Azure discovered that she was starving. And if she had any idea of getting something on with Lust Puppy, surely watching him eat ribs would bring her to her senses. A man with grease dripping down his chin and barbecue sauce up to his elbows was usually not the most romantic sight in the world.

IT WAS A COUPLE OF HOURS LATER when Lee pulled the Mustang into the Blue Moon's parking area and cut the engine. "Well. Here we are."

"Yes. We are."

"I—well." He cleared his throat.

Azure knew that she should get out of the car and walk inside, but she realized with a jolt that she didn't want to leave Lee yet. She also knew that she couldn't very well ask him upstairs for a nightcap with Paulette in residence. And maybe she didn't want to. Maybe she never wanted to see Lee again.

But he had passed the barbecue test. That there was such a test surprised her because she had never thought in terms of eliminating men from her list of dating prospects because of the way they ate barbecue. She had prepared herself to be revulsed. Yet Lee had eaten those ribs so neatly! It wasn't that he'd been prissy about it—far from it. It was more that he had bitten the meat off the bone carefully and not in large chunks. He hadn't ripped, torn, or gnawed. He had nibbled, licked, and sucked in a mannerly fashion without looking like the maw of a huge garbage truck, and grease hadn't run down his chin—not one drop.

Furthermore, the barbecue sauce had stayed on the ribs until he'd finished with them. He hadn't employed his tongue in place of a napkin, either. For some reason, his expertise in rib eating said a lot about the man. It bespoke an upbringing where manners were important. It showed that he was neat and methodical. In short, if the way he ate barbecued ribs was any indication, he was the type of man she liked.

But he was an unlikely ne'er-do-well! A corporate dropout! He worked as a painter, for heaven's sake! Was this someone who could appeal to her?

No.

Yes.

Well, maybe.

On the street, the overabundant neon of South Beach lent a glitzy glow to the night. Above them, the moon was a pale crescent swinging above the far horizon; palm fronds framed swirls of stars spinning through a cloudless sky. She sneaked a look at Lee's silhouette outlined in the pale bluish light, thinking how much she was attracted to him. She breathed deeply of salt air, acknowledging how much more salubrious it was than the fume-laden air of Boston. She felt so relaxed, for once calm and tranquil and not thinking about work. What she *was* thinking was that she wanted to be kissed.

"It's still early," Lee said carefully. "We could go for a walk on the beach if you'd like."

She thought about it for only a split second. "Okay," she said. She wasn't ready to go back to Paulette's claustrophobic apartment. She didn't want to abbreviate her feelings of well being and rare connectedness with another human being.

Lee looked jubilant, and she realized with a start that he'd thought she was going to say no. Only this morning, she would have. She couldn't have imagined at that time that she would want to be near this guy and moreover preparing to take a romantic walk down the beach with him. Usually a woman didn't walk down the beach with a man unless she wanted something more to happen between them. It was an intimate endeavor, a walk down the beach, and not to be entered into lightly.

It was also a chance to find out if his nibbling, licking and sucking abilities extended to his mastery of another skill—kissing.

5

A.J.,
Let me know as soon as you touch base with Santori. VERY
IMPORTANT.
Repeat: VERY IMPORTANT.
Harry Wixler

OKAY, AZURE THOUGHT as she and Lee kicked off their shoes at the end of the boardwalk, maybe having a fling while on vacation would get the lingering bad taste of Charming Paco out of her mouth. Maybe it was what she needed before she went back to Boston, where she saw Paco almost every day in the building where they both worked, not to mention Ms. 40DD. If she returned home with fond memories of her brief dalliance with a hunky beach boy, perhaps even showed pictures of the two of them together around the office, word would get back to Paco and he would realize that she was lost to him forever.

Be real, she scolded herself. *It's not about Paco. It's about me, and that's the best reason of all to be doing this.*

Lee strolled alongside her, his solid bulk outlined against

the haze of moonglow. Her eyes cut toward him and danced away before he noticed her looking. Not that he would mind, she was sure, that she thought he had an attractive chin—chunky, but not to the point of looking like a boulder that had attached itself below his mouth. She liked chins that were firm but not prognathously Neanderthal. She liked noses that were slim and elegant, not crudely bulbous. She liked eyes that held a hint of innate intelligence and a mind that knew how to put that intelligence to good use. Her friend Dorrie had commented several times that as single women who had reached the ripe and knowledgable age of thirty, they both knew too much about what they didn't like in men, and they often reminded each other that lots of women their age had not seen much about the opposite sex to like at all.

Azure had long ago realized that one of the advantages of being experienced with men is that each time one disappointed you, it became easier to cut your losses and move on. But Lee, having disappointed her right from the beginning, was a different kind of animal altogether, mostly because he got better instead of worse. This was unexpected as well as confusing and confounding and kind of crazy.

One thing was clear: They would have to go through all the polite preliminaries before getting down to what they both were here for—a kiss. It was part of the unwritten code once you got past ninth grade that certain niceties had to be observed between the sexes.

You couldn't simply, when the notion to kiss hit either party, glom onto each other and indulge. No, first there was The Look. Two sets of eyes had to hold long enough to express interest but not so long that the other person thought that kissing would be a sure thing. Then there was The Look With A Smile—not exposing a lot of teeth, and not a lot of look, either. After that some form of The Touch usually followed, and it might be the simple inadvertent brushing of hands or even the palm-to-palm intimacy of hand-holding.

Finally a more highly developed form of touching was necessary. It might be The Grasp Of Shoulders Or Forearms. It might be The Full-Flung Embrace, with arms twined around each other. And then there was the thrilling *Yow!* stage, when the kiss was all but inevitable. The general idea behind all of this was that lips couldn't meet lips without some other part of the anatomy meeting an equivalent part of the other person's anatomy beforehand. It was a matter of etiquette.

Did the touching when she and Lee were cleaning up back in the rest room of the commercial building in Miami count? Probably not. Too much time had intervened since then.

"Thank you for buying me dinner," she said, and not only because it was part of the expected protocol. She was grateful for the meal, especially since she had an idea that she was more qualified to pay the check than he was. Back in the restaurant after the check had arrived at their table, she had held her breath, unsure whether to offer to pay her share, but Lee had slapped the money down before she'd been able to get the words out of her mouth.

"You're welcome, Azure. I'm glad we went."

"I—um—I apologize for how I acted this morning. I was rude."

A faint smile played around his lips. "Were you? I thought you were only providing me with a challenge."

"You did? Really?"

"Yes, really."

"You didn't think I meant for you to leave me alone?"

"I thought *you* thought you really meant it."

This deflated her somewhat, but perhaps he was right. Maybe she hadn't been entirely serious about wanting him to go away. If she had been, she would have declined his offer of a ride and continued to search for another rental company that could deliver her car immediately.

She kept her eyes on the outline of a lifeguard stand ahead. Even the lifeguard stands here were art deco, she thought distractedly as they grew closer and she saw that it was painted sunshine-yellow with dark blue trim.

"Was I really so transparent?" she asked.

He grinned, and his eyes slid toward hers at the same time that she was looking at him. Good! The Look. They were making progress. "What do you think?"

"I think," she said evenly, "you're entirely too shrewd," and this provoked the next step: The Look With A Smile.

A wave washed up and threatened to reach their feet, and they both jogged slightly sideways to avoid it. Azure— by design or by chance—moved more slowly than Lee, and this resulted in their hands brushing. Fantastic! she thought. The Touch.

"Oops! Sorry," he said, reaching out to keep her from falling. She stumbled slightly and voila! The Grasp of Forearms. *Wow,* she thought, *this is going pretty fast.*

He said suddenly, "You know, Azure, I feel comfortable with you."

This, coming out of the clear blue as it did, caught her by surprise, and she didn't know what to say. "You do?"

"Yes, and I think you feel comfortable with me."

It occurred to her that she did. It was amazing and unexpected, but all this stuff about looking and hand-holding and touching and even kissing did not make her feel at all anxious as she usually did.

"You know," she said, her wonderment expressing itself in her voice, "I *do* feel comfortable with you, Lee."

"You seem surprised."

"I am, especially after—" She caught herself up short.

"After—?" He shot an emotionally penetrating glance in her direction, and for a moment their eyes locked.

"You probably wouldn't want to hear about it," she said, glancing away quickly.

He squeezed her hand in reassurance. "If it's important to you, I would."

She managed a rueful laugh. "It's not important anymore. *He's* not important."

"Oh," Lee said, his heart sinking. "A man." He should have guessed that there was someone else. Why wouldn't there be? Azure was beautiful and intelligent, the kind of woman any man would want.

"Yes, but he's past tense. He cheated on me with one of my best friends."

"I see," he said, although he couldn't imagine how anyone lucky enough to be the main man in Azure O'Connor's life could betray her.

"I've beaten myself up with wondering what I did wrong or if I could have done anything to keep him. I thought he loved me. I *knew* I loved him."

The pain in her voice gave him pause, made him look at her, really look at her. A tear slowly trickled down her cheek, and she brushed it away, reminding him of the day when he first saw her, her sister's wedding day. In that moment, his heart went out to her because now he knew why she had been so sad.

"He should have appreciated you more, loved you more."

She tried to make light of it. "Easy for you to say."

"I mean it, Azure. You're a kind, caring woman, and you're lovely besides."

"I know I concentrate on work too much." She admitted this stolidly, without emotion.

"That's no reason for a guy to cheat," he said.

"Still," she said. "If I hadn't been busy with work, he wouldn't have—"

"Azure," Lee said in measured tones. "Stop it. If he'd been a decent guy, he wouldn't have cheated on you. Period."

She was grateful for what he had said. For too long she had been blaming herself for Paco's mistake, and now Lee was giving her permission to think about the whole sorry episode in a different way. Not that she had needed permission. She could have stopped blaming herself at any time. But she hadn't until now.

He slowed his walk, stopped, faced her. His eyes seemed to have stolen the glow from the moonlight, and they mesmerized her with their magic. He slid his hands up her arms, generating a hum of electricity beneath the surface of her skin, and even though she was almost to the point of suspending all thought, she was luxuriously aware that they were rapidly approaching the *Yow!* stage.

As that realization settled into her mindset, she began to feel exhilarated beyond common sense. Something important, something earthshaking and significant was about to happen in her life—she knew it. How she knew it was certainly open to conjecture. Was it by telepathy? Intuition? Reading the body language of someone whose body might be more fun to read using the Braille method? Or what?

He moved so close that his breath caressed her lips. "Have you ever been totally out of control, Azure?"

"N-no."

"Would you like to be?"

"I don't know."

"We could start with a kiss and go from there."

"Yes," she said. "Are you, um, waiting for permission?"

"No," he said seriously. "I'm putting you on notice." And then he slowly wrapped his arms around her and drew her close to his chest in a Full-Fledged Embrace. She tilted her head back to look up at him, and when she looked into his eyes, they seemed so deep that all she wanted to do was sink into them. She felt slightly incredulous that he had awakened such a need in her, and her head angled into position almost without her direction. Lee's mouth closed over hers, gentle at first, tasting of the mints they had eaten at the restaurant, then exploring with exquisite skill. At his urging, her mouth blossomed beneath his until she found herself swept up into an arousing, overpowering kiss that made total surrender seem like a really great idea.

After one kiss? How could that be? She clutched at his shoulders to steady herself, but it only made him renew the kiss. Not that she minded. He was even better at kissing than he was at eating barbecue in a neat and mannerly way. There was nothing really mannerly about this kiss, however. It was a kiss that signaled imminent conquest, a kiss that made it clear what he wanted. But did she want what he wanted? Which was everything?

She opened her mouth slightly, inviting his kiss to lengthen, deepen. Her thoughts seemed to wash away with the tide, and the only remnant of consciousness that she had left became a slow tingle in her belly, working its way downward until she fairly ached with the longing to be touched.

His hands came around and skimmed the outsides of her breasts briefly, and she placed the heels of her hands against his chest and slowly pushed herself a few inches away. At that moment, a family group came laughing down a nearby boardwalk leading to a hotel, and Azure and Lee self-consciously broke apart.

When the family had moved on, Lee turned to her and said, "Well? Do you suppose we could get a beach blanket?"

Azure licked her lips. Due to the interruption, her heartbeat had stopped thundering in her ears, and she could almost think again. "What—what for?"

He slid an arm around her shoulders. "I think you know what for."

It was true. She did. She was already picturing that blanket in her mind and imagining what the two of them would do on it. Imagining her fingers tangling in his hair, his hands hot beneath her clothes, the shedding of clothing and sanity. Is that what she wanted? Wild sex on the beach? With a guy who wasn't her usual?

She bit her lip. "Couldn't—couldn't we go to your place?" It seemed like a reasonable suggestion, considering that wherever he was staying would be more private than the beach, though making love out under the stars had its romantic points.

Her suggestion seemed to give him pause, and she thought for a moment that a panicky look flitted across his eyes. "Not a good idea," he said gruffly. "My roommate will be there."

"Okay," she said. "Let's go back to the Blue Moon. I'll get a blanket from Paulette."

"Maybe she won't be home."

Azure glanced at her watch. "Oh, she'll be there at this hour. She had to take a lot of time off from Rent-a-Yenta during the wedding festivities, so she'll be in the apartment making phone calls and checking application forms."

They encountered the family whose passing had broken their lip lock earlier, and one of the women sang out, "Lovely night, isn't it?"

Azure replied with a smile, "Yes, it is," and they kept walking. But Lee couldn't help thinking how much more lovely it would be on the *Samoa* right now, not to mention convenient. Onboard, stewards attended to every wish. They disappeared discreetly when he was having a private moment with a woman. His bed in the master stateroom was wide and comfortable with smooth sheets of very high thread count, and making love was enhanced by the rocking of the ship at anchor.

But he couldn't very well take Azure there—it would be a dead giveaway. Plus he doubted Fleck's acting ability. Fleck might be able to play the part of a billionaire as long as he was on his own, but once Lee showed up, Fleck would falter in his unaccustomed role.

Azure led the way down a narrow alleyway where they soon came to the back door of the Blue Moon.

"Shh," she said as she punched a code into the lock. "You wait here, and I'll slip up the stairs without saying hello to Goldy. She's likely to be watching TV and probably won't hear me."

But as soon as the back door of the Blue Moon swung open, Lee's expectations plummeted as he recognized the O'Connors's Uncle Nate leaning on the counter above Goldy's desk and chatting.

"You were right about Leah and me," he was telling

Goldy. "Your tarot cards were right on the market when they said we were going to get married."

"Money, dear. You mean right on the money, not on the market. Isn't he cute?" Leah was stood within the circle of Nate's arm, beaming proudly. Her smile broadened when she spotted Azure.

"Azure! Why, we were looking for you!" she exclaimed, whereupon Azure shot an apologetic look over her shoulder at Lee and heaved an inward sigh of resignation. She loved her uncle Nate, and she thought she could grow fond of Leah, but the last thing she wanted was to be involved in a conversation with them at the moment.

Nevertheless, she presented herself for Uncle Nate's hug and Leah's air kiss, quickly pulling away and gesturing toward Lee, who had decided he'd better come inside. "You remember Lee, perhaps, from Karma's wedding?"

Lee stuck out his hand. "Yes, I'm Slade's college roommate. It was good to be at his wedding and to meet Karma."

"I'm happy to meet you," Nate replied, pumping his hand vigorously.

Leah spoke up. "Are you two going upstairs? I need to borrow a pottery catalog from Paulette."

Azure felt a stab of dismay at this development, and she tried to think of a polite way to tell Nate and Leah that this wasn't exactly what she had in mind for the rest of the evening. "Oh, but—"

"I think I'll run along," Lee injected smoothly. "I know you have some family visiting to do. How long will you be in town, Azure?"

Wondering how she could salvage time with Lee, she answered distractedly, "I have to stay until my client calls.

He's the guy who lives on the big yacht anchored off Fisher Island.''

The unexpected revelation hit Lee like a blow to the belly even as Azure went on talking.

"I thought I'd have heard from him by now, but I haven't. So I'm sure I'll be here at least for tomorrow." She gazed at him hopefully.

Her eagerness didn't escape him, but he was still flabbergasted to realize that Azure must be—had to be—the consultant from Wixler who was supposed to contact him. "I—I see," Lee said.

"Why don't you come upstairs with us?" her uncle suggested to Lee.

He appreciated the invitation, but he knew he had to think this through. He had to decide what to do. And it was for sure that he couldn't tip his hand now with all these other people around. It would be too embarrassing.

"Not tonight," he said as smoothly as possible. And then, because she looked so expectant, he said, "Azure, I'll call you."

Azure's heart dropped to the bottom of her stomach in consternation. It was a well-known fact among the single women she knew that men always said they'd call you, and few ever did. "Do you have Paulette's phone number?"

"It's 555-6734," Goldy said with a sidelong look up at Lee. "Would you like me to write it down for you?"

"I'll remember," he said quickly. Too quickly, Azure thought.

"You can call me on my cell phone," she said, reeling off the number.

"I'll remember that one, too."

For her part, Azure doubted that Lee would remember

either number. Most people wouldn't, so why should he be different?

"Thanks for everything," she said, knowing the words sounded lame but feeling hampered by the presence of everyone else. She hated to be saying goodbye to Lee— forever, for all she knew—in this brightly lit lobby with Nate, Leah and Goldy looking on. She hated saying goodbye to him, period. She'd had something else in mind, something thrilling and unexpected and entirely out of character for her. She'd wanted excitement, and now she was feeling vastly disappointed that circumstances had denied it.

Lee touched her hand briefly before he went on out the front door. *The Touch again,* she thought, feeling slightly more positive.

"Nice fellow," said her uncle, but then Leah began to fuss over her uncle and said that she didn't want him walking up all those stairs to Paulette's apartment, whereupon he said he'd done it many times and his doctor said stairs were fine, heart attack or not, and Leah said that was all very well, but doctors didn't know everything and Nate should take it easy.

As Azure, feeling that the evening had been hijacked, was trailing after the two of them, Goldy beckoned her back to her desk. Through the window she saw Lee's Mustang pull out of the parking lot and watched as its tail lights disappeared into South Beach traffic.

"That man Lee," Goldy whispered conspiratorially, "is hiding something. Mark my words, and it's something important."

This snapped her to attention. "What do you mean?" Azure said. "Like a corpse in the basement?"

Goldy shook her head, setting her dangly gold earrings

jingling. "No, no, it isn't anything bad. I don't know what it is. But it's something good. Something you won't mind."

"Thanks, Goldy," Azure said with a sigh. "I think."

"You're welcome. And don't worry. He *will* call."

And if he doesn't, I won't care, Azure told herself in a turnaround brought about by desperation.

But she knew she *would* care. A lot.

BACK ON THE *SAMOA*'S sundeck, Fleck was enjoying the taste of a good cigar complemented by the last of a bottle of equally good scotch. He greeted Lee effusively.

"Man, you should have seen the chicks crowd around at the marina when I stepped off the launch today," Fleck said.

Lee, hardly over his shock at who Azure was and his disappointment in how the evening had ended, eased himself down onto a deck chair and waited for the steward to appear. Right now he could use a drink.

Sure enough, the young Portuguese steward stepped out of the shadows. "Sir? What is your pleasure?"

Lee would have liked to say that his pleasure had been canceled by circumstances beyond his control, but he held his tongue. "I'll have what he's having," he said with a tip of his head toward Fleck's drink.

"Certainly, sir." Miguel hurried to the bar, pouring the drink and returning with swift efficiency.

Though Lee would have been happy with some quiet time for reflection, Fleck seemed determined to give him an update of his day. "I got into your Mercedes and took one of the girls with me," he was saying. "We drove up the coast for a while, stopped at a hotel, had a few drinks in the bar. You were right about the women, Lee. Money is the greatest magnet in the world." He took another drag on the cigar and blew a series of smoke rings toward the moon, which by this time hung high in the sky and threatened to disappear behind a cloud. *A great night for love-making on the beach,* Lee thought glumly.

"How did it go with you today, buddy?" Fleck leaned forward, ready for the scoop.

"Not at all as planned." His first sip of the scotch rolled smoothly across his tongue, and he hoped the alcohol would put him in a better frame of mind.

"What do you mean?"

"I found out that Azure works for Wixler Consultants, the company I've asked to handle the start-up plan for franchising. She's the consultant that Harry Wixler recommended so highly."

Fleck looked thunderstruck. "You didn't know this?"

"I had no idea. Apparently she's been waiting for me to call her, and I never got the message that I was supposed to. Miguel? Would you please come here?"

The steward hurried out from a pantry inside the salon. "Yes, sir, Mr. Santori?"

"Have you given me all the phone messages I've received since we've been anchored here?"

"I think so."

Lee knew that Miguel was new to the *Samoa* and not accustomed to the routine. "Would you mind checking to make sure?"

"Yes, sir, Mr. Santori." The man hurried away.

"I take it you got along all right with Azure?"

"In the first place, this morning when I stopped by Rent-a-Yenta, I didn't get a chance to give Paulette a piece of my mind. Azure gave *me* a piece of her mind. And then—"

Fleck aimed a wily leer in his direction. "Azure didn't give you a piece of anything else, did she?"

"Nope. No such luck. And I'd appreciate it if you wouldn't ask such pointed and crude questions about the woman I love."

The words had slipped out. He didn't know what to think after he said them, and from the looks of it, Fleck didn't, either.

"Love? Lee, holy sh—"

Lee cut him off. "Damn! I don't know where the infamous *L* word came from. I don't know why I said it." Bewilderment left him at a loss for more words.

Fleck stared at him incredulously. "You think you're in *love* with this O'Connor woman?"

Lee took a long pull on his drink as he stared at the lights from Fisher Island rippling on the water. He thought about how Azure had looked in her painter's coveralls, the end of her ponytail painted green. He remembered the way she had stared up at him in the moonlight, her yearning as strong as his after he'd kissed her, and how she hadn't turned him down flat when he'd suggested getting a blanket so they could make love on the beach. Was it possible to fall in love with someone you hardly knew over a few things like that? Or had he fallen in love with her at first sight?

"I love her," he said heavily, feeling even more helpless as the knowledge washed over him. Was he crazy? Had he taken leave of his mind?

Fleck's questioning was blunt and to the point. "You sure you don't just want to get her in the sack?"

The scotch had settled into Lee's stomach, its welcome warmth seeping soothingly through his veins. "I want her that way, of course. I also want a lot more than that."

"Okay, Lee. I'm trying to understand."

"So am I, Fleck," Lee said heavily. "So am I."

"And she still hates you?"

"No, she doesn't hate me. I'm pretty sure of that after tonight."

Suddenly Lee felt very tired. This business of pretending to be someone else had begun to wear on him earlier in the day, and now the prospect of keeping up the charade seemed exhausting.

Miguel materialized from the salon carrying a fistful of pink message slips. "Here you are, sir, copies of your messages."

Lee thumbed through them, finally finding one requesting him to call A. J. O'Connor at Harry Wixler's behest. He'd thought that during his brief conversation with Wixler about the matter, the man had said that his representative was going to call him. He wearily pinched the bridge of his nose between thumb and forefinger as he stared at the message, realizing that he was supposed to have called her. And Wixler hadn't mentioned who his representative was. If he had, Lee would have certainly picked up on the name O'Connor. It was clear to him that they had each been waiting for the other to call.

"All right, Miguel. It's my fault. The messages are all here, but I haven't been paying enough attention to them, obviously."

After the steward left, Fleck regarded him with uplifted eyebrows. "*Now* will you tell Azure who you are?"

"I don't know. Maybe it's time to come clean." Yet even as he spoke, he knew that things wouldn't be the same between them once he was Leonardo Santori and she was A. J. O'Connor. They would be required to relate on a business basis, and she would likely become nervous about who he was and what he could do for her company. They would not be able to laugh together in a humble barbecue place about splashing each other with paint; perhaps they would never get to walk on the beach in the moonlight once she felt self-conscious around him. They might never make love.

Lee drained his glass and heaved himself out of the deck chair. "I'd better rethink this."

"Look, buddy," Fleck said slowly, "how about one more day of switched identities?"

Lee thought for a moment or two. He saw no harm in it. "Okay, Fleck. You're on. One more day and then I spill the beans."

Fleck rewarded him with two thumbs up. "Right-o. See you in the morning, Lee."

Lee had serious misgivings about the scheme, but they were overshadowed by his desire to find out if the light in Azure's eyes when she looked at him could be rekindled by plain old ordinary Lee Sanders.

6

_____

a.j., where are you? earth to a.j., earth to a.j.! charming paco asked me if you were out of town and i said yes and he asked when you would be back. what should i tell him? that you're looking for a real prince?
luv,
dorrie

THE NEXT MORNING, AZURE spent forty minutes on the treadmill at the gym near the Blue Moon. She worked her abs, her glutes, her deltoids, her lats. And when she was through exercising, she treated herself to a sauna, where several other women were chatting as though they knew one another well. At first Azure wished that they'd be quiet so that she could enjoy the sauna in peace, but as they continued to talk, she became more interested.

"They say the *Samoa*'s the most enormous yacht to anchor near Fisher Island in years," said one, a redhead.

"The biggest since Aristotle Onassis's yacht back in the seventies," chimed in the woman in the striped bath towel.

"Leonardo Santori," said a third, who nearly swooned as she pronounced his name. "The Dot.Musix whiz."

Azure's ears perked up at this. This was the client who was supposed to call her. This was the guy that she was supposed to help with a start-up franchise business plan.

"He's *soooo* good-looking," said the redhead.

"I think I saw him running on the beach once."

"How do you know? He's plenty reclusive, and hardly anyone knows what he looks like. He never even gives interviews."

"Still, I hear he's got scores of girlfriends," said the one in the striped towel.

"That doesn't leave much chance for us, does it?" And they all laughed.

This overheard conversation started Azure thinking, though. Harry had said that she should wait for Leonardo Santori to call her, but she hadn't heard from him yet and she certainly didn't want to be blamed for letting him get away. Under the circumstances, wouldn't it make perfect sense for her to call the *Samoa?*

THE YACHT SAMOA, NEARLY the size of a small continent, gleamed blindingly white in the sunshine over near Fisher Island. The women gathered around the Sunchaser Marina's main dock were in their early twenties and very beautiful. When Azure asked about Leonardo Santori, they weren't reticent.

"We saw him yesterday," said one. She was wearing a blue hip-hugger miniskirt and a skimpy white halter top. She nodded toward a hibiscus bush bearing red flowers as big as saucers where one of their group was standing and listening to a portable CD player. "Ginger went for a ride with him in his Mercedes sports car."

The girl named Ginger unplugged herself from her earphones. "Leonardo Santori's no great shakes if you ask me. I'm not going anywhere with him again."

One of the others spoke up. "So why, pray tell, are you hanging around here today?"

Ginger shrugged. "I liked the looks of the guy who runs the launch. He said that maybe we could get together next time he comes to the marina." She tossed a head of blond curls.

"Right," said the other woman sarcastically. She called to two others who were sitting on a boat box and chatting. "You want to go get a drink out of the machine? A Coke or something?"

One of them lifted her hair up so that the breeze could cool her neck. "A cold drink would taste good. It's hot out here."

"Ginger?"

"Not me. It's about time for that launch to show up and pick up the daily supplies."

As the three women headed toward the drink machine, which was sheltered under a porch outside the marina office, Azure leaned against a dock piling. Scents of tar and brine tickled her nose, and a brown pelican swooped low over her head before skimming the bay in search of his dinner. In the distance, the *Samoa* rode easily on gentle waves, her flags fluttering in the breeze. No activity seemed to be taking place on deck, though the woodwork shone and the highly polished brass fittings gleamed brightly in the sun.

"That's some boat," Azure said, almost to herself.

Ginger clicked the CD player shut. "I know. I've heard there are marble bathrooms and solid gold fixtures shaped like swans. We all want to go on it." She sounded wistful.

"I don't want to see the yacht," Azure said carefully. "I only want to know how to contact someone on board."

"Oh, is that all? That's easy enough. I have a number for a phone there." Ginger seemed to be boasting or, at the very least, trying to impress Azure that she, in contrast to the others, had an in.

Azure tried not to show her surprise. "You do?"

"Uh-huh. The guy who brings the launch in—Mario— gave the phone number to me. He said to call and let him know if I'd be here today, and I did. I haven't told the others yet. They'd be *tooooo* jealous." Ginger rolled her eyes, and then she giggled. "I can't wait to see their faces when I step into that launch and ride off to the yacht with Mario. He's real good-looking."

"Ginger, I'm not interested in Mario, but I would like to have that phone number," Azure said quickly. She handed Ginger her card.

Ginger studied it. "You're not from around here?"

Azure shook her head and smiled. "No. I have no personal interest in anyone on the *Samoa*. My reason for wanting to contact the *Samoa* is purely business."

"I'll give you the phone number, but don't say where you got it. And don't tell the others." She glanced toward the three women. They were sitting around a concrete picnic table in the shade of a palm tree. "They're peeved because I went out with the great Santori yesterday. I thought he really liked me, but not all that much, as it turned out." She gave a little laugh and fished a scrap of paper out of her pocket. "Here's the phone number. Do you have a pencil so you can write it down?"

Azure produced a pencil from her fanny pack and wrote down the phone number that Ginger offered. "Thanks, Ginger. You've been a big help. And good luck with Mario."

Ginger shoved the bit of paper back into the pocket of her shorts. "Thanks." She settled her earphones over her ears before Azure set off down the dock.

"Giving up already?" one of the women at the picnic table called when she saw Azure headed toward the street.

"Yes. It hardly seems worth it to wait around here."

The three women exchanged knowing glances. "Oh, it is. Believe me, it is."

Well, maybe something was wrong with her, Azure reflected as she jogged back toward the Blue Moon. But she'd rather spend time with a beach bum who liked her instead of a billionaire who didn't give a hoot. And who had, apparently, no lack of gorgeous women in his life.

PAULETTE HAD NOT TAKEN any messages for her so far this morning, and neither had Goldy. A check of stored messages on her cell phone didn't produce any, either, but it was still early. Maybe Lee would call later.

Azure certainly didn't intend to tell Paulette that she and Lee had almost made love on the beach last night. It just slipped out as they were in Paulette's tiny kitchen drinking iced tea.

"You mean you wanted to?" Paulette said with frank amazement.

Azure, perched on a kitchen stool painted with orange and blue polka dots, stirred her unsweetened tea. While she'd been working out, she had decided to give up sugar, which made for flab. Which made for body anxiety. Which was not good when you were contemplating taking off your clothes in front of somebody for the first time whether or not he had a tattoo on his abdomen to distract you.

"Yes, I wanted to sleep with him. It was—" Azure groped for words. It was not easy to voice your exact feelings on the subject of why you wanted to have sex with a man. She hardly understood it herself.

"Last night was magical," Azure said, knowing that didn't cover the half of it. "It was mindbending. Marvelous. Memorable."

"It was Miami Beach," Paulette said flatly. "The tropical climate, the rush of the sea to shore, the freedom of being away from it all and on vacation. Sex with a new person seems special at the time, Azure, but you know as well as I do that these vacation flirtations don't last."

"Did I say I wanted it to last?"

Paulette shrugged. "From what I can tell, most women crave permanence. In the back of their minds there's always the possibility that a fling could be the real thing."

While she was thinking this over, Azure got up and rinsed her glass in the sink. "Not," she said, "after Charming Paco. That was supposed to be the real thing, and I thought it was a stable relationship. Then—boom!—a naked, wet Tiffany was being royally soaped by my equally naked and wet boyfriend in *my* bathtub. I ask you, how can I ever think anything is real after that?"

"Well, her *boobs* were real enough," Paulette pointed out.

"Right," Azure said with a sigh. She glanced at her watch. "Now that I've got a phone number for the *Samoa,* I'm going to call that client, despite what Harry said. I'd like to know what's what."

Paulette got up and began to load the dishwasher. "Say, aren't we going shopping today? I wanted to buy a pair of shoes to wear to the seminar."

"How about later? I'm hoping Lee will call."

"Did Lee actually tell you to expect a phone call from him?"

"He said, 'I'll call you,' and he has your number as well as my cell phone number. But you know as well as I do how men say they're going to call and never do."

"You know why? Karma and I did a survey on that for Rent-a-Yenta. It's because they didn't like the sex. They think it's polite to say they'll call afterward even when they have no intention of doing so. They have no idea how nerve-racking it is for the woman who waits by a phone that never rings." Paulette closed the dishwasher door and shoved the box of detergent back under the sink.

"But Lee and I have never *had* sex."

"Then he'll call. Chances on he'll keep calling until he gets you in the sack. He'll want to know if you're good at it."

"Is *that* what it's all about?"

"For a lot of guys it is. *Are* you good at sex?"

"Paulette!"

Her cousin only grinned. "Just curious."

"As it happens," Azure said with dignity, "I am *very* good at it. At least according to Paco."

"Who ran off with a pair of 40DDs." With a final knowing look, Paulette flounced off to her bedroom, where she commenced shuffling papers around on her desk.

Sometimes Azure didn't like this cousin of hers much at all. Also, she resented Paulette for raising the question of whether or not she was good in bed. Based on Charming Paco's enthusiastic response and the self-help tests she'd completed in *Cosmo,* she thought she was fine, even remarkably adept at times. And she enjoyed sex.

But would Lee think she was good at it?

And would her life be ruined if he never even had a chance to find out?

Well, no. We weren't talking ruined lives here if she

never heard from him again. But we were talking a ruined week or so, which was bad enough when that week was in Miami Beach and there was an ocean and a moon and stars urging you on to fulfillment of your heart's desire. Or at least what passed for your heart's desire while on vacation.

Memo to self:

1. Do I want Paco to know when I'll be back in Boston? What to tell Dorrie to tell him?
2. Don't answer calls from Harry Wixler until talk to client.
3. Buy revealing underwear so will look sexy for Lee. Check into thong panties if butt not too bouncy.

AZURE DRUMMED HER FINGERS on the arm of the lounge chair as she listened to the measured *bleep!* of the ship-to-shore telephone on the other end of her cell phone. She wished she were at the beach right now. But no. She was trying to reach Harry's elusive client.

The phone picked up. *"Samoa,"* said a nonchalant male voice.

"Hello, this is A. J. O'Connor of Wixler Consultants, and I'd like to leave a message for Mr. Santori."

A long silence, so long that she thought she might have been disconnected. Then, experimentally, "You've got Santori."

She hadn't expected this. She had expected to talk to an assistant, a steward, a secretary—not to the man himself.

She cleared her throat. "Mr. Santori, I'm hoping that we can get together soon to discuss your plans for franchising your Grassy Creek business."

Another long silence. ''Sure, that's a great idea. Uh, I mean, a good idea. To talk, you know.''

Azure frowned. Somehow all she had heard about Leonardo Santori had led her to believe that he was a man of well-spoken sensibilities. This man sounded ill-at-ease and, moreover, too tentative ever to have been head of a major company like Dot.Musix.

''Perhaps you could suggest a time?''

''What's good for you?''

Usually clients were more specific, since they knew they were calling the shots. ''May I take you to dinner on Friday?''

''Take me to dinner? Well, okay.''

''I'll be glad to pick you up, if you like, at your landing dock at the marina.''

''Kewl! Is seven o'clock all right?''

''Of course. I'll see you then.''

''Right-o.''

After they hung up, she sat for a moment shaking her head at her preconceived notions. Mr. Santori might be rich, but he sounded extremely unsophisticated. Well, he might not be what she expected, but at least they had an appointment.

When she went back inside the apartment, Azure booted up her laptop and checked her online mailbox for messages. Not surprisingly, there was one from her boss.

From: H_Wixler@wixler.org
To: A_OConnor@wixler.org
Subject: Re: Client

A.J., I cannot emphasize enough how important it is for Wixler Consultants to retain Leonardo Santori's goodwill. If he doesn't phone you within the next twenty-four hours,

I strongly suggest that you call him. STRONGLY, A.J.
Harry Wixler

SINCE SHE HAD ALREADY TAKEN action, Azure decided that
no response to Harry's e-mail was necessary, so she shut
off her computer and went shopping instead.

PAULETTE WASTED NO TIME in hauling Azure off to the
very boutique where the yellow crochet bikini was still part
of the window display, and she immediately located a version of it that seemed, to Azure's eyes, two sizes too small.

"Look at it this way, Azure," Paulette said impatiently
when Azure stood in front of her in the dressing room wearing the swimsuit. "You want to drive Lee crazy. This bikini
will do that. You look hot, hot, hot, girl."

"With the air-conditioning in here going full blast, I feel
cold, cold, cold." Azure twisted this way and that, the better to assess the ample amount of goosebumped skin reflected in the three-way mirror. The swimsuit showed off
her breasts to advantage, leaving little to the imagination.
The bottom was not much more than a few interwoven
threads that covered the essentials but left most of her hips
bare. She gave it a futile tug and sighed.

"You have a great figure," Paulette said, "and besides,
this outfit is the perfect look for South Beach. Why, people
are walking around in a lot less than that out on the sidewalk."

It was true. Skimpy boob tubes in Day-Glo shades, mini-
skirts with portholes of clear plastic so that skin showed
underneath, gauzy see-through pantaloons worn with little
in the way of underwear—Azure had seen them all.

"And," said Paulette in her most officious tone, "we'll
take the pareo that goes with the suit. And the—"

"Not the feather boa or the snakeskin boots," Azure said firmly, stopping Paulette in midsentence.

"Why not?"

"They're outrageous, and definitely not me."

"You said the bikini wasn't you, either," Paulette reminded her.

"The me I used to know seems to have evaporated in this heat," Azure said with a sigh. Paulette only laughed.

"You could try a new hairdo," Paulette suggested offhandedly from outside the dressing room door as Azure was getting dressed.

Azure stopped and looked—really looked—at her hair in the mirror. As usual, it was neatly twisted at her nape, and she thought it looked fine.

"I don't think I need a new hairstyle," she said to Paulette as she emerged from the dressing room.

"Try this," Paulette said, and before Azure could dodge out of her way, Paulette had pulled huge hanks of hair down on either side of Azure's face and was taking aim at the twist.

"Stop!" Azure yelped. "My hair is okay."

"So why should it be merely okay when it could be great?" Paulette said in midyank.

"Ow! What are you doing?"

"Finding the casual you," Paulette said before stepping back and admiring her handiwork.

"There is no casual me." With her hands full of garments that she'd tried on, Azure was unable to repair the damage to her hairdo. She rolled her eyes at her image in the three-way mirror across the narrow corridor between dressing rooms. The hair that Paulette had pulled out of the twist trailed around her face, wafting in the breeze from the air conditioner vent overhead. The twist itself was cockeyed, the hair that was still in it haphazardly held by the pins. "I look like a bimbo who just got out of bed."

"Oy! So what's wrong with that?"

"I have a serious job. I need serious hair."

"Not when you're on vacation."

Azure had to admit that the bedroom look was, well, sensual. Experimentally she drew her lips into a pout.

"There! That's perfect! You try that when you're wearing that yellow bikini and Lee will want to jump your bones."

This outburst brought Azure back to reality. "Paulette, you're incorrigible. Thanks for your help, and how about if I take you to lunch?"

But Paulette said she had to leave for the seminar late in the afternoon and still hadn't found the shoes she needed for her outfit, and if Azure didn't mind, she thought she'd better skip it.

After Paulette had left the shop, Azure, feeling deliciously wicked, hastily bought several pairs of thong panties, jiggling be damned.

"HI," SAID GOLDY, who was eating a kiwi fruit with a plastic spoon when Azure got back to the Blue Moon. "Anything new?"

Azure pulled the bikini from its bag and arrayed it on the counter for Goldy's inspection. "What do you think?" She left the panties in the bag, not wanting to appear as wanton as buying them had made her feel.

Goldy grinned. "I think you're going to give Mr. Lee Sanders an eyeful, that's what I think."

"*If* I even hear from him," Azure said, wrapping her purchase back up in the tissue paper. "*If* he's still interested."

"You'll hear from him. I'm sure of it."

"You phone me upstairs right away if you see Lee's red Mustang pull into the parking lot, Goldy. Please."

"I'll ring you as soon as I see the aura of that red convertible preceding it down the street," Goldy promised.

As soon as Azure got back to the apartment, she checked her cell phone to see if Lee had called. Again there were no messages. What if she had bought all this new underwear and the bikini for nothing? A yellow crochet number wasn't exactly something she'd want to wear at the health club pool in Boston, and as for her upcoming week on Cape Cod in August, forget it. Dorrie and their other friends would laugh their heads off if she showed up in a bikini that almost wasn't there.

Still, crochet bikinis and the like were what people wore here, so she decided to put it on. It exposed a lot of skin, that was for sure. Which made for getting a great suntan, so she settled a beach towel on the chaise longue on the balcony and lay back to soak up some serious rays. Bees were buzzing around the papery thin magenta flowers on the bougainvillea vine that climbed the side of the building, and somewhere someone was gabbling in exuberant Spanish. After a while a jackhammer started up across the street. Azure blotted out the sounds, trying not to think about work or whether she would hear from Lee.

It was an hour or so later when a foam cup weighted by a seashell flew over the balcony railing, startling Azure out of a reverie in which she was pleasantly dwelling on her recent vivid imaginings concerning Lee.

As soon as she saw there was a piece of paper wrapped around the seashell, Azure looked down and saw Lee's red car parked under the royal poinciana tree below in the parking lot. Goldy hadn't called to warn her! There was no sign of Lee, however, though she knew that must be who had thrown the cup.

She unwrapped the piece of paper and read it eagerly.

"Azure," it said. "Meet me downstairs. Believe it or not, I'm going to have my tarot read." It was signed, Lee.

"Having his tarot read?" she wondered out loud. But what did it matter? He was here, and he wanted to see her.

The pareo that went with her new bikini had a black background arrayed with wild tropical flowers, was not quite opaque and barely came to her knees. It took her a few minutes to wind it in an artistically saronglike way, first tying it experimentally between her breasts, then tugging it down to cover more of her thighs, and finally trying to make up her mind if its transparency was a plus or a minus. She finally decided that it was a plus and tied the corners around her neck, halterlike, before hurrying to the lobby, where she found Goldy slapping tarot cards down on the counter as Lee watched with an expression more skeptical than not.

"Hi," Lee said, and she was gratified that he looked her up and down and then up again in the manner of a man who wanted to see more. It was his Lust Puppy look, and it encouraged her considerably.

"Lee's getting a good tarot reading, Azure," Goldy said, looking over the cards.

Before she could reply, there was a clattering on the stairs. "What's going on, Goldy? I saw a red Mustang in the parking lot and—oh, hello, Lee. And Azure." Mandi, resplendent in vinyl shorts in an alarming shade of purple, a geometric-print top that was several sizes too small, and midcalf white boots, slinked up to the counter, which was just the right height to allow her to support her unfettered breasts on it only inches from the tarot cards.

"I'm reading cards for Lee," Goldy said without looking up.

"Hmm, let me see," said Mandi, craning so she could see the spread. "Isn't that the Emperor right there?" She pointed to a card whereon a man sat on a throne holding a large scepter.

"Mmm-hmm," Goldy said. "The Emperor is Lee's agent. It represents him as he as at present."

"Oooh," Mandi said, sounding impressed. "The Emperor is a powerful card, right, Goldy?"

"Yes indeed," Goldy said. She lay out a couple more cards, covering the Emperor.

"What do you mean by powerful?" Lee asked, looking turned off by the whole thing.

"The Emperor is the ruler of the world, possessing its highest attributes," Goldy intoned as she intently studied the cards.

Mandi huffed impatiently. "You're too shy to tell all of it, Goldy, so I will. The Emperor is the ultimate in masculinity and dominates sexually. See that thing he's holding?"

"The scepter?" Azure supplied in spite of herself.

"It's a phallic symbol. It's longer than a normal scepter would be, and the circle on top represents the part of the female that is penetrated by the male. The Emperor makes women ecstatic with his expertise. He—"

"Mandi, for heaven's sake." Goldy was blushing. "The important element is the crown that the Emperor wears. It bespeaks mastery over all. The Emperor is a powerful card, Lee. Very powerful."

"Good," Lee said, but Azure noticed that he was paying more attention to Mandi than was strictly necessary. How could he not, with her breasts on display like a tray of fruit?

Forbidden fruit, Azure hoped, but maybe not. Mandi was returning his interest unabashedly.

"The thing is," Goldy continued, sounding thoughtful, "Lee's obstacle card would seem to indicate a falseness of some sort." She glanced up at Lee. "Still, the future card shows sensual bliss and happiness and money in the bank. And a soul mate as well."

"Oh, Lee's future card is the ace of the deck," Mandi noted with interest. "You could say that it shows speedy orgasms, too. Though that might not mean sensual bliss for a partner, if you know what I mean." She shot a coy look up at Lee and laughed. The diamond in her nostril glinted in the sunlight pouring through the front window.

"Mandi! I should never have let you read that tarot instruction book!" scolded Goldy.

"I'm only saying what you can't bring yourself to talk about, Goldy dear. Say, Lee, I manage the juiceteria down the street. You want to come over and have a free smoothie on me? I could use a ride. My car's in the shop."

Azure's expectations dropped precipitously when Lee looked interested. "A juiceteria?"

"A fancy name for a juice bar. The kiwi smoothies are good, and we also make a terrific guava fizz."

"Azure? Would you like to go?" Lee smiled at her.

Mandi seemed surprised that Lee would invite Azure to go along and lifted one skeptical brow as she waited for Azure's reply.

Which, Azure decided in that split second, was no. Lee had tossed the note over the railing of the balcony and invited her to the lobby. Presumably he'd wanted to see her. She wasn't about to share him with Mandi Eye Candy, the complete airhead.

"I have work to do," Azure said loftily. "Maybe another

time." If Lee chose, he could take the hint and call her later. Or he could even change his mind about going with Mandi.

"Okay, whatever," Mandi said breezily. "Lee? Let's go."

"Are you sure you won't join us?" Lee said. To Azure's satisfaction, he sounded a wee bit anxious.

"No, I can't. Sorry."

"Come along, Lee, I don't want to be late for work." Mandi tugged at his arm.

He afforded Azure one last look over his shoulder. Azure, biting her lip in chagrin, thought that at least Lee looked regretful as he followed Mandi out into the heat of the day. He could not, she thought miserably, feel more regretful than she did at this development, but after all, he *had* had a choice. He wouldn't have had to let himself be manipulated by Mandi, though Azure supposed that the offer of a free smoothie had a lot to do with it. When you didn't have a lot of money, you tended to take people up on freebies.

"I tried to call you when I saw Lee's car pull into the parking lot," Goldy said. "You didn't answer the phone."

"I was out on the balcony. There was all that noise from the jackhammer across the street, and I didn't think to turn up the ringer on my cell or on Paulette's phone in the kitchen."

"Well, you got here and saw Lee, but why did you let him go off with Mandi?" Goldy scooped the tarot cards into a pile.

"I've never liked sharing my toys."

Goldy giggled. "Can't say that I blame you. Frankly, I'm surprised at Lee's reading. The Emperor is a powerful figure, so he must have a strong personality."

"If Lee's powerful, that's a surprise."

"Azure, don't count him out so quickly. And by the way, you look real nice in that new outfit. I think Lee noticed."

"He noticed Mandi," Azure said, feeling deflated. It didn't help that outside she could see the red Mustang as it zoomed out of the parking lot. Mandi's hair was flowing in the breeze, and she was talking with much animation. Lee wore his mirrored sunglasses, so it was impossible to read his expression.

"Between you and me," Goldy said conspiratorially, "I think Mandi is insignificant in his life. I didn't see her in the spread of cards."

Azure couldn't stop herself from asking. "And what about me? Did you see me?"

"Oh, you were there, all right. You're part of the influence on Lee's life that will come into operation soon. Maybe you're his soulmate, Azure. The cards definitely showed a soul mate."

"How soon is this influence supposed to arrive?"

Goldy looked mysterious. "Oh, I couldn't say."

"But not today, I gather."

"Oh, Azure, I wouldn't be so sure."

Nothing in life was sure, Azure thought unhappily as she went back upstairs to the apartment. Especially where men and, apparently, the tarot were concerned.

LEE WONDERED WHAT HE WAS doing driving down Collins Avenue in the company of a ditzy blonde who sported a jewel in one nostril and talked nonstop.

"Like I said, at the juiceteria we have avocado smoothies, strawberry fizzes, and something you might really enjoy, limeade made from Key limes. You know, those are the little limes, the ones they make Key lime pie from. I can make really good Key lime pie if you want to come over for dinner sometime. For today, maybe you'd like to try the passion fruit smoothie. I'll make it for you myself. Maybe you'd like that. Would you?''

Lee made a noise that he hoped was noncommittal. He was already contemplating how he was going to engineer his escape from this woman. Despite her considerable pneumatic assets, spending even one hour with her would be like walking forty miles in bad socks. But for the moment he was trapped, and all because he had wanted to see this juiceteria and compare it with what he had planned for Grassy Creek.

"Here we are," Mandi said. "Drive down this alley. Mine's the first parking space." He parked the car, and, treating him to much tossing of hair and swinging of hips, Mandi preceded him into a little hole-in-the-wall place with scarcely enough room to turn around. It had a bar equipped with stools, and a narrow counter where you could stand and watch people passing by on the street while you drank your juice. Grassy Creek was going to be much more upscale and health-food oriented.

"What will it be?" Mandi said after elbowing her assistant aside. "The coconut? The passion fruit? Although if you choose that one, it might make you more passionate than you would like," and she winked.

"I'll take the coconut," he said, studying the decor of the place. It was simple, with walls painted a bright Pepto-Bismol pink and gray tile floors. On one wall hung a framed poster showing an animal—it appeared to be a donkey—lying back in a beach chair with its hind legs crossed and blissfully drinking from a glass adorned with a tiny pink paper umbrella. His Grassy Creek store would have a scenic mural behind the counter and elegant light fixtures, not fluorescent lamps.

The roar of the juice machine interrupted his thoughts, and in a minute or so Mandi slid a glass across the counter toward him.

"I don't suppose you serve wheat grass juice?" he asked while he could get a word in edgewise.

She raised her eyebrows. "No. What's that?"

"Oh, a health food thing," he said before trying out his drink.

"Health food," Mandi said disparagingly, and then she was off on a new tack, one that seemed to be pointing toward the possibility of seeing him when she got off work.

He ignored her, drank half of his drink, decided that it was too sweet by far, and insisted on paying for it. This seemed to hurt Mandi's feelings, but he figured the couple of dollars he gave her were well spent on research. He had gained valuable knowledge about the competition hereabouts.

But now he was finished with business and could concentrate on pleasure. He would head back to the Blue Moon where he'd try again to connect with Azure. He'd been surprised when she'd refused to accompany him when he left with Mandi. Surely she knew that he had no interest in anyone but her. Didn't she? He'd been clear enough in his intentions from the very beginning. Hadn't he?

Maybe today's tarot reading had scared her off. Or perhaps Mandi's mindless prattle about speedy orgasms and phallic symbols had offended Azure. He had an idea she'd be a tigress in bed, though.

The thought was intriguing. He wouldn't disappoint her in the lovemaking department. That is, when he got a chance to show her that he could—what was it? Oh, yes, ''make women ecstatic with his expertise.''

He grinned to himself, already anticipating his own ecstasy as well as hers.

7

YOU'VE GOT MAIL!
To: D_Colangelo@wixler.org
From: A_Oconnor@wixler.org
Subject: Not-So-Charming Paco

Dorrie, I'm going to be staying in Miami Beach for a while because I won't be meeting with Leonardo Santori until Friday night. I might stay over the weekend, too. Guess what—I've met someone. And guess what else—you can tell Paco I've met someone. I swear, I can't figure out for the life of me why I ever thought Paco was charming in the first place.
More later—
A.J.
P.S. Yes, I've kissed him, and no, he didn't turn into a prince.

AROUND TWO IN THE AFTERNOON, Azure was on her way back to the Blue Moon after shlepping a stack of file folders over to a harried Paulette at the Rent-a-Yenta office when the red Mustang barreled around the corner. Lee swung it over to the curb and grinned at her, his smile as bright as the sun winking off the chrome wheels.

"Hi, gorgeous. Want to go snorkeling?"

She stopped in her tracks. With his crooked grin and

tousled hair, he looked about as scrumptious as a man could look. Still, it wouldn't do to appear too eager.

"Why should I?" she said.

"Because it's fun. Because I have snorkels and swim fins in the trunk of the car. And because what else do you have to do?"

"Now that you mention it, not much." She narrowed her eyes. "You're not planning on taking me to Haulover Beach, are you?"

He laughed. "No, I'll never go there again. I promise."

He looked so appealing that she found herself smiling, unable to stay angry with him. After last night, and she still remembered exactly how his kiss had broken down all the barriers between them, the only thing on her mind was resuming where they had left off.

"Hop in. You look beautiful, by the way." He leaned over and opened the passenger-side door for her, and without giving this jaunt another moment's thought, she slid in beside him. The car smelled of sun-warmed leather, of Lee, of adventure.

"Where's Mandi?" she asked.

He angled the car back into traffic. "I left her at work."

She turned toward him. "So. You're into providing a free taxi service for single women?"

He slid an amused look at her. "Did I say it was free?"

She enjoyed parrying with him. "You mean there's a price to pay?"

"Isn't there always?"

"Now that you mention it, maybe so."

"Are you interested in the price you'll have to pay to-day?"

She raised her eyebrows, pretending to consider this. "I'd say so."

"First let me explain that I wish you had come with Mandi and me."

"Oh." She couldn't think of a snappy reply. "How was the smoothie?"

"Fine, but I came to the Blue Moon today to see you, not Mandi."

"You didn't act like it. And besides, I thought you wanted Goldy to read the tarot cards for you."

"Believe me, the tarot was secondary." He would have loved to share with her his reason for accompanying Mandi to the juiceteria, but he couldn't do that without mentioning wheat grass. If he did that, she'd immediately know more about him than he wanted her to know.

"I guess I could have been more forceful about asking you to come with us to the juice bar," he said. He'd be glad when this playacting stint was over and he could talk with her about his plans for Grassy Creek. He hoped she'd be as enthusiastic as he was.

"I still wouldn't have gone," she said.

He glanced over at her and, taking note of the stubborn set of her jaw, decided to change subjects.

"What did *you* think of Goldy's tarot reading?"

At this, she softened. "I'm not into that kind of thing, but Goldy is a sweetheart and I don't mind going along with it."

"Have you ever had yours read?"

"No, and I doubt that I ever will. What if she declares that I'm going to be kidnapped by Elvis worshipers, and in a spaceship yet?"

He smiled. "Maybe it's better than being kidnapped by me in a red convertible. That's a very attractive outfit, by the way. I recognize it from the store window." He thought he saw the hint of a blush spreading upward from her neck—a very graceful neck, he thought.

"Paulette and I went shopping, and she insisted that I buy this. I'll never wear it again."

"You don't go to the beach when you're in Boston?"

"A group of us rent a house on Cape Cod for a week in the summer. It's not like here, though. Not nearly as hot, for one thing, and not as—colorful."

She herself looked very colorful today, Lee thought. The yellow bikini showed through the transparent wrap, and although her hair was piled haphazardly on top of her head, most of it had fallen out of its clip and swung around her face.

"I'm glad you decided to come with me today," he said.

She blew out a long breath, treating him to a hint of a smile. "I only hope I won't live to regret it. Where are we going?"

"There's a park at the end of Miami Beach. Fleck suggested it."

"Who's Fleck?"

Damn! He'd slipped. It was hard keeping his guard up when what he wanted to do was get to know her better. "Fleck's a friend. Does a lot of snorkeling and diving." Which was why there were snorkels and swim fins in the trunk of the Mustang.

"I haven't been snorkling since I went to the Virgin Islands with my friend Dorrie on vacation a couple of years ago," she said. Suddenly a thought surfaced out of nowhere. "I didn't bring my cell phone," she said. "Or my PalmPilot."

"So what?"

"So I might miss an important call. I might need to check my schedule."

"We have no schedule, and if you miss any calls, so what?"

She pondered this. "So what," she repeated. "You're right. So what?" She laughed again, something that she was prone to do when she was with Lee.

When they arrived at the park and he had pulled the car into a parking slot, she went around to the trunk to help him with the equipment.

"Here you go," he said, handing her a pair of swim fins and a snorkel.

"Want me to carry the towels?" she asked.

"No, I've got them." He tossed them across his shoulder.

The parking lot smelled of hot sun-baked asphalt, suntan lotion, and sea air. They'd had to park a long way from the beach, and when they finally reached the sand, there were several Latino couples with children not far away. A curious crab peered at them from the edge of its hole, then scuttled out of sight. Out on the sun-spangled surface of the bay, someone cut a frothy wake on a jet ski.

Azure helped Lee spread the towels on the sand, and Lee removed his shirt. At first Azure felt self-conscious about unwrapping the pareo and exposing herself to his eyes in full sunlight, but when she did, he didn't stare and he didn't ogle. That earned him a few points in her estimation.

He tossed her a swim mask. "This one should fit," he said.

She tested the mask and found it satisfactory. Then she tugged the swim fins on and stomped around experimentally, scaring away a flock of seagulls who were looking for a handout. "I feel like one of those sea monsters in old Japanese science fiction movies," she said jokingly, and he grinned at her through his own swim mask and retorted, "I feel like I just stepped off the spaceship that the Elvis worshipers are expecting,'' which made her laugh because he did look like something otherworldly.

Once they were in the water, she became more confident. She was an excellent swimmer, and she swam year round at her health club in Boston. Here the water was so warm and clear, and the salt water made her feel light and buoyant in her own skin. She adjusted the snorkel to fit her mouth and submerged, following Lee as he paddled toward the rocks of the manmade jetty.

At first they didn't see any fish at all, only a discarded fishing lure and an old lawnmower tire. But as they hovered over the rocks, Lee motioned toward a black-and white striped fish, and soon there were at least a hundred, their scales flashing iridescent as the school surrounded them. The currents stirred by their passing felt like silk against her skin. Before long, a bigger fish swooped out of a crevice in hopes of finding his dinner. The school of striped fish scattered, and the big fish hunkered down between the rocks, lurking in wait for his next opportunity.

Before she had ever gone snorkeling that first time in the Virgin Islands, Azure had thought that the underwater world might look something like scenes out of the Disney movie, *The Little Mermaid*. It wasn't like that at all. The denizens of the sea were reclusive, and if you suspected one was hiding, you had to wait it out, all the while looking as little like a preying fish as you could.

Azure found that she and Lee could communicate by hand gestures, pointing when there was something unusual to see, motioning in the direction toward which one of them wanted to swim. Once she caught him staring at her from behind his face mask and wondered how she looked to him;

underwater, did she look fat or too pale, or did she seem sexy?

But it was easy to forget her own self-consciousness, and in the end, it didn't matter anyway. In the end, the only important thing was that they had a good time.

After Lee at last motioned for them to swim toward shore, they surfaced side by side in the shallows. Azure pulled off her snorkel and mask. "Did you see that big stingray near the large boulder?"

"At first when I spotted it lying there half buried in the sand I thought it was a piece of old plastic. When it skedaddled away, it stirred up so much mud that I almost couldn't tell what it was. How about that blue fish hiding behind that log right after we saw the stingray?"

Azure grinned. "I almost stepped on him before I came up to clear my mask."

They splashed through the shallows onto the shell-strewn sand, where Azure eased herself down on the edge of a towel and pulled off her swim fins. Lee threw himself down on the beach blanket beside her.

From where they sat, they could see the ship channel leading from the Port of Miami to the ocean. A huge ocean liner was passing by, its decks lined with tourists. Azure had never been on such a big ship; she wondered if she'd get seasick. Feeling totally relaxed, she lay back on the blanket and lifted her face to the last rays of the late afternoon sun. "There were lots of fish. More than I expected," she said lazily.

"Not as—"

Lee caught himself before saying that there hadn't been as many as he'd seen at the Great Barrier Reef off Australia last year. "Not as plentiful as I've seen in the Keys," he amended.

''Have you been there often?'' Of course he would have; the Florida Keys were made for people who loved the sun and the surf.

''I spent Christmases there when I was a kid,'' Lee said, biting off the words in a way that made her open her eyes in surprise. He was gazing out over the water, a flinty look in his eyes, and she raised herself on her elbows to study his expression.

''And now? Don't you go there now?''

He forced a smile. ''My parents used to drag me down to Key West when I'd rather have been home in Michigan going ice skating and skiing with my pals.''

''You're an only child?''

He nodded, and he still didn't look comfortable with this topic.

Azure, coming from a big roistering family with few rules and fewer restrictions, couldn't imagine growing up all alone. She struggled to think of a consoling remark, but Lee went on talking.

''We'd spend the winter holidays in a rented cottage, and my parents went out every night with their friends. There were always baby-sitters or nannies, but I was lonely.''

''Your parents—where do they live, Lee?''

''Mom died when I was a teenager, and my dad lives in Grosse Point, Michigan, in a huge mausoleum of a house where I hate to visit. We're not on good terms.''

''I'm sorry,'' Azure said, and she was regarding at him with such sympathy that Lee wanted to tell her all of it— how his father had sent him to expensive prep schools and been livid when Lee dropped out of college to start Dot.Musix, how his father had never forgiven him for becoming a huge success despite the dire predictions he'd made concerning his son's future.

But as Lee Sanders he couldn't tell Azure those things.

Azure fell back onto the blanket and closed her eyes, listening to the swish of the waves upon the shore, the cries of gulls overhead, the rumble of a boat motor far away. Lee was quiet beside her, seemingly lost in his memories.

When he hadn't spoken in a long while, she opened her eyes and discovered that she was gazing directly into Lee's clear gray ones, which were thoughtful and filled with—what? She wasn't sure. Certainly she hadn't expected this close scrutiny, which seemed ill-timed. Suddenly feeling too exposed, she flipped over on her front, turning her head to the side with the intention of pillowing it on her crossed arms, but that only put her mouth within a whisper of Lee's.

Before she could turn away, her breath caught in her throat as the air seemed to scintillate between them, seemed to inexplicably draw them into a magical sphere. And then, before she could remember how to breathe, Lee brushed aside a wet strand of hair with one finger and then let that finger graze down her cheek until it tipped her head toward his.

She felt something akin to relief as his mouth found hers.

She'd been aware since last night of a certain edgy heat that would not go away, and she knew it wouldn't take much to whip that heat into an all-consuming flame. As illogical as this attraction was, she wanted to bring it to its logical conclusion. Not here, not now—but somewhere, and soon.

He kissed with great skill, and he tasted of salt, of excitement and possibility and heartfelt longing. Stunned by her own rush of feeling, she opened her eyes and stole a glimpse of his face intent above her, caught the concentration of his expression and also the passion that he didn't bother to hide.

As he ended the kiss, she pulled away. Then the children from down the beach ran past and sprayed them with sand, effectively ending the special moment.

"I wish we didn't have to, but I suppose we'd better go," he said.

She didn't want to leave, either, but judging from the complexity of emotions that she'd seen reflected in Lee's eyes, there would be another time and place.

On their way back to the car, she thought about how sad Lee must have been when he was a little boy. Since she'd grown up, she'd learned a lot about loneliness, about that hollow feeling deep inside that was never filled by friends or family no matter how much they loved you. Did Lee feel that too?

When they had stowed the snorkeling gear in the car trunk, Lee bought them cups of conch chowder from a vendor with a cart, and they perched companionably side by side on a table under a spreading ficus tree to eat it. In the distance, the rush-hour traffic was beginning to die down, and close by, people were returning to their cars after a day at the beach.

Lee asked casually, "When will you go back to Boston, do you know yet?"

Azure stirred little bits of conch up from the bottom of her cup. "I finally got tired of waiting for my client to contact me and gave him a call."

Lee's mind switched into overdrive. "And what did he say?" he asked cautiously.

"That we can get together on Friday. That suits me fine."

"I see," Lee said. Clearly she did not yet know that he was her client. On the spur of the moment, he could only think of one explanation for Azure's making an appointment to see him on Friday, and that was that she had somehow managed to talk with Fleck.

Azure went on talking, oblivious to the questions she had raised in his mind. "I have the next couple of days to do some sightseeing. I've told the rental company to cancel the car until Friday, and I'm going to make it a limo with a driver so I can pick up my client and impress him by taking him to dinner."

"Oh, a limo would impress him, all right," Lee said, trying to hide his astonishment at this unforeseen development and hoping that Azure didn't detect his wry humor. Fleck would no doubt be thrilled to be driven around by Azure in her hired limo.

"The account is very important to my boss."

As Lee digested this information, the parking lot lights began to wink on overhead, and the chowder vendor packed up his cart and left. A dog snuffled around beneath the nearby oleander bushes, and somewhere a child started crying. Lee knew he'd better talk to Fleck, and soon. He wished for his cell phone, and he thought about using a public phone to call Fleck on the *Samoa.* But if he used the public phone at the edge of the parking lot, Azure might want to listen. Not a good idea.

"Lee, this chowder is wonderful, but how about dinner? Paulette's left for a four-day seminar, and I was thinking that we could go back to her apartment and dig something out of the freezer. She saved leftover food from the wedding in neat little packets, all ready to pop in the microwave."

Lee thought that going back to the empty apartment with Azure seemed like a great idea, but if he did, how would he manage to talk with Fleck? Well, once they were there and she was preparing the food, he'd make an excuse to run out to the car and hunt up a pay phone on the street. Or maybe he'd be able to sneak the phone out onto the balcony while Azure was otherwise occupied and talk there unobserved.

Azure chatted most of the way back to the Blue Moon, saving him from making conversation. It was just as well, he thought, since he had perhaps said too much back at the park when he was telling her about his childhood. That time of his life had never been one of his favorite topics, and he seldom mentioned it. He was still surprised that he had wanted to talk about it with Azure.

When they reached the Blue Moon, Goldy was simultaneously scarfing down a take-out dinner from a carton and talking on the phone. She treated them to a friendly wave as they headed upstairs.

As they rounded the corner from the stairwell, they heard someone chanting a very long *"Ommmmmmmm,"* which Azure immediately identified as a yoga chant. To their startled amazement, a man was sitting in front of Paulette's door in a Half-Lotus position and a full-grown yellow chicken was pecking around on the carpet. The man wore his hair in a glossy slicked-back pompadour and looked vaguely familiar.

"Who are you?" Azure demanded.

The man opened his eyes. "I'm Kevin. I'm testing the vibrations in this hallway. The spaceship is supposed to land on the beachfront here, you know, and those of us who are believers want to rent rooms at the Blue Moon for the occasion. The rooms have to have the right vibes, though. Any room simply will not do."

"And the chicken?" Lee said warily.

"That's Fricassee. She needs a home."

"Oh," Azure said, remembering. "I've seen you before,

walking the chicken on a leash.'' It had been only yesterday, when she was waiting at the curb outside the Blue Moon for Lee to pick her up.

''That's me.'' The chicken pecked its way over to Kevin and hopped into his lap, where he petted it consolingly. ''Don't worry, sweetheart. We'll find you a home. And it won't be any old chicken coop, either.'' He blinked up at Azure. ''I rescued her from a box where people dropped in fifty cents and she played the piano. A chicken with this much talent shouldn't be in a carnival sideshow, right?''

''Right,'' Azure agreed. ''Um, Kevin, I don't suppose you'd consider moving so we could get into the apartment?''

This seemed to upset the man considerably. ''I'm supposed to chant seven more Oms and then I have to meditate for at least an hour. My crystals said that this is the place. If I move, I start all over again.''

Lee narrowed his eyes. ''Does Goldy know you're here?''

''I came up the back stairs. Goldy doesn't have to know everything. She knows me, though. I come here for the yoga class on the roof every Tuesday night. I'm a little early today, that's all.''

''Keep him talking,'' Azure whispered to Lee, who was starting to look annoyed. ''I'll go speak to Goldy.''

She ran down the stairs and reached the lobby desk as her uncle Nate came ambling through the front door. ''Azure, where have you been keeping yourself? You look wonderful, dear. Leah wants you to come for dinner before you go back to Boston.''

''Uncle Nate, I—'' She realized that Goldy was still on the phone, and since the woman was gesticulating wildly and treating someone to a discourse on the healing powers of copper bracelets, she doubted the wisdom of interrupting.

She turned to Uncle Nate. "We've got this guy who is meditating in front of Paulette's apartment. He won't move. His name is Kevin, and he's a little strange. He says he's here for the yoga class."

"Oh, Kevin. Everyone knows him. He's peculiar but harmless. Want me to come up and talk with him? He might want to join in a game of pinochle. I'm on my way to meet my buddies right now."

Azure grabbed her uncle's arm. "Will you? Oh, that's great."

Uncle Nate climbed the stairs behind her, complaining that he never got to climb stairs anymore because Leah wouldn't let him. "That woman—and she's a wonderful woman, mind you—she wants to make a lapdog out of me. I tell her, 'Leah, a man's got to be a man.' And then I go out and climb stairs anyway." He chuckled.

Kevin was still sitting in the Half-Lotus position and earnestly carrying on a conversation with Lee about the merits of liberating animals from places where they shouldn't be. This included insects, including a tarantula once kept as a curiosity in a roadside petting zoo west of town.

"Not that anyone petted the tarantula," Kevin said seriously. "But it didn't like being cooped up in a cage. So I let it loose in the Everglades. I'm sure it's much happier— oh, hello, Nate. I haven't seen you around lately."

"I been sick, but I'm fine now. Say, Kevin, the boys down at the café have been asking about you. How about coming along with me for a little game of—"

At that moment, the chicken, which had been hunkered down near the fire extinguisher, rose up in a flurry of feathers and squawked loudly. Then it flew directly at Uncle Nate, flapping its wings and cackling.

"Get this chicken off me!" Nate yelled, flapping his arms and batting it away.

Lee shoved Uncle Nate behind him, and Azure moved to help Kevin capture the chicken. The chicken subsided with a last resigned squawk and glared balefully at Nate from the protection of Kevin's arms while making disgruntled noises deep in its throat.

"What's going on here?" demanded Goldy, who was puffing her way up the stairs. "Did I hear a chicken? How could I hear a chicken? Oh, it's you," she said when she saw Kevin.

Uncle Nate ventured out from behind Lee. "I wish someone would tell me what I ever did to make a chicken hate a lovable guy like me," he said, looking hurt.

"Are you all right?" Azure asked anxiously.

"Of course I'm all right. I'm just surprised, that's all. And if Leah hears about this, she'll never let me out of her sight. Attacked by a chicken! In Miami Beach! It's a tapestry." He brushed off his shirt and looked indignant.

"He means it's a travesty," Azure said in a low tone to Lee.

Kevin, who had sprung up out of his yoga pose when Fricassee went into attack mode, sidled closer to Nate and sniffed. "It's as I suspected," he said. "You're wearing Old Spice aftershave. Fricassee hates Old Spice. The smell of it throws her into a rage every time."

"I never heard of such a thing," Nate said.

"Well, I never did, either, but who knows what torment she has known?" said Kevin, smoothing Fricassee's ruffled feathers.

"Well," said Nate. "There's torments and there's torments. You're tormenting yourself by trying to keep a chicken in Miami Beach.''

"She needs someone to love her," Kevin said in a wounded tone. He added hopefully, "Maybe one of you would like to keep her.''

"Chickens are not allowable pets at the Blue Moon," huffed Goldy.

"The chicken could stay for a while, couldn't it? While I take Kevin *out of here*—" Nate emphasized the last three words "—for a game of pinochle with my buddies?''

"I see the wisdom of that," Goldy said thoughtfully. "I suppose the chicken could stay in a box beneath my desk. Until you come back and get it, that is," she said to Kevin.

"I'm supposed to meditate, not go off and play cards," Kevin said stubbornly. "I'm supposed to go to yoga class.''

"You said you'd have to start your meditation over if you got up. You got up," Azure pointed out.

"And as for the yoga class, I heard it's been canceled," added Goldy.

Kevin looked disconcerted, then rallied. "Perhaps the crystals lied and this wasn't the perfect spot for my meditation. You think that could be it?''

"Definitely," Goldy said. "Crystals can be wrong.''

"Okay. I'll accept that. Let's go, Nate, I'll buy you a beer.''

"All right, but only if no one tells Leah about the beer. She thinks I shouldn't drink anything stronger than Kool-Aid.''

They all trooped downstairs, and Goldy found a cardboard box that fit under her desk. "The chicken will be perfectly safe here," she assured Kevin.

"Take good care of her, won't you?" Kevin said plaintively as Uncle Nate shepherded him out the door.

"No problem," said Goldy.

"That chicken would make great chicken salad," Lee muttered, but Azure shushed him with a look and hurried him upstairs before he got any ideas.

Once they were in the apartment, Azure went and changed out of her damp beach clothes. Then, while Lee poured them both a glass of wine, she dug the food left over from the reception out of the freezer. After she heated it in the microwave oven they both heaped their plates and feasted on health food hors d'ouevres until they couldn't eat any more.

After they rinsed the plates in the sink, Azure began to load the dishwasher in a series of moves that neatly delineated her derriere under the loose two-piece outfit she wore. Watching her, Lee felt a familiar stirring in his nether regions and promptly tried to quell it, more or less unsuccessfully.

She caught him looking at her. "Is anything wrong?"

He'd felt the beginning of the headache when they were facing off with Kevin. "Too much sun today, I think. I— well, I don't suppose you have any aspirins handy?"

"Sure."

Azure went to get the aspirins, and Lee washed them down with the rest of his second glass of wine.

"Come into the living room," Azure said. "You'll be more comfortable on the couch."

He followed her, and she arranged a couple of pillows under his head. The sunwashed scent of her almost got to him, and he would have pulled her down on the couch beside him but she deftly sidestepped his reach. He didn't know if her evasion was by design or not, but he rather thought it wasn't. If he had read the signs correctly, she wouldn't be averse to upping the sexual quotient of this relationship. He had intended to pursue that course, but the aspirins were beginning to kick in, and all he wanted to do was to lean back against the soft pillows and close his eyes.

She went away briefly. "How are you feeling?" When he opened his eyes, she was standing above him, her forehead furrowed with concern. With the kitchen light behind her, he could see the outline of her figure underneath her clothes.

"I'm a little sleepy," he admitted. Belatedly he remembered that he'd meant to call Fleck to find out exactly what he had told Azure while he was pretending to be Leonardo Santori. But at the moment, he didn't feel like moving from this couch.

He reached up and grabbed Azure's hand, pulling her toward him. "Sit down a minute?"

She did sit beside him, and he closed his eyes. This was so comfortable, so peaceful, and he was beginning to feel very mellow. After a few minutes, she began to smooth his hair back from his forehead. She stroked his head, his temples. Then he felt her lips, soft and gentle, upon his cheek.

"Azure," he said, opening his eyes, and it was as if he couldn't drink in enough of her beauty. He was startlingly, achingly aware of her in that moment, of her softly shadowed throat, her pale hair swooping down to brush against his face. She was so lovely she took his breath away, so beautiful that she made his senses spin.

She settled against him on the couch so that he could feel her body molding against his. Her lips were soft, provocative, and incredibly sensual. Before he could deepen the kiss, he felt her mouth opening to his, her tongue teasing. This wasn't the way it was supposed to be, he thought fuzzily. There was supposed to be a grand seduction scene, complete with candlelight and wine. He'd wanted to remove her clothes garment by garment, revealing her to his gaze bit by bit, and then when he couldn't stand it any longer, he would bear her away to bed. A big bed, maybe, strewn with flowers.

But now here they were with no candlelight and no romance. Just the two of them, just her lips and his, just long leisurely kisses, one melting into the next until he thought he would die of pleasure.

She didn't speak, though she did keep kissing him, until after a long time the kisses tapered off and they came up for air.

"Nice," he said, realizing that his left hand had worked its way under her shirt and was massaging someplace between her ribs and her breasts. She wore panties, he discovered when his hand ventured beneath the waistband of her shorts. But no bra.

"Mmm," she said, leaning into the caress. He thought he would close his eyes for a moment, just a moment, and then perhaps he would resume kissing her. Kissing her, and touching her, and loving her.

He drifted off to sleep, lost in a daydream that became a nighttime dream of the most delicious variety. He didn't even know when she slipped out from under his arm so she could stand up, or when she removed his shoes and lifted his feet up to the couch.

In his mind, she was sleeping beside him, her head on his shoulder, her hand curled upon his chest, and he was telling her about all the things he wanted to do to her, now and forever.

8

___

YOU'VE GOT MAIL!
To: A_OConnor@wixler.org
From: D_Colangelo@wixler.org
Subject: that paco!

a.j., you won't believe it but paco went ballistic when i told him you'd met someone. he acted like he couldn't believe that you'd actually take up with another guy. i said, well, didn't he have someone else, and didn't he think that was okay? he said he and tiffany are completely quits, finis, over. i didn't say anything about when you'd be back, a.j. you are coming back, aren't you?
luv,
Dor

To: D_Colangelo@wixler.org
From: A_OConnor@wixler.org
Subject: Re: that paco!

Serves Paco right, in my opinion. Right now the guy I'm crazy about is asleep on the couch alone. What happened is too long to tell, but suffice it to say that I had intended to be sleeping with him both tonight and last night (but did not due to circumstances). He's so adorable when he sleeps, Dorrie! He kind of snores, only it's more like purring. And he's nice, Dor, and he's personable, and—but I

*digress. Tell Paco I said to take a long walk off a short
pier. And you should try some of those thong panties if you
haven't already. They're not nearly as uncomfortable as
they look.
Love,
A.J.*

WHEN SHE WOKE UP THE NEXT morning in Paulette's bed
instead of on the pull-out couch in the living room, Azure
had to think for a moment to remember where she was.
Then it all came back to her—sun and fun, Kevin and his
chicken, and Lee falling asleep on the couch afterward.

She got out of bed and padded into the living room. Lee
slept with his mouth open, a position that she found attractive in few men but actually was becoming to him.

She went into the kitchen, started the coffee, and cut a
cantaloupe into wedges. As she was arranging the wedges
on a cut-glass plate, Lee stirred and slowly sat up.

"Good morning," she said.

"It's morning?"

"Look outside."

He did and saw sunshine. He groaned. "It's morning, all
right. I didn't mean to sleep all night."

"Oh, and what did you mean to do?"

"I meant to go on kissing you," he said. He swung his
feet over the edge of the couch.

Azure brought the plate of cantaloupe into the living
room and set it down on the table beside Lee. "Do you
have plans for today?" she asked as she walked back to
the kitchen.

He started to say no, but then he remembered the appointment with the man from the seed company. "I—well,
as it happens, I do."

Azure looked surprised. "Oh. Well, never mind, then."

He joined her in the kitchen. "How about dinner tonight?"

She turned away, fiddling with coffee mugs and sugar and spoons. "I'd like that. But not if you're busy."

"I won't be. This appointment today—it's important, or I'd break it." He had to talk with Fleck, too, and find out what had passed between him and Azure.

She handed him a mug of coffee. "It's about a job?"

"More or less." He hated being evasive. He hated pretending to be someone he wasn't. But he couldn't come clean. Not now, when things were going so well. Not now, when, if he read the signs correctly, she was beginning to care about him.

"A job—that's good, right?" She took her own mug and preceded him into the living room, where she sat on the couch with one leg tucked under her.

"Yes, it is." He sat, too, but on the chair across the room. He was eager now to get out of here, anxious about what Fleck had told her, worried that he had dug himself in too deep with this deception of his. By tonight, he'd have his facts straight and his course would be clear. He'd tell her who he was, tell her that he was in love with her, ask her if she felt the same.

"Help yourself to the cantaloupe," she said.

"No, I'd better go." He took his half-full coffee mug to the sink.

"I thought we could have a leisurely breakfast. I could fix eggs, toast—"

"I'm afraid I don't have time."

Her expression darkened. "Is anything wrong? Did I do or say something?"

At the door, he grasped her shoulders. They felt delicate

under her thin robe, and he imagined how it would be to brush the robe aside, to kiss the hollow below her shoulder, to feather more kisses up the side of her neck. "Everything is fine. I have something I need to do, that's all, and I'm looking forward to this evening. Pick you up at seven?"

"Seven is fine," she said, but her eyes were deep pools of concern.

"I—" he said, but he stopped short of what he wanted to say. There would be time for that later.

"See you tonight," was all he said, and then he left.

Azure closed the door softly behind him, wondering why he had bolted so quickly.

At least she would have time this morning to work out, she thought, and even though she wanted to, she resisted the urge to go out on the balcony and watch as Lee's red convertible pulled out of the parking lot.

"WHAT DID YOU SAY TO AZURE when she called me?" Lee demanded when he found Fleck lounging in the main salon of the *Samoa*.

Fleck clicked the remote control and brought the large-screen TV out from behind the folding doors that hid it from view when it wasn't in use. "Only that you'd have dinner with her on Friday."

"Friday," Lee repeated. He thought for a moment. "The day after tomorrow. That means that I have until then to be Lee Sanders."

"Is that a problem?"

"I don't know. I want to tell her who I am. I *need* to tell her who I am. This pretending to be someone else presents problems."

"I haven't noticed that," Fleck said with a straight face.

"Having fun, are you?" Lee couldn't help grinning.

"You'd better believe it. I found a beach bunny waiting in the Mercedes when I came out of the juiceteria yesterday. That wouldn't have been so bad, except that I had been chatting up this awesome babe inside, and she—"

"Awesome babe? Juiceteria? This babe wouldn't have happened to have a small diamond inserted in a hole in her left nostril, would she?"

"How did you know?" Fleck stared at him.

"A hunch."

"You don't have dibs on her, do you?"

"No, Azure is the one for me."

"Hey, Lee, are you going to tell Azure or not?"

"I'll tell her tonight, probably. But if she calls again, find some excuse not to talk to her. I don't want you messing things up."

"Right-o, buddy. Everything is kewl."

Including his head, Lee thought, which had better remain cool so that he could work his way out of this quagmire of deception.

THE PHONE AT THE APARTMENT was ringing as Azure let herself in after a full workout at the gym.

"Hello?"

"A.J.! Thank goodness you've finally answered!"

It was Dorrie, and Azure was delighted to hear her voice. "Is something wrong at work?"

"No, but Harry is agitated over this Santori thing."

"You can tell him I'm having dinner with Santori on Friday."

"That will relieve him a whole bunch, I'm sure. But what's with this guy of yours? The one you're so crazy about?"

Azure sank down on the couch and touched the cushion

where Lee had rested his head last night. It still smelled of him, or was it her imagination?

"I may have overstated things, Dor. I don't know what to think. He spent the night on the couch—"

"All night?"

"Yes, all night. I slept in Paulette's bed."

"Paulette's not there?"

"She went to a seminar in Orlando. Get this, Dorrie— he spent the night and ran off without even drinking all of his coffee this morning."

"Kiss or no kiss?"

"A brush on the cheek and a Shoulder Grasp."

"Ah, The Shoulder Grasp. And what did you do?"

"Nothing. I was too stunned that he was leaving. He asked me out for tonight, though."

"Hmm. What will you wear?"

"I don't know. I may have to go shopping again."

"Buy something very sexy. Something you're almost falling out of. And then fall out of it at an appropriate time." Dorrie laughed.

"What's all this stuff you keep writing to me about Paco? You know I'm over him."

"He's not over you, A.J. He went nuts when I told him you'd met someone. He yelped and spilled his café latte down the front of his pants. I hope it burned him in an inconvenient place."

"Me, too." She paused and glanced at her watch. "I'd better run, Dorrie, if I'm going to go shopping."

"Okay, but pick up your cell phone once in a while, won't you? And answer my e-mails."

Azure was hard put to explain how she only booted up her laptop once a day now and how her cell phone had lost its importance. She couldn't even explain it to herself, unless it was a result of being overcome by fresh ocean breezes, gaudy colors, and too much sun.

"Right. 'Bye, Dorrie."

"Goodbye, A.J."

After she had hung up, Azure went to find more clothes of Paulette's that would fit. She discovered a lime-green wraparound skirt in the back of the closet and a clingy black T-shirt with rhinestones around the neckline. With big sunglasses and hair piled haphazardly high with loose tendrils escaping around her face, she looked like a babe. A South Beach babe.

Which was proven when she sallied past Goldy's desk and Goldy called after her, "Oh, Mandi! Come here for a minute, please."

Azure turned back around. "I'm Azure. Did I fool you?"

Goldy appeared flustered. "You sure did. What's come over you?"

"A tropical depression, which I'm trying to alleviate by dressing for success. With Lee, I mean."

"I see. You look mighty cheesy, Azure."

"Thanks, I'll take that as a compliment and as a sign that I'm finally starting to fit in around here."

She heard a clucking from below the counter near Goldy's feet. Thoroughly inured to Miami Beach quirkiness by this time, Azure didn't bat an eyelash, nor did she remind Goldy of her own rule that chickens were not allowable pets at the Blue Moon.

LEE ARRIVED TO PICK HER UP for dinner a few minutes before seven. His early arrival might have knocked Azure off balance if she hadn't been ready and waiting for at least half an hour herself. Her hair was loose, cascading down her back in a shimmering free-fall, and she was dressed to stun in a new black slinky strapless confection that made the most of her breasts, which kept surging over the top of it like pink grapefruit bouncing out of a bowl.

Lee became properly bug-eyed when she answered the door, and the look on his face made all the money she had spent on her new dress well worth it. She'd invested in glittery mascara, too, after seeing a model in a store wearing it, and she'd bought a pair of strappy black sandals with impossibly high heels. She wouldn't be able to run fast in those shoes, and she hoped that Lee would realize that she didn't want to.

As for Lee, he looked suave and debonair in a pale gray sport coat worn over a white shirt thrown open at the throat. Below that he wore jeans and boat shoes without socks. She thought he looked fantastic, except for the no socks.

He held the door open for her as they left the apartment. "Want to try a new place around the corner? Goldy says it's good."

"That sounds wonderful."

Goldy was urging the chicken around the lobby on its leash when they arrived in the lobby. "I can walk her like a dog. Isn't that something? Where are you two headed?"

"Lu's Junkanoo, on your recommendation."

"Try their special drinks," she said.

"I take it you've decided to keep Fricassee?"

"Kevin hasn't shown up to take her back," Goldy said, but she didn't seem unhappy about it.

Lee chuckled as they left the building. "That Goldy. It's always something."

"Never a dull moment," Azure agreed, thinking that things were going smoothly this evening with Lee. The unaccountably sexy light in his eyes as he appraised her earlier, the eagerness with which he seemed to greet the evening, the attentive way in which he helped her into the Mustang—none of this bespoke a man who was tired of the chase.

The restaurant turned out to be decorated in pink and purple, and waiters wore straw hats and turquoise shirts with brightly patterned ties. Reggae music blared from speakers hidden behind potted palms, and they went into the bar and sat down at a tiny table.

Lee ordered a beer, and Azure ordered white wine at first. But Lee thought she was looking longingly at the drink that a waiter carried past them, one that came in a large frosty glass with a wedge of pineapple hanging over the edge. "Want one of those?"

She shook her head. "No, that's not necessary," she said, thinking that Lee's limited budget might not extend to fancy drinks, but Lee had already beckoned the waiter over to their table.

The waiter poised his pencil over his order pad. "We have a special on tonight. It's Lu's Mango Tango Surprise, and if you drink three of them you get the fourth one free."

"What's in it?"

"If I told you that, it wouldn't be a surprise," said the waiter with a wink.

"Go ahead, Azure, try it," Lee urged. He thought it was cute the way she squinched up her eyes and thought for a moment.

"All right. But I'll never be able to drink three of them." She settled back in her chair and smiled at him. "You know what I'm thinking?" she said.

"Not a clue."

"That I'm getting into this Miami Beach rhythm, finally."

The waiter brought her drink, and she took a sip through

the straw. Her eyes crinkled in delight. "Mmm, that's good. Know what? This drink is rather strong."

"Live it up, Azure. Let your hair down."

She fluffed her fingers through it. "It's already down anyway." She laughed. "I can't remember when I last felt so carefree. Plus I'm getting a tan that will impress everybody at the office."

"Do you like living in Boston?"

She considered this. "I think so. I mean, I was sure I did up until now. But when I think of going back, I seem to remember how drab all those gray buildings look when compared to the exciting colors of Miami Beach. The pinks, the turquoises, the bright greens and oranges—all jumbled together in a kind of tropical salad. It's so much more energetic, so—" She stopped and thought for a moment. "It's so titillating, I guess I'm trying to say."

Lee had an idea that Azure O'Connor had never used the word "titillating" in a sentence in her life. He leaned back and watched as she pulled the straw out of her drink, set the pineapple wedge aside, and tipped the glass up to drain it.

A waiter appeared immediately with another drink. "I didn't think I wanted another," she confided, leaning over the table toward Lee, "but they're awfully good." She had positioned herself so that he had a spectacular view of her cleavage, and he found himself shifting in his seat and thinking that he wouldn't mind being next to her so that he could slide an arm around her shoulders. But she had taken off on another subject.

"I told Karma that I didn't know how she could marry Slade and go and live on that ranch way out at the edge of the Everglades, but she was extremely happy about the whole thing. I guess when you meet someone special, you have to tailor your life to fit his. Hers. If you're a guy, I mean. Gosh, I think the drinks are getting to me. Is it possible to feel giddy after only one and a little bit of another?''

Lee signaled the waiter to bring him another beer. ''I'm not sure, Azure, but as long as you're having a good time, giddy is fine with me.''

''Maybe,'' she said, frowning slightly, ''we should eat dinner. But first I'm going to hit the ladies' room to freshen up.'' She got up and started across the room, and Lee thought he detected a definite wobble to her path.

While she was gone, he slipped the head waiter a twenty-dollar bill, and when Azure came back, they were led to the best table in the place, which overlooked a garden planted with orchids and banana trees and a lot of other tropical foliage that he didn't recognize.

''Nice restaurant,'' Azure said after they were seated. ''Tell me, Lee, have you ever been to Boston?''

''One or twice,'' he said.

''You could come for a visit sometime.''

He tried to imagine this and couldn't. He was so into his masquerade as Lee Sanders that it was difficult to picture going to Azure's apartment, watching her cook dinner for him, meeting her friends from work. But it was heartening to know that she would like him to come to see her. Would it actually happen? He didn't know. He only knew that he wanted her to be part of his life from now on, and when he returned to his Leonardo Santori persona, her perception of him would change.

He felt a certain regret at the inevitability of this. He liked things the way they were. He liked sitting across the table from Azure and watching her flip her long hair back with the thumb and forefinger of one hand. He liked anticipating making love with her. He liked his illusion that they could somehow create a life together—but was it only an illusion? Or could he make it real?

They ordered hearts-of-palm salad, to be followed by paella for two. By the time the entree arrived, Azure was on her third drink. Nevertheless, she attacked the paella with gusto, proclaiming it the best she'd ever eaten. "And we have great shefood—*seafood*—in Boston. Really great."

"I know," he said. He thought about tonight and the secret that he needed to reveal to her. There was no telling how that would go, he knew, but, assuming that she accepted who he was and what he was, he'd want to see her tomorrow.

"If you don't have any plans for tomorrow, let's get together," he said. He'd show her the *Samoa,* introduce her to Fleck. He'd ask for dinner to be served on the aft deck for only the two of them, a truly romantic evening.

She smiled. "I'd like that."

He gestured toward the mussel shells that she was lining up in a row across the tabletop. "What are you doing?"

"Making a barrier across the table. You cross it at your peril."

"And is there some reason you don't want me to cross it?" he teased.

"No, I want you to. It's a silly thing, this line. Because I've wanted you to cross it since the night before last."

"I can assure you that the line will be crossed," he said seriously. "You and I are going to resume where we left off."

"Left off. I left off something…but not my swimsuit. At the nude beach, I mean." She laughed, a tinkle of sound so melodious that it sounded like little bells.

"I told you I'd never go to that beach again, but if you

want to, I'll consider it,'' he said, holding back his own laughter. He was pretty sure that Azure didn't know what she was saying. By this time, she'd already downed three drinks, and the waiter was bearing another toward their table.

"Your free drink, ma'am," he said, setting it in front of her with a flourish. "Congratulations on finishing three Mango Tango Surprises."

"Congratu-gratu-lay-shuns to you for bringing four of them," Azure said to the waiter seriously, ending with a little hiccup.

"Would you care for dessert?"

"How about it?" Lee said.

"I am not getting dessert. I have run up a huge enough check already. And if I get fat, I jiggle. I worked out today, but not enough to go around eating desserts. You have dessert, Lee."

He signaled for the check. "No thanks. I think we'd better go."

"We should," Azure agreed. "Got to cross that line. But not yet, even though the tarot cards said that you are 'the ultimate in masculinity and dominate sexually.' Do you intend to dominate me sexually, Lee?"

"I think," he said seriously, "that a sexual relationship is something to be shared. I don't want to dominate anyone, Azure, and certainly not you." He paid the check with cash, not a credit card, which might draw her attention to the name of Leonardo Santori.

"That's good," she said dreamily. "If I were dominated, I don't think I could give you the sensual bliss that the tarot promised."

Was she serious? He didn't know. But she was *tipsy*, that was for sure.

"I'm thinking maybe we should go in the bar and dance," she said.

He recalled the obstacle card in his tarot reading. Maybe that was why things kept happening to keep them from making love. Still, dancing wasn't a bad idea. At least he would be holding her in his arms. "Would you like that?" He held her chair while she stood up.

"How else will I get to show off my rhumba?" she said, treating everyone in sight to a suggestive little wiggle that only whetted his eagerness to get her back to Paulette's empty apartment.

Before he knew it, she had dragged him to the middle of a tiny dance floor in the bar and he had his arms around her. But dancing slowly and holding her close was not to be. Salsa, this Latin music was called, and Azure flung herself into the merengue with wild abandon.

Lee was game enough. He had learned to dance all the Latin dances in Rio de Janeiro during a month-long stay, but even the South American women who had been his partners there didn't quite have the sexy moves that Azure did when she put her heart, not to mention her hips, into it.

"Where did you learn this?" he panted against her ear as she delicately bumped her pelvis against his. He had to admit it: this was his kind of dancing.

"Oh, you don't want to know," she said.

He swung her out and around, holding his breath as her breasts crested over the top of her bodice. "I *do* want to know," he insisted.

"From Paco. My unfaithful Argentinny—I mean Argenty—*Argentinian*—boyfriend."

The music segued into a soulful tango. "We used to dance a lot," she said. "The samba. Merengue. Flamenco.

And he may have been a jerk, but Paco could sure dance the tango,'' she said.

''So can I,'' he answered, prepared to prove it.

The tango was a sensuous dance, a passionate one, and as he led Azure through the steps, the dance seemed to mimic the sex act. Advancing to the throbbing beat, then retreating; caressing, then flinging themselves away from each other only to rendezvous again with more passion and soul. He thought that he had been mistaken when he thought that Azure was too reserved. Her usual demeanor might be cool as ice, but something had ignited a fire in her blood and he hoped it was her feelings for him.

As the last beat of the music died away, several onlookers clapped, and Lee was sure that more than one of them realized that he and his gorgeous partner were headed for a torrid session of lovemaking that night.

Azure stumbled against him as they reached the door. He gripped her arm firmly for support and wondered if four Mango Tango Surprises had been such a good idea. On the other hand, after a few drinks Azure had finally shown herself to be a wild woman at heart.

''Are you all right?'' he asked anxiously.

''I am quite all right,'' she said with dignity.

When they reached the car, he opened the door on the passenger side and waited for her to get in. But she didn't get in immediately. Instead, right in the middle of the parking lot with the sodium vapor lights glowing orange overhead and a clump of crispy critter tourists exclaiming about each others' sunburns as they passed, she flung herself against him, pressing so close that he felt her breasts full against his chest. She kissed him, an expert kiss involving teeth and tongue and her body molded against his all the way to his feet. His hand, moving of its own volition, swept up to cup the bottom of her breast, and she stopped kissing him to take a sharp little surprised breath, exclaiming, "Oh!"

He bent his head and breathed deeply of the scent of her soft skin as she arched her back in response. She smelled slightly of suntan lotion, of strawberry-scented shampoo, of tropical flowers. He wanted to bury his face in her breasts, could have become lost in her, wanted to take her right there and then, but he was brought rudely to his senses by the slam of a car door only a few feet away and the roar of the car engine to life. Suddenly they were illuminated in a pair of bright headlights, and he and Azure sprang apart, blinking.

He watched as Azure collected herself and slid into the car, then went around and got in beside her. When he glanced over at her, her head was lolled back against the seat, exposing her delectable throat and emphasizing her well-toned shoulders. And that dress, that beautiful dress—well, it showed so much of her breasts that he could hardly think straight. Lee swallowed; he didn't think he had ever been more excited by a woman in his life.

"Azure? Is everything okay?"

She opened her eyes, and he wanted to sink into their blue depths. "I was woozy for just a minute," she admitted. "I had a lot to drink tonight." She reached over and rested her hand on his thigh, and her touch sent a frisson of excitement zinging through his veins.

"Let's go break down all the barriers, Lee," she murmured. "All of them."

"You got it," he said, and he rammed the Mustang's gearshift into reverse. Which was not at all appropriate, he reflected, for a relationship that was at long last going forward.

GOLDY WAS OFF DUTY. Azure had to use a passkey to enter the Blue Moon, and the lobby was shadowed, quiet, and dark as they passed through. Once in the apartment, Azure turned on the glaring overhead light, then shook her head. "This won't do," she said, and she rummaged in a kitchen drawer until she found candles and matches. She went into the bedroom and lit some candles there, but when she came back into the living room and started to light the ones in the brass holders on the trunk that was the coffee table, her hand trembled.

She knew she shouldn't have had so much to drink. "You'd better do this," she said shakily, handing the matches to Lee.

She switched on soft music while he lit the candles, and when he had finished, she gazed at him across a distance of awe and wonder and held her arms open wide. He had been waiting, it seemed to him, far too long for that simple gesture and for the welcoming light in her eyes.

He went to her, enfolded her in his strong arms and listened to her pulse beating at her temple as he held her close. It felt right, this embrace, right and proper and true.

She lifted her face to his, and a slow heat seemed to emanate from her body and draw him in. "Azure," he said unsteadily, his voice rough with emotion. Not passion, he noted even as his lips took hers, though there would be that. The emotion that he was feeling was something finer and more real; a sparkling, shining, joyous delight that he was finally going to be one with the only woman who mattered.

He caressed her spine, slow and easy, taking his time with kissing her. Responding, she curved her body against his as though they had practiced this, but why wouldn't they know this dance when they had done the other so well?

He should have asked this earlier, but there hadn't been a good time. "Azure," he said gently, "are you protected?"

She shook her head, her eyes registering concern.

"I'll take care of it," he said.

"Thank you," she said, her voice no more than a whisper.

Somehow she slid fluidly out of her dress, somehow he was divested of his jacket, his shirt, his underwear, and when she stood at last before him totally revealed to his gaze, he could only say as she moved closer, "I never dreamed you would be so lovely."

She was staring at his tattoo. Or something in that general region.

"Somehow," she said slowly, "I don't think we need to talk about your tattoo for distraction." She ended her sentence with a little hiccup, and he was reminded of how much she'd had to drink.

"In fact, we don't have to talk at all," he said.

"Let's get on with this then," she said, and he almost chuckled at her urgency. She flowed smoothly into his arms, pressing her lips to the hollow of his shoulder, whispering his name against his hot skin. Her nipples rose into sharp little points against his hands, and her breasts felt warm and swollen and heavy. He wanted to taste them, draw them deep into his mouth, but she said, "Wait" and led him into the bedroom.

There seemed to be candles everywhere, on the dresser, on the windowsill, on the bedside table. Smiling up at him, she drew him down on the bed beside her, and he felt kindled by the light, energized and wholly aroused by it.

As she lay back amid the pillows, his heart began to beat so loudly that he thought it would burst through his chest.

He heard himself moan deep in his throat as her hungry mouth opened to his. And then, as he had imagined he would do, he was trailing kisses run together like a string of pearls to the hollow of her throat, his mouth moving lower, lower. She gasped softly as his tongue outlined the circle around one nipple, then the other. At last he cupped her breasts in the palms of his hands, and they were exactly as he knew they would be—round and full with dark areolae.

He took his time exploring her, wanting to know every part of her body. But she was eager, urgent, trembling beneath his touch. When he felt her hands clasp possessively around him, he knew he couldn't wait much longer. He caressed the soft cleft at the juncture of her thighs. "You're ready," he said, and she replied, the word a mere murmur, "Yes."

He knew he would remember this moment all of his life. Slowly he raised himself over her, felt her rising gracefully to meet him as he readied himself. He closed his eyes, steeped in sensation, lost in longing, and knew the agony of holding himself back for one more excruciating moment before he plunged into her with an exaltation that knew no bounds.

He thought she cried out at that moment, but he could not think, could not speak, could not do anything but thrust himself repeatedly into her, wanting to be enclosed by her, swallowed up by her. He felt her greediness, her abandon as they welded together in a heated collusion of bodies, flesh against flesh, heat against heat, two become one. And then, when he was lost inside of her, lost to himself and to the world, she cried out for release until he imploded in upon himself in a giant shock wave of heat and light, taking her along with him.

Together they spiraled gently down from that magnificent high, clinging to each other in moments of pure contentment and peace. Azure came to rest with her head upon his chest, listening to his heartbeat as it quieted beneath her cheek.

He traced her cheek with a finger. "My love," he said, but she thought he couldn't, didn't mean it. She remained silent, overwhelmed by the depth of her feelings for him and knowing that the landscape of her life had been transformed by this, by him.

He thought sleepily that this was the time that he had intended to tell her his real name. His eyes refused to stay open, and as he closed them, breathing in the scent of Azure's perfume, anticipating her surprise tomorrow when he took her to the *Samoa*. He smiled to himself, eager to see her reaction when she learned that he was the owner of it.

Azure, made stone-cold sober by the terrifying emotions called forth by his use of the L word, waited until Lee slept before pushing herself up against the headboard where she sat listening to the thrum of a steel drum band and the sound of traffic outside on the street.

Lee had called her his love, but how could she be? She had to go back to Boston, and the more she thought about it, the more her innate common sense told her that Lee Sanders with his hair bleached yellow by the sun and his red Mustang with the loose door handle wouldn't fit in there. Could she imagine him driving down Newbury Street with her in the passenger seat? Could she picture him at the symphony, an art gallery, a theater? Riding with her on a swan boat in the Public Garden? No, she definitely could not.

She had the sudden unsettling realization that she would have been better off to stick to her guns and not go out with Lee Sanders. Never mind that he was fun, he was considerate, he was a great dancer, and totally enamored of her. He was a boy toy for a night, and that's all. Nothing more. A vacation fling.

But he was wonderful. She was crazy about him. And she couldn't bear the thought of leaving him.

It wasn't until the wee hours of the morning before she finally fell asleep in exhaustion, and when she did, it was with a miserable feeling of impending doom.

9

WHEN LEE WOKE THE NEXT morning, Azure's hair was spread across his face, a sweet-smelling flaxen curtain separating him from the rest of the world. That was the romantic version; the reality of it was that he had to pick strands of hair out of his eyelashes and spit them out of his mouth, all without waking her. Not that he minded! He didn't. He had, ever since he first set eyes on her, wanted intimate knowledge of her hair. It—and the rest of her body as well—were as glorious as he had imagined.

She looked beautiful as she slept, her cheeks rosy with sleep and sun, the rest of her tanned body naked under the sheet. Last night she had been magnificent. He'd been right, he thought happily. She *was* a tigress in bed.

He didn't have the heart to wake her, so he tiptoed into the living room and pulled on his pants. He slid the sliding glass door open and took the phone out on the balcony before dialing the *Samoa*.

Fleck, summoned to the phone by Miguel, answered with a cautious, "Hi, Lee."

"Fleck," Lee said easily, pulling the glass slider closed to make sure there was no chance Azure would hear the conversation. "It's me. Would you mind letting the cook know that I'm bringing a guest to dinner tonight, and tell the stewards that she'll be staying overnight."

"Uh, Lee," Fleck said, sounding wary. "Your father is here. He arrived late last night."

"My father?" Lee was stunned. He hadn't seen Joseph Santori in over a year.

"Yes. Don't ask me why. And does he always look so annoyed?"

"Only with me," Lee said.

"He's already on Miguel's case for not bringing him clean towels. You'd better get back here as soon as you can."

Lee's mind raced. He couldn't take Azure to the *Samoa* until he'd calmed Joe down. He didn't want his courtship of Azure to be subjected to any disastrous explosions. With any luck, perhaps he could convince his dad to leave.

"Look, Fleck, keep things as normal as you can until I get there."

"All right," Fleck said doubtfully. "You still want me to tell the cook you're having company for dinner? And overnight?"

"Sure, go ahead."

"Right-o," Fleck said.

Lee quickly wrote a note and propped it on the bedside table only inches from where Azure lay. Then, resisting the temptation to kiss her goodbye, he dressed and left, thinking that maybe he could wind up this errand and be back in time to climb back in bed before she woke up.

The launch, with Mario at the helm, was waiting for him at the marina. "Your father you were not expecting?"

"Not at all," Lee told him as he prepared to board the yacht.

"He's in his usual stateroom," was all Mario said.

Joe Santori had only visited the *Samoa* once before, but as soon as they reached the boat, Lee set his lips in a grim

line and went to see why his father had decided to honor
him with his presence now.

AZURE, WAKING FROM A DEEP SLEEP, groped on the other
side of the bed, thinking she would encounter warm flesh
and a willing participant in certain delights. Her hand encountered only empty space.

"Lee?" She opened her eyes, which seemed to have
razor blades embedded in the eyelids this morning, and
closed them again. The light from the window pierced
through her brain like a red-hot dagger. She recalled drinking all those Mango Tango Surprises last night and realized
that she had been overtaken by the Hangover from Hell.

"Lee?"

Still no answer, so she raised her heavy head along with
the hammer that seemed to be pounding on it and looked
around. He was gone. Or was he? He might be in the
kitchen, making coffee, or he might be in the bathroom.

She hoped not. She needed to use it herself, and immediately. Her brain sloshed around inside her head as she
carefully dragged herself in that direction, her stomach now
getting into the act with its own queasy version of a wake-
up call.

The bathroom door hung wide-open, and the only live
thing in evidence was a spider that scampered down the
sink drain when her shadow fell across the room. *(Pound,
pound, pound.)* She took care of necessities, swallowed
three aspirin tablets, splashed water on her hot face, and
went back into the bedroom to grab the sheet off the bed.
Hoping that the whole world wasn't spinning like this
apartment, she wrapped the sheet around her and tried not
to stumble as she made her way into the living room.
(Pound, pound, pound.) On the floor was her black dress,

shapelessly puddled near the couch. Lee's clothes, which should have been close by, were gone.

Gone! Had he left? *(Pound, pound, pound.)*

He certainly had. She stood indecisively in the middle of the living room for a long moment, wishing her head would stop hurting. She hadn't had a hangover since she was a college student, and this one was ten times worse than any of those.

She tried to think past the pounding, but the only thought that seemed solid enough to contemplate was that Lee had taken what he wanted last night and then split. If what Paulette said was true, perhaps he had found her lacking in the fine points of making love. Maybe he hadn't wanted to see her again today, as he'd suggested last night. Maybe once with her was enough.

Azure made her torturous way back into the bedroom and sat dejectedly on the side of the bed. After her experience with Paco, she hadn't wanted to subject herself to any more jerks. She hadn't wanted to kiss any more frogs, and she had tried not to like Lee at first. She had attempted to frost him from the very beginning. Now she was sorry that she had given in to his persuasions, which, she thought with a surge of longing, were quite extensive. She might not have measured up to his standards, but he had certainly measured up to hers.

She felt tears welling in her eyes. She didn't want to cry over another dumb guy. She didn't want to hate him.

The problem was, she thought with brilliant clarity, that she didn't hate Lee nearly as much as she hated herself for being stupid, stupid, stupid.

Before she could break down and sob her heart out, she got up and turned on the shower. She'd wash all traces of him from her body, and she'd excise all pleasant thoughts of him from her brain. Which was now not throbbing so hard, thanks to the aspirin, but had settled into an annoying reggae beat, which might not be her brain at all but music from the street below.

But still, there was enough noise inside her head so that she didn't hear the faint rustle of paper as the corner of the sheet she wore caught on Lee's note, which fell unheeded and unread to the floor.

"I THINK," SAID JOE SANTORI, "that this has gone on long enough."

Lee leaned forward, his elbows on his knees, cradling a cup of coffee in his hands. "You want to clarify that?" he suggested cautiously.

His father, looking like an older, heavier version of himself, managed a tentative smile. "I want to bury the hatchet. I was wrong, son. I don't care that you didn't finish college. I don't care that you went into a form of business that I don't understand. What I care about is that you're smart enough to have made a success out of yourself even though you didn't do it the way I wanted you to."

Slowly Lee straightened. He stared at his father. "Dad—"

His father interrupted. "I haven't been much of a father to you, Lee. I hope you can forgive me and we can get past it."

"Any reason why you've had this change of heart?" Lee's own heart was in his mouth; he had never expected his father to make peace with him.

Joe Santori got up and walked to the rail of the deck. He stood staring at the greenery on Fisher Island, his eyes squinted against the sun. Lee looked more closely and saw that Joe's eyes were suspiciously damp.

"My friend Benny died last week, Lee. It happened suddenly, and he didn't have a chance to say goodbye to anyone. It made me think how short our lives are and how silly it is to hold grudges." He wheeled around and came to Lee, who stood up and smiled.

His father clapped a strong hand upon his shoulder, and then, before Lee could say anything, he was caught up in his father's big bear hug. It was the first time he could remember being hugged by his father since he was a small child.

"Okay, Dad," Lee said unsteadily. "I'm glad you're here."

His father grinned at him. "So am I. Now what do you say you and I sit down and you can tell me what you've been up to lately?"

Lee thought about Azure, realizing that he'd better call her and let her know he wouldn't be back any time soon. As far as he was concerned, they were still on for tonight. He couldn't wait to show her off to Joe, a businessman of the old school who would appreciate her career credentials, her beauty, and her charm.

But if he called Azure now, he might wake her up. And he'd left a note telling her that he'd talk to her later about tonight.

"Let's go in the main salon," he suggested to his father. "There's a lot to tell."

He'd check with Azure in a little while. He could hardly wait to let her know about this new development in his life.

"A.J.?"

Dorrie sounded entirely too pert when she picked up her extension at Wixler Consultants.

"Yes, it's me, and don't talk too loudly or my head will split open like a ripe watermelon."

There was a sound of a door closing, and then Dorrie said cautiously, "What's wrong?"

"Hangover of the tenth magnitude. And it looks like I've been seduced and abandoned by this guy."

"The one you liked so much?"

"The same. We went out, came home, made love like we were demented, and in the morning when I woke up, he was gone."

"Oh, no, not another frog. What happened?"

Azure blinked back sudden tears. She might be talking about the situation as if it were of little importance, but the fact was that she was crushed. She was hurt. She couldn't even think straight, which was why she had called Dorrie in hopes of solace.

"I don't know what happened. I—I was beginning to really care about him. Oh, hell, I think I've fallen madly in love with him." She swallowed, trying to keep this on track. "Anyway, I thought everything was fine. He pursued me until I caught him, and then—well, like I said, he was gone this morning when I woke up."

"Are you going to call him? Considering that it's love and everything?" Dorrie sounded slightly sarcastic.

"I don't even know where he lives," Azure said unhappily as she sank down onto a lounge chair on the balcony. She could see a sliver of ocean from here, and it was a deep sapphire blue this morning. As blue as she felt.

"I'm sorry, A.J."

"Maybe it's like Paulette said. Guys are interested until they get what they want, and then you never hear from them again. She says they disappear mostly because the sex isn't good enough. What makes sex good enough for a man? That's what I want to know.''

"A.J.!" Dorrie sounded shocked.

"Well, it seemed fantastic to me. He's good at it.''

"You make sex sound like a sport. Skiing or swimming or bowling or something.''

"Yes, and if it's a sport, Lee is an Olympic champion. Besides, Dorrie, there *are* certain learned skills involved. Kissing, for instance. I thought we kissed perfectly. You know how sometimes the tongues don't—''

Dorrie let out a scandalized gasp. "A.J., I'm at work. What if Harry Wixler happens to pick up the phone? I can't wait to hear your expert critique of—what's his name again?''

"Lee,'' Azure said miserably.

"—your expert critique of Lee's sexual skills, but not while I'm *here*. Call me at home later. Or I'll call you.''

"No, I'm not answering the phone. I'm going to conclude my business here in Miami Beach right away and come home to Boston.''

"I wouldn't come back without the Santori account, A.J., if I were you.''

Azure's antennae went on alert. "Why? Is Harry pitching a fit?''

"Worse than that. He's threatening to downsize, and you don't want to get the boot.''

Things, Azure reflected, were going from bad to worse.

"When will you be here?''

Azure pinched the bridge of her nose between her thumb and forefinger, ignoring the pain in her head. "As soon as I can see Leonardo Santori, I'll wrap things up with him and hop on a flight.''

"All right, A.J. I'm so sorry you've had a bad time.''

"Well," Azure said, blotting at her eyes, "I shouldn't have been so stupid. He was a Lust Puppy, not my type. I didn't want a fling. So what did I do? I went ahead and had the fling, and he's still not my type."

"Live and learn," Dorrie replied.

"Yup. Maybe I'd better have my tarot read after all. At least then I'd know what to look out for."

"Tarot? You never said anything about the tarot."

"I'll explain later. 'Bye, Dor."

She hung up, and then, full of self-righteous anger, she snatched the yellow crochet bikini off the back of the lounge chair on the balcony where she had hung it to dry yesterday. Then she tossed it over the railing, scoring a bullseye on the Dumpster in the parking lot below.

The gesture didn't help matters any, but it certainly made her feel better.

FLECK, WHO WAS WAITING nervously beside the phone in the media room on the *Samoa*, where he wasted a lot of his time viewing salacious music videos and waiting for girls to call, jumped when the phone actually rang. He dared to hope that the caller was Mandi, the chick from the juiceteria, who had been totally impressed when he told her he was Leonardo Santori.

But it wasn't Mandi. He recognized the voice right away as that of Azure O'Connor, with whom, he was fairly certain, Lee had spent last night.

"Mr. Santori?" she said.

Uh-oh. It sounded like Lee hadn't told her The Big Secret yet. Fleck looked around to see if Lee was in the corridor or anywhere nearby. He needed some direction here.

No Lee. No direction. As far as Fleck knew, Lee was

still huddled with his father in the main salon, and Fleck had no idea how *that* was going.

When he didn't answer, Azure went right on talking. "Mr. Santori, I'm sorry but I must meet with you right away. I'm going back to Boston due to unforeseen circumstances, and I'd like to move our dinner to this evening."

This evening, which was one day earlier than planned? What should he say? And did Lee know that Azure was planning to go back to Boston?

"I, um, don't know if that will work," he said, trying to think.

"Excuse me?"

"I mean, I can't." This seemed safe enough.

"You can't."

"No. It's impossible."

"Impossible."

Damn! This was like talking with the playback function on a tape recorder. "That's right. I can't possibly meet with you this evening. I'll call you later, how about that?"

"Perhaps another associate from Wixler could serve you better. I can arrange—"

"No!" he said, almost yelling. "I mean, you came highly recommended by Harry Wixler himself."

"Nevertheless, I can't wait until tomorrow evening to see you."

"You have to!" Fleck yelped. "You can't leave!" Not only because of the consulting job but because it occurred to Fleck that Lee probably *didn't* know that Azure was leaving. This was the woman he had claimed to love, after all. If he knew she were leaving, he would be with her up to the last minute, father or no father. Lee would have to be told what Azure had in mind, the sooner the better.

Azure's tone became very chilly. "I certainly *can* leave," she said. "You don't control me, Mr. Santori."

And then she hung up.

Fleck ran as fast as he could to the main salon, but a nervous Miguel barred his way to the door.

"You cannot go in there!" the steward hissed. "Mr. Santori and Mr. Santori—they left orders not to be disturbed."

Fleck, discouraged, decided to go back to the media room. He'd watch a couple more music videos, and then he'd try again.

THAT SANTORI! Who did he think he was, anyway? Azure bolted down a couple more aspirin, grabbed her gray gabardine suit off its hanger, and got dressed. While she was pinning her hair into a knot at the back of her head, the phone in the kitchen rang, but she ignored it. There wasn't anyone in the world she felt like talking to at the moment.

She hauled her briefcase down off the shelf where she had stowed it. A glance in the mirror confirmed that she looked like the wrath of God, but at this point, she didn't care. She wasn't trying to impress anyone. Her only goal at present was to hold body and soul together, and, incidentally, hang on to her job.

She stormed downstairs, hoping that it would not be necessary to make polite small talk with Goldy, who would be overly inquisitive about her date last night. Fortunately she realized as she rounded the corner from the staircase, Goldy had a visitor who was hanging over her desk and rapidly firing questions.

"What's the apartment number? What's the phone number? Can you at least tell me what *floor* she's on?"

That voice, that unctuous voice, that sonorous Argentinianly accented voice that Azure wanted to forget. She halted in midstep, taking in the visitor's rumpled suit, his bloodshot eyes, the air of exhaustion.

"Paco?" she said, stunned.

His head shot up. "A.J.! Where the hell have you been? You look awful." He strode forward, but she made her feet move toward Goldy.

"You don't look so great yourself," she pointed out, thinking that she had never seen him looking so unkempt or oozing so little charm.

"You wouldn't look wonderful either if you'd slept in a succession of airports since yesterday. I had to move heaven and earth to get here, A.J. I hope you appreciate it."

"Don't count on that," Azure said. And to Goldy, "Can't you make him leave?"

"He hasn't done anything wrong," Goldy said doubtfully. "He only wanted to see you."

"Hasn't done anything wrong? How about breathing?" Azure said.

"Come on, A.J., get off it. I'm through with Tiffany. I want you back, *mi cariña.*"

He was calling her his darling? Ha! "The problem here is that I don't want *you* back," Azure said scornfully.

"Come back to Boston and we'll discuss it." Paco made a conciliatory move in her direction.

She held up a hand to ward him off. "That's far enough. I'm not going back to Boston with you."

He grabbed her hand and pulled her to him. Goldy let out a little squeal of dismay. They heard a few interested clucks, and Fricassee the chicken peeked around the counter.

Azure tried to free herself from Paco's grasp, but he held

on with angry determination. On top of the remnants of her hangover and the burgeoning of her anger, the fact that he was trying to impede her progress out the door spawned a new determination to let him know that he was no longer of any importance.

With a foot whose strength, thanks to Paco, had been well-honed on flamenco moves, she stomped on his shoe, hard. At the same moment, the chicken let out an ear-splitting screech and went into attack mode. Paco released Azure's hand, and she stomped on his other foot for good measure. Then, without a backward glance, marching in time to the pounding rhythm in her head, she proceeded smartly out the door, thankful that Old Spice was Paco's favorite aftershave.

SHE KNEW BETTER THAN TO GO to the marina where the *Samoa*'s launch customarily landed. Instead she went to a smaller one where there were fewer boats and, she hoped, no groupies.

When she stepped out of the taxi, she looked around for a sign advertising boats for rent. There was none. The marina office was closed for lunch, so no information would be forthcoming from there. Azure refused to be discouraged, however, and hurried down one of the docks hoping to find someone who would deliver her to the *Samoa*.

"Are you out of your mind?" the first man she encountered said. "I don't want to tangle with Leonardo Santori."

The second one barked something similar and disappeared grumpily into his cabin when it looked as if she might try to persuade him differently. Finally, at the end of the dock, she saw an elderly fisherman unloading his meager catch.

"Excuse me, sir," she said. "Would you mind taking

me out to that yacht over there?'' She shaded her eyes from the bright sunlight with her hand and waved her briefcase in the direction of the *Samoa*.

''Take you to the *Samoa*? What for?''

''I need to meet with Mr. Santori.'' Quickly she explained who she was.

''How do I know you're not one of them young groupie ladies who keeps trying to meet him?''

''You don't, but believe me, if I were trying to get to know Leonardo Santori, I would wear something more comfortable in this climate than a gray business suit. Which is part wool, by the way.'' She thought that this statement gave her even more credibility; who would wear wool in Miami Beach in the summertime unless on business?

''I see. Well, this is only a rowboat. I fish over near the buoy almost every day, get me some fresh fish for dinner. Today I caught a nice snapper. Going to fry it.''

Azure let out a sigh of impatience. ''Wonderful, but I need to get to the *Samoa*. I'll pay you if you'll row me.''

''Nope, nope, I get plain tuckered from rowing out to the buoy and back. Exercise is good for a person, though. Everyone needs exercise.''

''How about if I pay you to use your boat?''

''You'd want to row way out there?''

''I can't say that I want to, but I need to see Mr. Santori. How about fifty dollars?''

''Fifty dollars? So you can row my old boat? Are you joking?'' He seemed taken aback.

She snapped a fifty out of her wallet and pressed it into his hand. Before he could recover, she was climbing into the boat and wishing she hadn't worn such expensive shoes. The water in the bottom of the boat would ruin them.

The breeze was coming from the direction in which she

was rowing, impeding her progress considerably. The fact that her muscles began to ache when she was halfway to the *Samoa* reminded her that she hadn't worked out enough lately. By the time she was three-quarters there, they were screaming in protest, and as she approached the yacht, it was all she could do to pull back on the oars. As if that weren't enough of a problem, blisters were raising on her palms, and the wind had capriciously torn her hair from its knot.

Once she was within shouting distance, the effort to row all the way out to the *Samoa* had made her so tired that she couldn't help slumping over her oars for a moment. A fine sheen of perspiration filmed her face, and her panty hose had sprung a run. She wasn't going to make a great impression on Santori, but why worry? On the phone he hadn't sounded like someone who observed the social niceties or cared how people looked.

She had not anticipated what she would do when she got there. Should she climb aboard? Should she wait until she was noticed? She pushed the loose strands of hair behind her ears and studied the yacht, which was truly huge. It was huger than huge. It was *enormous*. She could not imagine having so much money that you could travel the world in such a fashion.

"Yo!" she hollered up to no one in particular, thinking to attract some attention. "Anybody home?"

A surprised face surmounted by a thatch of kinky blond hair appeared above the railing and stared down at her openmouthed.

"Who are you?"

"A. J. O'Connor," she yelled back. She recognized the gritty voice as that of Leonardo Santori.

"Uh, wow. Would you mind proving it?"

She almost broke into hysterical laughter. She had rowed out here carrying a briefcase and dressed for success, and he was questioning who she was? Plus the rocking of the rowboat was beginning to nauseate her, underscoring the unstable state of her stomach.

"You've got to be kidding," she said.

He seemed to think this over. "Okay, okay. Maybe it's good that you're here. There's a ladder off the swim platform," he said, pointing. "You can climb up."

She looked where he was pointing. The ladder on the stern of the yacht appeared sturdy enough, so she maneuvered the rowboat closer. Above her, she saw Santori waiting, and at his side hovered a nervous-looking man in a white coat. A steward, probably, Azure thought, having seen enough movies to know that a yacht required several.

The rowboat rocked in a wake from a passing motorboat as she nudged it up to the ladder. The *Samoa,* big as it was, gave nary a lurch. Gritting her teeth, Azure rose in the rowboat, grasping the line in one hand and her briefcase in the other. She'd somehow have to hang onto both as she tethered the line to the ladder.

She looped the line around one of the rungs and prepared to board. As she was heaving herself upward, the rowboat gave a frantic bobble. Unfortunately the sudden motion sent her briefcase flying, and when she tried to recapture it, she did, too. Right into the drink.

She submerged along with a spate of bubbles, hoping that she didn't resurface under the rowboat. Fortunately she did not. Fortunately, when her head broke the surface of the water, she saw her briefcase snagged on a large clump of seaweed. She barely managed to pluck it up before it floated away.

"Are you all right?"

"What do you think?" Azure sputtered, struggling to tread water. This might not be the right way to do business, she reflected, but she was determined that Santori would talk to her, like it or not.

Her outstretched hand closed over a rung of the ladder. Hand over hand, somehow still wearing one high-heeled shoe, she made her way upward, water pouring from her clothes. Santori gave her a hand at the top, but the steward did little more than wring his hands and mumble disjointedly in a foreign language.

Finally she stood on the teak deck. Water poured off her and ran away in little runnels, pooled in her shoe, and no doubt made her mascara run. If she had any left, that is.

She eyed Santori warily. "Let's have that meeting," she said, wishing now more than ever that she wasn't chasing the tail end of a hangover.

"I think you'd better wait right here," Santori said.

The steward looked as if he were about to dissolve into hysterics. "But *he* has left the main salon," the steward interjected hastily. "I don't know where *he* is."

Who the mysterious *"he"* might be, Azure had no idea, but this missing person seemed important to Santori. "I'll find him," Santori said, and then, to Azure's utter amazement, he dodged past her and through a nearby door. The agitated steward followed, uttering what might be curses that she couldn't understand.

Azure, standing alone on the deck, wrung water out of her skirt and flicked a bit of seaweed from her jacket pocket. She couldn't help looking around her with curiosity. Too bad she couldn't have brought that groupie woman Ginger with her to see the yacht; it *was* magnificent.

She peered around the corner. Deck chairs were lined up neatly on the sun deck above, and someone was sitting in one. Because of the angle, she couldn't tell who it was, but then he spoke.

"Do you know when she'll be back?"

Azure felt her stomach swoop down to her wet feet and back up again, and this stomach discomfort wasn't due to her lingering hangover. It was because she knew that voice. It was the very same voice that had whispered so silkily in her ear last night, the voice that had called her, "My love."

The realization that this was Lee, the guy who had loved her and left her, was stupefying. What was he doing here?

Cautiously, not knowing what to expect, she made her way up a narrow teak staircase and sloshed lopsidedly around several deck chairs until he came into full view. She knew she must look a fright with her hair wet and stuck to her head, her expensive suit plastered to her body, and missing one shoe. Her appearance, however, was for once not uppermost in her mind.

"What are *you* doing here?" she said, staring down at Lee. He looked wonderful, all tanned and, wonder of wonders, his hair blown smoothly dry. He was wearing a white polo shirt thrown open at the throat and navy-blue shorts. The polo shirt's embroidered emblem said *Samoa*. His watch was a Rolex, and he wore deck shoes—expensive ones. No socks.

Where were his usual sleeveless tee and baggy Hawaiian print shorts? Where were the running shoes with holes in the toes?

"I have an idea," Lee said, a twinkle springing into those remarkable gray eyes, "that I belong here more than you do."

He belonged here? Since when? Caught off balance, she could only say stupidly, "What?"

"I live on the *Samoa*."

"But—" Words failed her. She fought for composure. "You're going to have to help me out here. I came here to see Leonardo Santori."

"Looks like you've found him," Lee said. He commenced to look her up and down, adding irrelevantly, "You should have called for the launch."

"You're—? No, it's not possible. It couldn't be." She tossed her sodden briefcase down on one of the deck chairs, and, still dripping copiously, eyed him with trepidation. "Why do I feel that I'm Alice fallen down a rabbit hole or something? This isn't real."

"It *is* real. I want to tell you all about it." He sounded worried.

"About—this?" She waved a hand at their opulent surroundings, at the shiny brass railings, the deck chairs, the table set up nearby and stacked with plates of fruit, roast beef and lobster tails.

"About me. Sit down, Azure. Please."

Her knees, which were feeling distinctly wobbly with the shock of all this, refused to support her any longer. She sat. Lee pulled his chair closer to hers and took her hands in his.

"I *am* Leonardo Santori, Azure. Will it make a difference?"

She snatched her hands away and, furious, said the first thing that came to mind. "I'll say. You can buy your own lottery tickets from now on."

He looked as if he might laugh. "I meant in the way you feel about me."

Her anger abated when she looked deep into his eyes. "Why, I don't know. I'm not sure I believe what you're saying."

The man she had thought was Santori emerged breathlessly from a hatch behind them. He stopped dead in his tracks when he saw them. "Oh! I've been looking for you, Lee." He stared at Azure and ran a hand through his wild-looking hair. "I might as well explain that Miguel and I wouldn't have let her come aboard, but I decided that if you love her, you'd want to see her."

"You love me?" Azure said to Lee in shock, not quite believing that she was asking.

"Yes, and now that I've found you, I'm never going to lose you," Lee said, his eyes never leaving hers.

"But if you're Santori, who is *he?*" Azure asked, staring at Fleck.

"Azure, meet Fleck. He's my first new employee at Grassy Creek."

"Nice to meet you," Fleck said. "I think I'd better go. Maybe I'll stop by the Grassy Creek store and take a look at it." He went, dragging the flustered Miguel along with him.

"You already have a Grassy Creek store?" Azure's mind was spinning with all this new information

"We painted some of it, remember?"

"Omigosh."

"And it took quite a bribe to buy the silence of Jake Gruber, who was going to report us to the contractor and possibly the police."

"Your first Grassy Creek store is going to be in Miami," Azure said. "Harry Wixler didn't mention that."

"He doesn't know. I didn't think it was important to tell him. I asked him for help in starting up my franchise operation because if the Grassy Creek store is as big a success as I intend for it to be, I'll have outlets all over the country. All over the world, maybe."

She pulled her hands away from his. "But why did you pretend to be a beach bum?"

He laughed and recaptured her hands. "You're the one who took me for a beach bum, dear. I let you go on thinking that because I never get a simple reaction to the real me when women know I'm Leonardo Santori. I like to call myself Lee Sanders when I first meet people. That way I know they like me for myself, not for my money."

"I see," Azure said, though she didn't really. She had little experience with billionaires, and none with billionaires who traveled incognito.

"Stop trying to take your hands away. I'll need to study them carefully so I'll know your finger size when I buy the ring."

"Ring?" she said. He wanted to buy her a ring? When only a few days ago she'd been doubtful that he could afford a one-dollar lottery ticket?

"Ring," he affirmed. "And soon."

"Soon?" The man had reduced her to a gibbering idiot.

"Today, maybe. I want to marry you, Azure."

He wanted to marry her. He wanted to marry *her?*

She closed her eyes and opened them. Much to her surprise, Lee was still there. She had thought that maybe he would disappear—*abracadabra!*—and she would wake up back in Paulette's bed with her hangover as fresh as ever.

"By the way, do you always put the cap back on the toothpaste? It drives me crazy when people don't." Lee regarded her with barely concealed amusement.

"Always," Azure assured him. "But you'll have to start wearing socks with your shoes. I hate it when guys wear shoes with no socks." She'd blurted this out without thinking.

"No problem."

''Do you want to be in the delivery room when our children are born?''

He looked taken aback. ''I don't know. I never thought about it.''

''You'd better.''

Lee became more serious. ''So now that we've settled most of the important things, will you? Marry me, I mean?''

''I have to go back to Boston,'' she said weakly. ''I have a job. I have an apartment.''

''You'll go back as Mrs. Lee Santori unless you feel strongly about keeping your own name.''

''I don't know. Azure Santori? A. J. Santori? Do you think maybe we could hyphenate?'' Over and above all this, she couldn't imagine Dorrie's face when she confronted her with a ring and a husband, not to mention a yacht bearing a resemblance to the Taj Mahal.

''You've thought long enough about becoming my wife. What do you say, Azure?''

''I think so,'' she whispered, still astonished at this whole turn of events.

He drew her to her feet and enfolded her, wet clothes and all, in his arms. ''I *know* so,'' he said, comfortably close to her ear. ''I've known it since the moment I saw you. Now that you've said you'll marry me, how about telling me you love me? I believe it's common practice, though we've put the cart before the horse in our case. And if you have any doubts, know that I adore you, Azure O'Connor. I idolize you. I love you with all my heart.''

''I love you, too,'' she said. ''It's just that I thought I loved a guy with no serious job, no prospects, no money.''

''I don't have a serious job, I do have certain prospects, and I've got gobs of money,'' he said.

"I've kissed a lot of frogs," she said unbelievingly. "How am I supposed to believe that finally one of them has turned into a prince?"

He laughed and swung her around. "Believe it, my darling. Now," he said. "I think it's time that we got you out of those wet clothes and into something more comfortable."

"Like bed?" she said, her hangover miraculously gone, replaced by a feeling of wonder as well as a desire to be held close and loved.

"You see? We think alike," he said, and he swept her into his arms.

He didn't set her down again until they were in a large mahogany-paneled stateroom with wide windows overlooking the ocean beyond the bay. "I'll find you something to wear," he said, flinging open a closet.

"Never mind," she said, demurely divesting herself of damp wool and panty hose. "I won't be needing clothes for quite some time."

He came to her then, all strength and warmth. And he was the Lee she had grown to love, not Leonardo Santori the billionaire, but the man whose affection and sense of fun had won her heart. She touched him, ran her hand over the smooth muscles of his back, down to his strong buttocks and around to his tattoo, making him tremble with desire. He smelled of soap and sunshine and of Lee, and when he whispered her name, she captured it in a deep and hungry kiss.

And then, ignoring the painful blisters rising on both her palms, she took his hand in hers and led him to the bed.

Epilogue

On the Samoa, *three months later*

"I NOW PRONOUNCE YOU husband and wife," said the judge who had been invited to perform the ceremony. "You may kiss your bride, Lee."

Lee took Azure in his arms, taking care not to rumple her exquisite white gown. It was made of silk organza, cut on the bias, and showed off her figure to perfection.

"My bride," he said. "My love." And then he kissed her, properly and thoroughly, taking so long to do it that everyone nearly let out a gasp of relief when he had finished.

Since they were being married in the elegant main salon of the *Samoa* and since their guests were all family and close friends, they dispensed with the receiving line after the ceremony and mingled informally with their guests. Azure thought she had never had a happier day in her life.

"I declare," Goldy said as she peered over the railing of the *Samoa* toward the ocean. "those tea leaves were right. I *am* attending a ceremonial occasion over water."

"The tea leaves didn't say anything about me," Mandi said with a pout. "Me and Fleck." She reached over and pulled Fleck to her, kissing him on the cheek.

"Aw, Mandi," he said. "I'm sorry I'm not the real Lee Santori."

"*I'm* happy enough with the real Fleck," Mandi said.

"And my daughter certainly seems delighted with the real Santori," said Saguaro, Azure's mother, balancing a glass of champagne with one hand and restraining a rambunctious small boy with the other. "Although I do wish she had let me bake the wedding cake. We're doing such fun things with wedding cakes these days. Why, I decorated one for a couple in Sedona that left little to the imagination. I ran out of flesh-colored icing, it was so *big*."

Azure broke away from Lee in order to cut off this direction of the conversation. "Come with me, Mom, Karma wants to talk to you. She says she's been troubled with morning sickness lately, and I told her you could clue her in to the right herbs to cure it."

"Oh, of course. Just think! A baby already!" And Saguaro trotted off with Azure to dispense motherly advice.

"The tarot cards showed all this, you know," Goldy said to Azure's father in all seriousness.

Eamon O'Connor raised both bushy eyebrows. "All what?"

"That Lee was powerful and rich. That he had a secret. That he would soon find his soul mate. I *told* Azure. The one thing the cards didn't tell me was that I would profit from their engagement. They both gave me their lottery tickets, and I won sixty-three dollars and seventy cents."

Isis came over and took her father's arm. "Goldy, what was Azure telling me about the chicken?"

"Oh, it's our new attack chicken at the Blue Moon. I wish I could have brought Fricassee to the wedding, but something tells me that she wouldn't like the ocean any more than she likes Old Spice."

Azure, back from making sure her mother found Karma,

grinned. "Fricassee certainly sent Paco packing, didn't she?"

"Did I mention that Paco has started wearing English Leather since that little incident in the lobby of the Blue Moon? It makes him slightly less charming, in my opinion," said Dorrie.

"And Tiffany? How about her?"

"Still a 40DD, and she's moved to Minneapolis."

"Good riddance."

Leah, Uncle Nate's wife, descended upon them. "Azure, this was the most elegant wedding. You O'Connor girls certainly know how to do things right."

"Stop your kvelling, Lee-Lee," Uncle Nate said affectionately. "*I'm* the one with bragging rights to these young ladies."

Karma, looking radiant in a flowing cerise dress, joined them and slid an arm around Azure's waist. "You've got to agree, Uncle Nate, that we O'Connors know how to pick great guys. Even though," and she nudged Azure in the ribs, "it takes kissing a lot of frogs to find one sometimes."

"Oh, I don't know," said Paulette. "How about giving Rent-a-Yenta some credit?"

"Sure, Paulette," chorused Azure and Karma, exchanging a look of extreme patience.

"So what do you do?" an attentive Joe Santori was asking Saguaro over near the stern railing.

"I bake cakes in the shape of body parts," she said brightly, smiling up at him in her most flirtatious manner.

"How interesting," he said. "And where do you live?"

"In Arizona."

He moved closer. "I'm visiting there next month. Perhaps we could have dinner."

"Why, what a good idea," Saguaro said.

Azure pulled Karma into an alcove in the main salon. "Did you see my new father-in-law chatting up Mom? What if—"

"—if *they* get together? It's fine with me." Karma smiled broadly.

When Azure found Lee explaining how the *Samoa*'s dining room table in the main salon used a hydraulic system to lower into the floor to become a coffee table, she joined him.

"There are lots of fun things about this boat," she said to the group of wedding guests. "Like the gold faucets in the shape of swans. Like the complete exercise facilities and the onboard masseuse."

"An onboard masseuse? No wonder you don't want to come back to Boston, A.J.," Harry Wixler said glumly. "No wonder you want to sail around the world on this tub."

"It's not all going to be vacation time," Azure informed him. "Lee and I will be working together to get the Grassy Creek franchises up and running."

"You lost him as a Wixler Consultants customer," said Harry. "For that I would have fired you if you hadn't already quit."

"Never mind," Azure said consolingly. "Lee's dad will be calling you on Monday to consult on one of his overseas businesses. And Dorrie is looking forward to handling the account."

"Azure, when are you going to throw your bouquet?" It was Dorrie, who nurtured great hopes of catching it.

"In a minute," Azure told her, and when she positioned herself in front of the bandstand on the aft deck where a dance floor had been set up, she honestly thought that Dorrie would. To her surprise, it was her mother who caught the bouquet, much to the delight of her daughters.

"Like I said, I'll be in Arizona next month," Joe Santori said with a suggestive gleam in his eye, and Saguaro had the good grace to blush.

It was later while they were dancing that Lee said to Azure, "Do you still feel like Alice falling down the rabbit hole?"

"More like Cinderella with her prince," Azure said, and he laughed.

"Who enjoyed pretending to be a frog."

"I only hope you won't turn back into one if I kiss you again," she said, smiling up at him.

"Let's try it," he said, and he stopped dancing and took her in his arms.

They kissed, taking their time about it, to the accompaniment of enthusiastic applause from the wedding guests.

"Am I still a prince?" he asked tenderly afterward.

"Yes, and I am overjoyed, my love, to be your frog princess," she said, kissing him once more.

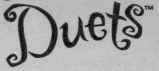

TWO ROMANTIC COMEDIES IN ONE FUN VOLUME!

Don't miss double the laughs in

Once Smitten

and

Twice Shy

From acclaimed Duets author

Darlene Gardner

Once Smitten—that's Zoe O'Neill and Jack Carter, all right! It's a case of "the one who got away" and Zoe's out to make amends!

In *Twice Shy,* Zoe's two best friends, Amy Donatelli and Matt Burke, are alone together for the first time and each realizes they're "the one who never left!"

Any way you slice it, these two tales serve up a big dish of romance, with lots of humor on the side!

Volume #101
Coming in June 2003

Available at your favorite retail outlet.

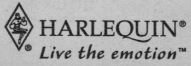

HARLEQUIN®
Live the emotion™

Visit us at www.eHarlequin.com

HDDD99DG

eHARLEQUIN.com

Sit back, relax and enhance your romance with our great magazine reading!

- **Sex and Romance!** Like your romance *hot?* Then you'll *love* the sensual reading in this area.

- **Quizzes!** Curious about your lovestyle? His commitment to you? Get the answers here!

- **Romantic Guides and Features!** Unravel the mysteries of love with informative articles and advice!

- **Fun Games!** Play to your heart's content....

Plus...romantic recipes, top ten lists, Lovescopes...and more!

Enjoy our online magazine today— visit www.eHarlequin.com!

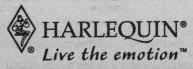

We've been making you laugh for years!

HARLEQUIN®

Duets™

**Join the fun in May 2003
and celebrate Duets #100!
This smile-inducing series,
featuring gifted writers and
stories ranging from amusing to zany,
is a hundred volumes old.**

This special anniversary volume offers two terrific
tales by a duo of Duets' acclaimed authors.
You won't want to miss...

Jennifer Drew's You'll Be Mine in 99

and

The 100-Year Itch by Holly Jacobs

With two volumes offering two special stories every
month, Duets always delivers a sharp slice of the lighter
side of life and *especially* romance. Look for us today!

Happy Birthday, Duets!

Visit us at www.eHarlequin.com

HD100TH